THE WARRIOR SPIRIT MURDERS

A LEILANI KEALOHA ISLAND THRILLER

BY

CHUCK MORGAN

This book is a work of fiction. Names, characters, places, and incidents are the product of the author's imagination or, if real, are used fictitiously. Any resemblance to events, locales or persons, living or dead, is coincidental.

Printed in the United States of America

First printing 2026

ISBN 978-1-968179-68-7 (Paperback)

LIBRARY OF CONGRESS CONTROL NUMBER

2026910864

Chapter One

The best part of the evening was that it had no agenda. Kai was long since asleep; the leftovers of takeout poke and half a chocolate haupia pie boxed in the fridge, and Leilani's living room, normally half storage locker and half evidence annex, felt almost like a place where people lived. She'd swapped the standard-issue HPD couch blanket for one her mother crocheted years ago, the color faded to the sweet spot between ocean and sky.

Isaac stretched his legs across the battered coffee table and scrolled mindlessly through the new crime stats on his phone. He wore a faded T-shirt with a print of a shark in sunglasses; Leilani was pretty sure she'd seen the same shirt on Kai a week ago. He looked comfortable in her house, comfortable in his own skin for once. It took a global smuggling case, three months of night shifts, and another bullet graze, but she guessed that was how these things worked.

"You ever think about quitting?" she asked, not looking up from her crossword. The paper was propped on her knees, pen hovering over 22-Across: five letters, island farewell.

Isaac didn't answer right away. He closed the crime stats and locked his phone, just to prove he was present. "Quitting the department, or quitting the idea that life is a perpetual open case?"

She grinned at the paper. "I was thinking the first one, but the second's good too."

"I thought about it after L.A. After the mess with Nani—" He let the name trail and started again. "It seemed easy to start over. Become a high school football coach. Sell solar panels to retired Navy personnel. Move somewhere dry."

"Don't think you'd last in Arizona," Leilani said. "You'd get hives and be on the first plane home."

"True," Isaac said. "Do you ever think about it?"

She looked at the crossword; the familiar itch of unsolvable clues was just background noise. "I did. When Kai was little. Every time I dropped him off with my mother so I could chase down a meth-head or fill out paperwork. But something stupid would happen, like a hotshot detective losing a drug mule in Chinatown or a tourist trying to surf with a selfie stick, and I'd want to be there. Even if I didn't admit it."

He nodded, solemn as a man could be in a shark T-shirt. "So, you never want to leave?"

Leilani set the crossword aside and looked at him, really looked. The bruise on his jaw was nearly gone. The stitches from the last scrape barely left a scar. His eyes were dark and tired, but when he was like this, at rest, with nothing to prove, he looked a decade younger.

"I've thought about leaving many times," she said. "But I always want to come back."

They sat with that for a while, no music, only the soft groan of the fridge and the slow drip of rain that hadn't made it inside. She watched him thumb at the scab on his wrist, watched him check his phone for the twentieth time. The house was quiet enough to make a secret of every breath.

"Do you think Kai will remember any of this?" Isaac asked.

She laughed. "He'll remember every embarrassing story and forget all the things that matter. That's how it goes."

"Still," Isaac said. "He's lucky."

"We're all winging it, though. Including my mother." Leilani picked at a loose thread on her shorts. "How's your mom?"

Isaac's expression did a weird thing, half pride, half panic. "She called last night. Wants to send another care package. Said she heard I was on TV."

Leilani laughed. "You looked like you were going to puke."

"I almost did." He reached for his water, remembered it was empty, and set it down. "I hate being the face of anything."

"Unless it's on a wanted poster?" she shot back.

"That's different. No one reads those."

Leilani got up to refill his glass. She watched the street outside: the sodium arc lamps, the slow roll of a late bus, and the hush of a city taking its last breaths for the night. She filled the glass, then leaned against the counter, half watching him, half watching the door.

Isaac set his glass on the table and kicked back. He smiled at Leilani. "I could get used to this quiet."

Leilani sipped her own glass and looked at him point-blank. “You want this to be a thing? Not just a we survived a cartel shootout and now we share takeout kind of thing?”

Isaac’s lips pulled tight, but he didn’t break eye contact. “I wouldn’t mind if it were more than that.”

She smiled, the kind that didn’t need to show teeth. “Good. Because I put your name on the parent contact sheet at Kai’s school. Welcome to the nightmare.”

He made a face. “Do I have to chaperone field trips?”

“Only if you want to win him over.”

Isaac groaned, but she could tell he liked the idea.

The mood was easy and warm. She almost forgot what it felt like to be hunted, to have every plan destroyed by someone else’s agenda. She wanted to freeze the moment, just for one night.

So, of course, the phone rang.

Chapter Two

She knew the ringtone before she looked at the screen. The low, metallic marimba she'd assigned to anyone with rank above Chief. She glanced down, saw MORI, and all the comfort bled out of her hands.

Isaac straightened without needing to be told.

"Evening, Chief," she said, pressing the speaker.

Chief Mori didn't do small talk. "Are you free tonight?"

"Was just finishing dinner. What's up?"

There was a pause, and a hiss of wind in the background. She realized Mori was calling from somewhere outside, probably her car.

"We've got three bodies at Kaena Point," Mori said. "Shallow graves. First glance, one has been down there a while; the others are fresh. HPD uniforms flagged the scene. They're asking for SIU."

Isaac whistled.

"Cause of death?" Leilani asked.

"Unknown," Mori said. "You'll see why when you get here. I'll meet you at the scene." There was another brief silence. "Lei, if this is what it looks like, we're going to have to be careful. Not with the press. With everyone."

"Meaning?"

"Meaning you know the history of that place. You know what it means if someone's started putting bodies out there again."

A chill zipped through Leilani's arms. Kaena Point wasn't only a remote stretch of coast; it was the end of the world, according to old stories. The place where spirits left the living behind. It wasn't the first time the department had found something grim there. But it was the first time since. "We're on our way," Leilani said.

"Text me when you hit Farrington. There'll be a roadblock, but you're cleared."

Mori hung up.

Isaac set the empty glass down, eyes already hard.

"What's Kaena Point?" he said.

She gave him a look, half apology, half admiration, and stepped down the hall to check on Kai. She found him curled in the dark, hair matted to his forehead, blanket tangled in a way only kids could manage. She brushed the strands aside, pressed a kiss to his temple, and pulled the blanket up. He murmured something, a line from a dream, or a sigh, and turned over.

Isaac joined her at the door, kept his voice down. "You want me to stay behind and keep watch?"

"He'll sleep through a hurricane. Besides, you heard Mori. If this is what I think it is."

"We do it together."

Leilani moved through the checklist without thinking, all muscle memory, and years of practiced hurry. She swapped her shorts for jeans, laced her boots, and placed her badge lanyard around her neck. The gun was already holstered, the spare mags loaded and ready. She grabbed her field notebook and the beat-up flashlight that had never failed her, though the tape on the grip was fraying.

Isaac was at the kitchen counter, typing the coordinates from Mori's text into his phone. "They're using an old parking lot for staging," he said, not looking up. "We'll have to walk the last half mile on foot."

"That's if we want the crime scene unscrewed," Leilani said. "Last time someone brought a four-wheeler out there, half the evidence was in a drainage ditch by morning."

He grunted in agreement, watched as she slipped a water bottle into her bag, and moved down the hall.

She checked on Kai again, this time with the light on. He hadn't moved; his breathing was slow. She lingered a second longer, then tapped out a quick message to her mother.

Got called in. Big case. Can you come sleep here tonight? Will bring donuts in the AM.

The reply was instant: *Always, Lei. Be careful.*

She closed the bedroom door softly, then padded across the living room, where Isaac was pulling on a jacket. He looked at her, one eyebrow cocked. "Are you good?"

"I was thinking about what Mori said." Leilani ran a hand through her hair. "If it's really ritual, or someone wants us to think it is, either way, it's going to be bad."

He zipped his jacket. "Guess we'll find out soon."

They walked to the door together. Leilani reached for her keys, hesitated, glancing at the side table. There, wedged between a drift of unpaid bills and a faded takeout menu, was a framed photo from five years ago: her, Naalei, and a younger Kai at the Waimea waterfall. They were all wet, arms around each other, faces split with laughter. She remembered the day—how her mother had insisted they go, though the weather was trash and Leilani had been half-distracted with a case. She remembered the feeling of being a child, not the parent, for once. The sudden, gut-deep certainty that nothing mattered more than the people in that frame.

She touched the glass, then pocketed her keys and stepped outside.

The air had cooled, that rare Honolulu hour when the world went quiet, the wet hush before dawn. Isaac headed to his car, a newer Civic, but he stopped at the curb.

"See you at the turnoff?" he asked.

She nodded. "Don't get lost."

He winked and drove off, taillights blinking through the mist.

Leilani started her own department-issue Explorer, the engine whining in protest before settling into its familiar rumble. She adjusted the rearview and caught the house in the glass. The porch light was on, the blinds drawn, and her world was safe and whole for now.

She let herself feel the tug, the gravity of what she was leaving behind, and forced her eyes forward. The clock on the dash clicked over to midnight.

She pulled out of the drive, her tires cutting a wet stripe down the block, and pointed the car west, towards the unknown. There were worse ways to start a night.

The city bled away in a rush of sodium lamps and tar-patched pavement, the edges of Honolulu blurring into long, dark runs of empty space. On nights like this, the island seemed bigger than it was. Every mile of blacktop, an invitation to get lost; every turn is a reminder that it all ended somewhere, probably sooner than you wanted. Leilani followed the GPS, which fought her at every roundabout, but she knew the way from memory: past the silent strip malls, past the clump of fast-food drive-thrus that marked the last real civilization, then into the wild.

Out here, the fog clung low, an animal's belly that scraped the road and erased anything beyond the next reflector post. The headlights hit mist, then nothing. If you cracked the window, you could taste the salt, the loamy rot of wet grass, and a sharp chemical scent from the runoff in the drainage ditch. She turned off the radio and listened to the engine, the squeal of the wipers, the rhythmic knock of her own pulse in her ears.

Every few minutes, her phone would ping with a new update from dispatch, a note from Mori, or a half-asleep meme from Kai, who, apparently, texted in his dreams. She let the phone buzz, fingers tight on the wheel, and focused on the road ahead.

Chapter Three

She reached the end of the county-maintained asphalt and saw the first set of blue strobes cutting sideways through the fog. High-visibility crime scene tape fluttered in the distance. A trio of cruisers clustered by the battered ranger station, engine blocks idling in the dark. Parked behind the last one was Isaac's Civic, the driver's side door open, and the cabin empty. She killed the Explorer's lights and sat, letting her eyes adjust.

Past the tape, portable generator floodlights blazed against the ancient banyan grove that squatted above the shoreline. The trees were so dense they turned the ground into a green cave, all buttress roots, and exposed black dirt, the canopy so thick you couldn't see the stars. The lights cast everything in hard shadows; nothing moved unless you made it.

She stepped out, her badge on her hip, and ducked under the first run of tape. An officer she didn't know tried to stop her; she gave him the look, and he let her through. She saw the crime scene in layers: the nearest forensics tech in a white coat and latex gloves, crouched by a patch of raw earth; farther back, a cluster of uniforms, three of them facing away, each locked on the spot where the body was. Chief Mori stood behind them, arms crossed, a to-go coffee cup in one hand. Her leather jacket was open, with a black T-shirt underneath.

Isaac was standing near the farthest grave. His jacket hung open, exposing the badge and the gun, but his hands were in his pockets. He'd gone into that state where he didn't blink, didn't talk, just absorbed everything.

Mori saw her and waved her over. "Evening, Lei."

Leilani saluted with her flashlight. "Chief. You beat me."

"Barely." Mori glanced back at the grave. "Follow me?"

Mori led her to the first grave, close to the front of the grove, thirty yards from the surf. The earth was still wet, spaded up in a rough oval, roots hacked but not removed. The body was male, mid-40s, dressed in a muddy golf shirt and expensive shorts, the kind you wore on a resort course. Rigor mortis had long since left, and there was a clean slice across the throat, dried black and gaping.

"ID?" Leilani asked.

Mori said, "Wallet and keys in his pocket. Name's Nathan Beckett. Local dentist. Reported missing two months ago by the wife." She pointed her chin at the body. "Never made it home from a hiking trip. HPD has an active missing person investigation running."

Leilani took a knee, careful to keep her boots out of the softest mud. She did a quick scan: hands tied behind with a cord, a thin tattoo ring on the left wrist, and knuckles scraped raw from trying to break the bindings.

"Time of death?" she asked.

"Coroner says 24 to 36 hours. Means he was alive when they put him here." Mori sipped the coffee, face grim. “There’s more.”

Leilani kneeled closer to the body. She sniffed something familiar. She stood and followed the chief.

They walked ten paces into the trees, where the next two graves sat close together, the dirt still fresh. Both bodies were smaller: one, a young woman; the other, a boy about eight. Both showed the same marks. Bound wrists, shallow cuts to the arms and legs, and throats slit but not deeply. The wounds were jagged.

“The other two?” Leilani said.

“Mother and son. She’s a Navy petty officer stationed at Pearl,” Mori said. “Missing since last Friday. No connection to the first, as far as we can tell.”

“Shit,” said Leilani.

Isaac looked at her. “What?”

“She Navy,” said Leilani. “That means we’ll have to deal with Castellano.”

“Who’s Castellano?” asked Issac

“NCIS,” said Leilani with a scowl. “Another fucking Fed.”

Chief Mori chuckled. “Play nice, kids.”

Leilani frowned and walked around the grave.

Isaac stepped over, his shoes caked with black mud. “It’s not the bodies,” he whispered. “There’s something off with the staging. Look.”

He pointed to the base of the woman’s grave. Pressed into the soil, three inches deep, was a knot of flowers—wilted plumeria, red ti leaf and a slice of dried breadfruit, all laid in a neat bundle at her feet. The boy's grave had a similar arrangement, but instead of plumeria, it was a strand of shell lei, clamped between his hands.

Mori said, "Whoever did this wants us to notice. It's not only a dump."

Leilani kneeled next to the graves and leaned close.

"What do you have?" asked Mori.

Leilani stood and wiped her jeans. "Saltwater. The bodies have been cleaned with saltwater."

Isaac looked at her, but she offered no additional information. Mori frowned.

Leilani nodded, then scanned the darkness beyond the floodlights. "Where's Mele?"

"Over by the bag station," Mori said. "She's taking samples."

Leilani made her way to the folding table at the scene. Mele stood hunched over a tray of vials, her long black hair in twin braids that glowed silver in the work lamp. She wore her usual: a white coat, jeans and a punk band tee visible at the collar. She barely looked up as Leilani approached.

"Tell me something good," Leilani said.

Mele slid a tray towards her. "I've got trace elements in the soil you don't see in this area. Sea salt, obviously, but also calcium carbonate. There's coral dust in the bindings and in the nostrils of the first vic. That means he used ocean water to wash the body after death, not before."

“Ritual cleansing,” Leilani said, mostly to herself.

Mele nodded. “Someone wanted them purified. Not only killed.”

She held up a bag of flowers from the grave. “The flowers are weird, too. They’re from three different islands. Not native to this exact spot.”

“Means the killer brought them in,” Leilani said.

“Yeah. And this.” Mele passed a swab, stained faint blue. “Indigo pigment on the boy’s palm. Not from his clothes or the mud. Probably ceremonial.”

Leilani looked back at the bodies, the surf pounding so loud now she felt it in her teeth. “Have you seen anything like this before?”

Mele nodded. “Closest was the Manoa case four years ago. The so-called ‘Kapu Killer.’ But that guy staged the bodies; there wasn’t any of the cleansing.”

Leilani thanked her and walked back to where Isaac waited. She filled him in.

“So, what’s the theory?” he asked. “You think someone’s reviving this Kapu?”

She exhaled hard. “It doesn’t make sense. Kapu was abolished by law in 1819. No one talks about it unless it’s for tourists.”

He waited.

“But people don’t forget. Not really.” She flicked her flashlight over the trees, the old roots that rose like petrified snakes from the mud. “My tutu used to say this was the place where everything ends. Kaena Point, the leap-off for souls. If you wanted to send someone to the next world, this is where you did it."

Isaac folded his arms. "So, someone's playing God."

She almost smiled. "Not God. Priest."

They approached the main grave, where Mori stood, the phone pressed to her ear. She was arguing in clipped, barely controlled tones with someone on the other end. Leilani waited for her to hang up. "Mele got salt in the soil samples, ritual cleansing." She turned to Isaac. "Call Tommy and have him track the victim's last movements. Also, have Tano and Akira dig up every recent case with ties to old religion or ceremonial practice, especially unsolved cases."

Isaac nodded, pulled his phone from his pocket and stepped away. Mori stared at Leilani. "There's more. We got a tip on the anonymous line. Someone claiming to know where the next body will be."

Leilani raised her eyebrows. "Next?"

Mori handed her the phone; the message popped up on the screen. It read in block capitals: **THREE DOWN, MORE TO FOLLOW. STOP ME BEFORE I KILL AGAIN.**

Isaac stepped up and read over her shoulder. "Someone's counting."

Mori said, "This is a top priority, Lei. Put everything else aside."

Leilani nodded; the heaviness of it settled right between her shoulders. "We'll start here. Work outward."

Mori gave her the tiniest smile. "I knew I had called the right team."

She moved off, leaving Leilani and Isaac alone with the graves.

Isaac looked at her, waiting.

She closed her eyes, then opened them to the surf and the stars, faint now, but still there, somewhere above the canopy.

"Worst part isn't what happens to the dead," she said, voice soft. "It's what comes next."

Isaac nodded, understanding.

They walked to the banyan grove and watched the horizon, where the fog gave way to open ocean and the sky hung heavy with the echo of the stories. Tomorrow will bring new bodies, new puzzles and new ghosts. But for tonight, the thing that mattered was not letting the island forget what it meant to watch and to remember.

The next case had started, and there was no turning back.

Chapter Four

Leilani's left eye wouldn't stop twitching. She'd slept less than three hours in the past two nights and felt every minute in her knees. The HPD conference room was packed. Uniforms, detectives, forensic techs, and a handful who didn't belong, shoulder to shoulder with a silent, electric expectation. The air was thick with burned coffee and the impossible scent of sea spray that seemed to follow her everywhere.

On the wall behind her, the whiteboard was a crime scene in itself. Photos of the three Kaena Point victims were taped side by side, each one showing the bodies as they'd been found: hands bound, wrists raw, salt-burned skin, and ceremonial flowers scattered at their feet. To the left, someone had scrawled VICTIM #1: BECKETT, NATHAN—MISSING 2 MONTHS in red marker. The other two were below, each in a column with every known detail: names, last seen, next of kin, points of connection.

Leilani faced the crowd, running her thumb over the faded bruises on her arm. Isaac sat to her right, eyes scanning the room. Espinoza and Tano stood behind, a half-step back, not quite at ease. Chief Mori leaned against the far wall, arms folded, and her mouth drawn in a flat line.

She sensed the mood shift before the door even opened.

A blast of refrigerated air, then the unmistakable staccato of military boots on vinyl. NCIS Special Agent Victoria Castellano strode in, trailed by her federal entourage in navy blue NCIS windbreakers. Vic, as everyone knew her, was the same height as Leilani, but carried a few more pounds. She had dark brown hair, cut short, and an olive complexion that gave her an exotic appearance. She also had a permanent scowl. Every movement, every clipped syllable she spat at her second-in-command said she owned the place.

Castellano's phone was plastered to her ear, and she didn't look happy. "No, sir," she said with a scowl. "I know we have a vested interest in this case, and I assure you, sir. We will get to the bottom of it even if we have to run over people." She listened. "No, sir. I won't let you down." She shoved her phone into her back pocket.

Without waiting for an invitation, Castellano moved to the head of the table, parked her hands on her hips, and let her badge swing like a challenge. The NCIS team fanned out: two men in identical windbreakers, and a woman in a bun so tight it looked like a threat. Every HPD cop in the room tensed, waiting for someone to flinch.

Leilani perceived the adrenaline trickle down her spine. She saw it mirrored in Isaac's body, his foot tapping faster, and his thumb running rapidly over the scar on his knuckle. The person who looked relaxed was Tano, who seemed amused by the entire performance.

Castellano started talking before Leilani could introduce her team. "We are taking over as of now. The base commander expects a preliminary report in three hours. You will forward all evidence, digital and physical, to our secure lab." She didn't look at anyone; she expected compliance, full stop.

Leilani crossed her arms. "We're happy to cooperate, but the victims include civilians. The jurisdiction is joint, per the mayor's office."

A flicker of something, impatience or boredom, crossed Castellano's face. "This is a matter of national security," she said. "If your department can't keep the scene from being trampled by reporters and tourists, I suggest you focus your resources on crowd control."

The room went deathly silent.

Isaac glanced at Leilani, a single raised eyebrow. Tano and Espinoza braced, arms folded, backs straightening in solidarity. Even Chief Mori's jaw flexed, as if daring Castellano to keep talking.

Leilani took a breath, then another. She kept her voice level. "Our forensic team preserved all the evidence. No press leaks came from HPD. If you want our files, you can have them, but we're running point until the mayor or the governor says otherwise."

The word governor had weight here. Castellano didn't like it, but she nodded, one quick bob of the head, acknowledging the line drawn in the sand.

Leilani kept her eyes fixed on the federal agent, not blinking. She gestured to the whiteboard. "The bodies were staged in positions that mimic ancient burial rites. Whoever did this wasn't improvising; they have deep local knowledge, or at least access to someone who does. If you have military suspects, we need to know which of them spent time in the islands or studied

Hawaiian history. This isn't just a random serial killer."

Castellano's mouth twitched. "Primitive theatrics. Designed to distract. The real pattern is in the victim selection."

She motioned to her aide, who passed around a glossy folder stamped NCIS: CONFIDENTIAL. "Every victim is connected to the military, either by employment, marriage or immediate family. Your so-called ritual is a smokescreen for a personal or ideological motive. I would recommend you spend less time analyzing flower arrangements, and more time on military base access and psychological profiling."

The insult hung in the air, waiting for someone to snap.

But Leilani had learned to hold steady, even when it felt like drowning. She pointed to the photos, this time using a metal pointer she grabbed from the chalk tray. "The murderer used saltwater for postmortem cleansing. That's not for show. The killer risked returning to the crime scene hours after the first burial. You don't do that for theatrics. You do it because you believe in what you're doing."

Castellano glared, but Leilani saw something else flicker in her eyes. Recognition or a challenge.

Mori finally stepped forward, her voice low but clear. "Agent Castellano, Detective Kealoha is our subject matter expert. She's solved every serial since the Kaimuki cases. We can brief you in twenty minutes, or you can read her file."

Castellano nodded once, eyes never leaving Leilani. She shrugged off her jacket, revealing an arm covered in old scars and tattoos. She took a seat at the corner of the table, chin up, every muscle coiled and ready.

Leilani didn't sit. She paced, her voice steady. "Victim one, Nathan Beckett. He was a civilian dentist and worked at Hickam. He also served on the joint advisory board for the Navy. He was lobbying for increased medical contracts. Missing two months before the body turned up."

She tapped the second column. "Victim two, Kaipo Ikaika. Active duty, but with disciplinary issues. His family lives in Nanakuli, which is a two-minute drive from the first dump site. He was last seen at an AA support group on the base."

She rapped her knuckles on the third column. "Victim three, Jessica Brown. She's a civilian but married to a junior officer out of Pearl. He's on assignment and the Navy is trying to reach him. Their son was enrolled at the base school. She worked part-time as a janitor at Hickam, fired two weeks before her disappearance. Security footage has her on base after hours."

She turned back to Castellano. "There's overlap, but nothing suggesting a direct connection. Unless you have something we don't?"

Castellano rolled her eyes, but one of her team passed over a printed sheet. internal emails from the base, all blacked out except for the dates and subject lines. "We believe all three received threatening communications. But without the bodies, no one took it seriously."

Leilani took the printout, scanning fast. She looked up. "You withheld this from HPD."

"Chain of command," Castellano said, her voice flat.

There was a low murmur from the room, a rustling of uniforms and quiet outrage.

Leilani felt her temper rise, but she kept it tamped down. "You have reason to believe more targets are planned?"

"We believe the killer is escalating," Castellano replied. She snapped her fingers at her aide. "Show them the file."

The aide flicked a laptop open, projecting onto the white screen on the wall. Images flashed, first the Kaena Point graves, then a series of anonymous threats sent to base personnel. Most were generic: "You will pay for your trespass." "The land remembers." A few, however, were specific, referencing bloodlines, old vendettas and phrases only a native speaker would know.

Isaac leaned in. "You think this is a local, or someone pretending?"

Castellano said, "A local. But with access to the base."

Leilani saw where this was going. She was being set up as the cultural interpreter, the one to root out a traitor from her own people.

She felt the muscles in her jaw clench. "If you think

someone from this department is involved, say it."

Castellano didn't flinch. "If I thought that, you'd be in cuffs already."

The insult rolled off, but Leilani noted the warning in the room. She felt the weight of every pair of eyes, her own team, Mori and the federal agents, all waiting for her to lose her cool.

She didn't. She took a breath, nodded once, and turned back to her whiteboard.

"We'll get you everything by noon. But I want every piece of threat analysis you've run, and a full base personnel roster."

Castellano stood and glared at Leilani. "We'll see if you can deliver. We're gonna go get some coffee in the breakroom. Back in ten."

She walked out, trailed by her team. The room held its breath until the door slammed shut behind her.

Leilani faced the board, letting her own heartbeat slow.

Mori was the first to speak. "If you need to hit her, warn me first so I can clear the cameras."

There was a round of nervous laughter, but it didn't break the tension.

Isaac leaned close. "She's going to be a problem."

"She already is," Leilani said.

Tano grinned. "I like the fire. But next time, don't mention the governor until you have the governor on the line."

Leilani forced a smile. "Noted."

The next thirty minutes went to triage. Espinoza and Tano started a database of all reported threats at the base; Isaac and Leilani huddled over the emails and printouts from Castellano's team. The office cleared out, slowly, leaving just the core detectives.

When they were alone, Leilani slumped into the nearest chair, rubbing her temples.

"Do you want to talk about it?" Isaac asked.

She shook her head, too tired for anything except the facts.

He handed her a coffee, extra strong. "You think she's right about the motive?"

"No," Leilani said, the word flat. "She wants to frame it as military-on-military violence. But there's a reason the rituals are so specific. She does this on every investigation we've been involved with. It's not just anger; it's a message. Or a warning."

"To who and what do you mean she does this all the time?" asked Isaac.

Leilani chose not to answer. Not yet.

She looked at the wall, the photos of the dead, and let her own mind go blank, just for a second. Then she squared her shoulders, tossed back the coffee, and got back to work.

The war had moved from the beach to the boardroom, and Leilani wasn't about to lose ground now.

Chapter Five

They reconvened after a break, the temperature in the conference room somehow even colder despite the growing crowd. Leilani hung back for a moment, arms folded, as Castellano commandeered the monitor at the head of the table and cued up a PowerPoint titled "OPERATION: LOKAHI."

She didn't bother with context. The first slide was a military-grade map of Oahu, with every base, and checkpoint marked in red. Castellano tapped the screen with a telescoping pointer, her voice snapping like a switch. "You see here, here, and here; these are the primary access points to the island's secure facilities. All three victims had access to at least two of these locations. If you cross-reference their movements in the days prior to their disappearances."

She clicked, moving to a spreadsheet dense with time stamps and acronyms. "You'll note that each of them entered a restricted area without clearance at least once. We're dealing with someone who knows their routines and the base's blind spots. Probably an inside operator. Could be active duty, could be retired. But it's someone with an axe to grind."

Every slide, every click, was accompanied by a hard rap on the table. Leilani watched Castellano's eyes, never on the evidence for long, always flitting to the HPD shield on Leilani's lanyard, to the three stripes on Tano's sleeve, and to the unblinking boredom of Akira, who was already playing some game on her phone under the table.

Castellano didn't miss the gesture. "Agent Akira, you'll be reporting to my technical team for the duration of this investigation. And Sergeant Pualani, your expertise in local customs will be invaluable. You're on loan to us, effective immediately."

A beat. Two heartbeats.

Leilani stepped forward slowly and placed her palm flat on the table. She let her voice go a half-octave deeper, even as her heart thudded with rage. "My detectives report to me, Agent Castellano. This is still our jurisdiction."

Castellano didn't blink. "This is a military matter now, Detective. Your team can assist, or you can step aside."

Leilani sensed the room lurch, every pair of eyes flicking to her. She looked at Akira, who stopped chewing her thumbnail, and then at Tano, who gave the world's tiniest nod.

She did not back down. "We're not tourists in our own city, Agent. If you want cooperation, you'll treat my people with respect."

"Respect is earned," Castellano shot back.

"So is trust." Leilani didn't move, didn't smile. "And I haven't seen any reason to trust you yet."

Castellano stepped closer, and for a second the gap between them was nothing. Leilani saw the faint stitches behind the agent's left ear, the cigarette burn on her index finger, and the way her hands never stopped moving.

Castellano lowered her voice. "You want to play

hero, that's your business. But if you get in my way."

"You'll what?" Leilani asked, equally softly.

Castellano's lips curled, almost a smirk. "I'll make it so you're chasing parking violations for the rest of your career."

Isaac finally intervened, stepping in with his palms open. "We all want the same thing, right? Catch the killer before another body drops?"

For a moment, the tension held. Then Castellano looked at Isaac like he were an errant child. "You must be Torres. I read your file. Didn't realize you were the peacekeeper."

He smiled, not flinching. "I just hate paperwork."

Castellano turned back to Leilani, squared off. "We'll be coordinating every move from here on out. You want to work the case, you run everything by me."

She strode from the room, her people falling in line. As soon as the door closed, the whole HPD squad seemed to inhale at once.

Akira spoke first. "I am not reporting to any desk-jockey Fed. Just saying."

Leilani shook her head, amused. "No one's going anywhere unless I say so."

Tano grinned, voice a low rumble. "You know, in my family, if someone disrespected you like that, you'd challenge them to a surf-off. No talking, just who can ride the biggest wave."

"That's not how it works in law enforcement," Leilani said.

Espinoza piped up from the back. “How does it work here?”

“It’s about who blinks first,” Leilani replied.

Torres, now leaning against the credenza, asked, “Do you think she’s right? About the inside connection?”

“I think she’s not wrong,” Leilani said. She thought of the rituals, the saltwater, the bundles of flowers that didn’t belong. “But she’s missing half the story. It’s not just military procedure. There’s a reason the killer goes through all the cultural steps. They want to be understood or remembered.”

Akira rolled her eyes. “So, we’re looking for a pissed-off soldier who’s also into flower arranging.”

“Or someone who wants us to think that,” Isaac said.

Mori’s voice cut through from the back. “I want a list of every base personnel who’s been on disciplinary leave in the last year, especially anyone with family from the islands. Tano, you take point. Akira, see if you can get those emails the Feds didn’t share.”

Leilani nodded, feeling the weight settle on her shoulders. “Torres, with me. We’re going to the base.”

He arched an eyebrow. “You think Castellano will let you on?”

“She’ll try to stop me. But she won’t.”

They all broke off, gathering their things with renewed purpose. As Leilani left, she heard Espinoza mutter to Akira, “She should’ve just punched the Fed in the face."

Akira snorted. "No, Lei's smarter. She'll break her from the inside out."

In the hallway, Isaac fell in step beside her. "Are you good?"

"Not yet," Leilani said. "But I will be."

They said nothing more as they walked to the elevator, both knowing the real fight had just started.

The elevator dinged, a soft but final note. Leilani and Isaac slipped into the small glass foyer at HPD headquarters, the sunlight knifing in at an angle that made them squint. They barely had time to check their phones, already filling up with calls from the press office, the ME, and Mori herself, before a shadow fell across the tile.

Castellano had been waiting. She leaned against the far wall, her jaw set. For a second, neither woman spoke.

Isaac cleared his throat and moved between them, the mediator's dance. He put both hands up, one to each rival. "Look, we're all on the same page here, okay? Nobody wants more bodies, and nobody wants the press getting wind of a turf war."

He glanced at Leilani, then Castellano, his voice even. "Let's do this the smart way. We formalize a joint task force. Every update, every lead, gets kicked to both sides, and nobody sits on anything. We agree to review evidence together before reporting up the chain."

Castellano considered him for a long, predatory

moment. "You think you can keep her on a leash, Torres?"

He smiled, all teeth. "No one ever could."

Leilani's fists clenched, but she kept her voice polite. "If you want a partnership, Vic, it starts with mutual respect."

"Fine," Castellano said. "But if you sandbag me again, I'll bury you."

"Deal," Leilani shot back. They shook on it, and the air was still. Then Castellano stalked off towards the waiting black SUV, her team in tow.

Isaac watched her go, then turned to Leilani. "You gonna keep it together?"

She was about to answer when Mori's voice, flat as a gunshot, called from behind. "Kealoha."

Chief Mori stood at the entrance to the stairwell, her face unreadable. She nodded for Leilani to follow. They walked into the cinder-block corridor, the whine of ancient fluorescents overhead making everything look jaundiced. Mori stopped, hands in her pockets, and leaned close.

"The mayor's office is already getting calls from the base commander. You need to find a way to work with NCIS without sacrificing our investigation."

Leilani tried to keep her frustration from boiling over. "I understand the politics, Chief, but Castellano is ignoring anything that doesn't fit her narrative. She doesn't want to hear about the rituals or the local angle."

Mori's gaze sharpened. "You don't have to like her, but you must be better. Castellano plays chess one move at a time. You play chess and see the entire board. If she pushes you, use it. Just don't get blindsided by ego."

Leilani nodded. "Understood."

"Find common ground, Detective. That's an order."

There was no room for protest. Leilani caught Mori's meaning: solve the case, keep the peace, or find herself sidelined. Mori turned, her shoes making no sound on the concrete, and left Leilani in the humming gloom. She waited for a beat, then stepped out into the light.

Back in the foyer, Isaac waited with his hands jammed in his pockets. "She chew you out?"

"She gave me a pep talk," Leilani said.

He grinned. "You're bad at lying."

She let it go, just this once.

They started for the car, ready to do it all over again.

Chapter Six

The following morning, they regrouped in the briefing room. A dozen desks had been pushed into a crude horseshoe, the central table now a litter of half-drunk coffee, evidence bags, and a growing stack of NCIS paperwork. The HPD team clustered together on one side, the Feds occupying the other, an imaginary border as obvious as a velvet rope at a club.

Isaac paced the perimeter, barely noticing the cold cup in his hand. Tano scrolled his phone, and Akira ran a quiet battle with the precinct's ancient printer, kicking it every few minutes to coax out a page. Leilani sat with her hands flat on the table, staring at the crime scene photos, willing them to yield something Castellano couldn't dismiss.

The door burst open, hinges groaning. Espinoza hustled in, a battered red folder in hand and sweat darkening the neck of his shirt.

"Got something," he panted, dropping the folder onto the table so hard that it scattered the paperwork. The HPD detectives closed in.

Espinoza flipped the folder open. "I started digging for anything the victims had in common besides the military. All three attended this special DOD workshop last summer. Some kind of Cultural Heritage Leadership Seminar." He tapped the cover. "Funded by the Office of Pacific Affairs, mandatory for certain staff."

Leilani snatched the curriculum packet. She leafed

through the printouts; the pages whispering under her hands, and her pulse quickened. It wasn't just diversity training. The roster included months of immersive seminars, field visits to sacred sites, even a guest lecturer with the words Kuleana Legacy handwritten next to his name.

Leilani ran a finger down the workshop schedule. "Here. Day Three—Kapu and Warrior Traditions. And this: the last session included a death-rite demonstration and comparative ritual burial practices."

The room fell still.

Castellano, at the far end, snorted. "Every base does these workshops. They're boilerplate. Mandatory PowerPoint and an awkward luau at the end."

Leilani locked onto her. "This wasn't some bland cultural awareness week, Castellano. The instructor is a kahuna. A real one. And the burial demonstration? Matches the body staging at Kaena Point, exactly."

Castellano didn't budge. "So, someone took notes at a seminar and acted out? That's not a smoking gun, Detective."

Akira chimed in, waving her freshly printed sheet. "They didn't just attend. All three victims sat on a panel together. It was called Improving Protocols for the Next Generation. That's a quote. The next scheduled event was canceled without explanation."

Tano leaned over the table. "Have you ever heard of this Kuleana Legacy group, Lei?"

"No," she said. "but I'll bet someone at the

university knows. Or the Office of Pacific Affairs. We need to talk to the seminar coordinator."

Espinoza tapped the victim list. "I pulled the full roster. There are nine other names that did the workshop, but three have gone missing so far."

Castellano flipped through the roster, clearly annoyed. "We'll have them all under protection by the end of the day. Or we'll get lucky and catch our killer waiting outside one of their houses."

Leilani took the list and ran her finger down the column, memorizing each name. "This is it. The connection we were missing."

She caught Castellano's gaze. "You still think it's a coincidence?" asked Leilani.

Castellano offered a lazy shrug. "Coincidence or not, we have a pattern. Let's use it."

For a heartbeat, it looked like they might agree on something. Then Castellano added, "But I still think you're chasing ghosts, Detective."

Leilani smiled, cold and real. "Sometimes, Agent, ghosts are the only ones who tell the truth."

They stared each other down, the battered red folder spread wide between them, a battlefield, a manifesto and a puzzle no one could solve alone. The briefing room pulsed with a new urgency. The case, and the competition, had just kicked into a higher gear.

Chapter Seven

Leilani hated the way her nerves felt whenever she pulled up to her mother's house, like she was parking in a churchyard, expecting to be ambushed by ghosts. The street outside was lined with tidy single-levels and hibiscus hedges, all cut to regulation height. Someone three doors down was burning kiawe in a backyard grill, the smoke mixing with the first tinge of evening rain. She killed the engine and waited a moment, letting the dashboard clock cycle its digital whine.

Inside, the house was exactly as she remembered. The living room was a relic, dark wood shelves bowing under the weight of salt-glazed figurines, yellowing class photos, and framed sheets of old hula chants. The corners glowed with tiny domestic shrines, each a complicated mess of shells, dried kukui nuts, votive candles and tiny clay images. Ti leaves braided into thick green ropes hung beside the door, and the air was sharp with the bite of ‘awa root tea and a vague, holy funk from the lingering smudge of incense. The world's only patchouli-hating kumu hula, her mother insisted on only sandalwood and pure ‘ala for the spirits.

She barely had time to kick off her shoes before Naalei emerged from the kitchen, cheeks flushed and hair pinned back in a loose gray bun. She wore her old blue muumuu and a mother-of-pearl puka shell necklace, same as always.

"You look like a wet cat," Naalei said by way of greeting. Her voice was gentle but precise. "Sit. I'll get you tea."

Leilani obeyed, sliding onto the vinyl-upholstered couch. Her mother's living room was so familiar that she felt the rules of childhood close in around her. She pulled out her notebook, then hesitated, not sure how to say what she needed to say.

Naalei returned, setting down two mugs of muddy tea. She folded herself into the chair opposite, one ankle tucked beneath her like a schoolgirl. "You said it was important."

Leilani exhaled. "I can't go into details. But I'm working a case with ritualistic aspects." She left out the word murder. There was no need.

Naalei's eyebrows lifted. "You always bring the good stories."

Leilani tried to smile but failed. She set her mug aside, flipping open the notebook. She sketched the layout from memory, three graves, bodies facing west, flowers, and tokens at the feet.

Naalei watched, eyes sharp behind their deepening wrinkles. "Kaena Point?"

"Yes," Leilani said. "The first one was an older man, hands bound, throat cut. They cleaned the body with saltwater. The others, a mother, and child. The same thing. Each grave had a different offering. Plumeria, red ti, breadfruit, shells. And blue pigment on the boy's hands."

Her mother inhaled long and quietly. Her hands trembled as she reached for the tea, then steadied. She sipped, staring at the sketch.

"Whoever did this," Naalei said finally, "knows old things. Things I haven't taught for years."

Leilani nodded. "I thought so. Some of it's close, but a few details are off. Modern. Like they read it in a book, then tried to make it real."

"Did they leave weapons?" Naalei's voice dropped, gone flat as stone.

Leilani shut her eyes, remembering the blood-clotted sticks, the jagged basalt slivers. "Yes. The kind you see at the Bishop Museum, not on the street."

Her mother's lips thinned. "Lei, you're not talking about a normal killing. This is intended for shame. For punishment."

Leilani splayed her hands, palms up. "That's why I came. I need to know how it should be done. Or how someone might misuse it."

Naalei turned away, gaze locked on the battered bookshelf. Her voice came low, more to the room than to her daughter. "In old times, when a warrior was defeated in great dishonor, by betrayal or cowardice, they were not allowed to cross to the next place. The bones would be arranged to prevent their spirit from leaving. The offerings you saw, those were not to honor, but to bind."

Leilani scribbled the words, but her pen shook. "Bind?"

"A curse," said Naalei. "It keeps the soul restless. This is not how we do things, not anymore. Only the most bitter would resurrect that practice."

She stood suddenly, as if the act of sitting was itself

a burden. She moved to the altar in the corner and, with careful hands, pinched off a sliver of sandalwood from the offering bowl. She struck a match, the sulfur catching and the scent rushed through the room. It was cleaner than incense from Chinatown, crisp, earthy, and sharp.

"Mom," Leilani said. Her own voice felt small. "Who would do this?"

Naalei cupped her hands over the tiny curl of smoke. "Someone who hates the living as much as the dead. Someone who's lost their own kuleana, who feels the only justice is in making others suffer."

She picked up a tattered, cloth-bound ledger from beside the shrine. "I will speak with the other kumu. Someone may know who is twisting the old stories like this." Her tone suggested both resolve and dread.

Leilani finished her tea in one gulp. The root numbed her tongue, yet her nerves kept firing.

"There's more," she blurted out before she could lose the thread. "The Feds, they're running the investigation like it's a military op. They think the killer is targeting people with military backgrounds. But to my eyes the rituals are the message. They want to be seen."

Her mother's face was unreadable, all the warmth pulled inward. "You must tread carefully, Lei. The people who keep these secrets do not fear the police. They fear nothing but being forgotten."

"I know," Leilani said.

A long silence pressed in, broken only by the quiet

fizz of sandalwood as it turned to ash.

“I’m sorry,” Leilani said, softer now. “To bring this to your house.”

Naalei shook her head. “You are my child. You bring everything home.” She crossed the room and touched Leilani’s hair, just for a second, the way she did when Leilani was small and sick.

They sat for a while, neither speaking. At last, Naalei took the burned wood, wrapped it in ti leaf, and set it on the sill. She looked older than Leilani had ever seen her.

“I will call tonight,” she said. “If anyone knows, I’ll find them.”

Leilani nodded and stood, tucking the notebook into her jacket. At the door, she hesitated. The garden outside was black with the coming rain; the frangipani blossoms closed against the damp.

“Be careful,” Naalei called after her, voice almost breaking.

Leilani tried to answer, but the words would not come.

Leilani barely made it to the front door before fifty pounds of denim and pre-teen bravado collided with her knees.

“You won’t believe what I found out!” Kai shouted, both arms locking around her hips.

“Let me guess,” she said, pulling him off with practiced ease. “You finally figured out which bug lives in your backpack?”

He made a face. "No. I mean, yes, but that's not it. It's for my project."

The house was alive with sound: television voices leaking from the living room, the neighbor's parrot squawking insults through the open kitchen window, and her own mother humming low over the stove. A fragrant tangle of dinner smells, garlic and something fried, filled the air. Leilani hung her jacket, feeling some of the cold from Naalei's house melt away.

Kai was already spreading his loot across the kitchen table: a poster board curling at the corners, sheets of ruled notebook paper peppered with cryptic notes, a battered laptop with the spacebar missing. He wore a t-shirt two sizes too big, sleeves rolled up to the shoulder, and there was a streak of glue running down his forearm. He buzzed around the table like a bee.

"It's about warriors!" Kai said. "Real ones, not the fake ones in games. Did you know the first Hawaiian army wasn't just all men? And they had, like, their own doctors and spies?"

"Espionage," Leilani corrected, grinning. "I believe it. Your tutu used to say there's nothing more dangerous than a Hawaiian grandma with secrets."

Kai snorted, already distracted. "I did interviews, too. With actual veterans. And Mrs. Borden at school says I can get extra credit if I find someone who was at Pearl Harbor, but that's basically impossible unless you know a time traveler."

He rifled through a folder, pulling out a crumpled page. "Look, Mom! Ancient warriors had to memorize chants before going into battle. Like a password, but for your brain. If you screwed it up, you got sent home."

Leilani scanned the notes, amused and more than a little proud. She spotted references to Kamehameha, to modern ROTC at school, even to the annual culture week the base ran every year for dependents.

Something on the last sheet snagged her attention. A handout with a logo she recognized from the HPD whiteboard—Office of Pacific Affairs, Culture Leadership Workshop. It was the same name Espinoza had dropped in the briefing.

She flipped the sheet over. Kai had highlighted the phrase, "Ceremonial burial demonstration—see page 12 for safe handling and best practices."

"You used the printer at school?" she asked, eyebrows arched.

"Of course." He shrugged as if that were obvious. "Mr. Alvarez lets us print five pages a week if it's for homework and not memes."

She paged through the bundle, her heart ticking faster as she recognized names from the case, victim, and witnesses alike, listed as panelists or guest instructors.

"Mom?" Kai tugged at her sleeve. "You're doing the cop thing. Where you stare and don't blink for like ten minutes."

She laughed, but the sense of ice was back. She kneeled, putting her face level with his. "Hey, did your teacher tell you how the workshops work? Like, do they do the demonstrations every year, or is it special?"

Kai shrugged, thinking. "I dunno. I only know because Nani's brother did one last year. He had to wear a lava-lava and do a chant, and then they taught them how to build a heiau with rocks. Kinda cool, but mostly boring, he said."

She nodded. "Do you remember who the teacher was?"

"Mrs. Kimo? Wait, no. She was the advisor. The head guy was from the university. He wore the funny beaded necklace."

She tapped the worksheet, picking out the name. "Dr. Kekoa," she read aloud. "Is that him?"

"Yeah!" Kai's face lit up. "He was kind of strict, I think. But everyone said he's like, the expert for old Hawaiian stuff."

The pieces slotted together, slowly but inevitably.

In the periphery, Naalei set a bowl of rice and fried fish on the table, her own face turned away. Leilani saw her mother's hands, quick and sure but clenched at the knuckles.

Kai chattered obliviously. "So, if you're doing something with real cops, can I interview you for my project? Mrs. Borden said it's okay if your family is interesting."

Leilani tried to conjure a smile, then tried harder. "Not for this one, Kai."

He pouted but accepted a forkful of food anyway.

She sat beside him, flipping through the highlighted printouts, the frantic scrawl of a child merging with the clean, institutional language of the workshop. Victim names reappeared: not just Beckett, but the woman and her son. Each one had attended the workshop. Every single one. She stared at her son, at the wild hair and impossible innocence, and wondered how close the darkness really was.

Kai chewed, considering. "You look worried, Mom."

She didn't want to lie. "Just tired, kiddo."

From the stove, her mother said nothing, but the scrape of the ladle on the pot was louder than it should have been.

They finished dinner together, the three of them, passing bowls and bad jokes and, for a moment, pretending the world outside their walls wasn't hungry for more blood.

When she tucked Kai in later, he clung to her longer than usual. "Night, Mom," he said, already half asleep.

"Night, bug," she whispered, and shut the door behind her.

In the kitchen, her mother waited.

"It's coming here," Naalei said, voice low and final.

Leilani nodded.

She glanced at the mess on the table, glue stains, history and the careless truth of a child's research, and saw how the pattern twisted tighter, night after night, around the things she loved.

She didn't sleep, not even after the house fell silent. Not with the printouts still lit on the table, not with the last words of her mother in her ears. It's coming here. And Leilani knew she was right.

Chapter Eight

The station was always too bright. Even in the dead hours, the fluorescent panels made everything look pale and unreal, as if the walls were scrubbed with bleach and the air itself was a kind of poison. Leilani walked in through the back, through a corridor that stank of mildew and day-old takeout, and let the noise of dispatch radios and desk phones crowd out the quiet her mother's house had left in her.

Her badge got her past the sleepy watch sergeant with only a grunt. She bypassed her own desk, ignored the sticky note pyramid that had accumulated in her absence, and headed straight for the evidence storage. Her sneakers squeaked on the floor, every step tight with purpose.

The evidence room was three rows of chain link cages and rolling drawer units, most of it packed with weapons, laptops, or whatever contraband the patrol units scooped up. The low hum of dehumidifiers ran beneath it all. She keyed the pad, punched in the code, and waited for the slow click.

Half the drawers were empty. The ones that weren't had new evidence tags, bright yellow, stamped with NCIS in all caps and a chain-of-custody signature that wasn't anyone from her department. She double-checked the log, her hand drifting to the grip of her phone, already halfway to calling Akira.

She heard someone behind her, a footfall, and a catch of breath.

It was Isaac, wearing a suit he'd already slept in, tie loose, hair a mess. "Are you looking for the murder book?" he asked.

"I was looking for the evidence," she said, keeping her voice low. "It's gone. All of it."

He didn't flinch. "Castellano ordered it up to their lab. Said the feds have a new protocol. Mori was outvoted."

"Since when?" Leilani felt her jaw tighten.

Isaac shrugged. "She made a move while you were off shift. Her techs boxed up everything, even the stuff you flagged for secondary analysis."

She pressed her hands flat against the drawer, trying to steady herself. "They took the flowers. The shells. Even the salt sample from the first grave."

"All of it," he confirmed, a dull edge in his voice. "You knew she would do it eventually. I just met her, but I can tell she plays for keeps."

Leilani leaned back against the caged shelving. "She doesn't care about the case. She cares about winning."

"Some people can't see the difference," he said.

They stood in silence, the noise of the compressors and the cold light pressing in.

Isaac nodded towards the door. "She's in the main conference. Brought her whole crew. If you want to throw down, that's where she'll be."

Leilani didn't answer, didn't need to. She strode out of the evidence room, down the central corridor, past the staring faces at every desk. A few uniforms looked away; a few watched with dark, calculating eyes like they were taking bets on who would win.

The conference room was a glass fishbowl in the center of the building, all sightlines and nowhere to hide. Castellano held court at the far end, her team hunched over laptops and coffee cups, some of them wearing gun belts even at the table. She saw Leilani, and her eyes lit up with the kind of welcome reserved for root canals and car accidents.

"Detective Kealoha," Castellano said, not bothering to stand. "Is there a problem?"

Leilani walked to the whiteboard, eyes on the case timeline. "You violated the chain of custody. Those samples aren't yours to requisition."

Castellano laughed, a sound as cold as the room. "Per the task force agreement, all physical evidence is now under federal supervision. If your team can't keep it from getting contaminated, maybe you're not as culturally competent as you think."

The NCIS agents around the table didn't so much as blink. One of them chewed on a pen, gaze flicking between the two women like a tennis match.

Leilani didn't shout, and she didn't pace. She fixed Castellano with the look that made rookies flinch and even Chief Mori think twice. "If you don't understand what you're looking at, you'll miss the whole point. These weren't random signatures. They were precise. Someone is trying to tell us something in a language you refuse to learn."

Castellano smiled, wide and sharp. "We're not here to chase fairy tales, Detective. We're investigating three homicides. Possibly four, if you count the one that's about to happen when you get yourself killed by making this personal."

A hush settled over the room. Even the printer in the corner seemed to stall, as if waiting.

Leilani stepped in, lowering her voice. "You can't just strip the culture from this and hope it solves itself. The person you're looking for is trying to draw you into the story. You'll never catch them if you don't read the words."

Castellano's eyes narrowed. "You're sounding like a suspect yourself, Kealoha. Is there something you want to confess?"

Leilani's fists clenched. For a second, she almost did something stupid.

Then Isaac's hand landed on her shoulder, a grip gentle but strong. He leaned in, close enough that only she could hear. "Not here. Not now," he whispered.

She didn't move, but her pulse slowed. She gave Castellano a last glare, then turned on her heel, exiting to the hush of the station beyond.

Isaac caught up, matching her stride. "You're going to get yourself benched if you keep that up."

She stared straight ahead. "I don't care. Not if it means letting her run the show."

He guided her into an empty interview room, shut the door, and stood in front of it. "Pick your battles," he said, softer now. "You're right. She doesn't get it.

She doesn't want to."

Leilani slumped into a chair, the plastic creaking. "So what? We just roll over and take it? Let them trample everything?"

He sat across from her, elbows on knees. "No. We work the case from our side. We keep digging. Off the grid, if we have to. The Feds are looking for a psycho with a checklist; you and I are looking for the truth."

The room was still and gray, except for the smudge of marker on the whiteboard and the faint dust on the window ledge.

Isaac reached across, fingers brushing her hand. "You're not alone, Lei. Not in this."

She squeezed back, then let go.

For a minute, neither of them said anything. Then, quietly, Leilani straightened, wiping a stray tear she refused to name. "If Castellano wants a war," she said, "she'll get one."

Isaac smiled. "I'll bring the ammo."

They left the room together. The station still buzzed and flickered with the usual energy, but the edge had changed. The lines had been drawn and Leilani felt ready.

She'd lost her evidence, her head start and her credibility. But she had the thing that mattered most: a partner who saw the world the way she did and a team that knew how to work together.

She grinned at Isaac as they stepped out into the blue-lit hallway, the badge heavy on her chest.

“Let’s get to work,” she said.

He didn’t hesitate. “After you, Detective.”

And together, they walked into the storm.

Chapter Nine

Joint Base Pearl Harbor-Hickam squatted on a broad stretch of the island's flank, a grid of low-slung buildings and neat rectangles of grass that looked nothing like the tangle of ferns and vines that crowded the highways on the way there. Leilani drove the last mile in silence, following the line of concrete barriers to the main gate. She watched the MPs pace behind thick panes of ballistic glass, their sidearms holstered and rifles strapped across their chests.

Isaac rode shotgun, his thumb tapping the case folder with a low, nervous rhythm. "First time I ever visited a base as a cop," he said. "Last time was as a kid, tagging along with my uncle for the air show. They used to let you eat freeze-dried ice cream in the hangar."

"Don't expect any at the security office," Leilani said. She eased the Explorer to a stop at the checkpoint, rolling down the window.

The guard, a woman young enough to still get carded, took their IDs with both hands, scrutinized the badges, and called back to the office with a clipped code that even Leilani couldn't fully parse. She handed back the IDs, gestured them through, and said, "Visitor parking's past the admin block. Don't leave the car unlocked."

"Roger that," Isaac said, all business.

Past the gate, the world tightened up. The parking lots were half empty; the buildings were identical but for stenciled numerals at each entrance. A flock of wild chickens lingered by the curb, pecking at nothing, their bright feathers out of place against the olive drab and concrete. Every hundred feet, a camera tracked their movements. Leilani noted the big, new dome sensors on the light poles. Nothing like what HPD could afford.

They passed the rec field, where a dozen men ran suicide sprints across the grass, shirts off, dog tags flashing. The American and Hawaiian flags whipped side by side above the admin building, both at half-mast. Leilani felt a weird flicker in her chest at that, a recognition that even in this hyper-ordered world, grief had to show its face.

She parked as directed, stepped out, and the wall of humidity hit instantly. She left the jacket in the Explorer and clipped her badge on her belt. Isaac did the same. They walked up the shallow steps to the entrance; the lobby was perfectly clean, but for the smell of floor wax and the faint hint of bleach.

A civilian secretary sat behind a desk encased in plastic sheeting. She asked, "How can I help you?" in a voice bored to tears.

"Detectives Kealoha and Torres, HPD," Leilani said. "Here to see the base commander about the Beckett case."

The secretary typed the names into a spreadsheet, not bothering to check the spelling. "He's expecting you. It's the last office on the left."

As they moved down the corridor, Isaac murmured, "Do you think they're going to be straight with us?"

Leilani smiled without humor. “Not in a million years.”

They split at the corner, Isaac peeling off towards the mess hall to find the colleagues of the deceased. Leilani squared her shoulders and rapped on the CO’s door.

A sharp “Enter.”

Inside, the commander’s office looked like a museum diorama of military discipline. Every photo hung perfectly level; plaques lined up like gravestones; a model of a B-24 perched on the bookcase with surgical precision. The man behind the desk had a jarhead’s buzz cut and a tan that looked like he’d spent a week on the beach. He stood when she entered but didn’t offer a handshake. He was tall and stocky. His air force uniform was perfect.

“Detective Kealoha,” he said, pronouncing her name as if he were reading it off a license plate. “Colonel McGrath.”

She nodded, remaining upright as well. The man gestured to a chair, waited for her to sit before retaking his own seat. “You wanted to talk about Beckett,” he said. “I’ll save you the time. This was not a military matter. The man was on leave. If you need access to his on-base files, you’ll need a court order. Right now, I can provide basic information only.”

He said it like he’d rehearsed, and maybe he had.

Leilani took out her notebook. “Beckett was missing for two months before his body was found. That’s a long time to slip through the cracks, even for a civilian."

McGrath's eyes narrowed, just for a second. "He told his section chief that he was taking family time. He filed a leave request. Nobody suspected anything until his wife reported him missing."

"Did he have enemies on base? Conflicts? Anyone angry enough to wish him harm?"

The Colonel smiled. "Everyone has enemies, Detective. But nothing out of the ordinary. Beckett was well-liked, a bit too chummy with his subordinates, but nothing actionable. As a dentist, people seemed to like him."

She studied his knuckles: squared off, nails cut to the quick. "I'm going to be blunt, sir. Beckett wasn't murdered. He was killed in a way that suggests a message, not an impulse. He was cleaned, arranged, and left with ritual objects."

The word ritual made McGrath blink but Leilani caught it.

He straightened the already straight pad on his desk. "That's not an area I'm familiar with, Detective. If you're looking for some kind of cult activity—"

"I'm not," Leilani cut in. "But I think the killer knew a lot about old ways. Pre-contact stuff. Beckett didn't grow up here. Did he have any involvement with the community?"

A hesitation, masked by a careful clearing of the throat. "We run a few programs for cultural integration. Workshops, mainly. Twice a year the Navy brings in speakers from UH. I believe Dr.

Beckett took part in a panel last summer, something about warrior spirit integration. I didn't attend."

She wrote it down. "Who else was on that panel?"

McGrath tapped a finger, as if typing in midair. "I don't recall. Our public affairs office organizes the guests. You could ask them."

"Did anyone get upset at the workshop? Arguments, walkouts, pushback?"

His lips thinned. "Some of our civilian contractors take this heritage stuff seriously. We've had minor conflicts, but nothing warranting an investigation."

The hair on her arms prickled. "If someone took it personally, would you know?"

"Detective, I know everything that happens on my base."

He said it with such finality that Leilani had to smile, even as she felt the lie.

She switched tack. "The victim's wife, did she contact you directly after he went missing?"

"No. She called his supervisor, then base security. By the time I got the report, it was a missing person case. We put out a BOLO. You can check the log."

Leilani made a note, even though she already had.

She glanced at the wall behind the desk. Medals, commendations, and a shadowbox with a sheathed ceremonial knife.

"Are you aware that the bodies were arranged in the style of ancient war captives? Bound, left facing west, with floral bundles?"

He flinched again, this time less expertly. "I don't know what to say to that, Detective."

"I think you do," Leilani said, keeping her tone flat. "If there's anything about your personnel, resentments or complaints, now's the time to bring it up."

He stared at her, two beats longer than necessary. "I'll have my adjutant forward the after-action reports from the workshop. And a list of everyone who attended. Is that sufficient?"

"For now," she said.

McGrath got to his feet, and this time she stood with him.

"Detective, I want to be clear. We are not hiding anything from your investigation. But this is an active base with security requirements. I expect you to respect that."

Leilani closed her notebook. "And I expect you to return calls."

She let herself out, walking through the hall slowly, letting the conversation replay in her mind. When she entered the lobby, she saw Isaac through the windows of the mess hall, seated with a group of young men in identical uniforms. He was talking, but mostly listening, nodding along as the men gestured and pointed.

Leilani waited for him outside, leaning on the sun-warmed rail. She checked her phone for messages, but found nothing new except a reminder about an upcoming after-work gathering at a new bar in the city.

Isaac joined her after ten minutes, his face set in a neutral mask. “Anything?” she asked.

“They respected Beckett,” he said. “But there’s a weird tension about the workshop. Some think it’s a joke; others are convinced it’s a political trap. One guy said it ruined the unit’s morale for a month.”

“Anyone stand out?” Leilani asked.

He nodded, thinking. “A Staff Sergeant, a Filipino guy, last name Perez, said Beckett got into a shouting match with one of the cultural advisors at the last event. Something about disrespecting the old warriors. He didn’t want to say more.”

Leilani turned the words over. “You ever notice how the people who claim not to believe in this stuff are always the ones who get the most bent out of shape about it?”

Isaac snorted. “Only every case. I’m going to talk to a few more people.”

Isaac headed back towards the mess hall, and Leilani walked to her car in silence, past the two flags hanging together, the sky behind them going that weird blue-violet that meant rain was coming.

She started the car and backed out of the parking space. In the mirror, she watched the CO’s office, a faint outline behind mirrored glass. She wondered what ghosts haunted a place like this, where order was the religion and anything that slipped through was denied, then buried. She drove away with more questions than answers, but at least now she knew where to look. The pattern was forming, and it was ugly as hell.

The education center was at the far corner of the base, away from the barracks and the firing range, as if to protect the softest part of the military from the noise of its own machinery. The building was a repurposed elementary school, linoleum floors scored from decades of chairs, walls painted a nervous shade of blue. In the entry, a wire rack held rows of glossy pamphlets: TUITION ASSISTANCE, EMERGENCY FAMILY SERVICES, WORKSHOP—WARRIOR SPIRIT INTEGRATION.

Leilani picked one up and fanned the pages. The photo on the cover was a local guy in a standard-issue T-shirt, arms folded, chin up, backed by an illustrated warrior from a pre-contact mural. Inside, the text mixed corporate-speak with faux-ancient platitudes: "Unleash Your Mana," "Embrace the Challenge," "Strengthen Body and Mind the Hawaiian Way." She nearly gagged at the page showing three junior officers, all haole, trying to tie barkcloth around their waists without help.

Farther down the main hall, she found the multimedia lab. The screensaver on the projector scrolled the logo for the "Integration Initiative." She pressed play on the nearest laptop, expecting the usual slideshow, but the video was more elaborate: quick cuts of sunrise over the Koolaus, slow motion men, and women running barefoot through tall grass, a deep baritone voiceover narrating the virtues of ancient warriors as footage of boot camp recruits flashed in sequence.

In one shot, a group of service members bowed their

heads, reciting what sounded like a chant. The effect was less reverent, more forced. Leilani's skin crawled. The video concluded with the text: "Building the Leaders of Tomorrow—With Honor."

She closed the laptop, resisting the urge to slam it.

A young airman sporting the rank of airman first class, with short hair and a hint of a mustache, appeared at her elbow. "You need help, ma'am?" he asked.

Leilani flashed her badge. "Looking for someone in charge of the Warrior Spirit program."

The kid's eyes grew big, then wary. "That's Dr. Lawrence's thing, but he's on vacation. The guy who started it quit last semester. I think he's around, though. They said he's still on the island."

"Name?"

He shrugged. "People just call him Coach, but the database says his name is Makanani Ka'eo. Or Makana, I guess."

She made a note. "Where can I find him?"

Another shrug. "He tutors in the library. Sometimes he eats lunch there. Not sure if he'll talk to you, though. He's kind of..."

The airman didn't finish, just pointed her down the hallway. She took the hint and left, walking the back corridor to the library annex. On the way, she passed a wall covered in framed quotes, mostly Hawaiian proverbs, some translated so badly that she winced.

The library was a single, high-ceilinged room, lined

with sun-faded banners and cheap metal shelves. Makana was easy to spot: older, broad-shouldered, skin the dark brown of old koa wood, and hair cropped close on the sides but still thick up top, the gray more salt than pepper. He wore a blue work shirt, sleeves rolled high, arms marked with old ink. At the study table, he hunched over a stack of books, ignoring the young airmen who clustered nearby, laughing too loudly.

Leilani approached, careful not to startle him. "Excuse me, Mr. Ka'eo? Detective Kealoha. Do have a minute?"

He turned, his expression patient but wary. "It's Makana," he said.

She smiled. "Do you mind if I sit and I'd like to record our conversation if that's okay?"

He made a go-ahead gesture but watched her phone like it might sprout fangs.

"Do you know why I wanted to talk?" she asked.

His nostrils flared, just slightly. "Because people are dead."

She nodded. "You know about the investigation?"

"Everybody does. They talk about it at Foodland, the post office. Even if nobody says the names."

She sat with her notebook open. "I want to hear your take on the program. I understand you were one of the first civilian advisors."

He closed the book and folded his hands; thick fingers gnarled from some old injury. "I was the first.

Helped them build the pilot. Wrote the chants, showed them how to make practice spears without hurting themselves. I thought it was a good thing at first."

"What changed?" asked Leilani.

His lips pressed together for a long moment. "You ever seen how they do team-building on the base?" He didn't wait for her answer. "They took the old stories, the sacred protocols, and made them into games. Who can scream the loudest, and who can finish the obstacle course? I told them, this is not how you respect the ancestors. They said I was stuck in the past. That I should get with the program."

He gave a dry, mirthless laugh. "When I objected, they told me I was too emotional. Then they stopped returning my calls. Said my services were no longer required."

"And the other Hawaiian advisors?" Leilani asked.

"They all quit. Some before me, some after. One was so angry she wrote to the governor, but nothing happened. There's never a shortage of people to run the show. Always a new Dr. Lawrence."

Leilani wrote the names as he spoke. "Did you know Beckett?"

He frowned. "The dentist? Only met him twice. He liked to talk about respect, but he didn't have any. Laughed when he thought nobody was listening. Wanting the short version, the simple answer. Didn't want to learn the real thing."

She tapped her pen, thinking. "Is there anyone from the program who took it personally? Anyone who might want revenge?"

He gave her a long, appraising look. "You think it's one of us?"

"I think whoever's doing this has very specific knowledge. I'm asking if there's someone you'd worry about."

Makana looked away, out the window. "People are angry, Detective. I'm angry. But nobody I know would do this." His voice was soft now, almost tired. "There're people who believe the old stories, yes. People who never forgave what happened to their families. But to kill, like this? Not for show. Not to be found."

She heard the real answer in his denial.

The silence stretched, giving him room. "Do you have a list of everyone who completed the program?" she finally asked.

He nodded, sliding a battered folder across the table. "It's all in there. The old list, and the new one. You should talk to Kapua Silva. She's the one who wrote to the governor."

Leilani pocketed the folder. "Thank you. If you think of anything else, if someone reaches out or says something, call." She pulled a business card out of her pocket and handed it to him.

He nodded, more grim than scared. "If I hear, I'll tell you. But they won't call me. They already know I failed."

She wanted to say something to ease it, but there was nothing.

She stood, shaking his hand. “Mahalo.”

He squeezed her hand, not hard, but with a bone-deep sincerity. “Be careful, Detective.”

Back in the car, she read through the folder. All three dead were on the roster. Not just as participants, but as volunteers for the ceremonial demonstration. Their names were circled in red.

She dialed Isaac, feeling the urgency rise. “Meet me at the office,” she said. “I’ve got something you need to see.”

As she drove through the base, she saw the flags still at half-mast, but the parking lot was almost full. On the rec field, the next batch of recruits ran their sprints. From this angle, it looked like they were chasing something invisible, always just ahead.

Back at the admin building, the air was colder, the AC jacked up high to battle a heat that never reached inside. Leilani found Isaac waiting by the front desk, reviewing her text on his phone. He looked up, nodded, and they marched together down the corridor, matching pace without speaking.

The Colonel’s door was closed; Leilani rapped twice, then entered before he answered. Inside, McGrath stood by the window, hands clasped behind his back, shoulders drawn so tight they might shatter. The office was as before, every surface gleaming, every object squared to a ruler’s edge.

Isaac closed the door behind them, lingering by the bookshelf.

“Detectives,” the Colonel said. His tone suggested

anything but a welcome.

Leilani stepped up to the desk, planting her badge on the corner. “We need the complete roster for the Warrior Spirit Integration program,” she said. “Not just the public list, but the instructors, the guests, everyone with access.”

McGrath didn’t turn. “I already explained. That information is restricted. You have what you need.”

Isaac interjected, “The last three murder victims all appeared on your internal demo team. The killer is targeting from within that group.”

The Colonel did not blink. “That does not justify breaching the privacy of dozens of service members and civilians. Many are still on active duty. I can’t allow it.”

Leilani opened the battered folder Makana gave her, sliding it across the desk. “We already have names, Colonel. We’re just giving you a chance to be helpful before you end up on the news as the man who stonewalled a murder investigation.”

His jaw flexed. “This is an internal military matter. You can file a request with legal affairs, and we will respond in due course.”

The door opened behind them with a snap. NCIS Special Agent Castellano strode in, two steps ahead of a base security officer trying to catch up. She looked at the Colonel, then at Leilani, ignoring Isaac entirely.

“Problem here?” she asked, voice cool.

“Nothing that can’t be handled in the chain of command,” McGrath replied, not quite masking his irritation.

Castellano smiled, sharp, mean, and unblinking. She held up her badge to the colonel. "Per Section 301 of the federal code, any ongoing investigation of this severity requires immediate access to all relevant records. You are not exempt, Colonel. In fact, I expect a higher standard."

He froze, the tension a single wire away from snapping.

She stepped past Leilani, planting her hands on the desk and leaning in. "We need every participant's name, rank, address and contact information. That includes civilian contractors and any outside facilitators. If you want to withhold, do it in writing, and I'll make sure the base commander sees it by dinner."

"You're NCIS," he said with a scowl. "You have no authority here." He looked smug.

Castellano stepped around the desk and glared at him. "This base is part of Joint Base Pearl Harbor-Hickam. The Navy has overall responsibility for the entire base, including your little piece of it. Now, do I need to call Captain Randolf, the base commander, or would you prefer I call Admiral Stevens, the fleet commander. I understand the admiral can be very persuasive."

A long, ugly pause as the smugness disappeared. The Colonel reached for his intercom. "Janice, print all records for the integration workshops, full staff, and guest lists. Bring them here. Now."

He kept his eyes on Castellano, who did not move and did not soften.

The silence settled, broken only by the printer whirring in the next room. When the assistant entered, she held the sheaf of pages with both hands, as if offering it to a firing squad.

Leilani took the printouts, scanning the names. She saw Beckett, Brown and Ikaika on the first page, highlighted. Instructors, guest speakers, and several local cultural advisors. Dozens of names, but one column marked "Special Demo Team" caught her eye. Several names were circled in red. Two of them had already been murdered.

She glanced at Castellano, who watched her with open disdain. "Thank you," Leilani said, voice level.

Castellano turned to McGrath. "I'll have my techs contact your staff for anything digital. Expect them within the hour."

The Colonel said nothing; the set of his mouth was the only reply.

As they stepped out, Leilani slowed just enough for Castellano to fall into step beside her.

"I see you're still allergic to the chain of command," Castellano said. "You could have called me first."

"Didn't think you liked phone calls," Leilani replied.

Castellano's mouth twitched. "I like results. Next time you try to break a base, bring donuts."

She walked ahead, cutting a line through the hall.

Isaac caught Leilani's eye. "You two gonna be okay?"

"Define okay," she muttered, thumbing through the pages.

They left the building, the late sun flaring in the glass behind them. For a moment, Leilani caught her own reflection—tired, hair in disarray, badge hanging heavy. The mirror image of Castellano, framed beside her, was crisp, put-together, and perfectly composed.

She almost laughed. Instead, she headed for the car, the names on the list burning a hole through the paper and straight into her head. Somewhere on that page was a time bomb. And she was running out of time to stop the next body from dropping.

Chapter Ten

They hit the H-1 as the clouds burst open, rain so thick it bounced off the hood in glassy sheets. The city in the distance fuzzed into halos of sodium light and chrome. Leilani gripped the steering wheel tighter than she needed to; the rush of wipers and water was loud enough to crowd out her thoughts.

Isaac rode quietly for the first mile, reading the roster aloud, each name landing with a heavier thud than the last. "Every single one was on the demo team," he said, "but none of the instructors. Whoever's doing this isn't targeting authority but the people who signed up for a line on the resume. Or because they needed to prove something."

"They're not even all Hawaiian," Leilani said. "One of them, Brown, she's from the Midwest, and why murder her kid with her?"

Isaac flicked on the dome light and checked the page. "You're right. There're three non-natives, five locals, and one from American Samoa. So, what's the link?"

"Anyone who volunteers for a team-building exercise at a military base has something to prove," Leilani said. "That, or they're trying to fit in. You ever hear of survivor's guilt?"

He made a low hum, thinking. "You think the killer feels like they're purging something?"

She shrugged, watching the water bead and smear across the windshield. "They're performing a ritual. A cleansing, but there's no sign of malice, just finality. Like they're setting things right."

Isaac didn't reply, just watched the rain as it knifed down the window, streetlights blending into rivers of yellow and white.

She broke the silence: "You ever regret transferring here and then quitting the FBI?"

He arched an eyebrow. "You mean, do I regret joining HPD, or do I regret joining you on this case?"

"Either," she said.

Isaac ran a thumb along his jaw. "No, to both. But I get why you're asking."

Leilani snorted. "Dating a colleague is complicated enough. Dating while hunting a killer who desecrates bodies takes it to another level."

He grinned, more at her discomfort than at his own. "You're doing fine."

She waited, expecting him to offer some easy platitude. Instead, he leaned back and said, "You want to know what I think? I think you're carrying so much of this you can't see where it stops and you begin. If you want out, just say so."

She shot him a look. "And you'll do what? Recuse yourself?"

He grinned again, this time softer. "I'll still bring you coffee every morning. I'll just do it in a less official capacity."

She let the moment stretch; the road ahead was a blur of gray and red brake lights.

"What if this is it?" she asked, voice dropping. "What if the killer doesn't stop?"

"Then we don't stop either," Isaac said, as if it were obvious.

The rain slowed, just enough to see the city's edge as it brightened under the next break of sun. The traffic tightened, and everyone bunched together in a cautious crawl. It mirrored the knot in her own stomach, hesitant and bracing for impact.

They sat in the slow drag of cars, the engine heat seeping up through their shoes. Leilani watched the faces in other cars, tired, distracted, all of them carrying burdens no one else would ever see.

Isaac reached for her hand, squeezed it, then let go.

"We'll get them," he said. "And if you want to talk about us, let's survive this first."

Leilani almost smiled. She was confused. Isaac had been pushing for more than a work relationship since their first case together. She was the one pushing him away, because with Kai and her job, she had enough on her plate, and here, suddenly, it's Isaac pushing her to wait.

She took the exit towards police headquarters, the wet road gleaming ahead, the distance between them measured not in miles, but in what they didn't say. She dropped Isaac off at the front door and headed home.

Chapter Eleven

The kitchen was a disaster zone; open textbooks, spirals of lined paper, a rainbow of uncapped markers bleeding onto the table, and a printout of a Kamehameha mural curling off the edge. Leilani set her purse on the counter and barely dodged an incoming glue stick, courtesy of Kai, who grinned without remorse.

"Check it out, Mom!" he said. "I built a fort for my report. Like the old warriors."

She scanned the pile: a lopsided cardboard rampart bristling with Q-tips and red string, tiny plastic soldiers perched between them. "Didn't know the ali'i had Nerf artillery," she said, dropping into the nearest chair.

Kai beamed, his face smudged with blue marker. "It's for the extra credit. Mrs. Borden said I need to explain how Hawaiians fought differently than the Americans. So I made both."

He pointed to two battalions, one neatly uniformed and marching in rows. The other, scattered and wild, and built for ambush.

Leilani bent close. "That's pretty accurate, actually." She picked up one of the plastic figures and ran her thumb over the chipped paint. "You know, when I was a kid, my tutu said Hawaiian warriors never fought unless they had to. They preferred to win without bloodshed. It was about brains, not just brawn."

Kai squinted at the array. "So why are there so many

battles in the history books?"

She thought for a second. "Because sometimes, even the smart ones get stuck fighting someone else's war."

He made a face like he got it, then went back to coloring the river blue.

She checked the clock, barely past six. Rain tapped at the windows, low and steady, a white noise that muffled the rest of the house. She set water to boil, opened the fridge for leftovers, and tried to block out the case notes running like a ticker tape behind her eyes. On the roster, she'd seen a name she almost recognized, and the memory gnawed at her all evening.

Kai shifted gears, as always. "Do you have to go to work tonight?"

"Yes," she said. "But you'll be with grandma, so it'll be fine."

He chewed his lip. "You gonna catch the bad guy?"

"Trying," she said, turning back to the stove. "It's a tough one."

He nodded. "Sometimes you have to team up with the enemy to win, right?"

She smiled, thinking of Castellano. "Sometimes that's exactly what you have to do."

A soft knock at the door and Naalei swept in, her umbrella dripping, and her arms loaded with Tupperware and a grocery tote. She shook the rain from her hair and shot a wink at Kai. "My favorite warrior!" she called.

Kai bolted for her, nearly taking down the recycling bin. "Tutu! I built you a fort!"

Naalei crouched to admire the chaos, pulling him in for a hug before setting down her haul. "You build it strong? Enough to keep out bad dreams?"

Kai giggled. "Nothing gets through! It's got double walls."

"Smart boy," Naalei said, then ruffled his hair. She caught Leilani's gaze, warm, but tight around the eyes.

They moved in their practiced rhythm: Kai dragging his fort to the couch, Naalei opening the containers, Leilani plating leftovers and pouring drinks. For a while, there was nothing but the clatter of forks, Kai's wild retelling of a playground drama, and Naalei's patient, steadying voice. For a few minutes, Leilani almost forgot the case.

Then Naalei glanced at her, and Leilani saw the question there: What did you find out?

After dinner, Kai headed off to his room to draw up a battle plan, leaving the women alone with tea and the drone of the old fridge.

Leilani said, "I talked to Makana. He says the program was a sham. Everyone local quit."

Naalei listened, silent. She poured a measure of tea, hands trembling just a touch. "And the pattern?"

"All three were on the Special Demo Team. Volunteers for the old rituals." She kept her voice level. "Whoever did it knows their stuff, but it's twisted. They're not honoring the dead—they're shaming them."

Naalei closed her eyes. "You saw the bodies, yes? You saw how they were left?"

Leilani nodded, jaw tight. "Mele thinks they were arranged on purpose. Even the flowers were brought in from other islands. Nothing was left to chance."

Naalei's voice dropped to a hush. "That's not a burial, Lei. That's a binding. The old kahuna did it to warriors who brought shame to the islands. It keeps the spirit here, trapped. No rest, not even in the next world."

Leilani felt her mouth go dry. "That's what the killer wants? To trap their spirits?"

A slow nod. "Someone believes these people deserve punishment. But not just in life, but in death. It's the worst curse."

Leilani remembered the blue pigment, the brittle flowers, and the saltwater washing away every trace of blood. Ritual, but not for healing. For vengeance.

She put her hands flat on the table, steadying herself. "I need to find out who else is on that list. Before it happens again."

Naalei stood, reaching for Leilani's face. Her hands were calloused, and her eyes were fierce. "You will. You're stronger than they know."

A soft whisper from the hallway. Kai sat in bed, holding his cardboard fort like a shield. "Are you talking about ghosts?" he asked, trying to sound casual.

Leilani sat on the bed and pulled him close, arms around his thin shoulders. "No ghosts tonight, kiddo. Only us."

He snuggled into her side, heavy with sleep, but still clutching his fort. "Promise?" he whispered.

"Promise," she said, holding him until his breathing evened out.

She tucked him in, hugged her mom good night, checked the locks, and set her phone to vibrate. The house settled, quiet and safe.

But when she lay in bed, the words circled her. It's a binding, not a rest. She peered at the dark ceiling, listening to the sound of the rain. Tomorrow, she would hunt, but tonight, she would remember what was worth saving.

Chapter Twelve

By seven AM, the air in the HPD conference room had already gone flat and metallic, thick with sweat and congealed coffee. The central table groaned under the weight of case folders, color-printed forensics, and the open wounds of a half-dozen spiral-bound notebooks. Leilani stood at the whiteboard, marker uncapped and poised in her hand, watching the last of the morning crew shuffle into their seats. The crowd looked rough: Isaac unshaven, tie abandoned for a plain black T-shirt; Tano rubbing sleep from his eyes; Akira with a Red Bull tucked discreetly behind her screen.

Leilani mapped the details on the board in three columns: EVIDENCE, RITUAL, MOTIVE. The markers bled through, leaving ghosts of old cases barely visible underneath. She tried not to read the afterimages, but they crowded in anyway.

Chief Mori entered last. She wore her hair tight and her jaw tighter, eyes scanning the room before she even hit the coffee pot. Behind her, Castellano strode in, trailing two NCIS agents and a combat-level disregard for the Hawaiian humidity. Castellano chose her spot and made a show of crossing her arms, phone face-up and unlocked beside her like a threat. Her mouth was already puckered in disagreement.

“Let’s do it,” Mori said, folding herself into the end chair. “Detective Kealoha, you have the floor.”

Leilani circled the board. The crime scene photos from Kaena Point were taped to the board, the corners curling as if to shield the bodies from the fluorescent light. She pointed to the first image, an overhead of Nathan Beckett's grave.

"Victim one. Beckett. Hands bound with braided cord, wrists raw, body positioned facing west. Grave included a bundle of wilted plumeria, breadfruit and red ti, all laid in a tight packet at his feet. According to Dr. Mele, the trace on the flowers puts their origin as three different islands. Not a coincidence."

She paused for effect, but most in the room waited blankly. Tano mouthed something at Akira, who just grinned.

Leilani moved to the next photo, the second, and third victims. "Victims two and three: Jessica Brown and her son, Maleko. Same burial orientation. Clean cuts at the throat, hands bound. Additional offering: a lei of shells, wrapped in the boy's hands. Bodies washed in seawater, per the coroner and supported by sodium concentrations in the soil."

A hand rose. Espinoza. "Why the washing? Doesn't that destroy evidence?"

Leilani nodded, flipping to the sideboard. "That's exactly the point. It's a cleansing, but also an erasure. In old times, it was used for two things: preparing a body for the next world or binding a spirit so it couldn't leave."

She paused, letting the silence hang in the air.

"The cuts on the hands and faces match what Naalei and two other kumu hula described as the shameful end, a death for someone who brought dishonor to the family or to the tribe. It's not a pretty tradition. But whoever's doing this is following the protocol to the letter."

She uncapped the red marker and scrawled CEREMONIAL in a looping script across both columns.

Akira raised her hand, then spoke. "Doesn't it bother you that they're getting it right? Like, really, right? Even the cleaning with saltwater?"

"It's not common knowledge," Leilani said. "You don't pick it up on a Bishop Museum audio tour. You either learn from a true source, or you're copying from a detailed historical record."

Isaac shifted forward in his seat, elbows on the table. "Are there records that specific? Could someone find them online?"

"Some," Leilani said. "But the offering bundle, the order of flowers, the pigment, those are family specific. Mostly oral traditions. Unless someone's digging through restricted archives, or they had an insider."

She took a breath, feeling the edges of her own voice shake. She pushed on.

"Which brings us to the forensics." She motioned to the side, where Mele hunched behind her stack of vials and annotated photos.

Mele nodded, pushing her glasses higher up the bridge of her nose. "We analyzed plant fibers from all three scenes. They match native flora; no substitutions. Whoever made the cords used the traditional wili technique. Took me half an hour to match the knot." She displayed a high-resolution close-up of the binding. "This is not decorative. It's functional, and it's period-correct."

She clicked to another slide. "We also found traces of blue pigment on the second victim. The binder had a dusting of indigo mixed with local clay, used for ceremonial marking. Difficult to come by unless you know a source."

Espinoza interrupted, "Could a regular person buy this pigment?"

Mele shook her head. "You'd have to grind it yourself or buy from a specialty art store."

Leilani chimed in. "The killer is not just copying. They're living it."

Tano looked up, his voice carrying a skeptical edge. "So what? We're looking for a reenactor? A cultural nut?"

"A devout one," Leilani answered, refusing the easy joke. "But there's more."

She pulled a second batch of photos. "Every victim was cleansed, but only after the wounds were inflicted. That means the killer wanted them to experience the pain, and only then be washed."

She let that land. The silence thickened.

Castellano spoke without looking up from her phone. "You're putting a lot of weight on island myth, Detective. What's your tangible link?"

Leilani drew herself up. "The tangible link is this:

all three victims took part in a military workshop called Warrior Spirit Integration. They weren't just random. They were on a demonstration team that handled sacred objects as part of a team-building exercise."

She laid the workshop roster next to the photos. The same names, circled in red, reappeared. In handwriting that wasn't hers, the word "Kapu" had been scrawled beside two of the entries.

"Who else was on this team?" Mori asked.

Leilani pointed. "Seven others. Five are still on the island. All have military connections. Three have been cited for minor disciplinary issues in the last year, but nothing else jumps out."

Chief Mori rubbed her face, tired. "And the cultural advisor for this workshop?"

"Makana Ka'eo. He quit last year after a dispute over protocols. He's local but says he's never met any of the victims outside of training. No record, and no motive."

Castellano closed her phone, finally looking up. "Are we running protection on the remaining team members?"

Isaac answered, "We put uniforms on their houses and got in touch with base security. Two of them live on the base. One's on deployment. The rest, I can interview today."

Castellano turned to the rest of her team. "I want electronic surveillance on all personnel who touched the demonstration. Pull emails, texts, anything referencing this so-called kapu ritual. If anyone contacts the survivors, I want to know before they do."

Leilani's jaw tightened. She said nothing.

Mori scanned the room. "Is there a consensus on motive? Is this a cultural extremist, or is the ritual a cover for personal revenge?"

Leilani spoke without hesitation. "It's both. The rituals are too precise for a cover. But the killer is using them to send a message, to shame the dead, not just to punish."

Tano folded his arms. "But why these people? If it was about desecration, why not target the guy who designed the workshop?"

Akira, her eyes bright, chimed in. "Could it be a test? Perhaps the killer wishes to confirm if others adhere to the protocols, not solely the supervisor."

For a second, the room drifted, everyone following their own thread.

Mele set down her notes. "If you want my opinion, the killer is only getting started. There's enough pigment left for dozens more. And the way they cleaned the wounds? There's almost no sign of hesitation. The cuts are perfect."

That finally silenced even Castellano.

Chief Mori nodded, as if bracing for impact. "Okay. Torres, you and Tano track down the other names. Keep a visible presence; no surprises. Akira, coordinate with the Navy and NCIS for digital surveillance. Detective Kealoha, you're the point on the cultural angle. Find out if anyone else is talking about this, or if there are any old grievances we missed."

Leilani inclined her head. "Yes, Chief."

The team scattered, chairs scraping on the linoleum. Mele packed her samples, murmuring about the need for more tests. Tano and Isaac were already huddled, plotting their approach. Even Akira moved with a new sense of purpose, her grin gone feral and focused.

Leilani let herself sag against the board, uncapping a blue marker and idly sketching a wave across the bottom edge.

Castellano approached, voice low. "You really believe the next target will be from that list?"

Leilani didn't look up. "I don't believe. I know."

Castellano paused, as if weighing an apology, then thought better of it. "You're good, Kealoha. Better than you give yourself credit for."

Leilani almost laughed. "You don't believe a word of this, do you?"

A shrug. "I believe in people. They're predictable, even when they pretend to be ruled by the supernatural. But I trust your gut."

Leilani nodded, accepting the rare concession.

When the room was empty, she wiped the board, leaving only a single name underlined twice: Kapu. She checked her phone. Nothing but a missed call from Naalei, time-stamped at 6:07 a.m. She took a slow breath, capped the marker, and turned her back on the board. Outside, the sun was just cresting the spines of the Koʻolau. The entire city is still damp and raw. The work, at least, was real. She stepped out, shoulders square, ready to walk into whatever was waiting next.

Chapter Thirteen

The team had reassembled in the HPD conference room at three PM for an end-of-day debrief. Fresh printouts spread over the old mess. This time, Leilani walked in with the stride of someone who knew the ground would shift beneath her feet.

She had the first slide queued before anyone had buckled in. The room dimmed; the only light came from the projector, and a streak of sun slicing across the whiteboard.

"We missed something," Leilani said, straight to the point. "Not who they were, but what they did."

She let the slide hang. A color shot of the Warrior Spirit Integration workshop last year. A dozen men and women in formation, all in faux-kapa loincloths, mid-chant. The faces of Beckett, Brown and Ikaika hovered near the center, looking uncomfortable and out of place.

Next slide: a close-up of a large, black stone, half-swaddled in ti leaf, sitting at the center of a makeshift altar. "This is a ki'i pōhaku," she explained. "A sacred stone, used in pre-contact times to mark the spot for rituals—warfare, birth, death."

A third image, grainy but damning: Beckett and Brown, standing over the stone, both with hands on it, grinning for the camera. A third figure in the background is making the shaka sign and laughing. Bile rose in Leilani's throat.

"According to a witness," she said. "They tried to

move the ki‘i pōhaku as part of the team-building. The stone broke. The workshop leaders tried to glue it back together with Gorilla Epoxy."

Tano winced; Akira covered her mouth, her eyes wide.

Leilani kept going. "The grave positions match the way they displayed the bodies in the workshop demonstration, down to the direction, the order of the flower bundles, even the pigment marks." She cycled through comparison slides: the panel reenactment, the fresh crime scene photos. "The killer isn't just copying. They're correcting what happened. Restoring a wrong with the same players, the same ritual, but for real."

Castellano's eyes narrowed. "Forgive me, but that seems—"

"Don't," Leilani said, her voice as sharp as a knuckle. "You think it's a joke, but to a practitioner, it's a sacrilege. You want to spark a vendetta, that's how you do it."

A silence hovered, except for the faint grind of the projector fan.

Mori sat forward. "You're saying this is revenge for breaking the artifact?"

Leilani nodded. "Every detail matches. Even the ceremonial salt came from the same source as that used in the workshop. Whoever is doing this has a connection to both worlds. They understand the protocol, but also the insult."

Castellano smirked, fingers drumming on her phone. "Or it's just a military nut with a flair for drama.

We've seen this before. Theatrics to throw us off a standard-issue revenge motive. Probably someone Beckett pissed off who wants to muddy the water."

Leilani glared. "You think a disgruntled ex would spend weeks researching chant protocol and drive a hundred miles for the right flower? No. This isn't the work of a hack. It's personal, and it's sacred. Even you should see that."

"Sacred or not," Castellano fired back. "It doesn't change the outcome. Three dead, all military-affiliated, and every base on Oahu on edge. If we chase after every cultural lead, we'll lose the actual killer in the noise."

The words stung, but Leilani forced herself to focus on the evidence. "This is the lead, Vic. You can run your standard revenge angles, but if you ignore the cultural trigger, you're missing half the motive."

Tano jumped in, hands open. "Can't it be both? Someone took offense, but also had a personal beef?"

Akira nodded. "That's how I'd do it. Hide in plain sight."

Castellano turned her glare on the others, but Mori cut in. "Enough." The word ricocheted around the room. "Detective, what's your next move?"

"As we talked about this morning, we maintain surveillance on everyone from the demonstration team. Every. Single. One. So not just protection. Meanwhile, I want to meet with the university experts and see if anyone could've coached our killer through the protocols."

Mori fixed her gaze on Castellano. "And you will coordinate, not compete. That's an order."

For a moment, Castellano just seethed, her fingers white around the phone. Then she smiled—thin, professional, and icy.

"Of course, Chief," she said. "But I stand by my analysis: this is military business. The rest is distraction."

Leilani's hands curled, but she held her tongue. If it came down to a war, she'd fight it on her own terms.

The meeting dissolved into logistics, phone numbers and a list of names. Leilani barely noticed as the others filtered out, or how Mori and Isaac lingered to exchange low-voiced plans.

It was Castellano who finally made her way over, moving with a grace that was almost predatory. She leaned closer, her voice for Leilani alone.

"These killings aren't about your island superstitions. They're about the chain of command, about who gets to have the last word. You want to play priestess, fine. But leave the actual police work to us."

Leilani's jaw set, hard enough to ache. She said nothing, but she imagined the old ancestors, the ones whose stories had survived only in whispers. She would not let them down.

Castellano gave a quick, satisfied smile, then breezed out, her presence lingering in the stale air.

Leilani studied the crime scene slide; the broken stone now forever marked with the hands of the dead. She could feel the anger in her bones. She uncapped her pen and wrote in the margin: Not superstition. Survival. Then she started planning her next move.

The hallway outside the briefing room ran cold; the tile floor still wet from the night janitor's half-hearted mopping. Leilani barely made it two steps before the sharp crack of Mori's heels closed in behind her.

Mori didn't bother with pleasantries. "Kealoha. Office. Now."

Leilani followed without protesting. Mori's office was tidy to the point of discomfort with a single photograph of her police academy graduation breaking the plane of the desktop. Mori shut the door with her foot and rounded to face her, the energy in the room snapping like a live wire.

"I get that you and Castellano don't mix," Mori said, her voice as level as a rifle barrel. "But we have three bodies, a fourth almost certain, and every federal agency breathing down my neck. So you are going to play nice. Or I will replace you both."

Leilani swallowed her anger and managed a nod.

"I mean it," Mori said, her voice lower. "I can't afford an ego war. I need a solved case." She paused, then added, "I know you're right about the cultural stuff. I trust you. But you must convince them, not fight them."

"I know, Chief," Leilani said. "I'll keep it in line."

Mori's gaze softened for a nanosecond. "If anyone can, it's you."

She jerked her chin, signaling Leilani to leave. In the hall, Castellano leaned against the door frame, arms crossed, mouth set for a fresh argument. Before either could speak, the glass in the corridor rattled, and Isaac appeared, half jogging, face flushed.

"Team meeting. Conference B," he called. "It's urgent."

Leilani followed the bounce of his badge as he darted ahead. She tried to slow her breathing, to shake off the last of the fury.

Conference B was a box of a room, ringed with battered rolling chairs and a wall-mounted TV stuck on the city's cable access feed. Everyone was already there, including Tano and Akira, who sat with their laptops open and eyes wide.

Isaac slapped a folder onto the table. "Fourth victim," he said. "Or missing. Marcus Chen, petty officer second class. Didn't report for duty, and he didn't answer his phone. His roommate last saw him last night, said he was in a weird mood, and was packing a go-bag. Shore patrol finished canvassing the barracks. No sign of him."

Tano tapped on his laptop. "He's got family in Manoa. I'm sending a uniform over now."

"How come you got this before me?" asked Castellano, the annoyance clear in her voice. Her phone chimed with an incoming message, and she unclipped it from her belt. She read the message and frowned.

"I was on the phone with base security," said Isaac. "I was following up on Jessica Brown when the SP let them know the barracks inspection was a bust. They filled me in, and I told them I'd connect with you."

Castellano bristled. "Last known GPS?"

"He turned his phone off at 2:04 a.m.," Akira answered. "North of Kaena Point. It pinged at Barber's Point near the first grave site."

Mori strode in, gaze sweeping the team. "Is it true we may have a fourth victim?"

Leilani looked at her and wondered if she had a bug planted in the room. Leilani nodded. "Missing sailor, Chief." She faced the table.

"Tano," said Leilani. "You and Espinoza check the last ping. Akira, see if you can trace his social or credit card usage. Vic, can you run point with base security and run a full sweep of the base? Please coordinate with the team. No one goes alone."

"Isaac," says Leilani. "Can you work with Vic and search his house and anywhere on the base he might hang out?"

"No problem," says Isaac. "I'll head over there now to get started." He picked up his folder and raced out the door.

Mori looked at Leilani, her eyes clear and hard. "You've got the best gut in the room. Use it."

"Will do," Leilani said, ignoring the way her hands trembled.

The room emptied in a blur of motion. Leilani ducked into a side cubicle to grab her badge, phone and a fresh pack of notebooks. She was halfway to the door when her phone buzzed, sharp and insistent.

Unknown number. No text, only an image attachment.

She opened it. The picture showed a ti leaf, bound with red thread, set atop a gray basalt slab. Scratched into the stone were three symbols: a wave, a spear and a crescent. She recognized them immediately. They'd been painted on the face of the first victim.

Her throat went dry. This wasn't a warning. It was a challenge.

Castellano's voice, loud in the hall: "You okay, Detective?"

Leilani looked up, fixed her face into something calm, and held up her phone. Castellano looked at the photo. "Fuck," she said. "Do you think we have time, or is he already dead?"

"We'd better follow Tano to the original grave site."

They left the station together, the competition now irrelevant. Their sole focus was on getting to Chen before the next ritual could begin. Leilani climbed into her Explorer and raced out of the parking lot followed by Castellano in her SUV. As Leilani drove, she replayed the symbols in her head. Not just for the dead, but for her. She kept her eyes on the road, but she knew: the killer was watching, and the game was only getting started.

Chapter Fourteen

The road to Kaena Point cut through what was left of the island's last wilderness, a band of wet asphalt flanked by bone-white sand, dune grass, and the looming mass of the point itself, shrouded in the gray fog that made every breath feel like a dare. Leilani's Explorer fishtailed on a patch of slick gravel near the ranger gate, and she let it slide, counter steering by instinct. Beyond the turnoff, every landmark was lost in the soup; even the ocean, just yards from the trail, was more rumor than fact, its presence announced only by the roar that carried onshore in thick, bell-shaped pulses.

She saw the flashers before she saw the people. Blue and white, strobing through the mist. The crime scene tape was rigged between two ironwood trunks, already sagging from the weight of dew. Tano was on his knees in the middle of a muddy clearing, hands deep in a patch of earth so raw it still steamed. Espinoza, face drawn and pale, was helping, scooping out hunks of black loam with a folding entrenching tool. Neither noticed Leilani's approach until she killed her headlights and stepped out, boots squelching in the half-drowned undergrowth.

Castellano arrived seconds later, flanked by a pair of NCIS techs in windbreakers. The federal agent's jaw was set; her eyes were red-rimmed, but her posture betrayed nothing except the expectation of an immediate result.

Leilani slipped under the tape. "How long?" she

called out.

Tano answered without looking up, his breath a white thread. “Maybe twenty minutes. The ground’s soft, but it goes deep. Whoever did this, they wanted it to last.”

Leilani moved to the hole and peered down. The depression was three feet wide, but the angle of the soil and the way the root mat caved around it told her everything she needed: this was recent. A stray stick jutted from the pile, snapped by hand.

She kneeled, gloves already on, and joined the dig. Espinoza gave up the trowel without a word.

Together, they worked in short, violent bursts. Every scoop brought up more details. First a section of wrist, then the suggestion of a blue shirt sleeve, and then the fine white arc of teeth where a mouth hung open, caked in grit.

When they exposed the face, everyone stopped digging. Tano fell back, wiping a muddy palm over his jeans. Even Castellano, normally quick to close gaps, hung back.

Leilani didn’t hesitate. She leaned in, head nearly touching the ground, and used her hand to clear away the last of the mud. The face was distorted by swelling, eyes already clouding, but the hair was intact, short, black, and spiked flat to the skull. There was a tattoo behind the right ear, a small Chinese character half-hidden by blood. Leilani squinted, memorized the lines, and thumbed her phone awake, navigating to the PDF in Chen’s personnel file. The birthmark matched. The haircut matched. The tattoo was a family honor;

the caption appeared in his HR folder, and it matched.

She checked again. She looked until her eyes watered.

Castellano appeared at her side, knees planting in the muck. "Is it him?" she asked, her voice soft.

"Yeah," Leilani said. "It's Chen."

A long moment. The only sound was the surf and the slow, congested breathing of the people behind them.

Castellano didn't touch her, but she hovered close, her hand braced on the rim of the grave. "How did you know?"

Leilani slid the phone over, held it so both could see. "His tattoo. Same as the file. And his face is still..." She didn't finish.

Castellano exhaled, slow. "Sorry. I know this one was a long shot."

"It's never a shot if you care," Leilani said. She held Castellano's gaze for a full second, then broke away.

She stood, stretching the ache from her back. "Is Mele on her way?"

Tano nodded. "ETA fifteen minutes. She's got the tent and all the gear."

She turned to Tano and Espinoza. "Good job," she said. "Go help with the perimeter, please. And get fresh gloves."

Tano made a face, but nodded. Espinoza looked grateful to be given something to do.

Leilani and Castellano stepped away from the grave and checked the area for secondary evidence. All they found in the immediate vicinity were a few roots, some torn cloth, and the compacted impression of a size nine boot heel on the north side. She took a photo, marked it on her phone, and pinged Mele with the location tag.

Castellano kneeled by the hole and her gaze swept over the face.

"You want to take a print?" Leilani asked, low.

Castellano shook her head. "You're better at this than I am. Always were."

Leilani didn't have an answer to that, so she moved to the edge and waited for the sound of the next car on the access road. When it came, she could hear Mele's laugh, even over the rumble of the engine, and for a second she felt almost normal.

Mele's van rolled up, blue flashing lights stuttering in the gloom. The forensic team spilled out—three techs in Tyvek suits, all business. Mele led them, pulling her case behind her like a stubborn dog.

She saw the grave and nodded. "Let's do it cleanly, people," she said. "We get full scans before we touch the scene. No exceptions. Jerry, get me lots of pictures as we remove the dirt."

Leilani stepped aside so the techs could photograph from every angle. She kept her eyes on the horizon, where the fog had thinned just enough to show a line of blue water and the broken bones of the reef beyond.

They worked in silence for several minutes, documenting, confirming, cross-referencing with old notes and photos. The sunrise fought its way up through the fog, and the light changed the color of everything; the grave now a dish of gold and shadow.

She stepped out beyond the tape, breathing in the cool air, and dialed Akira. "Hey A. Please run a full background check on Chen and go deep," she said. "It's definitely our guy."

Akira didn't say anything for a second. Then, "You want to know something weird?"

"Always."

"I checked the demo team list. Chen wasn't on the original panel. He was a substitute. Got called in last minute after the previous guy got sick. He didn't even want to do it. He wrote about it in a Reddit post. I can forward."

"Do it," Leilani said, feeling the chill all over again.

She disconnected and found Castellano standing in the clearing, arms folded, watching the water. "You heard?"

"Yeah." Castellano kicked a rock, hard enough to send it skidding into the brush. "It never makes sense until it does."

Leilani wanted to say something about the pattern, or the way the killer had adapted, but Castellano spoke first.

"I'll run point with the Navy," she said. "Coordinate with the base, get the rest of the panel under wraps, and I'll make the notification. See what the wife has to say."

"Thanks," Leilani said.

"Don't thank me yet. There's going to be hell to pay. Nobody likes a serial on their watch." Castellano paused, then looked up. "Don't let them take you off the case."

"I won't," Leilani said.

The fog was gone now, burned off by the sun, but the air was still raw, and the silence of the point hung heavier than before.

They stood like that for a long time; the wind flattening their hair, both staring at the blue line where the island ended and the ocean waited beyond. Leilani turned back towards the grave.

By the time the evidence tent was up, and the first ring of white Tyvek suits moved in, the evening sky had gone from steel to black, everything sharp and reflective under the tower of work lights. Dr. Mele Tatana ran the operation like a field surgeon, her gloved hands pointing, slicing, annotating, her voice never raised above what the occasion demanded.

The initial grid of the grave was mapped in string and numbered flags. Every bit of disturbed ground was vacuumed and bagged, each clod of dirt handled as if it held a secret. The entire team radiated a hunger for detail, a refusal to let the killer win so much as a hair's breadth of deniability.

Mele slid into the whole first, the knees of her Tyvek suit caked with mud, and her breath short from crouching so long. She worked her hands around the perimeter of the burial, tracing the flower arrangement before anything else moved.

"Start here," she said, motioning the nearest tech to photograph in tight sequence. "It's textbook. No, better than that. It's art." She adjusted the focus on the team's macro camera and thumbed a measurement caliper open. "Look, alternate plumeria, red and white. The ti is fresh, not wilted. It means it was placed no more than three hours before we got here. The ulu is sliced in perfect quarter-inch sections, fanned clockwise. Every element is deliberate."

Leilani squatted beside her, careful not to interfere. "You see the same pattern before?"

She didn't move until the techs had documented everything, bagged and labeled every clump of dirt, every fragment of cloth. Mele kneeled at the rim, close enough to the face that her hair brushed the tips of the grass. "Clean cut at the neck," she announced, not needing to measure. "The angle looks identical to the others. No sign of hesitation. I'll know more once I get him on the table."

She looked up, her lips pressed tight. "It's not rage," she said. "It's doctrine."

Leilani glanced at Castellano, who met her look, then back at Mele. "Anything different this time?"

Mele pursed her lips, running a gloved finger around the line of salt. "There's more detail. Whoever did this is getting better with practice. There's a string of flowers under the body. Ti leaves, plumeria, and something that looks like ulu."

Leilani ducked under the tape and crouched to see

for herself. The flowers were arranged with clinical precision, every stem lined up, the blossoms alternating yellow-white and blood-red. The breadfruit was sliced, not whole, and layered in a fan. "It's almost beautiful," Leilani murmured, surprised.

Mele shrugged. "If you ignore the context, it is."

Mele nodded, hair straggling loose from the braid. "Not just on this case. I saw this kind of precision once in grad school, at a repatriation for iwi kupuna. Only back then, it was preservation, not retribution." Her fingers never stopped moving, drawing an invisible diagram in the air. "Whoever's doing this, they're escalating the ritual each time. The first victim's arrangement was loose, almost random. Now, it's as formal as a funeral for a chief."

Leilani nodded back. She didn't need to look at the body anymore, but she found herself drawn in by the details: the position of the hands, palms flat, arms straight at the side, the angle of the head, forced to look west even in death. A careful line of salt had been poured over the lips and eyes, the granules glittering like quartz.

They cleared the flowers only after a complete digital scan, top, side and close-up of every blossom and leaf. The salt line was lifted with care and sampled twice, once for isotope analysis, once for trace elements. Only when the last petal was documented did Mele nod to her second-in-command, who produced a surgical saw and began working on the arm of the corpse, freeing it from the compacted soil with a series of precise, shallow cuts.

With the body exposed, the stench of saltwater intensified. It caught in the back of the throat, a rot-sweet bite that instantly separated the veteran from the greenhorn. Espinoza gagged and turned away; the youngest tech, her face blotchy and sickly, had to back off entirely.

Mele ignored the smell. She lifted the head by the crown, tilted it so the neck wound gaped under the lens. "Depth, three centimeters, angle matches the others. Blade was serrated this time, like a utility knife. See the drag on the edge?" She pointed but didn't wait for a response. "Hands folded, not bound. This one was unconscious or compliant at the end."

"Not compliant," Leilani said. "Drugged."

Mele shrugged, approving. "Could be. We'll know after the tox panel."

They extracted the body, peeling away the last of the dirt, and laid it on the tarp with the flower arrangement carefully set at the feet. Leilani watched as Mele used a swab to lift blue residue from beneath the dead man's fingernails.

"Ceremonial pigment again?" Leilani asked.

"Same as before. I'd bet on it. But this time it's under the nails, not on the surface. It's possible he attempted to scratch the murderer, or himself."

"Or the killer made it part of the pattern," Leilani said.

For a long beat, neither of them spoke. The only sounds were the muted whine of a drone taking overhead shots and the faint roar of the surf, now drowned in the logistics of evidence management.

Leilani slipped her phone from her pocket, scrolled to the text she'd received: the ti leaf bundle atop a slab, the trio of carved symbols. She walked over to the flower arrangement, compared petal for petal.

A chill wormed up her arm. The arrangement here was a perfect match to the one in the photo. Not the order, but the spacing, the angle of the ti. Whoever had sent the message had either been present or had access to a prior site. She flagged the images and sent them to Akira for analysis, then turned to Castellano, who hovered just outside the tent, arms crossed.

"Vic," Leilani said, gesturing her over. "You need to see this."

Castellano didn't flinch at the odor, didn't blanch at the sight. She crouched next to the tarp, eyes moving in quick, mechanical flicks as she scanned the flowers, the arrangement, the precision of the salt and pigment.

"You're telling me this is a signature?" Castellano said.

"It's more than that. It's a message. The killer isn't just copying old protocols. They're recreating them exactly."

Castellano nodded, eyes distant. "I see it now. The pattern's not window dressing. It's the reason for everything."

Leilani held up her phone and showed her the side-by-side. Castellano's mouth twisted, not quite a frown, nor an admission.

"I need to check the victim's quarters," Castellano

said, her voice clipped. “If the killer had this kind of access to ceremonial material, they also watched the victim for longer than we thought.”

Castellano straightened and called out to her team. “Pack it up, guys and let’s move to base housing.”

Mele, finished with the first round of sampling, zipped her kit and stood. “You want the full report as soon as possible?”

Leilani nodded. “Sooner if you can.”

Castellano led her agents to the SUVs, heads bent together as they planned the next move. Tano and Espinoza packed up the perimeter, rolled up the tape, and collected the spent gloves in biohazard bags. For a moment, the grave clearing was quiet, the bustle suspended. Mele stood with Leilani, their shadows merging in the wet, trampled grass.

“You going to be okay?” Mele asked, her voice so gentle it almost didn’t sound like her.

Leilani nodded. “This is the work. We keep the records. We honor the dead. No matter what.”

Mele smiled, tired and true. “Then let’s get the bastard.”

When the documentation was complete, Mele and her team lifted Chen’s body onto a black body bag laid out on the stretcher, careful not to break the flower arrangement. The scent of saltwater grew sharper as they moved him, and Leilani had to turn away, heart kicking in her throat.

Leilani walked towards the vehicles, leaving the tent and its silent witness behind, ready to chase the ritual into whatever darkness was waiting next.

Chapter Fifteen

The housing cluster where Marcus Chen lived was a clone of every other military barracks on the west side: blank-walled, sand-colored rectangles stacked two stories high, hedges sheared to regulation length, and not a single window that wasn't locked tight. There was no siren, no flashing light to announce the latest death to the neighbors. A single shore patrol car out front, the only hint that anything was off schedule.

Castellano's team, two NCIS techs and a fed analyst with thick glasses, parked a full block away to avoid drawing notice. She walked the last stretch in silence, boots clicking on the walk. The day's humidity pressed on her shoulders, a second skin she couldn't peel off.

At the door to 202-B, the shore patrol had cordoned off the landing with a strip of caution tape. A bored sentry recognized Castellano's badge and let them through. The inside was cooler; the hum of the central air making the entire space seem oddly deserted.

Isaac was already there. He'd lost his jacket, and his holster rode high, but he looked more relaxed than any of the agents. He greeted Castellano with a half-nod, all business.

"Detective," she said. "You start?"

He smiled, but not with his eyes. "Did a walk-through for anything obvious. His belongings are in the bedroom. There's a computer on the desk, powered off. You want to take point?"

Castellano shook her head. "This is joint. I'll have

Agent Timmons sweep the room for anything physical. You take the digital."

Isaac moved for the laptop without another word.

The NCIS analyst, Agent Timmons, headed for the closet and bathroom, gloves on and evidence bags already clutched in one hand. Castellano herself checked the windows and door latches, then followed Timmons to the closet, keeping half an eye on Isaac at the desk.

Isaac plugged in the power and hit the ON switch. The machine booted up, an ancient HP model, fan whining louder than it should have. Castellano watched as he bypassed the login. His hands were deft, and even though she hated to admit it, she respected the skill. Within minutes, he was digging through email folders, searching for keywords, the entire act as calm and systematic as folding laundry.

"Find anything?" Castellano asked, hovering just enough to let him know she was there.

Isaac didn't glance up. "He was researching the case. He started a private folder called Justice for the Fallen. He clipped news articles, public notes and a bunch of amateur theories from Reddit and Quora. A lot of mentions of you." He turned the screen so she could see: a grainy image from a TV segment, Castellano's face frozen mid-sentence.

"Obsessed?" she asked.

Isaac shrugged. "Could be, but it's more than that. Look, he corresponded with someone at the University, using a Proton Mail address. Discussing the rituals, why the killer chose the victims. Here, he references a Professor Makani, says the guy used to work as a consultant for the Warrior Spirit Integration workshops on base."

Castellano narrowed her eyes. "Forward that to me and Dr. Mele. And print it to the evidence folder."

He tapped a few keys, sent the message, and kept scrolling.

In the bedroom, Timmons called out. "I've got something."

Castellano crossed the narrow hallway. The closet was a mess of uniforms, duffel bags, and a portable safe with the lock busted off. On the shelf above, there was a neat stack of shoeboxes, but nothing seemed out of place.

Timmons pointed down. "This board is loose. Look." She bent and pried up a section of the floor, standard OSB, painted to match the carpet. Beneath, wrapped in a hotel laundry bag, was a sheaf of printouts and hand-scrawled notes.

Castellano kneeled, careful not to touch anything. "Bag it and log the location," she said.

Timmons used fresh gloves, dropped the bundle into an evidence pouch, and sealed it. She handed it off to Castellano, who flipped the top edge for a look.

It was photocopies of official records including base rosters, security memos, and most damning, a file on a Lieutenant Commander James Holt, with the words KEY TO ALL written in Sharpie across the cover sheet.

Castellano's pulse ticked up. She paged through and found a personnel file, old disciplinary records, and a few blurry photographs from what looked like a bar fight. Every page had underlines, exclamation marks or notes in a tight, upright print. Some pages had sticky notes with names and dates, linking Holt to at least two of the known victims.

She took her phone from her belt, snapped a quick set of photos, and emailed them to herself and the NCIS evidence locker. When she stood, she looked at Isaac, who watched her with that tired, amused detective's stare.

"You know the name?" she asked him.

He pursed his lips. "Never met the guy, but he's got a reputation. He retired early after a command incident. Something about excessive force on deployment, but it never made it to a court-martial."

Castellano's mind spun through scenarios. "You think Chen was going to expose him?"

"I think Chen was in way over his head," said Isaac. "But yeah. He was chasing something. Or someone."

She glanced at the bundle, then at Isaac. "We follow both. You work Makani, I'll take Holt."

He grinned, all teeth. "Race you to the next corpse?"

She ignored him and turned towards the living room.

Timmons had spread the rest of the evidence on the kitchen table. "There were printouts from the Warrior Spirit training manual," said Timmons. "Some pages are bookmarked and annotated in Chen's handwriting.

One section was flagged with a sticky note, and someone had written a note that said, binding rituals for punishment of warriors, not for honor, but for disgrace. The protocol is public, but the intention makes it lethal. In one margin, Chen had written: Ask Makani, he'll know if this is true."

Isaac snapped a photo of the page, then pulled out his own phone, dialing the university's main line. Castellano watched him as she dialed her own contacts, punching the digits so hard her screen registered a double input.

At the other end, Isaac smoothed his voice. "Hi, this is Detective Torres, HPD. I need to speak with Professor Makani Ka'eo. It's urgent." He listened and jotted down a number. "Can you tell me if he's on campus today? Thank you."

He hung up and looked at Castellano. "He's teaching a class at 2 p.m. I'll call Leilani and have her meet me there. What do you want to do about Holt?"

She had her phone to her ear, and she held up 1 finger. She spoke into the phone, her voice clipped. "This is Special Agent Castellano. I need to fast-track a warrant and surveillance package for a former officer. Yeah, I'll email you the specifics." She fired off the email before the operator had even finished responding.

Isaac, hands free again, watched her work. "You really think Holt is our unsub?"

She considered. "If he is, he's good at hiding in plain sight. If he isn't, he's at least what the killer wants us to see. Either way, I want him boxed in before sundown."

She turned to Timmons. "Sweep the place again. See if there's any digital trail on the safe, or if the victim used other devices. I'll set up the interview with Holt's old COs."

Isaac grabbed his keys. "I'm heading to the university. If the professor bolts, I want to be there to greet him."

"Call me if he runs," Castellano said. "Or if you get anything from the interview. I'll coordinate from the office."

She packed up the evidence pouch, triple-checked the seals, and headed for the door, not looking back.

Out on the landing, she squinted against the sunlight, already mentally outlining her follow-up: track down Holt, run his military record through every database available, and prep a parallel profile of Makani for good measure.

Behind her, she heard Isaac calling to Leilani, his voice easy but edged. "You want to call the professor, or do you want the element of surprise?"

She didn't catch Leilani's answer, but she could picture the way the other detective would handle it, fast, direct, already a step ahead. Castellano liked that in an adversary.

She took the stairs two at a time, boots thudding with purpose, already dialing the next number on her hit list. The names and motives, the scraps of ritual, the failures of the chain of command. She'd fit them together.

In the parking lot, the air smelled of hot grass and the faint bite of spilled gasoline. For a second, she let herself close her eyes and map the angles of the case, the victims, the rituals and the points of intersection. It was nearly a grid, except the lines wouldn't stop moving.

She got in the car and turned the key; the engine caught in a single, angry note. She wouldn't let the case get away from her. Not now, not ever.

As she pulled into traffic, she checked her mirrors and caught sight of Isaac already loading up, his face a mask of resolve, ready for the next confrontation. In her gut, Castellano knew the endgame had started, and she was damn well not going to blink first.

She hit the accelerator and vanished into the heat, hungry for whatever came next.

Chapter Sixteen

The path to Makani Ka'eo's home curved off the main road, winding up through an overgrown curtain of red ginger and wild banana. The driveway was packed dirt, its edges softened by moss and a half-century of tropical rain. Leilani let the Explorer coast to a stop beside a battered, wood-sided Toyota with a bumper sticker for every election since '94. She and Isaac stepped out and stood in the humid air, both momentarily silenced by the sense of encroaching green.

Makani's house was a low, battered bungalow set back from the road, its battered screen door patched with wire and careful knots of fishing line. The porch was small, but every surface was covered with plants; potted ferns, spindly papaya and a hibiscus with petals like torn silk. An empty beer bottle stood at the top of the steps, its label faded to anonymity. Somewhere inside, a ukulele played, plaintive and half in tune.

Leilani led the way up, shoes thumping the hollow boards. The air smelled like old wood, ash and the faint, musty funk of mildewed books. Before she could knock, the door cracked open, and Makani Ka'eo peered out. He was shorter than she remembered from the photos, his hair longer and streaked gray, a papery mustache shading a mouth pressed into a thin line. His eyes were sharp, but ringed with fatigue.

He recognized her in a blink. "Detective Kealoha?"

She nodded, her badge out. "And Torres, my partner." Isaac offered a gentle smile, hands open, cop-soft.

Makani gave them both a hard look, then stepped aside, motioning them in. “Shoes off, please. And mind the book piles.”

Inside, the air was cooler. The living room overflowed with the detritus of two lives: a battered sofa, a TV stacked with VHS tapes, and piles of printouts and spiral-bound reports. Shelves lined the walls, overstuffed with paperbacks, academic journals and binders. Several implements, gourd rattles, a shark-tooth club, and unfinished wood carvings, hung by their cords, some mid-restoration. In one corner sat a desk heaped with loose papers, the surface crowded by teacups and ballpoint pens. The place felt not lived in, but survived in.

Makani gestured to the sofa and vanished into the kitchen. Leilani heard the clatter of cups, the hiss of a kettle. Isaac scanned the shelves, stopping at a faded photo of Makani in a graduation lei, flanked by younger, sharper versions of himself.

They sat. The sofa exhaled a cloud of dust and sage when Leilani leaned back. She picked at a thread on her jeans, planning her opening. She looked at Isaac. He raised his brows: Let him go first.

Makani returned with three mismatched cups and a battered teapot painted with faded koi. He set them on the low table, pouring with a steady hand, and sat opposite on a wicker chair. For a moment, he eyed the tea, then the cops.

“I was expecting you sooner,” he said, voice quieter now, less wary. “The Navy’s already called twice this morning."

Leilani sipped. The tea was earthy, shot through with ginger and lemon peel. "We'd like to hear the official story, but mostly, we want to understand what happened in the workshop."

Makani made a noise between a grunt and a sigh. He looked down at his hands, browned, leathery, and scarred with old splinters and a constellation of blue ink. "You know I quit a year ago?"

She nodded. "We saw the file."

"You know why I stopped." He glanced up, eyes glittering. "They wanted a kahuna, but not the truth. They wanted to put on a show. The Navy's culture team, the contractor, that bastard Holt. They all said they wanted respect, but the first time I told them no, I was out like that."

Isaac leaned forward, elbows on knees. "Can you tell us about Holt? Was he the one who pushed the traditions?"

Makani's mouth twisted. "He was obsessed. Not with the real ways. With what he thought they meant." He flexed his hands. "He used to sit in my office after every session with questions and wanting the backstory, the parts I said should stay private."

Leilani set her tea aside. "What did he ask for? Details on rituals, or more than that?"

"Everything." Makani blew air through his nose, irritated. "He'd say he wanted to restore honor to the command. He said that the men had forgotten what it meant to be warriors. The language he used..." Makani trailed off, hands hovering over the table as if searching for the right arrangement. "He sounded more Hawaiian than my own cousins, but it was all fragments. Borrowed words that were out of order. When I corrected him, he got angry. But always quiet, never loud."

He reached for a cord hanging from the wall, a long strip of sennit twisted tight and black. He rolled it in his palm, fingers fidgeting with the braid. "I tried to get the workshop changed. Cut out the fake rituals or at least make it about genuine history. Holt wouldn't let up. He started inviting people to private events. Night sessions. I wasn't allowed."

"What did they do at night?" Leilani asked, notebook out.

Makani looked at the floor. "They said it was for discipline; for team-building. But I heard stories from the juniors, marching in the dark, screaming, and some kind of chanting. One time, the morning after, I found the practice field covered in lines of salt. They said it was for the ants."

He snorted. "Stupid, but he made the men do it."

"Did you see anything yourself?" asked Isaac.

Makani shrugged. "Only once. I stayed late, wanted to confront Holt. I found him in the locker room, making one man kneel in front of a bowl of water. The man had cut his hand. Holt was cleaning it with saltwater, not medical, but like a," he hesitated. "Like a punishment."

Leilani looked up. "Was it a ritual?"

Makani nodded. "But not a real one. He was making it up. The way he poured the water, the way he made the man repeat phrases, it was all wrong. But he believed it." He stopped, his knuckles whitening around the cord. "That's when I quit. Sent my notice that night."

He set the cord down, hands shaking. "You ever hear someone try to speak your language, but every word is a knife? That's what it felt like."

Leilani let the words settle, the only sound the ticking of the ancient wall clock and the thrum of the fridge cycling on. "Did Holt ever threaten you?" she asked, tone soft.

Makani shook his head. "Never direct. More like a stare, or a smile when he thought I was weak. But I heard him talk to the men. He said they needed to be ready to cleanse the dishonor. That they would be remembered as the ones who brought back the code."

He pointed to a shelf, where a battered copy of Malo's Hawaiian Antiquities leaned out. "He used to read that book like a bible. Underlined everything about war, about loyalty, and about punishment for traitors."

Isaac finished his tea in a gulp. "Have you ever seen him outside the workshops? At your house, or following you?"

Makani hesitated. "One time. At Foodland. He watched from the other aisle but didn't buy anything. Stared for a minute and left." He looked embarrassed at the admission. "Probably nothing."

Leilani flipped the page. "Can you tell us about the last workshop you ran? Anything unusual?"

Makani frowned. "It was the panel for the civilians. They asked me to show the traditional way to wash a body after death. I said no. I said, you can't do that for real people, only with a carving or a gourd. But the coordinator, a woman from the mainland, pushed me." He pulled at the cord, twisting it around his finger. "Holt brought in a pig's head. He said it was for the demonstration. He made a big deal out of it, had the men watch as he poured salt, then blue paint over the eyes. I walked out. I told them they would regret it."

He looked up, meeting Leilani's gaze for the first time. "I never thought someone would try it for real."

There was a long silence. Outside, the rain started, soft at first, then hammering the tin roof with the force of a drum line. Leilani noticed the air shift.

"Did you ever see Holt lose control?" Isaac asked, his voice a thread.

Makani nodded, slow. "The last time we spoke, he told me he had a destiny. He said it was his kuleana to restore order. I told him he was sick. He told me I didn't understand what a warrior's life meant." The hands in his lap tightened into fists. "He said I was already dead."

For a while, no one moved.

Leilani stood quietly. She closed her notebook and offered a business card, which Makani took but didn't look at. "If he reaches out, or if you remember anything else, call me. Even if it's small."

He nodded, his eyes fixed on the braid in his hand.

Isaac hesitated at the door. "Makani, do you know if Holt was ever in contact with anyone else? Anyone who believed the way he did?"

Makani snorted. "There's always someone. But nobody like him. Not since the old days."

He gave a bitter laugh, then met Isaac's eyes. "If you find him, be careful. He knows what he's doing. Even if it's all wrong, he believes it."

Outside, the rain had already formed tiny rivers down the driveway. The Explorer was spotted with leaves and flower petals, shaken loose by the sudden downpour.

Leilani and Isaac got in, closing the doors on the echo of Makani's warning.

She started the engine and sat a moment, her hands steady on the wheel.

"Thoughts?" asked Isaac, his tone careful.

"He's not lying," Leilani said. "He's scared. And I think he's right about Holt. You don't fake that kind of obsession. Either you're sick, or you're a believer."

Isaac pulled up the evidence photo on his phone: the first grave, salt poured in a straight line over the lips and eyes.

"It matches everything," he whispered. "Even the pigment. Especially the salt."

They sat listening to the drum of rain on the roof. Leilani thumbed the business card she'd taken from the desk. The number of the woman who coordinated the panel was scrawled in pencil on the back. She felt the knot tighten in her chest with cold certainty. They were already two steps behind, and they needed to find Holt.

Chapter Seventeen

Castellano's office on the fourth floor of the old administration annex was barely big enough for the desk, two chairs, and the battered safe that took up half the floor. Every wall was cinderblock, painted the off-white of every government building since the fifties; the light came from a buzzing fluorescent bar, which hummed in tandem with the fan in her desktop computer. Outside, the view was just a parking lot and the haze of diesel smoke from the morning shift change. She liked it this way. Nothing to distract her, or to remind her she was more than a function of the job.

She worked through the personnel file first. The manila folder was crisp, but the contents weren't. The first several pages were typed summaries; the rest were handwritten notes, mostly addenda from superiors or recommendations for further review. Castellano scanned fast, noting the key dates, enlistment, officer school, BUD/S training, SEAL Qualification training, his first deployment, and his first disciplinary flag. The first ten years were exemplary, with lots of redacted mission information. During the next five years, things got weird.

By year sixteen, Lieutenant Commander James Holt was running unauthorized warrior spirit sessions for his command. The complaint logs were alternately blunt and baffled. He encouraged recruits to take part in unsanctioned nighttime training and claimed it would instill ancient discipline. He refused to provide after-class summaries and claimed warriors do not question orders from the ancestors. He insisted on regular saltwater cleanses for disciplinary issues with no medical personnel present.

Castellano thumbed the margin and read the scrawled side notes from the chain of command. *Nothing dangerous, but the guy gives me the creeps. May be over-identifying with the role. Watch for escalation.*

She flipped forward. The next file was a PDF printout of scanned journal entries from Holt's government-issued laptop. The language was obsessively formal, full of capitalized concepts like HONOR, RESTORATION, BLOOD DEBT and CLEANSING. More than once, he referred to the coming reckoning, as if prepping for some metaphysical battle. Castellano marked the odd phrasing for later, then reached for her notepad and scribbled a list of every oddball complaint. She circled two of them. *Forced subordinates to bury animal remains in ritual patterns* and *rehearsed mock executions with blunt instruments for morale*.

The last page in the folder was a single sheet of navy blue, official, stamped as a Personnel Action Notice. It detailed Holt's abrupt retirement following an incident on a Pacific training mission. The code word was *cultural miscalculation*, but the rest of the sheet had been heavily redacted.

Castellano set the folder down and leaned back, closing her eyes to the hum of the light. She thought about her first conversation with Leilani, the pushback over who ran the investigation, the way the detective looked at a thing sideways and then somehow ended up being right. She felt a strange prickle of respect, then irritation that she'd noticed it. There was a rap at the door, not a knock, more of a professional warning.

"Come," she called, and the door opened.

A woman in dress blues, one of the Navy's clerical support staff, hovered just inside the threshold. Her head was down, and her arms held a fresh stack of paper.

"Agent Castellano? These just came through the psych eval database. For your subject." She didn't quite make eye contact.

Castellano gestured towards the corner of the desk. "Leave them."

She did, then hesitated. "If I may, ma'am. There's some strong language in the findings. You might want to read it yourself before you show your team."

She gave her the same hard stare she used on subordinates and suspects. "Thank you, Petty Officer. That will be all."

She left fast, letting the door clatter shut behind her.

Castellano opened the top file. The summary was stamped in red: CLINICAL REVIEW—MANDATORY. She skipped straight to the diagnosis.

Subject exhibits symptoms consistent with Obsessive Ritualistic Disorder, compounded by combat-related PTSD and a history of religious zealotry in early upbringing. She skimmed. *Not recommended for leadership roles. Potential danger to self or others if provoked.*

There were case notes. She forced herself to read them in full, line by line.

Lt. Cmdr. Holt frequently speaks of ancestral obligations and restoring order to a corrupted world.

The subject believes ritual is the only path to truth.

When challenged, the subject retreats into archaic or pseudo-Hawaiian speech; at times, appears disassociated.

The subject described the need for ritual sacrifice to ensure the success of future operations.

The last was underlined and highlighted in the scan. Castellano's mouth tightened.

She paged through the after-action notes from the Pacific incident. Most of it was blacked out, but one sentence stood free. *After losing several unit members in a hostile exchange, subject forcibly stripped insignia from the fallen and buried them in traditional arrangement; local guides intervened to stop further escalation.*

Castellano read it again, then underlined the word forcibly.

The next sheet was a psychiatric memo, even more direct. *Subject displays a dangerous fixation on ritualistic punishment and the erasure of dishonor through symbolic violence. Particularly susceptible to triggers involving perceived disloyalty or cultural disrespect. There is reason to believe the subject may blend military discipline with religious fervor, resulting in erratic or extreme behavior*.

For a moment, Castellano glared at the wall, her

teeth grinding in her jaw. “How the fuck did this guy make it as a SEAL?” she asked herself.

She opened a new browser window. A quick check of the command directory confirmed what the report hinted at. Holt had taken early retirement the year before and had received an honorable discharge. There was no reason given for the retirement, and Castellano wondered if the military was moving a problem into someone else’s space. Holt was still on-island, working as a civilian contractor for the same Warrior Spirit program, but now on a volunteer basis.

A single word hung in Castellano’s mind, escalation. She set the files in a neat stack, rubber-banded them, and shoved them into her bag. Then she hit speed dial, calling her second-in-command.

“Timmons,” she barked. “We’ve got a live one. I’m sending you an address. This guy is a former Seal, and he might have a few screws loose. Prep for a takedown, but do it quiet.”

She hung up, then flicked off the light, letting her office fall into the blue shadow that always followed the end of a long shift. On her way out, she paused in the hallway, watching the movement of sailors and civilian staff, all busy with their routines. There was an edge to her posture now, something new, a tightness under the skin. She set her jaw, shouldered her bag, and moved into the stairwell. Her orders were clear; her target was locked. All that remained was to see how far down the spiral Holt had already fallen.

***

Leilani turned off the ignition a full block from the

target, letting the engine tick as she sat and scanned the modest housing complex. From this distance, it looked almost peaceful. There were several rows of small, weathered stucco homes in various pastel colors of blue, pink and orange, with small concrete walkways running between them, and a few palm trees leaning together like conspirators. The complex north of the base looked like it had been built in the fifties. Faded red clay pots lined the entrance, the survivors of decades-old plantings gone leggy or wild. A few cars lurked under the attached carports. A couple of battered sedans, a van with base access stickers on the glass, and a truck that might have been used for construction or for carting bodies into the wilderness. She clocked every point of egress, the angle of each shadow, and only when satisfied did she get out and walk.

She kept her badge visible and her weapon holstered but ready. Every step brought the now-familiar itch between her shoulder blades, the sense that the air itself was bracing for violence. She waited for Isaac and Castellano to arrive and was surprised to see several government SUVs pull onto the street and multiple agents in ballistic vests pile out of the vehicles. Leilani slid out of her vehicle and looked around.

"I thought we were going to make a friendly approach first," she said. "Looks like you brought the whole fucking Navy."

"I got more details after you and I spoke," said Castellano. "This guy has the training to be considered armed and extremely dangerous. I don't want to take any chances."

"That's fine," said Leilani. "But we are not on the base. We are in my jurisdiction, and no one moves without my approval."

Isaac walked up, pulling on his ballistic vest as he approached. He looked around. "Geez, what did I miss?" he asked.

Castellano handed Leilani the file, which she glanced at and handed to Isaac. "Okay. I don't have time to call SWAT, so your guys cover the back of the house and before we go in hard, let's try a softer approach first."

Castellano nodded and sent three of her team around the buildings to cover the back. She had three more agents stand by in the street with Isaac in case backup was needed in a hurry. She looked at Leilani who nodded, and they walked up the walk and approached the front door. They stood on either side of the door, and Leilani knocked. They heard no response, so she used the side of her fist in a classic cop knock and banged on the door.

"Honolulu Police!" she yelled at the top of her voice.

The unit's exterior was unremarkable except for the strange neatness of its doormat, perfectly aligned, no sand or leaf debris. She waited, then tried the knob, which turned. The door swung open two inches on the first try.

That's when they drew their weapons, clearing the barrel with a slow exhale.

"HPD," she called. "Anyone inside, make yourself visible." She pushed the door open all the way, and they stepped across the threshold and moved to opposite sides of the door.

The hallway was empty. It opened into a living room bright with late morning sun, the windows unshaded, the entire space curated like a military museum. Every piece of furniture was at parade rest: a couch against the east wall, rattan chairs squared to a bamboo coffee table, and on every surface, not just art, but artifacts.

The first thing Leilani noticed was the wall display. Six weapons, each mounted on custom racks and tagged with tiny printed labels. There were three lei-o-mano, shark-tooth clubs, wicked and old. Above those, a hardwood throwing spear, polished to a mirror finish, the tip inset with dark, greasy basalt. Lower down, what might have been a reproduction of a gourd calabash, but when she leaned in, she saw the stains of real use.

They cleared the house, and Castellano had her team stand down. She holstered her weapon, her eyes scanning for movement, then eased into the room. The air smelled of sandalwood and something sharper, like ammonia but not bleach. Every breath carried an acidic undertone, as if the entire place had been wiped down with brine.

Across the back of the couch, a length of tapa cloth draped, patterned with zigzags and the inked profile of a ku—war god, and not a gentle one. On the end table, instead of magazines, there was a half-burned candle and a scatter of shells, some broken, some still caked with sea grit.

She advanced towards the kitchen, expecting a body, but found only more order. Every dish was dried and stacked, with nothing out of place except for a single, heavy chef's knife by the sink. The blade was clean but for a trace of blue pigment at the tip.

She kneeled, gloved, and swabbed it with a tissue. The color matched what Mele had pulled from under the last victim's fingernails.

She backed away, adrenaline spiking, and moved down the narrow hall to the bedroom. Here, the tableau was more shrine than home. The bed itself was stripped and remade, military corners on the sheet, a single pillow centered just so. The closet, left half-open, showed nothing but pressed uniforms—camo, dress blues and civilian workout gear. No clutter. Nothing to hide.

But at the foot of the bed stood a low altar. It looked handmade, plywood stained dark, and on top, several objects. A battered field journal, two bundles of dried ti leaf, a wooden bowl crusted with salt, and three plumeria blossoms already wilted brown.

Leilani focused on the journal. She pulled her phone, snapped a photo of the scene before touching anything. The cover was standard-issue, government inventory sticker still attached. She removed her nitrile gloves, pulled a new pair from her vest pocket, and put them on. The first several pages were lists of names, dates and brief phrases in all caps: PREP, CLEANSING, RESTORE. The next were diary entries, dated and sometimes time stamped. She photographed each page.

She read one aloud. "8/17. The spirit in the group is weak. Discipline lacking. They must experience rebirth through trial. Use water, then salt. Blood is a last resort."

She kept flipping. "8/22. Met with Makani. He refuses to teach the real thing. I will learn from the ancestors. The blue is the sign; the loyal warriors mark the body and mark the grave. Next time, do not hesitate."

And then, in bold marker: "HONOR CAN ONLY BE RESTORED THROUGH THE OLD WAY."

She looked up and froze. Standing in the doorway, framed by the cheap molding and a triangle of sunlight, was Castellano.

The agent holstered her gun as she pushed into the room.

Leilani raised her hands, palms open. "It's clear," she said.

Castellano advanced, her shoes squeaking, and swept the room with a cop's precision. Only when she was satisfied did she lower the gun.

"Anything out back or in the truck?" asked Leilani.

"No," said Castellano. "Looks like we missed him. I've got my guys canvassing the neighbors to see if anyone might know where he is."

Castellano turned her attention to the altar. She made a sound, half disgust, and half something closer to pain. "You see the weapon display?"

"Yeah," Leilani said. "All real, all sharp. But look at the journal."

They crowded together over the notebook, reading the next few entries in silence. Each one ramped up in intensity, the script wandering into a fever dream. *Blue for shame, red for blood, white for peace. Prepare the flowers. The next one must be ready.*

Castellano tapped her phone, shooting photos for the file. "He's got the pattern planned out. I bet every entry is a blueprint for a kill."

Leilani agreed, then motioned to the journals back cover, where a hand-drawn map detailed the island's west coast, with four X's marking prior crime scenes. A fifth was penciled in, no label, just a date, tomorrow.

"Shit," said Castellano. "He's going to do it again. And soon."

They worked quickly. Castellano bagged the knife, the flowers, and every visible object on the altar. Leilani found a USB drive taped under the coffee table and pocketed it, making a mental note to have Akira dump its contents as soon as possible.

Castellano returned to the living room, arms full of evidence. For a second, she glanced at Leilani, not as a rival, but as another professional. "Anything else?"

"Yeah," said Leilani, pointing to the altars. "He's mixing it up. Some of these are real, some totally fake. The ti leaves, the pigment, that's all period correct. But the way he uses the blue paint? It's wrong. No one would have done that, not even in the old days."

Castellano shrugged. "Doesn't matter. The victims

wouldn't know the difference."

"But the killer does," Leilani pressed. "That's the whole point. He's rewriting the rituals for himself. Not for tradition, but for control."

A long silence, broken only by the whine of a distant lawn trimmer and the drone of midday cicadas.

Castellano's face softened, just a fraction. "You're right. That's what the psych file said, too. He's obsessed with the script, but he's always the author."

"Means he'll improvise," Leilani finished.

They looked at each other, two women, both half-salted by the job, both blinking away the strain.

Castellano shook her head. "You ever get tired of being right, Kealoha?"

Leilani laughed, but the sound died in her throat. "Never. But I do get tired of chasing ghosts."

They bagged the evidence, tagged the scene, and called it in to the watch desk. Every move was efficient, automatic, the muscle memory of people who'd done this too often.

At the door, Castellano stopped, her hand braced on the frame. "We run this together?"

"For now," Leilani said. "But if you mislead me again, I'll make you regret it."

Castellano gave her the ghost of a smile. "Deal."

Outside, the sky had gone glassy with heat; the sunlight bouncing off the pavement so hard it hurt to look at. They stood a minute, neither wanting to break first. Castellano pulled her phone, called the shore patrol and set up an APB on the base for Holt, in case he tried to get on the base. Isaac called dispatch and had them issue an APB for Holt. He wondered where Holt might have gone without his truck. He called Mele and asked her to send a forensic unit to the address and called for a uniform to be positioned outside the house in case Holt returned.

Leilani heard the faint squawk of the dispatcher, and she felt the knot in her chest tighten. Somewhere out there, Holt was preparing his next scene, and the clock was running.

Chapter Eighteen

The call came in just as Leilani pulled into the station parking lot, engine still rumbling, and the dashboard clock reading 14:33. She glanced at the caller ID—an unknown local number, but the first three digits flagged it as the Department of Education.

She answered. “Detective Kealoha.”

A pause, then a nervous man’s voice: “Um, Ms. Kealoha? This is Mr. Dunn. I’m the head of campus security at Kahala Elementary. Sorry to bother you, nothing urgent, but I’m hoping you might have a minute to talk.”

“Go ahead,” she said, setting the phone to speaker as she gathered her bag and evidence packets.

A longer pause. “It’s regarding your son, Kai. Nothing’s wrong! He’s fine, but it’s about his search history. Our IT Department flagged some unusual queries from the school network. I wanted to ask if there’s something going on at home, or if it’s just...well, I’m not sure.”

She felt her scalp prickle. “What sort of queries?”

“Some of it is normal for a history project. Hawaiian culture, ancient warriors, stuff like that. But today, he spent over an hour looking up things like ritual execution in old Hawaii and how to make ceremonial saltwater and the best flowers for grave offerings. There were even some images. We check for anything like self-harm or—”

Leilani heard herself laugh, but it came out dry. "He's ten. He doesn't know what self-harm is. He's researching for his project, like you said."

"Right," said Dunn. "That's what his teacher said, too. But he also tried to access restricted case reports on the murders from Kaena Point. Those are only referenced by reporters or LEOs. So, we're obligated to flag it."

Leilani felt the chill hit her spine, radiating outward. "What time did he run those searches?"

"Lunchtime. The computer lab logs every half-hour. We can get you exact times."

She forced her voice to stay easy. "I'll talk to him. If there are any other issues, please let me know."

Dunn sounded relieved. "Thank you. I just wanted to check, because sometimes kids..." He trailed off. "Anyway, we're always here to help."

She hung up and sat for a minute, the air in the car suddenly too still, too heavy. She thought of the journal entries in Holt's apartment, the way the killer tracked the news coverage of his own crimes.

She texted her mom a heads-up that she was swinging by the school and would grab Kai herself. Then she started the engine and peeled out, tires chirping on the sunbaked asphalt.

Kahala Elementary was built in the seventies, when the theory was that open-plan, brightly painted corridors would make education feel like a theme park. The outer walls were blue and gold, mottled with spray paint and sun-fade; the interior was a strange riot of modular classrooms and wall-length murals. Today, it was near-empty except for the distant sound of basketballs and the faint clatter of a distant music class.

She signed in at the front office. The woman behind the desk recognized her, smiled with that peculiar blend of pity and fear reserved for parents who were also cops. "You're here for Kai?" she asked, already paging the teacher.

"Yeah," said Leilani. "I'll just wait out front."

She stood on the covered walk, sweating, replaying the officer's words in her head. She scanned the street, the grounds, even the roofline, searching for a car or a face that didn't belong.

The classroom door opened, and Kai bounded out, his backpack slung across both shoulders, and his hair sticking up in all directions. He looked fine, but his smile faded as soon as he saw her face.

"Did I do something?" he asked, his voice small.

Leilani tried to soften her expression. "No. I just finished early and wanted to pick you up myself." She ruffled his hair. "You hungry?"

He nodded, though it was less hunger and more reflex. She led him out through the shadowy breezeway and towards the lot. Her eyes never stopped moving.

They made it to the car. He dumped his pack in the back seat, but before he climbed in, he turned to her, squinting into the light.

"Mom, can I ask you a question?"

She braced for anything. “Always.”

He shuffled his shoes on the curb. “You know the pictures you had on your laptop? For work? The ones with the flowers and the grave stuff?”

Leilani’s mouth tasted like dust. “Yeah?”

Kai glanced over his shoulder at the school. “I saw that guy. The one in the blurry picture. He was in the field during lunch watching. He wrote in a little notebook and left.”

Her heart pounded against her ribs.

“Are you sure it was him?” she asked, keeping her voice steady.

Kai nodded, all solemn. “He looked like a teacher, but he wasn’t. He watched the playground for a while. He didn’t talk to anyone. But he saw me, I think.”

Leilani put a hand on his shoulder and squeezed. “You tell anyone else?”

He shook his head. “Should I?”

She shook her head. “No. You did the right thing.”

She looked around one last time. No strange cars, no unfamiliar faces in the teacher’s lounge windows. She loaded him into the front seat, fastened the belt herself, and locked the doors.

“Where are we going?” he asked, nerves finally showing.

“We’re taking a drive before we go home. And after that, you and I are going to work on your project together.”

She started the car, breathing slowly. Her hands were steady on the wheel, but her mind was running every scenario, every way Holt might have found them, and every breach in the armor she thought she'd built.

She dialed Torres on speaker, not taking her eyes off the road.

He picked up on the second ring. "Isaac."

"Holt was at my son's school. Kai is fine. We're heading home. Have Espinoza pull the cameras from all around the school, especially the parking lot by the playground," she said, her voice clipped.

"Okay. I'll ping Castellano and Tano."

She hung up, pulled onto the main drag, and merged into the early traffic. Every car in the mirror was a threat. Every pedestrian was a potential watcher. But as Kai's hand found hers, small and trusting, she let herself believe for a second that she could keep him safe. Whatever Holt thought he was going to do, he'd have to come through her first.

Chapter Nineteen

Naalei Kealoha's house always felt too warm, like the humidity had pooled there over decades, distilled into a syrup that stuck to your skin. The front door was half-shut, the screen letting in the afternoon's noise. distant lawnmowers, shouts from the neighbor's TV, and the rattle of a rusted delivery van's suspension. Leilani pushed through the door, hard enough that it rattled in the frame, and called for her mother.

She found Naalei in the kitchen, sleeves rolled and wrist-deep in pale mochi flour, hands working dough into precise, stubborn balls. The sight should have calmed her, but Leilani felt her pulse throb in her neck. Kai was perched on the stepstool, his shirt already dusted with flour, eyes tracking her like a bird expecting a storm.

"Mom," Leilani said, but the word came out raw. "We need to go. Now."

Naalei's hands paused mid-roll, then she finished the ball, set it gently on the baking sheet, and wiped her fingers on a rag. She didn't ask why. She just stared at Leilani's face, then at Kai, and said, "Go wash your hands, baby. Grandma will pack snacks."

Kai vanished, the thud of his feet echoing down the hall.

Naalei stepped closer, her eyes on Leilani's face. "It's him?"

Leilani nodded, but she couldn't say it yet.

“Did he see the boy?” asked Naalei

“Yes. At school. Today. He watched from the fence.” The words came out jagged, chewed up by a throat gone dry.

Naalei’s expression darkened, every crease in her face tightening. She moved with purpose, snatched a Tupperware container from the shelf, and started stacking cookies inside. “You drive to the station. I’ll take Kai to Makoa’s place on the North Shore. He’ll be safe with his uncle.”

Leilani knew better than to argue. She tried to keep her voice level. “We need to go now before the school lets out. If Holt’s tracking us—”

“He won’t get past Makoa. Your uncle’s got more firepower than the Kamehameha statue. And he owes me three favors.” She pressed the cookies into Kai’s backpack, zipped it, then reached for a battered wooden box on the fridge. From inside, she pulled a small pendant, a tiki, rough-carved, its surface oiled and dark.

Naalei closed her hand around the tiki, kneeled by the counter, and whispered three words into her fist. She tucked the pendant into a side pocket of the backpack, zipping it so that the cord trailed out. “He won’t know it’s there,” she said, almost to herself. “But the ancestors will.”

Kai reappeared in the hallway, his hands still damp. He eyed the tension, the speed at which his mother and grandmother moved, and said nothing. Instead, he hoisted the backpack, rolling his shoulders like he were preparing for a field trip.

Leilani crouched to his height. "Hey," she said. She reached out, brushing a lock of hair from his forehead. "You're going to stay with Uncle Makoa for a couple days, okay? I'll call every night." She hesitated, searching his face for cracks. "Only until we catch the bad guy."

Kai's voice was small. "Is it because he was at my school?"

Leilani almost broke. She shook her head, forced a smile that tasted like metal. "He won't hurt you. Never. I promise."

Kai nodded, eyes cast down.

Naalei snapped the backpack over Kai's shoulders, patted the pocket with the tiki. "Let's go, my warrior. You get to eat all the malasadas you want tonight."

She herded him out the side door, every motion economical, with no wasted time. Leilani followed, pausing only to grab her own jacket and check her sidearm—twelve in the well, one in the pipe.

At the curb, Naalei gave Leilani a look that was all warning, all love. "Call me when you're ready. And don't do anything stupid."

Leilani swallowed her pride. "Never."

She opened the rear door, watching as Kai slid into the seat, legs swinging. Naalei buckled him in, muttering a quick pule, and shut the door with a finality that stung.

For a long second, the two women just stared at each other, mother to daughter, warrior to warrior. Then Naalei said, "You're stronger than this man.

Even if he's a demon."

Leilani shook her head. "He's just a man. But he's making a run at my family."

Naalei's smile was cold. "Then he's already lost."

The car started, coughing on the first crank, and then Naalei and Kai were gone, rolling down the street towards the highway, sunlight blinking off the rear window.

Leilani stood in the open doorway, hand on her weapon under her jacket, and scanned the street, every parked car, and every silhouette. The neighbors were invisible behind their curtains, but she could feel them watching. She waited, her heart heavy, until she was certain no one had followed. Only then did she let herself breathe.

Chapter Twenty

The joint task force room was more holding pen than conference space, with whiteboards scarred with old case numbers, coffee ring constellations on every surface, and the air alive with the desperate hush of professionals who'd been up too many nights in a row. Leilani walked in with her badge clipped and her jaw set, aware that the room took her mood and amplified it.

Castellano was already there, arms crossed, back to the window, her expression tuned to somewhere between predatory and bored. A couple of HPD detectives and two NCIS support staff huddled over laptops, their screens reflected in the icy blue of the overheads.

Leilani made her announcement before the door had closed. "My son is being moved to a safe house under family care. He'll have protection. I need one officer to coordinate the handoff, then return to the case. I can't leave him exposed."

It was an order, not a request. Castellano didn't let it stand. She uncrossed her arms, leaned forward, and said, "You want to use case resources for personal protection? With a killer on a timetable, targeting military assets? That's not happening."

Leilani kept her voice even. "He's already found my son. At school. It's a liability for everyone if we pretend otherwise."

Castellano smiled. "This unsub isn't interested in

collateral damage. He's after ritual, not revenge on your family."

Leilani didn't blink. "Until I'm the next name on his list, and my kid is the reason. You want me distracted, Vic? That's how you get it."

Leilani let the silence build, then added, "It's about the case. Holt is watching for weakness. This isn't a personal favor. It's about plugging a hole in the investigation."

A chair scraped as Castellano stood, closing the distance between them by two feet. Her voice dropped. "If you want to stay on the case, you don't get to play by your own rules."

Leilani felt the old familiar heat at her temples, the pressure of being boxed in by someone who didn't know the territory. She stepped closer. "You want to see what happens if I'm not here, Agent? Try me."

The standoff might have gone nuclear, but the door to the chief's office across the hall slid open with a click. Chief Mori walked across the hall and entered the conference room with one hand on the door, and her eyes fixed on the two women. The hush in the room collapsed inward.

Mori's voice didn't rise above a whisper, but it cut cleaner than a Ginsu knife. "Problem?"

Neither of them moved.

Castellano said, "Kealoha is diverting resources."

Leilani answered, "My son is a witness now. This is protocol."

Mori looked from one to the other, then said, "Torres, do you have a minute?"

Isaac materialized from the kitchenette, coffee in hand. He approached like a man walking into an unexploded minefield. "Yes, Chief?"

Mori gave him the floor. "You know this case better than anyone. What's your read?"

Isaac didn't hesitate. "Holt's fixation isn't random. If he's already targeting Leilani's family, that means he's using them as leverage, or as a message. Either way, leaving the kid unprotected is a mistake. But we don't need the entire squad. One or two officers, tops, as a visible deterrent. It's about optics and peace of mind. I can pull a couple of plainclothes officers from the surveillance unit. That won't hurt our investigation, and it will give us trained eyes in case Holt shows."

Castellano opened her mouth, but Mori lifted a hand, silencing her. "Thank you, Detective. Make it happen." The silence linger a moment, then said, "We're on the clock. Everyone needs to be at their sharpest. If the detective needs a detail for her family, she gets it. No further debate."

Castellano's face was unreadable. "Understood."

Mori turned and slid the glass panel shut; the matter was closed. Leilani exhaled, felt the line of tension from her jaw to her back go slack, just a little.

Castellano leaned in, voice pitched for her alone. "You know he's watching for this kind of weakness."

Leilani met her gaze, her eyes dark as obsidian. "Let him. He won't find any."

Castellano gave a curt nod, a slight grin flickered before she reset her face to neutral.

Isaac drifted over, hand steady on his coffee. “You good?” he murmured.

Leilani nodded once. “Never better.”

He smiled, the way people do when they're counting their own lies. They turned to the board, the new hierarchy clear and the next moves already spinning into place.

The forensic lab felt like an icebox, over-lit and over-air conditioned. Mele had set up her briefing at the end of a battered steel workbench, a trio of monitors glowing with close-ups of dirt samples. She wore a faded blue lab coat and a T-shirt for some band nobody'd heard of, and her hair was twisted into a pair of black braids.

Leilani, Isaac and Castellano crowded in, breathing fog into the frigid air. Tano and Espinoza hovered in the doorway, not quite inside, but not willing to miss anything.

Mele fired up the projector, clicking through slides with a remote that looked one spill away from death. “I'll keep this quick,” she said. “Four graves. Four soil samples, taken from under the victim, not the surface. All have the same signature, fine red basalt, high potassium, flecks of olivine, and the weird part, micro-fragments of chromium and nickel.”

She zoomed in on one image, a tangle of black and green crystals glinting like confetti. “This shouldn't be here, not unless someone trucked it in from Koko

Crater or Mokuleia. But get this. The trace mineral ratios don't match those quarries. They match a specific volcanic layer, mapped by the USGS forty years ago."

She spun the map on the next slide. "There are only three places on Oahu with this exact composition. Here," she tapped the first. "The military reservation at the end of Barbers Point. Next, a cultural site at Kaneana Cave, on the west shore. And third, the old heiau ruins above Pupukea, which are now partially fenced off by the Feds."

She let the map linger, then said, "All four victims were buried on Kaena Point. This dirt doesn't come from there, meaning they were killed at one of three other sites and brought to the point for cleansing and burial."

She turned, expecting questions.

Leilani stepped forward. "It's not just geography. It's intent. The killer is picking these places for a reason."

Castellano shifted, unconvinced. "You're telling me our unsub is a geologist, or does he like the view?"

Mele shrugged, unbothered. "Or he wants the dead to anchor something bigger. Old ground, old gods."

Isaac looked at the map, then at Leilani. "You think Holt knows this?"

Leilani nodded. "He's obsessed with protocol. He doesn't pick his victims randomly."

Castellano folded her arms. "So what's the play? Stake out all three? We're thin as is."

Leilani didn't flinch. "I think we need to. He'll go to all of them in order, or pick one to finish the cycle."

Mele, ever the scientist, added, "I'd bet on the heiau. Plus, the last entry in his journal referenced something he called the altar."

Castellano frowned, but said, "Fine. We split the team. Torres, Tano and Timmons, you take Barbers Point. I'll handle Kaneana with Waldorf and Simms. Kealoha, you get the heiau with Espinoza and take at least one uniform with you."

Leilani nodded, already thinking through the terrain, the trails and the best place to watch without being seen.

Mele smirked, proud of her handiwork. "Bring back a live suspect this time, yeah?"

Leilani managed half a smile, and pivoted, ready to move. But Castellano caught her at the door, voice soft. "You're sure about the heiau?"

Leilani looked her dead in the eye. "I know how he thinks."

Castellano held her gaze, searching for doubt, and found none.

"Don't get yourself killed," she said. "I don't have the patience to solve this case alone."

Leilani almost laughed, but it came out as a grunt. "I'm not planning on it. Now let's get the topographic maps and lay out our approaches and get as much detail as we can on this guy."

Chapter Twenty-One

The conference room had gone full command center. Digital maps stretched across two screens, and printouts taped and double-taped to every vertical surface. The overheads were dimmed, but the blue glow from the monitors turned every face into hard angles and tired eyes.

Isaac worked on the central laptop, his hands never stopping. He dug through military personnel records, flagging every reference to Holt and cross-referencing them with flagged incident reports. Leilani hovered close, her own phone open to a growing folder of images and old deployment logs.

She found the photo first, a sepia-washed snapshot from an overseas tour, Holt kneeling beside a stack of human bones, the other soldiers smirking, one giving a mock shaka to the lens.

Isaac leaned over. "That's Afghanistan. What's he doing there?"

Leilani scrolled down, reading the attached notation. "Locals accused them of desecrating the grave. Holt wrote in his report that he was restoring order to a site defiled by enemies of the state."

Isaac scanned the page. "He saw himself as a protector or a priest."

Leilani kept digging. "There's more. His parents died when he was six. Raised by a grandmother in Honolulu. She's listed as pureblood Hawaiian in the census. Strict. No record of a father."

Isaac nodded, lines deepening around his mouth. "So he's half in, half out, and trying to prove himself to the old world and the new. That's why he's obsessed."

She let that settle. "This trauma and his heritage make the perfect storm. He doesn't see himself as a killer. He thinks he's cleaning up a mess."

Isaac grunted, half in agreement and half disgust. "And he's escalating. Each kill becomes more precise. More like a ritual. Next one will be the magnum opus."

The door opened and Castellano entered, less of a storm than before. She moved to the board, studied their progress, and said, "I talked to my contacts in Navy psych. Holt was on a suicide watch in 2019, right after his last tour. They said he wrote manifestos, pages of them, about rebirth, cleansing, and fixing the bloodlines."

Isaac glanced up. "He was flagged?"

Castellano nodded. "But they let him finish his tour. Deemed him functionally sane." The scorn in her voice was sharp as glass. "He went to ground after his discharge. No family, no friends, just the gym and church and then he found the warrior groups, and he found a new home."

She met Leilani's gaze, and something in her posture was less brittle, more respectful. "You were right about the ritual. He's not copying. He's inventing."

Leilani squeezed her eyes shut for a beat, saw the graves, the careful lines of salt and flowers, and the way each victim's face was turned to the sky. "He's writing his own story. He thinks it's the only one that matters."

Isaac straightened, hands bracing on the table. "So we need to rewrite the ending."

Castellano allowed herself a thin smile. "Then let's get to work."

The three of them bent over the maps and dossiers, the only sound the tap of keys and the slow, hungry tick of the wall clock, each second counting down to the next confrontation.

Chapter Twenty-Two

By the time the sun ducked behind the Koʻolau, the conference room looked more like a war bunker than a station office. Three topographical maps blanketed the far wall, marked up with color-coded pins, highlighter streaks, and annotated Post-its. The air vibrated with radio chatter as officers checked in, prepped their gear, confirmed fuel in the SUVs and the batteries in the handhelds.

Isaac manned the whiteboard, scrawling last-minute updates as Castellano fielded a call with the Navy liaison. Leilani mapped the flanking trails at the heiau site, using the satellite overlay to mark every entry and exit. Tano and Espinoza hovered near the door, ready but trying not to look overeager.

Leilani circled the main table, where all three teams would converge for the final briefing. "We're rolling out in threes. You all have your assignments. Communication is radio-first, but we use cell backup in case Holt tries to jam us. If you see anything, a fresh flower, a line of salt, even just a disturbed patch of ground, you call it in, no solo heroics."

Isaac nodded. "Base security is the backup at Barbers Point. HPD will have units in close proximity to support Kaneana, but the heiau is on you, Lei and your team. It's too remote to stage back up. You sure about that?"

She tapped the map, her finger pressing the spot above the old shrine. "He's not expecting a cop to know the land. And if he does, I'll smell it before he does. Besides, I've got Espinoza and Sergeant Jerry Powell from uniform to keep me company. Powell's got twenty years on the streets."

Castellano grunted, then turned to Isaac. "You trust her?"

Isaac grinned, all teeth. "She's gotten me out of worse."

There was no time for ceremony. They broke, each team heading for the supply closet, grabbing body armor, med kits and thermal scopes. Leilani took a minute to pull Espinoza aside, reviewing the plan in a low, even voice.

"You see anything weird, you stay back. Don't touch artifacts. Even a rock in the wrong place could trigger something."

Espinoza, not usually a believer, nodded so hard his sunglasses slid down his nose. "Got it, boss."

Leilani smiled, fleeting and hard. "Let's make sure we're not the next offering, yeah?"

Powell entered the room and took in the scene. At six feet-four and two hundred-fifty pounds, he made quite the impression walking through the door. Leilani introduced him around the room, and she gave him a quick debrief on the plan. Powell carried his ballistic vest in one of his huge hands and an AR-style rifle in the other. He was ready to go to work. When everyone was geared up, the teams assembled at the exit, the air thick with anticipation. Castellano did a quick comms check, her voice sharp and clear. "All channels are live. Listen for the codeword. Move only if you're certain that you have him. Consider him armed and extremely dangerous."

Isaac, already on the move, called back to Leilani. "See you on the other side."

She watched the others peel away, then took her own pack and headed out. The station felt too empty in their wake, the world outside darkening by the second.

They were two blocks down and past the last streetlight when the first call came in. Leilani answered, expecting a status report, but the voice on the line was unfamiliar and urgent.

"Detective? This is Officer Nobriga, central desk. Tripler Army Hospital just reported a trauma. Female, mid-twenties, with ritual injuries that match your case. She's still alive."

Leilani's heart kicked into gear. "Name?"

"They don't have it yet. She was found on a hiking trail above the Pali. Runners called it in."

Leilani snapped her fingers for Espinoza to start the car. "We're en route. Alert Castellano and Torres. This could be our best shot."

She hit the siren and peeled onto the main drag, city lights flicking by in quick, electric bursts. Next to her, Espinoza murmured a prayer under his breath, and Leilani, for once, did the same.

Chapter Twenty-Three

Tripler Hospital's emergency room was at capacity, every cot, and gurney jammed with a body, some whimpering, some angry, but most silent with pain. Paramedics cut through the chaos, barking patient info over the clatter of med carts and the wail of a kid who'd caught a skateboard to the teeth.

They brought Olivia Makasi in the back way, two military EMTs rolling her through the corridor at a dead run. The girl looked gone already; her skin was gray, her lips blue and the front of her uniform was soaked a black so deep it barely registered as red.

Leilani reached the doors at the same instant as the trauma team. She kept her badge high, voice even as she announced, "This is a victim in our ongoing investigation. Chain of evidence, please." No one argued.

Inside the trauma bay, they cut away the uniform, layer by layer, exposing arms cross-hatched with bruises and cuts. One deep gash scored from clavicle to sternum, but someone, possibly the killer or the EMTs, had packed the wound with cloth to slow the bleeding. Across her chest, in blue pigment and salt. The beginnings of a ritual sigil that waited to be finished.

Castellano arrived, breathless but all business, phone recording. "We need her name for the log. Fast."

A nurse checked the dog tags, then said, "Senior Petty Officer Olivia Makasi. Navy. Catholic, O positive. Someone call for a priest, stat."

Isaac, standing behind her jotted it down as another nurse picked up the wall phone and requested a priest. "She was one of Holt's demo team. Only one we couldn't locate. Hikers found her on the trail above the Pali, at the base of the old heiau."

The lead doctor, a woman with a marine tattoo inked on her inner forearm, called out orders, hands never stopping: "Pressure here. Get an IV. Notify the OR that we are on the way, stat. Call the blood bank and get ten units of O positive. She's shocky. Let's move, people."

Castellano stepped aside as the medical crew lifted Makasi, moving her to a fresh bed. There was so much blood, it dripped off the mattress and pattered onto the linoleum.

Leilani edged closer, careful not to touch anything. She caught a whiff of the salt, real, not hospital-grade, mixed with the faintest stink of smoke and pigment. She studied the wound patterns, matching each mark to the old diagrams from the files.

Isaac stood by her side. "He didn't finish. Something interrupted him."

Leilani nodded. "Or she fought him off. That's even better."

A nurse wiped Makasi's mouth, and for one moment, her eyes flicked open. She looked straight at Leilani, terror, and shame tangled in her stare.

Leilani leaned in, voice gentle. "Olivia. I'm Detective Kealoha. You're safe now. Can you tell me who did this?"

Makasi tried to speak, but her throat was raw; her words little more than a croak. "It was... Holt. Said I...dishonored... the old traditions." Her hand trembled, fingers clawing at the air. "He's not done. Said he needed... a witness."

The doctor swept in, pushing them back. "She's going under. Clear the room."

They rushed into the hallway.

Castellano broke the silence. "She's alive. That changes the case. He can't hide behind ritual now."

Isaac let out a long, shaky breath. "He'll try. But he's running out of places and time."

Leilani watched the medical team do their jobs, the old ache settling in her chest. "He's running out of stories to tell himself."

Outside, the corridor buzzed with a different energy. Determined, but not desperate. Leilani texted the chief an update, her eyes locked on the trauma bay as they wheeled Makasi towards the surgery wing. For the first time in weeks, she felt like they were ahead.

Chapter Twenty-Four

The drive up the old access road was like driving into a green canyon. What the satellite called a road was a tunnel of banyan and tangled passionfruit trees; the forest older than anything in the city and meaner, too. Branches clawed the roof of Leilani's Explorer, scraping paint and glass with such insistence that Espinoza, riding shotgun, kept flinching. In the back, Powell rode with both hands on his rifle, the muzzle angled towards the transmission tunnel, eyes flicking to every shape out of place.

Leilani drove with the windows down, letting the wet rot and ginger-laced breath of the interior jungle into her lungs. Sweat ran from her temples down the hollows of her cheeks; the AC had been no match for the terrain, so she shut it off. Up ahead, the canopy pressed down until even the late sun couldn't get through. A thousand birds screamed and fell silent as the SUV rumbled past. Every time the headlights knifed through the gloom, a flock of ghosts scattered, feral chickens, lost cats, and once the flick of a wild boar's black tail.

Espinoza checked the handheld radio clipped to his vest. "Still got a bar," he muttered, then hit the transmit button: "Unit B, two minutes out from target location. Copy over."

Nothing but white hiss.

Leilani kept the wheel straight. "You'll lose it for good a hundred yards from here. There's an old lava tube under us. It plays hell with anything electronic."

Espinoza tried again anyway, then gave up and started narrating for the dash cam. "This is Detective Espinoza, heading up the Ridge Access Road to the old Pupukea Heiau with Detectives Kealoha and Powell. ETA less than one minute. Will update at approach." He clicked off, checked the battery, clipped it to his vest, and pulled his weapon.

Powell leaned forward, the bulk of his vest creaking. "What are we looking for, exactly?"

Leilani spotted the gap in the undergrowth that passed for parking, nosed the SUV in, and killed the lights. "Ritual prep. Flower petals, pigment or evidence of a kill kit. If he's here, he's setting up a show. And if he brought a victim, he won't take long to start."

They exited in silence, Espinoza first, then Powell, then Leilani. The jungle took them like a tide. Darkness fell between the trees, and the air was alive with insect wings and the rip of geckos feasting. They moved without words, their boots soft on the leaf mold, and their senses tuned to the expectation of violence.

The heiau itself was older than the road, older than the city, the ranchers or the long-vanished farmers who'd terraced the hills. It squatted at the top of a bluff, half-swallowed by elephant grass and the roots of a rain tree that had gone feral centuries ago. The main altar, a platform of stacked basalt slabs, as big as a coffin, was slick with moss and dark from years of rain. Smaller broken trees jutted at odd angles from the ground like broken ribs; some toppled, and others slowly reburied by vines.

Leilani walked point, her headlamp off, trusting her eyes to adjust. She knew this place; her grandfather used to bring her here before it was fenced off by the State. She stepped through the boundary wall, three feet high, lichen-crusted, once meant to keep out the unworthy, and felt the hairs on her arms stand up.

Powell's voice was a low rumble behind her. "Fucking hell," he muttered. "Do you ever get the feeling something's watching you?"

Leilani didn't answer, just kept moving, her eyes darting to every break in the foliage. Ten meters inside the wall, she stopped and held up a fist. The other two froze.

She pointed towards the ground. A line of pure white, like the snarl of a chalk strike, arched across the old stones. Not paint or powder, but salt.

Espinoza whispered, "Didn't Mele say the killer used Morton for the others?"

Leilani crouched. This wasn't supermarket stuff. The grains were crystalline and irregular, the kind you got from coastal evaporators or ground up yourself with a mortar and pestle. She ran her finger along the line, careful to disturb it as little as possible. Fresh. The humidity hadn't melted it yet.

"He's here," she said, rising. "Or was, less than an hour ago."

She swept her light up and down the line. At either end, a spray of blue pigment dusted the leaves, a hint, barely there. She fished a sterile swab from her vest and took a sample, then bagged it. Espinoza bagged a pinch of salt.

Powell swept his light to the tree line. "There's a path here," he said. "Looks freshly cut."

They followed. Where once the grass and ferns tangled above their knees, now a narrow corridor had been carved out. The work was recent; the stubs still oozed clear, wet sap.

Fifty feet along, a pile of leaves masked a shallow pit. In the center, a star of flower petals, red ginger, white plumeria, and the crushed yellow of day-blooming cereus. In the middle, a ti leaf bundle, tied with white cord. Leilani kneeled, examining it with her headlamp angled. "This is for cleansing," she said. "But see the knots? It's a variation. Never saw it this way before."

Espinoza kept his hand on his holster, his other holding the light. "The killer's improvising?"

"Or getting closer to what he thinks is the real thing," she replied. She pointed to the base of the tree near the pit, where a fan-shaped stone had been set upright, deliberately. On its surface, blue pigment had been ground to a paste and smeared into the stone's grooves.

"He's building a gate," Leilani whispered. "It's not for the victim. It's for whatever he thinks is coming next."

A branch snapped to their right, sharp and clean. All three moved into a crouch, their eyes on that direction. Nothing but dark, moving shadows, and the hiss of a million insects.

Powell murmured, "You want to go loud, or keep quiet?"

"If he hears us coming, he'll bolt. Or he'll kill the witness. We move up fifty yards, then sweep in a fan," she said.

Powell grunted assent. "If you get eyes on him, do not engage. Hold and observe."

Leilani nodded, but inside she knew it was bullshit. Comms would be dead already, and if Holt was anywhere near the altar, he'd be armed and running on a religious high. She sensed the weight of her sidearm and wished she had grabbed the shotgun out of her office.

They fanned out, Leilani in the center, Espinoza left, and Powell to the right. The air was thicker here; the ground soggy underfoot. She followed the line of cut grass, reading the subtle cues. A broken branch, a smeared patch of pigment on a fern, and the scuff of a boot on an exposed root.

Another pit, shallower, marked the midpoint. This one was filled with water. It could have been filled by rain or as part of the ritual. Floating in the water, a layer of salt, iridescent in the flashlight beam. She was about to call out when her boot snagged on something rigid, half-buried in the mud. She crouched, brushing away the dirt with a gloved hand. A knife. Or, more accurately, a lei-o-mano, a wooden handle with shark teeth lashed along the edge with sennit cord. The blade glistened wet, but not with water. Blue pigment smeared along the edge, and at the tip, a trace of red.

Leilani bagged the weapon, her heart stuttering. She

looked ahead and saw the shadowed outline of the heiau's main platform. Two torches flanked it, set in steel sleeves hammered into the stone, and their flames were just visible, flickering in the thick, windless air.

She clicked her radio, just in case. "Approaching the main altar," she whispered. "Two torches. Could be occupied."

Static, then silence.

She heard a hiss from her right: Powell, crouched and gestured with the barrel of his rifle. She moved to his position, keeping low.

Powell pointed: "Footprint. Big."

He wasn't kidding. In the soft loam, a single print, boot size twelve or better, and fresh. She measured it against her palm. The mud had barely rebounded from the weight. She motioned to Espinoza, and the three of them inched up, using the fallen stones for cover. At the platform, Leilani stopped, held up a hand, and signaled Espinoza and Powell to flank wide. She'd go up the center.

The platform's top was flat, fifteen feet across, and slick with lichen. At its center, a rectangle of disturbed earth. Leilani saw the outline of a body, covered with a white shroud, cloth, or paper; she couldn't tell which. Next to it, a bundle of flowers, plumeria, and red ginger tied with twine, and a black ceramic bowl, half-filled with water. Leilani stepped out, slow and deliberate, her weapon in her hand and hanging along her right leg. Nothing moved.

She crept closer. The shroud was a hotel sheet, crisp

and clean, the edges tucked military tight under the body's weight. She leaned in and peeled the edge back. Underneath, a face, pale but alive, eyes rolled up and out of focus. The skin on the man's arms and chest was scored with fresh, shallow cuts, each one lined with salt. She pressed two fingers to his neck. A pulse, faint but present.

Behind her, Powell called out in a harsh whisper: "Clear, nothing left side. You got eyes?"

She replied just as something hit her from the right. A tackle, fast and silent, bowling her off her feet and into the mud. She barely had time to get her arm up before a hand closed around her throat, big as a clamp.

She choked, lashed out with her left hand, found an ear, and dug in with her nails. The grip loosened just enough for her to breathe. She twisted, rolled, and glimpsed the man's face in the torchlight: wide nose, sunburned skin, head shaved and oiled. His eyes were wide and crazed, and his lips moved in silent prayer.

She brought up her sidearm, but he slammed her wrist against the stone, numbness shooting up her arm. He reached for her pistol lying on the ground, but she rolled to her side and bit his hand, hard enough to taste copper.

He grunted, pulled back, and she drove her knee up, catching him in the ribs. He stumbled, just a second, as Leilani grabbed her weapon from the dirt and brought it up. He rolled back and landed in a crouch.

He was fast, already moving, but Powell's silhouette loomed behind him, rifle raised. "Drop it!" Powell barked. "Down! Now!"

The man froze, then smiled, slow and mean, his mouth red with blood, his or hers, she didn't know.

He raised his hands, but in one he held a blade, a serrated diving knife, dark and slick. He charged.

Leilani took the shot. Two rounds, center mass. The impact spun him sideways, but he kept moving, staggering towards Powell. Powell fired three times. The man dropped, smiling and clutching the blade.

Espinoza sprinted in, cuffed the arms, and kicked the knife clear. Powell covered the body, eyes sweeping for any other threat.

Leilani crawled to her knees, wiped blood from her lips, and turned to the shrouded man on the altar.

He was awake, eyes now frantic. She cut the cords at his wrists and ankles and rolled him onto his side. His face was streaked with pigment, mouth stuffed with a ball of rice cloth.

She pulled it free. He gasped, then said, "He was going to cut out my tongue."

Leilani looked up at the dead man, his mouth fixed in that awful grin.

She radioed in, got nothing but static, so she called out to Powell: "Jerry, can you help the victim to the Explorer, then see if you can get a radio or cell signal out. Call Isaac or Castellano and tell them to send forensics and EMTs. Espinoza and I will secure the scene."

Powell nodded, picked up the limp man like a child, and moved off through the forest. Espinoza grabbed a thermal emergency blanket from his backpack and covered the body. He pulled out an evidence bag and secured the knife. Leilani swept the site, bagged the bowl, the flower bundle and the ti leaf charm.

At the SUV, Powell loaded the victim into the back seat, checked his airway, and did a quick field dressing on his wounds. Powell tried his radio and his cell phone, and had no reception. He spotted a trail leading up the hill, and he took off at a run, watching his radio the entire time and waiting for a single bar to appear.

Leilani listened to the sounds of the forest, but the sounds had all disappeared, leaving a deep silent void. In the torchlight, the stones seemed to move, shadows twisting, the old gods unsettled and waiting. Espinoza looked around. He felt the strangeness, too. He looked at Leilani for reassurance, but her face was not reassuring. He moved towards her, but she held up her hand.

"I don't think we're alone," she whispered.

Espinoza covered the area with his pistol as the last rays of the sun disappeared behind the mountain. He swung from side to side, his eyes like huge pie plates. Leilani's mind wandered, and she wondered if the spirits of the elders were angry that the ritual had been stopped. She didn't believe in ghosts, but she had seen things over the years that were hard to explain. They'd stopped Holt, but the ritual wasn't finished. Not for her, not for the island, not for anyone still alive in the aftermath.

They could feel movement all around them, and they stepped closer together with their backs to each other and waited. They sensed something was coming, and it would not be good.

Chapter Twenty-Five

Isaac Torres checked his phone for the third time in as many minutes, thumb flicking over to the time, then back to the dispatch app, then over to his encrypted texts with Leilani. Still nothing. Her last pinged location had come through ten minutes ago, exactly where she was supposed to be, and then the map icon just froze. The next message was a generic "out of service area" bounce, which could mean anything from a dead battery to the inside of a shipping container.

He stepped away from the cliff, his eyes scanning the black line where the ocean met the sky. He keyed his radio and tried the main channel. "Kealoha, this is Torres. Report status." He waited, listening for a hiss of static, a clipped reply, anything.

Nothing.

He forced his voice to be steady. "Espinoza, Powell, Kealoha update."

A beat later, Powell's voice came over the radio. The static made it difficult to hear. "This is Powell. Holt is dead, repeat, Holt is dead. We found another victim alive; need air medivac. Heard shots coming from the area we found Holt. I can't leave the victim, so I can't investigate. Comms are not working up here. The forest is moving. Shadows everywhere."

"Powell," he yelled into the radio. "Powell, respond!" There was nothing but static. He wondered what Powell meant when he said the forest was moving.

Castellano's voice came over the radio. "Torres, do you copy?"

Isaac keyed his mic. "Torres, go."

"I've called for a Navy medevac," said Castellano. "What's going on up there?"

He kept it crisp. "No idea. That radio call from Powell was the first in an hour. No contact with Kealoha or Espinoza. I don't like that Powell reported gunfire."

Castellano cursed, sharp enough to crack the phone's speaker. "We need to maintain coverage at all three sites. Holt could double back. You leave your post, he might slip through."

"He's not coming back here," said Isaac. "Powell reported Holt is dead. We need to head to the site. Something else is going on up there."

"Take your team and head up there," she said, but her voice was brittle, all the toughness in the world unable to hide the fear. "See if your uniform division can divert some of their close assets. We're heading to the vehicles now and we'll head that way."

Isaac didn't say "roger," or "copy," or anything else. He disconnected and started the engine. Tano and Timmons jumped in and buckled up. The Subaru's tires slid on the gravel before grabbing hard. He hit the lights and siren and floored it, ignoring every posted limit and a couple of road barriers, the rush of night air so dense it felt like the car was plowing water. While Isaac focused on the road, Tano used the radio and called for uniformed backup.

Chapter Twenty-Six

He hit the forest road in under twenty minutes, which would have been a record if there had been anyone to clock it. The Subaru was designed for off-road, but he forced it up the slope, fishtailing around root humps and overgrown culverts. With every swerve, he replayed the last time he'd seen Leilani. The unspoken tension, her hands steady on the wheel, that look she got when she was seconds from going over the edge. The jungle pressed closer. The sound of insects and birds cut off, replaced by the weird roar of his own blood in his ears.

He pulled to a stop next to Lealani's Explorer and spotted Powell working on the victim. Powell pushed out of the SUV and approached the Subaru as everyone piled out.

Isaac keyed the radio again, dropping his voice to a whisper: "Kealoha, this is Torres. If you can hear me, click twice on your mic, no voice."

He waited, holding his breath. Nothing but the faint squelch of distant comms, too far away to matter.

"What happened?" asked Isaac.

"We found the altar and a live victim," said Powell. "He's in bad shape. Holt attacked, and Lei and I put him down. We had no comms, so I carried the victim up here and climbed the ridge until I got a signal."

Isaac, Tano, and Timmons grabbed their gear from the back of the Subaru and headed down the trail. As they moved into the forest, they could hear a chopper coming in low and fast over the ridge. They moved slower than Isaac wanted, but he remembered the last time he'd blown a search by going too loud and too fast. There was no room for error here. He moved along the path, following broken fern stalks and the scuff of boot prints in the mud.

At the first ring of fallen stones, they found Espinoza lying against a large stone, his gun next to him on the ground. Espinoza's shirt was torn at the elbow, and blood beaded along his forearm. He had a large purple bump on the side of his head. Isaac kneeled next to him, pulled out a flashlight and put his hand on his shoulder. Espinoza opened his eyes and grabbed his head.

"Fuck, that hurts."

"Where is Leilani?" asked Isaac.

Espinoza shook his head and winced. "I don't know. After she and Powell took out Holt, the forest around us came alive. There were shadows everywhere."

"She told me to head back to the Explorer," Espinoza said, his voice shaking. "I was worried when I heard shots fired, so I doubled back and something hit me."

Isaac's own pulse hammered in his jaw. "Which way?"

Espinoza jerked his chin. "Follow the salt, then the flower petals. That will take you to the altar where we found the victim."

Isaac slapped his shoulder. "Timmons, stay with

him and stay alert. We have no idea what we are up against."

Timmons nodded and raised her rifle into the low ready position. She kneeled next to Espinoza.

Isaac and Tano headed deeper into the forest. The trail narrowed, and the air grew cold and slick. The ground underfoot gave way to stone and moss. He turned off his flashlight and let the meager moon guide him. The first thing he saw was a cluster of red, like the spatter of a paintbrush. Blood. Not a lot, but enough to be fresh.

He whispered to Tano. "Looks like blood."

They moved slower, weapons tight to their chests, and their hearts pounding so hard they thought someone would hear it. They reached the clearing and spotted the altar, just as a wind licked through the stones and set the torches sputtering.

Next to the altar was a large shape. Isaac lit his flashlight. The body was human and dressed in ancient Hawaiian ceremonial clothes, right down to the flower cape and headdress.

Isaac crossed the last twenty feet in a crouch, eyes darting, every nerve screaming that this was wrong. He holstered his weapon, kneeled, and rolled the body up onto its back. Tano stood by on high alert.

The body was painted like a warrior or a priest, but what struck Isaac was that the man on the ground was Hawaiian. Holt was a white man with no island features.

"Shit. That's not Holt," he said.

Tano stepped over and shined his light on the man's face. "Fuck. Who the hell is this guy and where's Holt?"

A voice rolled out of the dark, booming but contained. "You defiled my offering."

Isaac's muscles locked. The words were English, but the accent was island, deep and old, so thick it sounded like it came from the bottom of a well.

They pivoted with guns raised and saw a shadow materialize from the forest. Holt rose from behind a toppled stone as if he'd grown there. The man was enormous, his body painted with blue and black stripes, wearing nothing but a barkcloth malo and a cape of red and yellow feathers. In one hand, he held the shark-tooth club. In the other, a modern tactical knife, matte black and so sharp the moon glinted off the edge.

Something in the tableau held him back. Holt wasn't advancing; he just stood, bare feet sunk into the moss, looking like a pillar of the goddamn mountain.

"Where's Kealoha?" said Isaac, his gun steady.

"She broke the ceremony. She has to pay," said Holt, smiling.

Isaac wanted to stall, but he needed to find Leilani and try to talk him down, but he felt the moment slipping. He heard the crunch of steps behind him, probably Castellano.

He said, "It's over, Holt. We know about the rituals, the plan. You're done."

Holt's smile didn't change, but his eyes became sad.

"I'm never done," he said. "Not until the island is clean again."

With a speed that should have been impossible, Holt raised the club and brought it down hard on the altar. The stone shattered, sending a spray of salt and bone and god-knows-what into the air. The sound echoed for a full three seconds, longer than any gunshot. In the confusion, Isaac's finger jerked the trigger, but the round went wide, flattening against a tree trunk.

Holt turned, glided, and disappeared into the forest.

Castellano burst from the trail, her gun drawn. "Where is he?"

Isaac pointed, already running. "He ran into the forest!"

They ran, all three, through the maze of stones, ducking under fallen logs and following the sound of breaking branches. Holt was big, but he knew the terrain and knew how to vanish. They tracked him by the crash of his passage, the occasional glimpse of blue paint on bark, the stink of sweat and salt.

At the crest of the bluff, Holt stood, silhouetted by the city lights far below. He held the club in one hand, the knife in the other, chest heaving with each breath.

Isaac slowed, closing the gap to twenty feet. He holstered his weapon, hands up.

"Holt," he called. "You're cornered. You have nowhere left to go."

Holt shook his head, feathers shuddering in the wind. "There is always somewhere. The old customs never die. You just forgot them."

"You're not a priest. You're not even a true believer," said Castellano, circling left. "You're a murderer. Let it go."

For a second, something in Holt's face crumbled, like he wanted to cry or laugh or both. He said, "You will never understand. Not you. Not her."

He turned, not to fight, but to jump. For a heartbeat, Isaac thought he'd go over the edge, but Holt stopped at the precipice and turned back, teeth bared.

There was no warning. He lunged, faster than anything his size had a right to, straight for Castellano.

She fired twice; the first round missed. The second hit him in the shoulder, but he kept coming, the knife low, the club high. She ducked, but Holt caught her with the flat of the club and sent her sprawling.

Isaac closed in and tackled the man from behind. It was like wrestling a tree. The two of them crashed down in the wet grass, rolling, every muscle in Isaac's body on fire as he fought for the knife hand.

Holt hissed something in Hawaiian, low and fast, and Isaac recognized the words: "Kapu loa. This is forbidden."

They rolled again, and now the knife was free, arcing towards Isaac's side. Isaac caught the wrist and twisted it. He felt the bones grind, felt the heat of blood where the blade slipped, then finally, the snap as Holt's hand gave way. For a second, everything stilled. Isaac drove the man's face into the mud, pinned the arm, and brought his knee up, breaking the grip on the knife. He rolled clear and pulled his pistol.

Holt was spent, but he still tried to rise, his arms trembling. Castellano came up behind him and aimed her pistol at the center of Holt's back.

"Don't," said Isaac, though his voice was gone.

Holt spat blood, coughed, then smiled, all teeth. "You have stopped nothing. There will always be more."

Isaac shivered, not from cold, but from something deeper. "Where is Kealoha?"

Holt looked up, locked eyes with Isaac, then fell sideways, landing in the ferns with a thump. "By now the forest has consumed her."

"What the fuck does that mean?" screamed Isaac. "What have you done to her?"

Holt closed his eyes.

Castellano checked for a pulse and found one. She pulled a sat phone off her belt and called the base. She requested a shore patrol unit and search dogs. Isaac nodded, then stumbled back towards the altar, back to the last place anyone had seen Leilani. Back to the reality of what they'd done.

Behind them, in the darkness, the jungle pressed close, watching, waiting. The ancient ways weren't gone, not really. They just wore unfamiliar faces now. They felt like they were being watched by a thousand eyes.

He reached the altar and stopped short. Leilani stood there, covered in mud and blood and who knew what else. She had blood dripping from the side of her head, and her left arm hung limp at her side. She kneeled next to the body of the man they had killed. She looked up at Isaac, tears streaking her face. Isaac wanted to rush to her and hold her, but the look in Leilani's eyes told him that this was neither the time nor the place.

Castellano walked up and touched her shoulder. Leilani looked at the blood on Castellano's shoulder and half-smiled. "We're a sight, eh?"

Castellano laughed. Leilani looked from Castellano to Isaac. "Holt is not in this alone." She pointed at the body on the ground. "This was one of his priests, but there are others. Our job isn't over yet."

And then, when the wind shifted, they heard it. The faint, impossible echo of drums.

Not from memory, but from the hill, and the jungle, and from the bones of the island itself. The drums were all around them. The case was closed, but nothing was finished. Not for them.

Chapter Twenty-Seven

Leilani stared into the battered mug like it might offer her a version of herself she could tolerate. The coffee was bitter, but she kept drinking, letting the heat pin down the dull ache in her jaw. Her cheek was swollen, and purple spread like a bruise-shaped continent across her cheekbone. When she shifted, a spasm caught at her ribs and she tried not to let Isaac see her wince.

But of course he saw. Torres had a knack for reading faces. He sat across the desk, sleeves rolled up, two fingers tapping out a rhythm on the lid of his cup. He waited, patient as a statue, for her to get through the start of her story in her own time.

She let out a breath and looked at the wall behind him, at the bent department commendation plaque that always hung a few degrees off square. "You want to hear it all?"

Isaac's voice was gentle. "Start wherever you want. I'm not going anywhere."

She nodded, knuckled her good hand along her brow, and tried to reconstruct the thread from the night before. It didn't come in order, but in sense-memory fragments. The mineral stink of old blood, the white shimmer of salt under moonlight, and the way her arms had locked around a throat and wouldn't let go even when her brain told her she was dying. She skipped the worst parts, or at least she tried to.

"We got to the altar, and the first thing I saw was

the arrangement. Someone had made the cut flowers and the ti bundle in the exact pattern as at Kaena. Even the blue paint was the same, but the air was so wet it was dripping off the rock."

She flexed her fingers as she spoke, the memory of the place making her want to stretch every joint. "Espinoza spotted the victim first, a sailor, his work uniform cut to shreds. He was alive, but out cold. Drugged. The flower pattern was a mat, like a nest for the offering."

Isaac scribbled something in his pad, but she couldn't read his handwriting. "What about the killer?"

"I was broadsided by someone huge," she said. "I thought it was Holt. I fought him off, but he rebounded and charged us. He was wearing a ceremonial cape and helmet and carrying a club and a knife. I fired twice, and Powell fired three times. The guy dropped."

She made a loose fist, her fingers mottled with half-healed scrapes. "The victim was awake and frantic, so we untied him. He was hurt badly, so Powell picked him up and headed for the Explorer to get him clear of the scene and to get a signal. Comms were dead. That left Espinoza and me, and that's when we realized the forest was alive with movement, all around us."

Isaac's brow furrowed. "You think they had someone watching from the start?"

She nodded, then regretted the movement. "It was a trap. I should've seen it." Her hand trembled as she pressed it against the side of her head, just above the hematoma. "I told Espinoza to head back to the Explorer and see if he could call for backup. He raced off, and a few minutes later I heard several gunshots. Then another guy, dressed in feathers stepped into the torchlight, and he said something in Hawaiian, but it was twisted, like old church Latin but meaner."

Isaac looked up. "What did he say?"

She tried to recall the cadence. "Something like, the shame is not yours, but it's you who will suffer for it. Then he lunged. He was fast. I didn't think I'd get my pistol out in time, so I dove low. Took out his knee."

She set the mug down and, with her left hand, pantomimed a sweep and grab, then locked her forearm as if it were pinning someone's leg. "Hapkido and lua mix. Grandpa taught me the combination. But he just shrugged it off. He swung a club at me, and I blocked it with my arm." She showed him the purple, slightly misshapen forearm. "That's where I lost my grip on the gun. Suddenly there were more people on me, punching and kicking. I got in some good shots, but it was hopeless."

Isaac didn't interrupt, only reached for the coffee carafe and topped her mug with a fresh shot of black.

"So now it's just hands, and he goes for my throat. I threw an elbow at the bridge of his nose, then tried for the eyes, but he caught my hand and twisted it until something popped. I couldn't use it after that. He smiled again, as if it was a game. That's when I realized he must want me alive."

She looked at her hand, and at the scarred knuckles on her right hand. "He didn't kill me. Only choked me out. I remember his hands; they were cold and smelled like ashes."

Isaac set his own mug aside and finally spoke, voice steady. “What happened next?”

She shrugged, tried to make it seem casual, but the motion hurt. “I woke up in the dirt must have been fifty or sixty yards from the altar. It was dark, and my arms were behind me, wrists wrapped in something. At first, I thought it was rope, but it was vines, woven so tight it cut my circulation. I was lying against a log with my head spinning.”

She ran her tongue along the inside of her cheek, testing the new tender line where tooth had met flesh. “I could hear the drums. Not from the hill, but down in the valley. It was more like a pulse than a rhythm. He wasn’t alone, Isaac. There were others. Not many, but enough.”

He leaned forward. “How many attacked you, and could you see their faces?”

She thought hard, trying to reconstruct the event. “There must have been half a dozen of them. One or two women. One had a bandana over her dark hair. She was carrying a bundle, more flowers, but I couldn’t see what else. The other was taller. They all had painted faces. Solid blue. The others I couldn’t identify.”

She reached for her mug with her good hand but winced as the motion twisted her torso. “They circled me but didn’t talk. They kicked and punch once I was on the ground.”

Isaac’s eyes were dark. “How’d you get loose?”

She shrugged, which was her way of saying she didn’t want to think about how close it came to not happening. "There was a rock, sharp as a shark's tooth, set in the ground near my hip. I used it to rub the vines against until they snapped. It took forever. My wrists were numb."

She looked at the wall, not at him. "When I stood up, I almost passed out. I had blood in my mouth, and I didn't know if it was mine. It was dark as a cave, and I wasn't sure which way was up until I heard the commotion, so I headed that way. That's when I heard you and Castellano fighting someone. The rest you know."

He grinned, but only for a second. "What do you think he wanted? Why not just kill you?"

Leilani noticed the heat rise under her scalp. "He wanted to prove a point. Or just to show he could. He might have been saving me for later. We interrupted his ceremony twice. He wasn't going to let that stand."

She let the words settle in the space between them. Isaac nodded, looking out the window as if to check for specters in the parking lot.

"How are Espinoza and the victim?" she asked.

"Espinoza has cracked ribs and a concussion. The victim lost a lot of blood, but the Navy doctors think he'll be okay," said Isaac.

"Have we identified the big guy we thought was Holt?" she asked.

"Guy's name was David Tatana. A retired Navy SEAL. He had some missions with Holt, but Castellano is having trouble getting his unredacted file. Been out about two years. He's divorced with two grown kids. They live on the mainland."

She let herself breathe again; the whole retelling leaving her emptier than when she started. She stared at her hands. "We're not done. Not even close."

Isaac nodded. "Holt is at Queen's Hospital, under guard. Castellano is already prepping for a full debrief. And the chief wants you to sit this one out, for a week. Heal up."

Leilani gave a huff. "Sure. Let me run that by the ancestors."

Isaac snorted, and stood, collecting both mugs. "Let me get you something stronger than coffee."

As he left the office, Leilani studied the pale banding around her wrists, the marks the vine had left, and thought about how some bindings were permanent, long after they were removed.

Chapter Twenty-Eight

The interview room in HPD's basement had all the ambiance of a meat locker. The walls were the same government-issue green, old enough that you could find the original paint peeking through where the newer coats had peeled. The overhead fluorescents flickered on and off at irregular intervals, creating a visual stutter that turned even simple movements into something threatening.

Leilani sat at the metal table with her hands folded, knuckles still scabbed, jawline a mapped archive of purple and blue. Castellano was next to her, her windbreaker thrown over the back of the chair. A large black and blue mark above her ear and the corner of a white bandage sticking out from under the collar of her shirt. The two women didn't talk, only breathed, collecting the ambient hostility in the room and turning it over in their heads.

Holt was already there, hands cuffed in front, his orange jumpsuit an obscene note of brightness in the drab room. His face was swollen, and the cut over his eye was stitched with half-dissolved sutures. But he sat up straight, chest out, chin high. The effect would have been impressive if you hadn't known what he'd done.

Leilani watched him through the glass of the carafe in front of her. The warped reflection split his face, giving him two sets of eyes, one placid, and one quivering with madness.

The door opened behind her, and Isaac came in with a stack of folders and a fresh legal pad. He didn't sit, but positioned himself at the wall, out of Holt's direct line of sight. He gave Leilani a micro-nod, and she took the cue.

She started with the basics, like it were any other day. "Please state your name for the record."

Holt looked straight at her. "James Edward Holt."

She clicked the pen, not writing, but letting the sound fill the next few seconds. "You understand why you're here?"

Holt shrugged, the cuffs rattling. "You think I killed those men and women. And you think I did it for a reason."

Castellano, who'd been massaging the bridge of her nose, finally spoke, voice hoarse from too many cigarettes and too little sleep. "Stop playing. We know it was you. We have you at the scene. DNA, footprints, the whole deal."

Holt's mouth twisted. "Evidence only proves I cared enough to do what you people won't."

Leilani watched him for tells. The way he held his hands, never relaxed, but always cocked like he was waiting to break free. The way he leaned forward enough to put his face in the hard pool of shadow cast by the fluorescent above. He was putting on a show, and he wanted her to see it.

She tried a different tack. "Why them, Holt? Why those people?"

For the first time, Holt looked slightly pleased, like a kid who'd found the grown-ups finally understood the rules of his game. "They were corrupt. Liars.

Pretenders. They wore the uniform, but not the honor. They desecrated everything about warrior culture."

Castellano scoffed. "You mean the Navy's cultural education program? That's what set you off?"

Holt gave a slight shake of his head, as if disappointed. "It's not the program. It's what they did to it. Turned it into a sideshow for the tourists. Forgot what it was really for."

Leilani tried to keep her tone neutral. "You think they needed to die for that?"

He didn't answer immediately. Instead, he met her gaze, and for a second she saw it, the flicker of shame, or regret, buried under the sediment of fanaticism. "Yes. If you don't restore the ancestral path, you lose everything. You become nothing."

Standing with his back to the wall, Isaac's face was carved in shadow. Leilani imagined the room full of onlookers, possibly even the chief, but none of it mattered. Here, in the glare and hum, only three people existed.

She pressed on. "Were you alone? The crime scenes suggest more than one person."

Holt smiled, slow and tight. "You think I'd trust anyone else with this?"

Castellano leaned in, her presence expanding, and her voice pitched low. "Cut the shit. Kealoha was attacked by multiple people, and we have a dead guy named Tatana who was dressed like you at the altar. We're tearing that altar area apart looking for prints or DNA. You want to take the fall for the rest of your merry little death cult? Be my guest, but they're going down with or without you."

He sat back, his expression flickering for a microsecond before it resettled into calm. "There are always others. But they don't know what I know. I taught them only what they needed. They can't finish what I started."

Leilani noted the pressure behind her eyes mount, but she kept her voice even. "What did you start?"

Holt gazed at her. "A reckoning. A cleansing of the blood. The old code says there is a debt to be paid for every shame, every lie, every theft from the ancestors. If I hadn't done it, someone else would have. You know that."

He sounded almost pleading, and she recognized the desperation. The same need for legacy, for the story, that had animated every megalomaniac she'd ever locked up.

She kept her voice gentle, the way she would with a skittish child. "You're saying you're the first."

He gave her that ugly smile again, showing all his teeth. "You should be grateful, Detective. I did your work for you. Now the rest is on you."

Castellano's jaw ticked. "Who's next, Holt? Who picks up your sick little flag?"

Holt didn't break eye contact with Leilani. "You know how it is. Once you light the torch, others will carry it. Could be someone in this building." He turned his head and looked at the two-way mirror. "One of your own."

Leilani's fingers tightened on the pen. She didn't want to give him the satisfaction of a reaction, but the words dug under her skin.

She leaned forward, elbows on the table, face only a foot from his. "Why me? Why did you let me live?"

This time the smile was softer, less rehearsed. "You carry the burden. You know what it's like to walk alone in the dark. I wanted you to understand."

Silence filled the room for a long, aching moment.

Castellano stood, pushing her chair back with a scrape that made everyone flinch. She pointed at the folder in front of her. "You're never seeing daylight again. I'll see to that personally."

Holt ignored her, eyes fixed on Leilani. "You'll never stop the next one, Detective. They're already out there."

The words hung there, cold and absolute.

Leilani stood, her body stiff with pain and adrenaline. She collected her notes, closed the file, and with a last glance at Holt, left the room. Castellano followed a few beats behind. In the hallway, the air appeared colder, the light less forgiving. Isaac was the last to leave the interrogation room, his face a question mark.

"He's not alone. He never was," she said.

Isaac put a hand on her shoulder, squeezing hard enough to remind her she was still here, still breathing. Castellano peeled off, muttering something about filing the report, but Leilani could see her hands shaking as she walked away.

Leilani fixed her gaze on the smudged glass wall, watching her own battered reflection, and tried to imagine how many more torches might already be burning.

Chapter Twenty-Nine

The conference room on the fourth floor had the staleness of an old library. At one end, crime scene photos, maps and autopsy reports wallpapered the board, weighted down with magnets shaped like sushi and rainbow animals. The table was covered with evidence bags, half-empty coffee cups, and three laptops bleeding power from a tangle of extension cords.

Leilani sat nearest the evidence, her hands resting on the worn wood, while Isaac and Castellano filled the space with the tension of two magnets forced together. Espinoza, arm splinted and eyes puffy, hovered by the window, nursing a soda and not quite sitting. The air smelled of menthol and dry-erase markers.

Castellano led, even though her hair was matted and there was a tear at the shoulder seam of her shirt. "We got the bastard," she said, with all the satisfaction of someone lighting their last cigarette after a war. "But he didn't do it alone." She nodded at Leilani. "You were right. The pattern was too clean. The attack, too coordinated."

Isaac pointed to a photograph on the board. "Footprints, here and here. Two different sizes, at least one woman. The drone photos from the trail show three figures splitting off before the altercation." He slid a folder across the table. "Plus, this. Surveillance from the base gate. You can see a woman in blue scrubs enter the site three times, always at shift change. Never leaves through the front."

Castellano tapped the file. "She's not Navy. No badge, no credentials. Might be a local civilian. Or she's a ghost."

Leilani turned the photo so she could see it upright. The woman's face was a blur, but her posture, a certain way of carrying her shoulders, head dipped but eyes straight ahead, felt instantly familiar. "I saw her," she said. "At the demonstration months ago. She asked questions afterward about the old death rites, but it was like she already knew the answers."

Espinoza nodded. "There's more. The night of the last kill, the motion sensors picked up two figures leaving by the north road, but only one set of tire tracks. If it was Holt, he had backup on foot."

A pause. The room's only sound was the hum of the cooling fan in the old wall unit.

Leilani glanced at Castellano, who looked as if she'd been forced to swallow something sour. "It's not one fanatic," Leilani said, voice low but steady. "It's a network. Not a formal cult, but a team. They're organized and they believe what Holt believes, but they're smart enough to stay invisible."

Isaac tapped the keyboard, scrolling through the background checks on all the participants in the cultural training program. "There are two other outliers, one guy who left after the first session, and another who was dismissed for disruptive conduct. Both went off the radar six months ago. Neither has a fixed address."

Castellano licked her lips. She looked at Espinoza. "Get with the base MPs and canvass every participant and their families. Hard, fast, and no phone warnings. You got it?"

Espinoza nodded, the relief at having something concrete to do softening his expression for the first time all day.

Leilani stood and stepped to the wall, her eyes skimming the pattern of crimes. Each grave, each flower arrangement and each mark of pigment. It wasn't only a ritual; it was communication. Signals left for those who understood the language.

"There's a motif in the way the bodies were staged. A triangle, always pointing west, always aligned with sunset." She ran her finger across the photos. "Holt was obsessed with the old stories, but he missed something. This symbol isn't his; it's older. There's someone else out there, someone who knew exactly how to use him."

Isaac looked at her, eyebrows raised. "You think he was a pawn?"

She shook her head. "More like a tool. A true believer, but not the true leader. The person we need is the one who wrote the script."

Castellano's jaw ticked, but she nodded. "We find her. Or him. Or whoever's smart enough to stay out of the photos and keep their hands clean."

The door at the far end of the room clicked, and the chief entered. Mori's suit was sharper than anyone else's by an order of magnitude, and her eyes, even more so. She took in the scene, then spoke without preamble.

"Update."

Castellano spoke first, succinctly. "Holt's locked up. He's confessed, but we have credible evidence of at least one accomplice, probably more. We're cross-referencing all Navy and civilian contacts, and we're flagging anyone who fits the ideological profile."

Mori didn't blink. "Full-court press. I want search warrants, background checks, and all social feeds scraped and analyzed. And Leilani. Take the point on the community angle. Use whatever resources you need, but I want a report on my desk by morning."

Leilani nodded, the charge igniting something that had lain dormant under the pain. "Yes, Chief."

Mori turned to leave but paused. "If you get tired, Kealoha, let Torres drive. Otherwise, try not to break the furniture this time."

A ripple of laughter filled the space. Enough to ease the edge.

The chief was gone, but her shadow lingered.

They worked for another hour, reviewing the notes, plotting the network, and arguing about the motive. At some point, Espinoza left for the hospital, and Isaac got a phone call that made him curse under his breath. Castellano typed up the draft report, her fingers blurring on the keyboard.

When Leilani was alone with the mess of the case, she took the last of the evidence bags and spread the contents on the table. There, among the salt and flowers, was a small wooden tag, painted with a spiral symbol. It wasn't part of the killings they'd tracked, and it didn't match Holt's signature. It was new.

She ran her thumb over the surface, experiencing the grit of the pigment, the lines burned into the wood. The hair on her arms stood up, and for a moment, she felt watched, as if the person who'd made it was standing behind the glass, waiting to see if she understood.

She reached for her phone, ready to dial, but stopped. Instead, she let her eyes close and tried to see the world as Holt did. Not as a series of crimes, but as a ceremony, a cycle, an island forever trying to balance itself. When she opened her eyes, she wasn't sure if the fear belonged to her, or to the island itself.

In the corridor, the lights flickered again, and somewhere below, she could almost hear the echo of drums. It would be a long night. But it wasn't over yet.

Chapter Thirty

The sun had left the western ridge when Leilani hiked up the last fifty meters of the trail, each step a hard reminder of the fight that still throbbed through her ribs and cheek. The night air was thick with the smell of wet grass; the torches were out now, and only the crime scene lanterns cut through the shadowed jungle.

Castellano was already at the heiau, standing on the platform's edge, her body squared to the altar and her jaw set. She wore gloves, boots and a professional chill, but Leilani caught the dark bruise blooming above her shirt collar, a leftover from the brawl with Holt. The rest of the site had been roped off and grid-flagged by the forensic team, but only Leilani and Castellano were allowed inside the ring.

Leilani passed under the crime scene tape and took inventory. The lines of salt had been laid clean and true along the stone perimeter. The scattered petals of red ginger and frangipani were set in concentric circles around the altar, and the heap of ti leaves neatly folded and bound in a way she hadn't seen since her last funeral. In the center, what remained of the altar bore a flat bowl, still half-full of saltwater, and a lei-o-mano club with shark teeth dark from use.

She moved slowly, aware of the ache in her left arm, and pulled her gloves from her pocket. Castellano watched impassively as Leilani circled the scene, taking her own notes on a battered Rite-in-the-Rain pad.

"You see what I see?" Castellano asked, her voice clipped, the accent showing more east coast than island now.

Leilani didn't look up. "I see a confession."

Castellano grunted. "I see a goddamn mess. But yes, it's methodical." She pointed to the ti leaves, then to the salt. "He followed a pattern, right up to the end."

Leilani crouched beside the lei-o-mano. "He wasn't improvising anymore. This was the real ritual."

Castellano stepped closer, peering at the blue paint stains on the altar's edge. "Explain it to me," she said. "Like I'm stupid. Humor me."

Leilani glanced up, and for the first time, Castellano's eyes weren't narrowed in skepticism, but open and waiting. "He set the salt as a barrier. It's an old method to keep the spirits in or out, depending on the intent. The ti is for cleansing. The flowers are an offering for whatever comes next." She pointed to the bowl. "That's for the final blessing or, in this case, a curse."

Castellano looked at her, at the altar, and at the evidence bag she'd been rolling in her palm. "Your background. It's why you tracked him, isn't it?"

Leilani shrugged, the motion more painful than she'd expected. "I knew what he wanted. I didn't expect him to go all the way."

Castellano scanned the site, letting the silence stretch before she spoke. "The way you handled yourself with Holt—" she broke off, as if the words cost her. "It was smart. You got him to reveal more in ten minutes than we did in three hours."

Leilani allowed herself a half-smile. "Different methods. Same goal."

They moved through the scene in a deliberate orbit, each collecting evidence and sealing it with the care of bomb techs. Castellano started with the salt lines, photographing and collecting small vials of the substance at intervals. She held the vial to the lantern, and to her nose, the gesture at once clinical and oddly reverent.

"Not Morton's," Castellano muttered. "Smells like sea salt."

"Hanapepe," Leilani said. "It's a small-batch. There are only three vendors on Oahu. I can get you the names."

Castellano made a note. "You always this detailed?"

Leilani touched her bruised jaw, the memory of Holt's grip fresh enough to taste in her mouth. "It comes with the job. And the lineage."

Castellano stooped to examine the ti leaves. She picked up a bundle and held it up to the light, studying the knots. "Why the cord?"

Leilani reached for the evidence bag, then stopped herself. "Binding. For the spirit, or for the ritual. He's keeping the past from getting loose."

Castellano studied the leaves, then looked at Leilani. "You think it worked?"

"No one ever asks if the ritual's supposed to work,"

Leilani replied. "They do it because someone before them did." She bagged the club, careful not to jostle the teeth.

Castellano drew closer, voice low. "Can I ask you something?"

Leilani nodded, sealing the evidence bag.

"What do you think it did to him?" Castellano said. "Holt. Did it make him crazier, or did it keep him sane?"

Leilani considered the question as she watched the moths flit in the lantern light. "It gave him structure. A reason. But it didn't make him less dangerous."

Castellano was quiet, her posture softening for the first time. "I grew up thinking rituals were..." She trailed off. "I never thought they'd matter in a case."

Leilani smiled, the motion stretching her bruised cheek. "They always matter. Especially when you ignore them."

They finished cataloguing the scene. Castellano sealed the ti leaves and placed them in the kit. She lingered at the altar. Leilani stood back, watching her work.

"You know what I respect?" Castellano said, not looking up. "You didn't sandbag me. Not once. You could have, but you didn't."

Leilani wiped her forehead with the back of her glove, sweat, and blood mixing at her hairline. "Didn't have to. You'd have doubled down."

Castellano grinned, all teeth. "You're not wrong."

The lantern light shifted, shadows swinging wide as the breeze changed. Around the altar, the air seemed cleaner, the mugginess lifting, as if the place had let go of something heavy.

Leilani peeled off her gloves and dropped them in the biohazard bin. "We done?"

"Yeah," Castellano said. "Unless you want to lead the next briefing."

Leilani hesitated. "I'll write it up. But you get to answer the Chief's questions."

Castellano scooped up the evidence kits, shouldered them, and glanced over her shoulder. "You ever want to go for a drink, off duty, let me know."

Leilani smirked, the tension broken, at least for the moment. "Only if you buy."

They walked out together, not quite side by side, but close enough that the distance no longer mattered. Behind them, the heiau glowed in the lantern light, stripped of its terror, nothing left but stones and silence.

At the parking lot, the rest of the team was waiting, but no one interrupted as Leilani handed Castellano the final evidence bag. Castellano took it, nodded, and for the first time, her respect was real, not something she put on for show.

They climbed into separate vehicles, but as the engines started, Leilani caught Castellano's reflection in the rearview mirror, a small, quick smile, gone as soon as it appeared. It was enough. The work was unsightly, but it belonged to them, and for the first time, it seemed like they stood together on the same side of the tape.

Back at the station, the night was young, and there was a mountain of paperwork to climb, but Leilani didn't mind. Her cheek ached, her arm throbbed, but something inside her had changed and she wasn't walking the perimeter alone.

Chapter Thirty-One

The HPD's second interrogation room was little more than a bunker painted institutional green. A space that could wear down a suspect's will to resist or, in Leilani's experience, just drive everyone inside slowly mad. The overhead light buzzed and flickered; the plastic chairs wobbled with every shift in weight, and a narrow metal table bore the scuffs and cigarette burns of three decades of confessions.

Holt was already seated when Leilani entered, flanked by two station officers who looked like they'd drawn the short straw. The man seemed smaller in the orange jumpsuit than he had in the first interview; his shorn scalp turning his head into a pale, angular wedge. His hands, cuffed to the table, were bruised and scraped, remnants from the night on the mountain. His eyes, though, were the same, sharp, unyielding, and fixed on the spot just to the left of Leilani's shoulder.

She took her seat across from him, settled with care, letting her battered ribcage guide her into the right position. The click of her pen was the only sound for a moment. She felt Isaac take up his spot at the wall behind her, a deliberate move. Not at her side, not looming over the suspect, but a subtle presence, anchoring the room's gravity.

Castellano was invisible, but Leilani knew she'd be watching from the other side of the glass. The psych team had insisted she stay out of this one as her presence agitated Holt too much, but Leilani could feel Castellano's attention as surely as if she'd been breathing down her neck.

"Mr. Holt," Leilani started softly. "Thank you for agreeing to speak with us again."

Holt's lips curled. "Like I had a choice."

She ignored the dig. "You remember Detective Torres. I'll be recording, but this is for clarity, not pressure. If you want to stop, say so."

He shrugged, the cuffs rattling. "We're past the part where you pretend it's my choice."

Leilani tapped her notebook, flipping to a blank sheet. "Last time we spoke, you mentioned honor, restoration, and that you were carrying out a reckoning. Can you tell me why?"

For a long beat, he said nothing. "You know why. You saw it yourself."

"I want to hear it in your words," she pressed.

He looked at the table. "I grew up split," he began. "Grandmother was Hawaiian, pure blood. She taught me what she could, but my mother ran the house, and she was ashamed of the past. Dad was military. Discipline and order, nothing more." He turned, his gaze suddenly fixed on her face. "No matter what I did, I was always a bastard. Not enough haole, not enough Hawaiian. Something to push around."

Leilani nodded, letting the silence drag, waiting to see what else he'd yield.

Holt's tongue worked at the split in his lip. "I enlisted in the Navy. Worked harder than anyone. They said I was a perfect recruit, but every time they saw the name or the skin, it was there. The look. You know it."

She didn't react. He'd try to personalize it, make her the mirror. Fine. She'd give him nothing.

"I got out," he continued. "Did security, did contract work, got bounced between offices until the base picked up the Warrior Spirit integration. They said they wanted to help. Bring the culture back, they said. But it was a joke. The haole officers didn't even bother showing up."

Leilani scribbled a line and nodded for him to continue.

"I met Souza there. The professor." Holt's voice softened, reverent. "He knew the real history. Not the sanitized shit they tell at the Bishop Museum. He knew about the blood rituals, the way the ali'i handled shame. He told me I could find peace by finishing what the ancestors started."

She caught the use of the past tense. "Was Professor Souza the first to tell you about the reckoning?"

Holt flinched, not quite an answer. "He gave me readings, yes. Told me how it worked in the old days. Not all of it was pretty."

"Did he encourage you to act on it?"

Holt shook his head, almost imperceptibly. "He just showed me what was missing. I did the rest. It had to be me."

Isaac, silent until now, shifted against the wall. Leilani glanced up and saw the brief raise of his eyebrows. He was clocking the changes, too.

She flipped to the next page. "You said in your statement that the military took your honor. What did you mean by that?"

Holt's hands twisted on the cuffs. "You serve, you fight, you bleed, and in the end, they tell you to forget everything you were. No past, just the uniform. They take your name and your story. When I tried to bring the old customs, they made me the problem. Labeled me unstable. Sent me for a psych eval. If you're loud about it, you're defective."

"And the people you killed," she prompted. "What did they do?"

He glared at her. "They were traitors to the code. Pretenders. They said they cared about culture, but they didn't. They just wanted the grant money, or the medals, or the look. Not one of them knew what the ti leaf was for. Not one. They played at being Hawaiian." The last word came out bitter as ash.

Leilani let him vent, let the momentum carry him. "And your victims. How did you choose them?"

"Easy. They were the ones who put themselves above the rest, who talked the talk and walked none of it." He spat, the word nearly a curse. "Hypocrites."

She flipped through her notes. "The third murder. The victim at Barber's Point. Why did you bury him there? It doesn't match the pattern of the others."

A flicker of confusion passed across Holt's face. "It was supposed to be on the base. But it was locked down, so I did what I could. It still worked. The ritual doesn't care about geography."

She made a mark in her notebook, then paused. "Your background says you never completed a single Hawaiian language class, but the rituals you followed used precise, ancient terms. Who taught you that?"

He glanced at the glass. "I read and listened. My grandmother spoke in her sleep sometimes."

"That's not enough," Leilani pressed, voice still gentle. "Not for the precision of what you did."

Holt grew silent, jaw working. He stared at his hands. "It doesn't matter who gave me the words," he said at last. "They were true. The blood, the salt and the flowers. It's all true."

A pause. The AC unit rattled, the only sound in the dead air.

Leilani closed her notes. "You said last night that you never belonged in either world. Which one failed you first?"

For the first time, Holt's composure slipped. The mask faltered, just a flicker, but enough. "Both," he whispered. "Always both."

They let that land; the heaviness growing between them. Isaac scribbled something in his notebook, then straightened, signaling it was time.

She stood, ready to leave it there. But Holt looked up, and in the harsh overhead light, his face was less wolf and more scared, like a cornered dog. "You understand," he said. "You get it, don't you? That's why you caught me."

Leilani said nothing. She just nodded once and let herself out, her footsteps echoing down the cold hallway.

Outside, Castellano was waiting. She'd propped herself against the wall, arms crossed, eyes red but steady. "Will he flip on Souza?"

"He thinks he's the last one with the code. He'll go to his grave with it, unless Souza outs himself," she said.

Castellano's jaw ticked. "You believe him about the old traditions?"

Leilani shrugged. "I believe he needed it. That's enough."

She walked away, Isaac beside her, the station's air less sour now, the fluorescent lights less brutal. There was still a knot in her chest, unsolved pieces, and open loops, but for tonight, at least, they'd gotten something done.

Not justice, not yet. But the truth, at least. Or the version of it that Holt will share. In this line of work, that counted for more than most would ever know.

Chapter Thirty-Two

Most of the detectives working the night shift barely registered the knock at the glass doors, but Leilani heard it, even over the drone of the vending machine and the hiss of coffee brewing in the break alcove. The sound was insistent, and when she opened the door, she found her mother, Naalei, standing in the building's vestibule with a woven basket cradled in both arms. The basket was covered with a tea towel, and the smells coming from it were wild and green, utterly at odds with the reek of floor cleaner and microwaved kalua pig that dominated the station.

Leilani led Naalei through the bullpen, past a cluster of uniforms reviewing body cam footage, and into the main conference room, where the air held onto the day's heat like a stubborn memory. Espinoza was there, bruised and pale but still upright. Isaac leaned over the far end of the table, riffling through some printouts. Tano hovered near the window, scrolling on his phone.

Naalei set the basket down and pulled the towel away, revealing ti leaves, bright and glossy, bundles of sea salt wrapped in brown waxed paper, and a small bowl holding a chunk of ʻawa root. At the bottom, Leilani saw a pair of votive candles and a strand of knotted kukui nuts.

Chief Mori appeared in the doorway, arms folded, her suit crisp and unwrinkled despite the hour. She gave Leilani a sharp nod, then spoke to the room. "I authorized this for the record. No social media, no press. Let's be quick and quiet about it."

She retreated, leaving the door open.

Naalei set to work with the same efficiency she'd brought to every family holiday, no wasted movement, and everything in its order. She swept the table clean, placed ti leaves at each corner, and sprinkled a fine dusting of salt at the threshold and the center of the room. The ʻawa root she sliced thin, arranging the pale discs in a circle around the bowl, and then filled it with water from a glass pitcher she'd brought herself. When she finished, she looked up, scanning each face in the room until they met her eyes. Even Castellano, lurking in the corridor, seemed drawn in by the gravity of the scene.

"E hoʻolohe," Naalei said, her voice low but resonant. She raised her hands, palms out, and began a chant, a long, rolling oli, the syllables round and tidal, moving in waves that reverberated off the tile and drop ceiling. The sound was unlike anything Leilani's coworkers had ever heard, and even Tano set his phone aside. No one said a word.

When the chant ended, Naalei spoke in English, clear and deliberate. "We do this to honor the ones who died, and to cleanse this space of the darkness that came with the last weeks. If you do not believe, that's fine. Listen and remember what was lost."

She moved clockwise, flicking drops of saltwater from her fingers at each wall. The fragrance of ti was strong, and it crowded out the sterility of the space, the old coffee, and even the tang of the sweat. As she placed the bundles of ti at the four corners, she recited a second chant, softer, almost a whisper, and when she was done, she motioned for Leilani to come forward.

Leilani stepped in, bowing her head. Naalei pressed a cold ti leaf against her bruised cheek, and spoke in Hawaiian, the words a private balm. She did the same to Espinoza, who blushed deeply, and to Isaac, who accepted the touch with the dignity of someone unsure of the rules.

When Naalei approached Castellano, the agent straightened but hesitated at the threshold. Leilani caught her mother's eye, and with a gentle gesture, Naalei invited her in. Castellano stepped over the line of salt, awkward but willing, and bowed her head for the touch of the ti. After a moment, Naalei murmured a phrase, short, guttural, and final.

The silence afterward was profound. Even the vending machine in the next room seemed to hold its breath.

Naalei gathered the last of her implements and nodded to the room. "We are done."

The spell broke. Tano exhaled, rubbing his eyes. Espinoza smiled, and Isaac let out a low whistle. Leilani noticed something inside her unclench. She looked to Castellano, expecting a joke or a hard-won dismissal, but the agent nodded, a real nod, the kind you couldn't fake.

When most of the others had filed out, Castellano lingered by the table. She traced the ti leaf pattern with her finger, and looked up at Naalei. "What was that second chant? You said something about remembering."

Naalei smiled, lines fanning from the corners of her eyes. “It’s for forgiveness. For those who did not find peace in life. Sometimes you need to tell them it’s okay to move on.”

Castellano blinked. The question caught in her throat. “Did it work?”

Naalei shrugged. “Time will tell. But it’s better to try than to let the darkness stay.”

Leilani watched them, her mother and the mainlander, both survivors, both changed by what had happened in the last few weeks. She saw in Castellano’s face the same hunger she saw in herself. Not just for answers, but for the grace that came from knowing when to let go.

The night outside was still. In the lobby, the guard was asleep, and the rest of the building glowed with the false sun of overworked lighting. But in the conference room, for once, it felt like the island was watching over them, instead of waiting to pounce.

Leilani gathered the ti leaves, careful not to spill the salt. “I’ll clean up,” she told her mother.

Naalei smiled, then paused at the door. “You did good, Lei. All of you.”

As she left, Leilani felt the weight lift. There was more work ahead; there always was, but for tonight, the old gods could rest, and so could she.

Chapter Thirty-Three

By the next afternoon, the station had mostly shed the aftershocks of the case. The conference room smelled faintly of bleach and flowers; the recycling bins overflowed with battered paper cups, and the detectives who'd pulled double shifts now loitered in the lot with the stares of men who'd seen enough.

Leilani was at her desk, ice pack pressed to her jaw, when Isaac knocked on the door. He held a thin blue folder, stamped with the Navy insignia, and a to-go cup of actual coffee, the expensive kind.

"Truce offering?" he asked, holding up the drink.

She grinned, painful but worth it, and motioned him inside. "You always know how to find my weak spots."

He sat and dropped the folder on the desk. "New development. The Navy's shutting down the Warrior Spirit program. Full review. Everyone involved is restricted to base pending an investigation." He sipped his coffee, then looked her in the eye. "You did that. Not Castellano and not the base commander. You."

Leilani peeled the ice from her face and scanned the document. Most of it was CYA language, but the intent was clear. "So, we win?"

Isaac shrugged, but there was pride in his smile. "For now."

She reached for the coffee, then caught him watching her, something on his mind. "Spit it out," she said.

Isaac hesitated. “How’s your arm?”

She flexed it, the bruise, a blue-black ring at the elbow. “Not broken. Bruised.”

He nodded, tracing a finger along the rim of his cup. “You know, I was sure you were going to kill him. Holt, I mean.”

“Part of me wanted to,” she admitted. “But I didn’t want him to think that’s all there was. Some debts you pay by walking away.”

Isaac’s smile was soft. “Ever wonder if that’s enough?”

“It’s not my job to decide,” she said. “I keep the scales from tipping all the way.”

He leaned back, more relaxed now, with his hand close enough to hers that their fingers brushed as she set the coffee down.

Chief Mori swept in, a force of nature in a tailored pantsuit, her hair pulled so tight it looked lacquered. “Good, you’re both here,” she said, bypassing greetings. “I received a call from Castellano’s boss. They want a training protocol based on how you and Castellano ran the case.”

Leilani glanced at Isaac, eyebrows raised. “Together?”

Mori’s lips quirked. “Apparently, it’s called hybrid investigative methodology now. And you’re the template.”

Isaac grinned. “You’re going to be a teaching

module."

Leilani made a face. "You want me to sit in a classroom with Castellano?"

Mori deadpanned, "Try not to kill each other." She paused. "You both did good. Even when you hated each other, you kept the mission first. Some people in this department could stand to learn from that."

She turned to go but stopped in the doorway. "Heal up, Kealoha. You're no use to me dead."

The door clicked shut. Isaac exhaled, and touched her hand for a second, but warm and real. "You ever take a vacation?" he said.

Leilani rolled her eyes, but the smile stayed on her lips. "I'm not sure I'd survive the boredom."

"You could give it a shot," he said.

He stood, hesitated, leaving her with the folder and the last of the good coffee.

Alone, Leilani perused the stack of case files and noticed the fatigue finally land. But it wasn't heavy this time. More like the moment after a storm, when the air was clear and you could see all the way to the next horizon.

She let the ice melt on her desk, turned her chair to the window, and watched the day roll on. The drums, for now, are quiet.

Chapter Thirty-Four

The air in the kitchen was thick with the scent of browning onions and the sharp bite of chili pepper water. Leilani stirred the pot with her good arm, cradling her ribs with the other, and watched as Kai assembled his tri-fold presentation board at the table. His tongue poked from the corner of his mouth in concentration, each letter he printed as carefully as if he were etching it in stone.

He looked up, beaming. "Mom, look! Grandma said if you use ti leaves and salt you can keep bad spirits away, but you have to be respectful. You can't just do it for show."

Leilani smiled, the motion tugging at the healing bruise on her cheek. "She's right. That's how it always was. It's not a magic trick. It's about doing it for the right reason."

Kai nodded. "I wrote that in the report." He pointed to the middle panel, where in block letters he'd added: HONOR IS MORE THAN FIGHTING. "That's what Grandma said."

He grabbed a marker, switching colors. "But the old stories say sometimes the warriors had to be tough. Did the guy you arrested do it wrong? Was he a bad warrior?"

Leilani thought about how best to answer. "He wanted to be strong, but he forgot what it was for. It's not about hurting people. It's about protecting."

Kai nodded again, satisfied. "Like you."

She snorted, then winced as her side twinged. "Not every day."

He looked at her, head cocked. "Are you going to be on the news again?"

Leilani grinned, stirring the pot. "I hope not."

They finished the project together, taping printouts of warriors, artifacts and old petroglyphs onto the board. At the top, Kai pasted a photo of himself from the last school luau, standing next to Naalei. They wore homemade feather capes. The caption read: ME AND MY GRANDMA: KEEPERS OF THE STORY.

When the last piece was glued down, Kai cleared his throat, stood tall, and read the entire project aloud, voice strong but high with nerves. He hit every Hawaiian word, even the tricky ones. At the end, he bowed, just like Naalei taught him.

Leilani clapped, even though it made her hands sting. "You're ready," she said. "Even the ancestors would be proud."

They ate dinner at the small table, Kai narrating every bite as if it were part of the presentation. "Did you know some warriors used blue paint? Grandma says it means kapu, forbidden. Like a warning sign."

Leilani laughed. "She knows her history."

Kai's eyes widened. "Do you think the old gods get mad if people mess it up?"

Leilani considered. "It's possible, but I think they want people to remember. That's the most important thing."

He finished his food, then ran off to finish his homework. Leilani tidied the dishes, the ache in her body gradually replaced by a deeper, softer tiredness.

Her phone rang, an unfamiliar number but a familiar prefix. She answered, expecting a work call.

"Detective Kealoha," she said.

A beat, then Castellano's voice, low and dry. "Not interrupting dinner, am I?"

Leilani smirked. "Depends on who's asking."

"Are you still up for a field consult? I've got a new one, someone painted petroglyphs on a warehouse, real old-school. Navy says it's nothing, but the pattern matches one of your cold cases."

Leilani leaned against the counter, watching the reflection of her bruised cheek in the dark window. "You need help or just someone to argue with?"

"Help, this time," Castellano admitted. "They want a hybrid team again. And, uh, I could use a translator for the old rituals."

Leilani almost laughed. "I'll see you in the morning."

She hung up, set the phone aside, and finished putting away the leftovers.

Later, as she tucked Kai into bed, he asked, "Will you be home tomorrow?"

"Not right away. I have to help a friend. But I'll be back for dinner."

Kai yawned. "Will you tell me a story when you get

home?"

She brushed his hair back. "Every time."

He was asleep before she turned off the light.

Downstairs, Leilani gathered up the finished project, set it by the door, and took a last look at the neat lines and the collage of photos. She felt the old fear stirring at the edges of the next case, the next danger and the next night alone, but tonight it was quieter, a ghost softened by the smell of food and the echo of Kai's voice.

Tomorrow, she will hunt the past again. But tonight, Leilani allowed herself the comfort of knowing she'd brought her son, and herself, safely through another day. The island outside was silent, and this time, the quiet felt like peace.

Chapter Thirty-Five

Leilani passed through the access checkpoint with the heavy, hollow drag that came from too little sleep and the full awareness that she was driving into a hornet's nest. The early morning haze still shrouded the low cinderblock buildings, making the base seem almost deserted. The radio hissed static as she parked by the designated Quonset warehouse, her tires crunching the unpaved shoulder. A dull ache ran up her right forearm from yesterday's gym session, and she rubbed it absentmindedly as she took in the crime tape already strung across the chain link perimeter.

Castellano stood just beyond the tape, arms crossed, windbreaker zipped to the throat, a lone wolf in a pack of mostly bored base security. She had the bearing of someone who'd rather be cleaning her pistol, or shooting it, then explaining herself to rent-a-cops. Her hair, darker than usual in the dew, stuck out in sharp, precise spikes from a hastily done bun. Leilani recognized the look: ready to pounce on any whiff of insubordination, already bracing for a fight.

She let herself through the tape and offered a nod. "Heard you called in for a cultural consult. Didn't expect you to need me for art appreciation."

Castellano's mouth ticked into a not-quite smile. "Cute. Let's see how funny you find it when you get a look at the wall."

She led the way around the end of the warehouse. The outside was as bland as government money could make it. Whitewashed cement, battered steel doors, and patches of mildew in the perpetual dampness. Except for the east-facing wall, where someone had spray-painted a sequence of images. At first glance, a mess of lines and circles, but as Leilani closed in, the shapes resolved into something older, deeper, and so intentional it made her scalp prickle.

The main image stretched across twenty feet of wall, three rows of glyphs stacked above a band of red ochre triangles. Someone with an expert's hand had drawn the heads and torsos in the old style, showing exaggerated arms, conical headdresses, and crescent-bladed clubs. Intermixed were geometric signatures, spirals and chevrons. Some had been stylized versions of the war god's profile, complete with fangs and a row of what looked suspiciously like shark teeth. Below the row, a second band of black symbols, smaller, denser, and more like a written code than decoration.

Leilani whistled low, reaching for her phone to snap pictures. "They teach you at Quantico how to spot the difference between a real petroglyph and a knockoff?"

Castellano produced her own phone, already recording the scene. "I go by whether base security loses their shit. And this?" She jerked her head at the mural. "It's got every historian associate with the base playing phone tag."

Leilani stepped in close, ignoring the puddle at her feet. The paint smelled sharp, new, and the over-spray dusted the gravel with tiny neon droplets. She ran her eyes over the symbols, the spacing and the careful mimicry of the old basalt carvings found on the northwest cliffs. But whoever did this wasn't just copying; they were blending multiple traditions, mixing heiau iconography with motifs from burial caves and old surf stones, like a greatest hits album for the worst omens in the Hawaiian playbook.

She pointed at the tallest figure, its chest marked with an X over the heart. "That's a vengeance mark. Old school. But whoever did it got the direction wrong. They meant it to read as a challenge, not a warning."

Castellano's eyes narrowed. "You're sure?"

"Yeah. If it were to scare the Navy, you'd see a generic tiki face or a standard skull motif. But this?" She traced the black band below the triangles. "This is an invocation. See the double triangles? This means the act is already in motion. Not a threat. A declaration."

One of the base security officers, an older local guy with a belly like a prize-winning melon, stepped in. "We had two different witnesses walk by here around midnight, and they saw nobody. But when the first patrol rolled at oh-six hundred, the wall was like this. The paint is still wet. Had to be after midnight."

Leilani nodded, still staring at the second band of marks. "Any security footage?"

Castellano cut in before the security guard could answer. "Checked every camera within a quarter mile. Whoever did this either wore full camo, moved in the blind spots, or used a blackout kit. No faces. No plates on any of the cars that passed during that time window."

Leilani shrugged. "So someone who knows the base. Or gets tips from someone who does."

Castellano's mouth twitched, annoyed at having missed it. "That's why I called you. I thought, if anyone can tell a copycat from the cult, it's you."

Leilani ran a finger along the edge of one painted club. "This isn't a cult, not in the movie sense. Whoever did this knows their history, but they're rewriting it. These glyphs don't match the textbook. See this hook here?" She tapped the arched symbol near the bottom. "That's a death-canoe. You don't see it except on burial markers on Molokai."

Castellano scribbled in a pocket notebook. "What does it mean?"

"It means someone's promising to send a body to the other side. Not tomorrow. Soon. They're advertising."

A silence fell as they both took in the wall, the shiver of sea air, and the way the red triangles seemed to almost vibrate in the rising sun.

Castellano's voice softened, just a hair. "Did you see the case files before you came out? Holt's confession, the evidence wrap-up?"

Leilani shook her head. "Didn't need to. I saw the bodies up close, remember?" She turned back to the mural, letting herself fall into the rhythm, the obsessive repetition and the careful layering of shapes. "This isn't his hand. Different left-right bias, different grip."

Castellano grunted, but she was listening. "So you're saying it's a follower, or a partner."

"Not necessarily. It could be someone inspired by the media coverage or a survivor." She hesitated, then said, “But I’d bet my last paycheck this is the real deal. It’s a recruitment poster, not a performance piece.”

The security guard said, “We’ve had some guys at the barracks saying they’re scared to walk the quad after dark. I figured it was just stories. But this feels personal.”

Leilani nodded, the back of her neck prickling. “That’s the point. It’s not a call to arms, it’s a challenge to someone.”

Castellano stared at her. “To who?”

Leilani let her eyes follow the mural’s line, then down to the ground, where a smudge of blue pigment marked the curb. “To us. To law enforcement, to anyone who thinks the case closed with Holt in cuffs. They’re daring us to see the next one coming.”

Castellano’s teeth flashed in a smile that was more wolf than woman. “You’re not like most consultants, Kealoha.”

“Not a consultant,” Leilani said. “I live here.”

A beat passed, then Castellano drew her close, lowering her voice. “I’ll help you because I do not want another murder to pop up in my jurisdiction just because we didn’t see the signs.”

Leilani matched her stance. “Works for me, but we play it my way.”

Castellano considered, then nodded. “Fine. We start with the oldest living experts. Anyone who could’ve taught this level of symbology. And we cross-reference with every one of Holt’s contacts, in prison or out.”

She turned, calling the base's security chief. "Get a list of all recent civilian visitors. Also, any suppliers who delivered within forty-eight hours. And pull anyone who ever did grounds maintenance. I want the personnel files for the last ten years."

The officer hurried off. Castellano looked back at Leilani. "You got a name in mind, or you just plan to read the glyphs until they spell it out?"

Leilani traced the last black symbol, a tight spiral ending in a triangle. She felt her mouth go dry. "No name. Not yet. But this one." She pointed. "This is the same as the tag on the last victim's grave. Not publicized, not even in the reports. Someone's showing off."

Castellano's face darkened. "So you're saying we might have missed something. But we have a signed confession."

Leilani let herself smile, small and tight. "Well, something's amiss and we need to figure out what it is."

Castellano scoffed. Okay. I'll help you with what I can, but as far as the Navy is concerned, this case is closed.

They stood a moment, side by side, facing the wall, until the wind picked up and set the caution tape snapping. For the first time since the case broke, Leilani sensed not just competition, but a kind of respect in the way Castellano regarded her. They might not trust each other, not yet, but it didn't matter. The mural had forced their hands.

They peeled off, Castellano moving with quick, hard steps, Leilani trailing just far enough back to keep her in focus. Neither said another word until the warehouse shrank in the rearview mirror and the radio came alive with new alerts. They were back on the Holt case, for better or worse, and whatever came next, it wouldn't be solved by the book.

Chapter Thirty-Six

The HPD conference room had all the charm of a high school detention hall, and the only sign of life came from the scatter of Post-it notes that covered every inch of the dry-erase wall. Leilani sat at the battered table, three different case files open in a fan before her. The sole source of natural light came through a narrow window, making the room's yellow bulbs feel even more artificial.

She flicked her pen, marking the evidence grid for the third murder, the one at Barber's Point. Something didn't sit right. Holt's confession described the crime in detail, but the language read like a fever dream, all about cleansing the shame and setting the spirit free. The ritual elements matched, mostly: the ti leaf bundle, the positioning of the salt, and the blue pigment. But with placing the victim, Holt had said, "He faced the rising sun, arms outstretched." But the body, as photographed, faced west. And Holt's narrative mentioned an artifact at the scene, a wooden bowl full of saltwater, that hadn't existed, not at that location. The writeup from the forensic techs confirmed it. No such bowl existed, only a ring of salt in the dirt.

She pushed back from the table, the wheels on her chair screeching, and added another Post-it to the growing tangle. *Holt error, site #3. Why*?

The door opened without a knock, and Isaac entered, a paper bag balanced on his left arm and two coffees in his right hand. He placed one next to her elbow, then perched on the table, scanning the wall of notes.

"You always pace your caffeine intake, or is this just for show?" he asked, dropping into a seat with a tired smile.

"I like the way the old cases make sense," Leilani said. "This one doesn't. Not really. Look at this." She slid the file towards him, tapping the highlighted paragraph. "Holt's statement about the third murder is off. Not just the facts. The sequence, the ritual, and the tools. Half of it reads like a guess."

Isaac sipped and shrugged. "He's lying, or the details blurred together. Most serial killers blend the scenes after a while."

She shook her head. "Not if they're religious about it. Every case up to that point matched the old rites. This one just misses."

He accepted the printout, eyes tracking the words. "You think it's a copycat for that one?"

"It could be a decoy or someone wanting us to believe they're connected."

The door banged open again. Castellano strode in with the unrestrained energy of someone itching for a fight. She wore the same navy suit as the morning, but now the sleeves were rolled, revealing a forearm tattoo, a thin black snake or a chain. "You know this isn't your private seminar," she said, zeroing in on the evidence board.

Leilani set her pen down. "Trying to square Holt's confession with the scene reports."

Castellano stopped, arms crossed. "We have a

signed confession, DNA on the weapon, and witnesses who saw Holt's car at two of the sites. What am I missing here?"

Isaac said, "Her instincts are usually right."

Castellano snorted and pointed to the board. "Look, I don't care how you parse his poetic bullshit. Holt confessed. Case closed. If we have a copycat, we need to work that out, but I'm not reopening the Holt case."

Leilani stood, moved to the whiteboard, and pointed to her notes. "If he's our guy for all of them, why does his description of Barber's Point differ from every other site? Why does he mention a ceremonial bowl that was never there? Why the reversed direction for the victim?"

Castellano shrugged. "He's a nutcase, or the stress made his memory spotty. Does it matter?"

"Yes," Leilani said, her voice steady. "Because that's the only murder where the blood work showed a secondary donor at the scene. The others, nothing. But this one? Unmatched DNA on the handle of the lei-o-mano. Partial, but not Holt's."

Castellano moved in close, her breath sharp with cinnamon gum. "You think he's taking the fall for a partner?"

"I think the evidence says he didn't kill that one. And whoever did knew the rituals, but not well. They made mistakes. Deliberate or not, I don't know."

Isaac, always the peacemaker, said, "We should at least run down the secondary DNA. Could be another victim, or—"

Castellano cut him off, eyes locked on Leilani. "You want to waste time on a technicality, fine. But don't drag me into it. I'm not giving the Feds or the Navy any excuse to think we botched the case."

Leilani bristled. "I don't care what the Feds want. I care about not charging the wrong person for the wrong thing."

A heavy silence settled. The air in the room felt dense, waiting for someone to break it.

The door opened and Chief Mori stepped in, her presence like an electric current. Her tailored suit seemed to soak up the light, and she didn't waste a moment. "Brief me," she commanded.

Castellano deferred to Leilani, but not without rolling her eyes. "Detective Kealoha believes there's a discrepancy in the Holt confession, specifically on the third murder."

Mori raised an eyebrow. "And?"

Leilani spoke quickly, hitting every point. "Details in the confession don't match the forensic findings. The ritual elements are inconsistent. There's an unknown DNA at the scene, and the MO is sloppy compared to the other murders. I want to check for accomplices or copycats."

Mori looked at Isaac. "Torres?"

He nodded, backing her up. "It's worth pursuing. At a minimum, we should compare the secondary DNA with databases and look for any other ritual-style attacks in the last year."

Mori turned to Castellano, whose jaw flexed. "Do

it," the chief said. "But keep it tight and do not let this slow down the review process. If there's a second perp, I want an ID as soon as possible. Understood?"

Castellano set her jaw but nodded.

"Good," Mori said, then left as quickly as she'd entered.

Castellano lingered for a moment, then addressed Leilani directly. "For the record, if you're wrong, I'm not bailing you out when IA comes calling."

Leilani didn't flinch. "If I'm wrong, I'll eat it. But if I'm right, it means we missed someone. Someone who's probably not finished."

They held each other's gaze, neither blinking, until Isaac cleared his throat and began stacking the case files. Castellano left, her steps quick and hard down the corridor.

Leilani exhaled, the adrenaline still singing in her hands. She sat and pulled the third victim's file closer. Isaac set the coffee next to her, careful to avoid the mess of notes.

"Glad she's on your side?" he asked.

Leilani snorted. "If she ever is, I'll buy you dinner."

He laughed, low and genuine. "Good luck. You want help running the DNA?"

She nodded, suddenly grateful for the familiar, measured tone of his support. "Yeah. Let's pull every flagged case in the last two years with similar MOs, and see if any of Holt's old associates went missing or got moved."

They set to work, each falling into a rhythm, Isaac on his laptop, Leilani on the phone and digging through printouts. The room felt less like a detention hall, more like an outpost on the edge of something unknown. As the sky outside the window shaded from gray to orange, the evidence wall filled with new connections, and the difference between case closed and case solved became, for the first time, all the difference in the world.

Chapter Thirty-Seven

The air in Halawa Prison's visitation wing smelled of an antiseptic so strong it smothered even the reek of sweat and despair. The guards ran her through the usual protocol, bag check, frisk, and then another sign-in on a digital tablet that lagged half a beat behind every tap. Leilani walked the corridor past the rows of shatterproof glass and battered chairs.

Holt was already seated at the table, shackled at the ankles, the sleeves of his prison-issue t-shirt tight against a physique that had not suffered since the trial. He held himself with an eerie patience, almost ceremonial, as if he'd waited there all morning not for her, but for some ancient appointment. When Leilani entered, he looked up and smiled, the corners of his mouth not quite aligning with the rest of his face.

She sat, let her gaze take him in, then placed her yellow legal pad flat on the metal table. "You know why I'm here."

Holt nodded. His fingers, calloused and tan, made a steeple on the tabletop. "I expected you sooner."

"You got lucky," she said. "My schedule's been hell." She opened the pad and flipped to a flagged page. "Let's talk about the Barber's Point murder. The third one."

Holt leaned in, folding his hands as if at confession. "That was a necessary step."

Leilani watched him for micro-tells, but if he had any, they lay buried. "Your statement describes the victim as facing the sunrise. The scene showed him facing west. That's not the only mismatch, but it's the most obvious. You want to explain?"

He considered. "The direction is symbolic. East, west, it matters only to the dead."

She tried a different tack. "You also said you left a wooden bowl at the scene. The forensic sweep found only salt rings. Nothing else."

Holt didn't flinch. "Sometimes the offering disappears before you see it. Someone else might have taken it."

Leilani leaned back. "Is that your way of saying you had help?"

Holt's smile turned playful, the glint in his eye almost charming. "You know the old stories. The hero never acts alone. There's always an ali'i, a priest, a witness."

She waited, letting the silence gnaw at him, but he simply watched, head canted slightly, as if admiring the patience of a hunting dog.

"You want to tell me who the priest is?" Leilani asked.

"If there is one," he said, "I couldn't say."

She moved her finger down her list. "You were meticulous for the first two, but the Barber's Point site had mistakes. You made none before. Why start now?"

He licked his lips, the only nervous movement she'd seen. "I was tired, or I wanted you to see through it."

Leilani didn't buy it. "I think you're covering for someone. Someone you owe or someone who threatened you. I think the ritual mattered to you, but you couldn't stomach the third murder."

Holt looked amused, almost affectionate. "That's good, Detective. Better than the others."

"Who are you protecting?"

His eyes sharpened. "I'm protecting the truth. The ancient traditions." He leaned closer, lowering his voice. "You still don't understand. It's not about me, or the body count. It's about restoring the balance. If I didn't finish, someone else would. That's the point."

She met his gaze hard. "You want to be a martyr?"

He shook his head slowly. "No. Martyrs die for someone else's cause. I just wanted to fix what was broken."

Leilani tapped her pen. "Fine. Let's play it your way. Where did you learn the rituals? Not from your grandmother. Everything we found in your house said she didn't know the burial codes. The Bishop Museum would have been an option, but those records are sealed."

Holt's expression flattened. "You ask too many questions, Kealoha. That's why you're always one step behind."

She let the jab slide. "So, who taught you?"

He glanced at the guard near the door, then back to her. "The teacher becomes the student, and the student becomes the teacher. That's how knowledge is preserved."

She said nothing. Let the words hang.

He shifted his hands so that the shackles clicked softly against the metal. "Sometimes you have to lose everything before you see what matters. I learned that from my ancestors. Someday you will too."

She fought the urge to roll her eyes. "You're not a kahuna, James. You're a guy who got caught."

He smiled again. "You ever wonder why I let you catch me?"

She let herself smile back. "Let me catch you? I think you weren't smart enough to stay free."

He shrugged, his shoulders moving slowly and deliberately. "Or I needed to get here to finish the work."

Leilani closed her pad. "If you want to be cryptic, fine. But you're not the only one who can read between the lines."

She pushed away from the table, gathering her notes. Holt straightened; the interview clearly over. As the guard stepped forward, unlocking Holt's chair from the floor, he looked at her with something like respect, or a warning.

As she walked towards the end of the corridor, his voice echoed off the linoleum. "Ask your mother about Professor Souza. He understands the old rituals better than most."

She hesitated, then kept walking, her skin crawling.

Outside, the afternoon sun had turned the prison parking lot into a heat mirage. She pulled her phone from her jacket, scrolled through her contacts, and found her mother's name. For a second, she hovered, thumb poised above the call icon, then slipped the phone back into her pocket. Instead, she sat in her car, windows down, listening to the hum of insects and the distant drone of traffic, thinking about teachers, students and the ancient math of revenge.

Chapter Thirty-Eight

Naalei parked in the shadow of a banyan that stretched from the music building clear across two parking stalls, its roots buckling the blacktop. The walk to the anthropology department felt shorter than she remembered, but the building itself had not changed. A hulking slab of 1960s concrete, humid in all seasons and redolent of old paper and fried teriyaki from the student union below.

Souza's office sat on the top floor, at the end of a hallway lined with dusty display cases. He'd left the door ajar, and she could hear the brisk clatter of a typewriter even over the hum of the air conditioning. She knocked, and the sound startled him from his work. Professor Tao Souza rose from his desk, a man of compact build and ageless brown skin, with his hair pulled into a scholar's topknot. He wore a faded aloha shirt over pressed khakis, and his bare feet seemed to have never known a shoe.

"Naalei Kealoha!" He beamed, crossing the tiny, paper-choked space in two steps. "It's been too long."

She allowed him the two-cheek kiss, then stepped back and surveyed the office. It looked as if a hurricane of cultural detritus had passed through. Woven mats and feathered capes draped over the bookshelf, lava stones, and gourd drums crowding the floor, and a fat sheaf of grant proposals threatening to collapse from one chair. Tacked to the cinderblock wall above the desk, a riot of color photographs: Souza posing at sovereignty protests, hunched over fieldwork with keiki on the Big Island, with his arms raised at some midnight ritual.

"I see you're still the keeper of chaos," Naalei said, smiling.

"Order is for Western minds." Souza gestured at a chair, cleared a stack of essays with one deft motion. "How can I serve the kumu of Diamond Head?"

Naalei eased herself down, wishing she'd chosen a darker muʻumuʻu. "I need your expertise on a sensitive matter." She reached into her tote, produced a slim folder with some of the news articles and her own notes on the recent ritual murders.

Souza's eyes flicked over the headlines, then up to her face. "You wish to understand the rites, or the mind of the killer?"

She hesitated, then decided on the half-truth. "Both, if possible. I consult for the local PD now and then. Some elements of the crime scene reminded me of your writing on warrior death rites. But there are deviations."

Souza leaned back, his hands forming a steeple at his chin. "The media never gets it right, and they are always looking for cannibals and curses. Never the subtleties."

He scanned the printouts, then pointed at a line in her notes. "Ti leaf bundles, salt lines and blue pigment." He smiled, but the smile felt a shade too eager. "Classic signatures. But which tradition? The island histories disagree."

Naalei let him elaborate. She figured the less she

revealed, the more Souza might say. He launched into a dazzling recitation of the differences between upland burial, sea burial and battlefield sacrifice, sprinkling the lecture with terms she hadn't heard in years. But beneath the performance, his questions felt designed to probe more than inform.

He set the folder down and asked, "And the third victim, the one at Barber's Point. Was it west-facing, as the papers claimed?"

She froze. "The police reports are vague on that."

He studied her, and for a beat, the mask dropped. "You can tell me, Naalei. Off the record."

She forced a neutral smile. "Let's say I'm not at liberty."

He laughed, but the sound was forced. "Always the guardian."

She allowed the silence to build, then tried a different approach. "These killings. Do you think it's one person, or is this a coordinated thing? A cult?"

Souza shrugged. "We have no true kahuna anymore. Only men with fractured memories and books." His fingers drummed the armrest, as restless energy coiled beneath the surface. "If I were to guess. A single mind, but many hands. The leader would hide behind ritual, make the students do the dirty work."

Naalei nodded and let her gaze drift to the wall. The photos had more meaning now. Souza at a tent encampment holding a megaphone, Souza in a crowd of tattooed men brandishing clubs, and Souza, years younger, sitting cross-legged on a lava field with a cluster of young men in camouflage. Her mind put the pieces together. She felt uneasy.

Souza rose, went to a shelf, and retrieved an ancient, battered text. He set it before her. "If you want to read between the lines, study this. The old priests wrote in metaphors. Most of what you need is here, if you know what to look for."

Naalei leafed through the first few pages. The margins brimmed with Souza's own handwritten notes, in English and Hawaiian both.

He lingered behind her, then said, almost casually, "If your police friends want more, I can host a workshop. Some things are easier to show than explain."

She stood, closing the book. "I'll let them know, but for now, I should go."

He smiled, but his eyes didn't. "Of course. I would never keep a kumu from her calling."

She thanked him, and walked to the door, the hair on her arms prickling with old instinct. Outside, the hallway felt colder, emptier. She glanced back just once. Souza stood at his desk, his hands behind his back, and watched her until she turned the corner.

She walked the stairwell to the ground floor, clutching the text to her chest. She waited in the parking lot for several minutes, trying to decide whether to call her daughter right away or wait until she'd found the words that wouldn't sound like pure paranoia. Above her, at a top-floor window, Souza watched, unblinking.

Chapter Thirty-Nine

When Leilani reached her desk, a manila folder, the color of dried mustard sat on the battered surface, propped against the cold remains of a coffee. Isaac waited nearby, slouched against the partition, thumb scrolling through emails but his eyes locked on her as she dropped her tote and slid into the chair. He said nothing, just nodding towards the file.

She flipped it open. Inside, there is a short stack of printouts, mostly transcripts, but at the bottom, an event flyer: Cultural Authenticity in the Modern World: An Evening with Prof. Tao Souza. The date on the flyer put it several months before the first murder. Highlighted underneath, a name: JAMES E. HOLT.

Leilani snorted. "You found his RSVP?"

Isaac's lips twitched. "He attended three of them, per the sign-in logs. Sat in the front row. Took notes."

She paged through the rest. Photos of Holt at the lectures, stone-faced and listening. In one, Holt and Souza stood together after the session, hands clasped, both smiling at the camera. A Post-it flagged the back: Original source: U of H faculty blog.

"Souza taught the ritual. Holt brought it to life," she said.

Isaac nodded and leaned in. "It gets better. Souza was on the mailing list for the Warrior Spirit pilot program at Pearl. He was also the guest of honor at three of the base's early cultural events, always with the same angle, reviving the true traditions, not the watered-down museum versions."

Leilani let the words sink in, felt the dots connecting themselves all at once. "We need to call my mom."

Isaac didn't even blink. She pulled out her phone, found Naalei in the contacts, and put it on speaker.

The phone rang twice. Naalei picked up with her usual efficiency. "Lei?"

"Hey Mom, quick question. When you met Souza, did he ask you anything about the murder scene? About how they were set up?"

Naalei exhaled, the sound sharp. "He asked for every detail. He even wanted to know which way the bodies pointed, what plants surrounded the sites, even the time of day."

Isaac shot her a look, and Leilani nodded. "Anything else weird?"

A pause. "He said if you needed help interpreting the rituals, he'd be glad to do it. He seemed excited. It made me uncomfortable. He said he was working on a scholarly paper and that the recent murders would be a nice addition to a continuing story."

"Don't talk to him again until I say so, okay?"

"Understood," said Naalei.

They hung up and Leilani shut her eyes for a second. "He's not just the brains. He's the recruiter. The one who put the kill list together."

Isaac made a noncommittal sound, then motioned to the envelope at the far side of her desk. "Found something in evidence you should see."

She opened it. Inside, a battered black composition book. Holt's journal. They'd run through it already, but this time she opened the back cover, her fingers searching the cardboard lining. A small seam peeled up. With a nail, she pried it loose. A second, hidden cache: folded paper, a few photos and an SD card taped to the inside.

She unfolded the photographs. The first, a blurry telephoto shot of Kai, taken from across the playground at his school. Dated six months before the first body. The next one showed Naalei at the cultural center, pouring salt in a circle on the floor, unaware of the camera. A third, Leilani herself, walking out of HPD at dusk, hair in a bun, and her hand on her badge.

She fought down a shudder. "He was tracking us. Before the killings started."

Isaac took the photo and studied the date stamp. "Holt wasn't even in Hawaii in May. He was on a security contract job in Korea, per his pay records."

Leilani sorted through the photos, her heart thudding. There were more. She and Kai at Ala Moana Beach Park, a towel thrown over her shoulder, Kai halfway up a monkey bar. One of Naalei at the Safeway, and another at a beach-side shrine. Each shot marked with a red dot on the back, sometimes a crude symbol, a spiral, a triangle, or a star.

On the back of the one with her and Kai together, someone had drawn a circle with a slash through it, then, in blue pen, the word KUPONO. She whispered it. "Worthy opponent."

She looked up at Isaac. "He had someone leading

him. This is way more organized than one crazy ex-military guy."

He didn't need convincing. "You think Souza's the mastermind?"

"Or the next in line. Either way, we need to bring Castellano in on this. She's not going to like it, but she's got the Feds' leverage to make this official."

Isaac nodded. "Let's do it."

They grabbed the evidence and headed for Leilani's Explorer.

Chapter Forty

They found Castellano in the glass-walled office she'd claimed as her home base. She barely glanced up from her laptop as they entered, but something in their faces pulled her attention. "Got something?"

Leilani tossed the journal onto her desk, then spread the photos before her. Castellano's gaze sharpened. "Is this your family?"

Leilani nodded. "And Holt couldn't have taken them. Not unless he teleported."

Castellano took her time, studying the dates, the markings and the strange care with which the photos had been notated. "You think this Souza guy did it?"

"I think he's either running the show or serving a higher-up. Either way, my family is under surveillance."

Castellano leaned back, tension rippling off her in waves. "We need to move. Now."

Leilani stood, packed her laptop and the photos. "We have a theory of the case. But not enough for a warrant. We need to get leverage, something he can't explain away."

Leilani felt adrenaline sparking, the sick thrill of a new hunt, but this time with the unmistakable edge of fear. She ran through every moment of the last few weeks, every random car, every face in the crowd at Kai's school, every flower left on the hood of her car and saw them all now for what they were.

A pattern. A warning.

She grabbed her keys, ignored the tremor in her hands. “I’m going to get my son.”

Castellano nodded, not arguing. “We’ll meet at your mom’s place. Bring the journal.”

Isaac touched her shoulder gently. “We got this, Lei.”

She let the words settle, then walked out, the sound of her boots sharp and certain in the corridor.

Outside, the air crackled with late afternoon heat. Somewhere, a drummer kept a steady beat, the old rhythms echoing from the bandstand at Kapiolani Park. She tried to picture herself and Kai walking there again, free from eyes in the trees, and free from history’s shadows. But for now, she had a job to do. And this time, she wouldn’t let the past catch her from behind.

Chapter Forty-One

The HPD conference room felt smaller than usual. Someone had taped butcher paper over the dry-erase wall, a mess of maps, crime scene photos, and hand-drawn diagrams paper-clipped in loose rows. Chief Mori leaned back in her seat, her arms folded, and her lips pressed into a line as thin as fishing line. Isaac flanked her on the left, his pen already tapping his notepad. Castellano claimed the end nearest the door, all coiled muscle and crossed arms, her face set in a mask that read "I'm only here because protocol requires it."

Leilani stood at the front, close enough to the wall that the corners of the paper curled into her shoulders. She felt every pair of eyes locked on her, but forced herself to keep her voice calm.

"First, a recap," she said, pointing to a timeline sketched in black marker. "Holt confessed to the five base murders and two attempts. Every site had consistent ritual elements, salt lines, ti bundles, pigment and weapon type. He even volunteered details only the killer could have known."

Castellano cut in. "But he's a liar. No shock. He's already confessed to five murders. Why split hairs?"

Leilani ignored her, flipping a photo of the third murder site to reveal a second shot beneath. "But here's where it breaks. Holt described setting a ceremonial bowl here, but the evidence sweep found only salt. His version says the victim faced the sunrise. The body, as found, faced west."

Castellano rolled her eyes. "So he got his east and west mixed up in a panic, or he's showing off for the trial."

Leilani snapped a second photo to the wall, this one of a wooden bowl, slightly scorched on one rim. "This bowl was found, but not at the third site. It showed up at the second, three miles away, after Holt's arrest. DNA results from the rim and inner surface don't match any of the victims, and they don't match Holt."

Chief Mori's eyebrow went up, but she said nothing, just kept her fingers drumming in a slow, steady rhythm.

Leilani continued, "Holt's confession contains other gaps. He describes the third scene as if he saw it on TV, not as someone who lived it. And there's the surveillance issue."

She stepped to the end of the board, peeled away a folder, and thumbtacked a glossy 8x10. "These are surveillance stills. These were found tucked in a hidden compartment in Holt's journal, printed and dated. But the timestamps place several of them before his return to the island. In May, he's in Korea. Yet here, this photo." She tapped the next one, a grainy image of herself and her son at a playground. "Someone took this in May."

Castellano stood. "So what? He had a pen pal? Someone bought them off the dark web? You're reaching, Kealoha."

Isaac cut in, "It's not just the photos, Vic. The quality on some is professional. These aren't phone snaps; they're long-lens, high-res, properly framed.

And Holt didn't own the camera these would have needed."

Castellano let out a dry laugh. "Plenty of camera shops in Honolulu, or are we now profiling every auntie with a Nikon?"

Mori silenced her with a wave. "Detective Kealoha, are you saying there's a second actor?"

"At a minimum, a surveillance expert, or a handler. And—" Leilani paced back to the first column of the board, tracing a spiral symbol on the margin of one photo—"the tag used on all three scenes matches the one in these photos, in blue ink. It's a mark of authorship, or at least of someone orchestrating."

Mori's eyes narrowed. "Could the suspect have coordinated with someone off-island?"

Leilani nodded. "If the accomplice supplied the surveillance, the accomplice could have directed the victim selection. The killings all align with targets critical of the new cultural training at the base."

Castellano butted in, her tone clipped. "Now you're pitching conspiracy theories. Every case I've seen, when a perp says he had help, he means imaginary friends or someone he wants to pin it on. It's classic misdirection."

Leilani ignored the interruption. "Except the patterns hold. The ritual elements have evolved. At the third murder, the ti bundles were knotted in a way consistent with an obscure burial tradition, and there are only a handful of experts who know it."

She paused, letting that hang. "And one of them is

Professor Tao Souza, the man who advised on the military's cultural program. The man who mentored Holt at every pilot training. Souza's name is all over the planning documents for the first two training modules."

Mori sat forward, hands now flat on the table. "You're suggesting we question him."

"At least background him." Leilani forced herself to look Castellano in the eye. "You wanted my theory, that's it. Holt was a pawn. Souza might be the king."

Castellano's jaw flexed, and her knuckles blanched. "You realize how that sounds, right? You're accusing a respected academic of masterminding a serial murder ring because some flower knots matched?"

Isaac kept his voice even. "That, and because his email appears on every chain that also went to Holt in the run-up to the killings. Also, his phone pings off the same towers near each of the crime scenes on the relevant nights. That's not theory. That's records."

Mori pinched the bridge of her nose and let out a slow breath. "So, you want to reopen the investigation, add Souza as a person of interest, and brief our federal partners?"

Leilani nodded, but Castellano slammed the table with an open palm. "No. We don't need a media circus, and we don't need to open a fresh can of shit with the Navy when we are safe on base again. If you want to play cop, fine, but don't drag the whole department through another island-wide panic without something concrete."

Leilani perceived her pulse beating in her temples, but she didn't move. "I'm asking for permission to surveil Souza. Enough to see if he's planning anything."

Mori considered, fixing her gaze on Leilani. "You need to be damn sure before we tell our military partners another killer is at large."

The words landed like a stone in water, sending ripples down the length of the table.

"Understood," Leilani said.

Mori stood. "I'll authorize a quiet review. If you find anything actionable, bring it straight to me. Torres, work with Kealoha. Castellano, assist as needed. But keep this inside the department. No leaks, no off-the-record briefings."

She turned on her heel and exited, Castellano close behind, muttering under her breath. The room emptied, leaving Leilani alone at the front, the photos curling on the wall behind her.

Isaac approached, his hand resting lightly on her shoulder. "You okay?"

Leilani didn't answer right away. She gazed at the wall, jaw tight. "I have no choice. If Souza's out there, he's not finished."

Isaac squeezed her shoulder. "Let's catch him before he is."

They stood there for a moment, letting the silence work. They gathered the evidence, ready to move before the story broke, before the next body fell.

Chapter Forty-Two

The station's third shift settled into the usual rhythm of tapping keyboards and slurping instant ramen. In the back corner, Leilani, and Isaac shared a battered desk that still smelled faintly of a decade-old diet cola spill. The precinct had gone quiet except for the humming of the ancient AC and the tap-tap of Isaac's fingers moving across his laptop.

A stack of files squatted between them, each one stuffed with schedules, training agendas and personnel rosters from the Navy's cultural education program. Leilani paged through the first section, half the names circled, others underlined in red or annotated with her quick, narrow script.

"Let's start with the consultant list," Isaac said. He dragged a roster into the middle of the screen and angled it for her to see. "Half these names are dead weight. Only three stuck around for the duration of the program, and two of those are in admin. We've accounted for everyone during the Holt investigation except for Professor Tao Souza."

Leilani didn't look up. "Souza's famous in some circles. He wrote the book on contested burials and has a knack for pissing off anyone in uniform."

Isaac clicked a link, pulling up Souza's university profile. The man's face stared out, weathered and deliberate, black hair pulled into a tight bun. "You ever meet him?"

"Not directly," said Leilani. "My mom crossed

paths with him a couple times. He's the guy who can start a shouting match at a funeral and somehow leave with more friends than he started with."

Isaac scrolled through a timeline of Souza's public appearances, each one matched with local media coverage. "He left the Navy project before it went live," he said. "Here." He pointed to a personnel action form with Souza's signature at the bottom. "Resigned six months before the first murder, no reason given."

Leilani snorted. "He likes being in charge. If they didn't do it his way, he probably told them to shove it."

They went back to the folders, cross-referencing emails, seeing which ones got Cc'd to both Holt and Souza. A few patterns formed, the kind that didn't announce themselves but whispered if you looked long enough. "Every field trip for the training program went to one of three historic sites," Isaac said. "All three became crime scenes."

He pulled up a batch of social media photos. "This is from the pilot, a month before the first murder. That's Souza, and that's Holt, right?"

Leilani leaned in. "Yeah, that's him." Holt looked younger, clean-shaven, and nervous in his aloha shirt. Souza had his arm around Holt's shoulder, guiding him like a docent showing off a prized artifact.

Isaac flicked through more photos. "And here, the same two, but this time they're at the Makaha site, the one that got hit second."

The silence stretched. Leilani paged through the stack again, then said, "Souza was everywhere Holt went, even after he quit the project. That's not accidental."

Isaac drummed his pen on the desk. "He's not in the system for anything criminal. Nothing more than a couple of trespassing raps from old protests, and those are expunged."

"He's got friends who can make that happen," said Leilani. "He plays the activist card, but he's old guard. He knows how to pull strings."

Isaac opened a second tab, typing in quick bursts. "Let's see what he's up to now." He found a personal blog, photos of Souza at a recent protest, and an open letter denouncing the "militarization of Hawaiian identity." In one photo, Souza wore a red shirt with a black spiral, the same one Leilani had noticed on the murder scene evidence.

She jabbed a finger at the screen. "There. That logo. It's not just a mark, it's a signature. That's his crew's symbol."

Isaac dug deeper, searching through a handful of public records and news archives. "He's connected to at least three different sovereignty groups, all nonviolent, at least on the surface. But two were cited for aggressive disruption at Pearl's visitor center, and one of those got shut down after a bomb threat."

"He's the guy who gives the cops just enough trouble to make them look stupid," said Leilani.

They kept at it for another hour, flipping through printouts, connecting dots, and talking it through. At some point, the overhead lights flickered, plunging the room into strobe-lit half-darkness.

Isaac clicked off his monitor and turned to Leilani. "You think he's running the show, or just running interference for whoever is?"

Leilani pressed her palms against her temples. "He's too smart to get his hands dirty. But if he wants to make a statement, he'd pick a fall guy like Holt and orchestrate the whole thing from the shadows."

Leilani's phone buzzed with a text from her mother. *Checking in. When are you coming over for Kai's finished project?*

Leilani studied the message, looking back at the stacks of paper, her mind cycling through every encounter Naalei had ever described with Souza. She tapped a response before putting the phone down.

Isaac noticed. "What's up?"

She gave a tired laugh. "I think my mom knows more about this guy than the whole state database."

"You want to pay her a visit?"

Leilani nodded, rising from the chair. "She'll talk if I bring good coffee. But first, let's ping the cultural center, see if Souza's due to appear anywhere in the next week."

Isaac fired off a quick email to their contact at the Hawaiian Studies department. "If he's planning something, you think he'll do it soon?"

"He likes big audiences. The anniversary of the Overthrow is coming up." Leilani gathered up the key files and stowed them in her bag. "If he wants to make a scene, that would be a good choice."

They walked out together, the flicker of the old lights chasing them down the corridor.

Outside, the air was cooler; the city humming at half-speed. The station lot was empty except for two squad cars and a lonely night guard on his phone.

Isaac said, "You want me to tag along tomorrow?"

"No," Leilani replied. "Monitor the feeds. If Souza so much as sneezes online, I want to know about it before it hits the street."

Isaac nodded, then hesitated. "Be careful, Lei."

She looked at him, his brow furrowed and worry written all over his face. "Always."

She turned, the files tight under her arm, and headed home. The work had a long way to go, but at least now it had direction and so did she.

Chapter Forty-Three

Castellano's office looked like the inside of a submarine: a long stretch of gray wall, a forest of framed commendations, and a steel desk so old it rattled every time she set down a file. Night pressed at the windows, warping her reflection until she barely recognized herself.

On the desk, the case file from Leilani had exploded into a debris field: mug shots, site diagrams and pages of annotated ritual details. At the far edge, her own service record glared at her, a photo from FLETC graduation where she still looked like a believer. She tried not to look at it.

She thumbed through the latest crime scene stack, her eyes cataloging every grotesque detail with professional detachment. Every so often, she scribbled a note or flicked a page into the outbox. The lamp overhead cast sharp shadows on her hands, making her knuckles look like broken glass.

She picked up the surveillance photos, the ones Leilani insisted were too good for a DIY stalker. Castellano turned them over in sequence, watching her own skepticism chip away, frame by frame. Holt was a narcissist and a warrior, but he hadn't taken these. Some were telephoto; others looked like they came from hidden trail cams. She noticed now, in the margins, something she'd missed the first dozen times: the spiral mark in blue ink, always tucked away, like a tag. The same as the one found at the last scene.

She sat back, the chair creaking. The air vibrated

with the buzzing of her government-issued phone, cutting through the silence. Castellano grabbed it, thumbed the green button.

"Agent Castellano."

"Where are we?" The voice on the other end belonged to Special Agent Finley, who ran NCIS Hawaii from a windowless office in Pearl City.

"I'm reviewing the case file," she said. "I have concerns about—"

Finley steamrolled her. "Our contact at Pacific Command wants this closed. They're getting heat from Washington, and nobody wants to hear about a cell of Hawaiian militants during an election cycle. Wrap it up."

She kept her voice neutral. "Sir, Kealoha found credible evidence of an accomplice. And the timelines on some of the pre-murder surveillance don't add up."

"Are you questioning the confession?" Finley's tone got flatter.

"I'm questioning the narrative," she replied. "There's a Professor Tao Souza, involved in the program development, and his signature shows up—"

"I know who Souza is," Finley cut in. "He's a flake and a showman. You will not tag him as the mastermind in an active-duty murder without bulletproof evidence."

"Sir, there's evidence in the file—"

He exhaled, not even pretending to be patient. "Close the file, Castellano. That's an order. If you want to play consultant for the HPD afterwards, fine. But you don't bring this to the base commander unless you want your career to take a permanent vacation in Nowhere, Nebraska."

Castellano locked her eyes on the phone, her mouth twitching. "Roger that."

The call went dead.

She tossed the phone onto her desk, where it slid across a photo of Souza, grinning at a protest rally, arms around two men who now sat in Halawa lockup. She pulled it closer and studied his face. Nothing about him seemed violent, but the eyes gave away nothing. She lined up the crime scene diagram next to a scan of Souza's book on pre-contact warfare.

The words from Leilani's notes scrawled in the margins. Ritual as symbol. Symbol as threat. The resemblance to the third murder was uncanny. Same layout, same mix of salt and pigment, the same blue spiral.

She circled the pattern, her teeth clenched. "Son of a bitch," she muttered.

Castellano reached for her laptop and pulled up the most recent fusion center alert. Her fingers flew over the keys, searching, connecting, and triangulating. She got a hit. Souza's name showed up on a Department of Defense watchlist, flagged for potential radicalization. Less than a week old.

Castellano went rigid. The case file, with her boss's order to bury it, was now hot as hell in her hands.

She pulled out her phone again, but before she could

dial, it buzzed with a new message. She glanced at the screen. It came from Finley. The message was easy to interpret. CLOSE THIS CASE. NOW.

She gripped the phone so hard that the plastic flexed. For a moment, Castellano felt every frustration she'd ever swallowed since she put on the badge. She dialed anyway.

"Torres," said a sleepy voice on the other end.

"It's Vic. Tell Kealoha I'm not a hundred percent on board, but I think she may be onto something about Souza, and if we don't get eyes on him, we're going to lose the whole thing?"

"Copy," Torres replied, instantly alert. "You coming in?"

Castellano let out a thin smile. "I never left."

She killed the call, stuffed her files into her bag, and grabbed her sidearm from the drawer. She paused only once, looking at her old Quantico photo, then at the chaos of evidence on her desk. It was a hell of a way to make a living. She clicked off the light, left the office in darkness, and headed out.

Chapter Forty-Four

A downpour hammered the empty walkways of the Manoa campus, turning the sidewalks into running streams that overflowed the curb. Leilani hustled under the canopy of palm and shower trees, the bag with her case files pressed tight to her chest. It was past eleven, but the campus was still alive, pockets of graduate students holed up in their offices, maintenance staff hustling to fix a roof leak, the faint scent of steamed rice drifting from the late-night cafeteria window. Her jacket was instantly soaked, but she didn't slow down.

The Hawaiian Studies building loomed, blocky and low-slung, with hand-carved ki‘i sentinels posted at the entryway. The doors, though locked after hours, opened to her ID badge. Someone had left them on day mode for finals week. The halls inside ran with puddles and dripped with the smell of wet earth and old paper. Leilani paused, checking the wall directory, then headed for the top floor.

Artifacts lined every surface. Kapa drums, kukui nut leis, ancient fishing lures in glass display cases. Each one a piece of history. She felt their eyes on her as she hurried down the hallway, her shoes squeaking. At the end, Souza's office looked dark. No tell-tale sign of light coming from the door.

The door hung open an inch. She hadn't noticed while walking down the hallway. Inside, the light had been left off, but the weak spill of the exit sign was enough to sketch the outline of chaos: bookcases emptied, piles of loose-leaf paper on the floor, and a battered duffel bag zipped and abandoned under the desk. A mug of black coffee, still warm, sat on the shelf. The air was humid and wrong, like the room had been closed for months instead of hours.

Leilani took a cautious step inside. Her flashlight beam cut the darkness, catching the corners of the room where textbooks and field journals had fallen like dead leaves. She pulled her pistol from her holster and held it in the low ready position. She reached beside her, found the light switch and flipped it on, keeping her flashlight on and covering the room with her pistol. Seeing no one in the room, she holstered her pistol and slipped on a pair of nitrile gloves. She moved to the desk, tracing the edges with a gloved hand. Every drawer had been yanked and emptied. The computer tower was missing; the monitor yanked from its cables, the plastic casing still warm.

She stooped to the bottom drawer, which stuck a little, then gave way with a metallic clunk. Inside, a tangle of cable ties and a small tool roll—surgical scissors, black gaffer's tape, a bottle of blue pigment labeled Moloka'i Original. Next to it, a single sheet of white paper with torn edges.

She read the text in the faint light.

Always the student, never the teacher. But the lesson survives.

Her skin prickled. She checked the duffel bag. Empty, except for a hotel key and a mostly empty pack of cigarettes. Nothing that would give forensics a good place for fingerprints, not even the decency to leave a last note.

She ran the beam over the desk again and the credenza behind it. That's where she saw it. Carved into the wood, just beneath the lip was a tight spiral ending in a triangle, the exact symbol from the murder scenes, freshly incised, the shavings still dusting the floor. The lines were precise and angry, dug deep with a sharp knife or a letter opener.

Her phone vibrated in her pocket. She fumbled it out and thumbed to the call.

"Lei," said Isaac. His voice was tense and too awake for the hour.

"I'm in," she whispered. "The office has been cleared out, but he was here tonight. Within the past couple of hours."

"Same at his house," said Isaac. "Neighbors say they saw him load a car around dusk, not the usual ride. We pulled his bank records. His last purchase was a camping supply shop in Kapahulu. Looks like he's planning to go off-grid."

Leilani pressed her hand against the desktop, the carving biting her palm. "He's leaving a trail, but it's meant for us to find. This symbol, the way he leaves the sites. I think he wants us to follow so he can finish the story."

"You want me to come to you?" said Isaac. "Or wait for Castellano? She called me a little while ago and is on her way to meet me here."

A beat. Leilani looked at the carved spiral, the clean sweep of the empty shelves. She closed her eyes, breathing in the stale air. "Stay with Vic, but keep it low-key. No uniforms. Search everywhere. Call Akira and have her run his social media sites. See if we can get a line on where he might be going."

"Copy that," said Isaac.

The call ended. Leilani thumbed the flashlight off, letting her eyes adjust. The blue pigment, the empty desk, and the carved spiral seemed like a challenge, or an invitation.

A student walked past in the hall, oblivious, headphones on, and the glow of his phone painting his face a sickly blue. Leilani waited until the footsteps faded. She took a picture of the carving, the timestamp burning into the photo's metadata, then pulled the desk drawer shut, erasing the spiral in shadow.

She lingered in the silence, letting herself feel the absence that Souza had left behind. Not just the physical emptiness, but the sense of something uncoiling and ready to strike. She wondered if this was how Holt felt, knowing he was just a ghost in someone else's story.

Leilani stepped into the hall, phone in one hand, a sheet of paper in the other. She walked past the cases of artifacts, past the silent kiʻi, and into the rain. It hit her face cold and sharp, stinging her back to the present. But as she walked to her car, Leilani sensed the spiral's pull. Souza wasn't running; he was waiting. For the right time, the right witness and the next lesson.

She texted her mother: "*Be safe. Lock the doors. I'll call soon.*"

Inside her car, the world shrank to the drumming of

rain and the blue glow of the phone. She closed her eyes and let the island's old gods whisper through her for a second. She started the engine, the mission clear. The storm lashed the city, erasing footprints before they could be traced. But Leilani knew the marks would last in the wood, in the memory, and in the blood. She would not let Souza become another ghost story. She would see him caught, or she would burn the spiral closed herself. The hunt was on.

Chapter Forty-Five

Leilani parked at the curb, the engine off, and the window cracked to let in the salt-heavy evening. The lights inside her mother's house flickered through the old bamboo shades, and the familiar orange door hung open, spilling lamplight across the walkway. She heard the faint whine of Kai's cartoons from the back room, and, over that, the syrupy tremolo of Naalei singing to herself. Even from the driveway, the air held a clash of plumeria and fresh ginger tea, sharp, sweet, and grounded by the herbal undercurrent of some ancient homebrew.

She straightened her jacket, tucked the manila folder under her arm, and headed up the walkway. Naalei's slippers waited at the stoop, perfectly aligned, as if they expected her to slip them on before crossing the threshold. Leilani did, not out of respect for the floor, but because tonight she needed every ritual she could get.

Inside, the living room looked the way it always did, with shelves crowded with jade plants, wedding photos, and a century's worth of hula trophies. The ceiling fan stirred the air, and the table under the window overflowed with bundles of mail and puakenikeni. Naalei sat on the couch, cross-legged, needle and thread in hand, stringing white crown flowers into a lei. Her hair, still damp from her post-halau shower, glinted in the lamplight, a storm cloud broken by streaks of gray.

She didn't look until Leilani set the folder on the

coffee table. With the slow, deliberate care of a judge reading the sentence for her own trial, Naalei picked it up and opened it. The folder bulged with color printouts, most grainy and rushed, but clear enough to make the point: Souza on a megaphone at the gates of Schofield Barracks, Souza at a sit-in near Wheeler Field, and Souza's face overlaid on a forum post calling for perpetual kapu against all military presence on Hawaii. There were PDFs of meeting minutes from sovereignty groups, and printouts of Facebook posts where Souza's pseudonym was circled in yellow highlighter, annotated with the word, match, in Torres's handwriting. The top sheet was a still frame of Souza, fist raised, head thrown back, with his mouth open in mid-chant.

Naalei's hands trembled. The thread snagged on her thumb, and a loose bloom rolled off the lei, landing in her lap. She closed the folder, set it aside, and looked at her daughter for the first time.

Leilani said, "I need you to be straight with me, Mom. How long have you known Professor Souza?"

Naalei pressed her lips together, drawing her fingers away from the damp flowers. "We met at the Bishop Museum in '02. The contested burial issue. He wrote the position paper; I organized the mediation. He was passionate, but so young, so angry. Like most men who think their knowledge is a weapon."

"That's not what I asked," Leilani replied, softer now. "I need to know if he's ever involved you in anything. Anything that crosses the line."

Naalei's eyes went to the folder. "You believe

this?"

"It's more than belief," Leilani said. "I've seen the crime scenes. The ritual elements aren't from a book. They're too precise. He's using the details only someone like you, or someone you've taught, would know."

A pause. Kai's cartoon reached a crescendo, and for a moment, neither woman said a word.

Naalei picked up the unfinished lei, set it on the table with more force than necessary, and brushed the fallen petals into a small white pile. "I told you he called me last week," she said. "After the arrest, after your chief put the case on the news. He said he wanted to talk, but only about the past. Not the killings. Never the killings."

"You met him at the university, and then what?" Leilani asked.

"Yes. I already told you I met him at the university," Naalei said, not ashamed but not proud, either. "I wanted to hear his side. We talked in his office for ten minutes. It became uncomfortable, and I left. That's it."

Leilani's shoulders went tight. "Mom, this is important. Did you ever give him access to our personal archives? The family chants, or the stuff you keep at the community center?"

A spark of irritation flared in Naalei's eyes. "You think I'm an idiot? I never share that with anyone, not even you. He can recite protocol from memory, but he'll never get our lineage."

Leilani exhaled. “He’s implicated in the murders, Mom. Holt named him. He didn’t say it outright, but he described someone who guides from the shadows and makes the others believe they act alone. Holt’s a killer, but Souza gave him the script.”

The needle in Naalei’s hand snapped, the tip flicking onto the glass table. She noticed the cluster of petals at her feet, each one bruised and flattened.

Leilani took her mother’s hands. “He played you. Like he played the Navy, the university and everyone.”

Naalei’s voice came out thin, as if pulled through a sieve. “He’s not a bad man. Not in the way people think.”

“He’s not the man you thought,” Leilani said. “You told me you felt sick after that last meeting. You said you thought he was hiding something.”

Naalei’s face crumpled, her mouth a line of pure regret. “I should have trusted my bones.”

“It’s not your fault, Mom.”

A bitter laugh. “Every mother’s worst excuse.”

Leilani let her mother sit in silence. Sometimes, there was nothing left but to outwait the pain.

Finally, Naalei said, “What do you need from me?”

The kitchen had always been Naalei’s sanctuary. Even now, after the long night, she clung to her routine, boil water, rinse the teapot, then set out two cups. The bulb in the overhead fixture threw down a circle of light, and the house faded to shadow. From where she sat at the breakfast bar, Leilani watched her mother's hands shake as she tipped water from the kettle into the cup. More landed on the counter than in the mug, a trembling river that ran to the sink.

"Let me," Leilani said, rising.

But Naalei only shook her head and set the kettle down, the clang ringing sharp as a bell. "I can still make tea, Lei," she said.

They sat in silence while the leaves steeped. From the fridge, Kai's class photo smiled at them. In the shot, he stood between two chubby boys in matching Dodgers shirts, his own face caught halfway between pride and nervousness.

Naalei didn't look at the photo. She looked at the space above the stove, as if searching for a prayer that could undo the past. She took a shuddering breath and said, "He asked such specific questions about the ritual arrangements."

Leilani took a seat beside her, close enough for their knees to touch. "What did he want to know?"

Naalei's composure slipped, leaving her smaller, older, not the indomitable kumu but someone's frightened auntie. "He said he was writing a paper. Wanted to honor the old warriors by making sure the ceremonies were authentic." Her laugh sounded hollow. "I felt proud at first. No one wants the past remembered wrong."

She looked at her hands, pale and cracked from years of lye and salt, and forced them to stillness by gripping the counter. "He started asking about the crimes. He wanted to know how the bodies would be prepared. Which plants mattered. How the chanting worked, where to set the salt, how to mark the direction."

She paused, lips quivering. "I thought he was trying to help the police, or you."

"He told you it was for a paper?" Leilani asked.

Naalei nodded. "He's always working on a paper."

Leilani pushed a mug towards her, not that it mattered. The tea had already cooled.

After a moment, Naalei stood, walked with slow purpose to the end of the counter, and pulled open the junk drawer. She rummaged through batteries and coupon flyers until she found a black-and-white composition book. She set it between them.

"This is what I wrote," Naalei said. "Every question he asked. Every answer I gave."

Leilani paged through the book. The first entries, careful and measured, described traditional chants and burial arrangements full of footnotes and marginalia. The later pages got darker, diagrams of body positioning and notations on the meaning of blue pigment and the correct way to braid ti for a restraining knot. The handwriting wavered, and steadied, as if each new horror demanded a steadier hand.

She compared one diagram to the memory of the second murder scene. They matched in a way that felt like a punch to the gut.

Naalei watched her daughter's eyes move down the page. "I didn't think. I thought he was just a historian. That's all he ever was, to me."

Leilani closed the book, then set her hand over Naalei's. "You didn't help him kill anyone, Mom."

"But I gave him the keys," Naalei said, the words barely audible.

A moment passed, and the kitchen filled with the click of the fridge cycling on, the buzz of a late moth at the window screen.

Leilani leaned in and held her mother's gaze. "You taught me the old rituals. They're not weapons. They're guides. If he twisted them, that's on him."

Naalei blinked, the tears not falling but painting her eyes glassy. She managed a laugh, then wiped her nose with the back of her hand. "You always were the stubborn one, just like your father."

Leilani grinned. "You mean the brave one."

"Same thing," Naalei said, and for a second, the old strength came back.

They sipped the tea in silence, neither tasting it. Eventually, Naalei got up and took her phone from the charger. "There are others," she said. "If he got to me, he got to them, too."

Leilani nodded. "Warn them. If he reaches out, tell them to avoid him. Or call me."

Naalei's thumbs flew over the screen, tapping out a group text. She rattled off a list of names, the other culture bearers, hula elders, and even the old men who fished the sacred ponds. "We will not let him claim our history," she said.

Leilani watched her mother, the resolve knitting her

back together, piece by piece.

After she sent the texts, Naalei looked up. "Are you scared?"

"Yes," Leilani admitted. "But that's not the part that matters. We're going to stop him."

"I believe you," Naalei said.

They cleared the table together, moved in tandem as if rehearsing for some family pageant. When the kitchen was clean, Leilani slung her bag over her shoulder and headed for the door. Naalei pressed the composition book into her hand at the threshold.

"For when you need to remember what's true," she said.

Leilani hugged her mother tightly, something they rarely did. Neither wanting to let go first.

Out in the Explorer, she opened the notebook and paged to the last entry. It contained a list of Hawaiian words with their meanings, one circled in blue ink. She ran her finger over it and committed it to memory.

The porch light came on behind her as she started the Explorer. Naalei stood in the doorway, her arms crossed and her shoulders set. Warrior, historian, mother, but always the guide, never the student.

Leilani let the car idle. In the notebook, one phrase stood out, written in a careful, tight script: If you give someone your trust, make sure they're worthy. She smiled. She would finish this. For Naalei, for Kai, for everyone who'd ever believed history could be bent, but not broken.

Chapter Forty-Six

By the time Leilani hit the basement level of the Navy building, the day had already soured. The morning sun was up and burning, but the concrete corridors below it never lost their chill. The NCIS conference room, repurposed from an old supply cage, was already alive with tension. Evidence boards hung wall-to-wall, computers hummed with the latest dumps from military intelligence, and the overhead lights buzzed loud enough to kill conversation.

Castellano leaned against the long side of the table, her arms folded, her fingers drumming out a staccato that telegraphed three hours of sleep and a lifetime of being let down by everyone around her. Her face looked more gaunt than usual, and she hadn't bothered with even a token touch of makeup; her eyes read full-court press and no time for dignity. Two men in blue service uniforms sat at the table, not speaking, both wearing that default here under protest posture shared by every officer above pay grade O-4.

Leilani clocked all this as she entered; Isaac half a step behind, had the folder of Naalei's notes tucked under his arm. He nodded at the others, tried a smile, but nobody offered one back.

Castellano pointed them to seats. "Glad you made it. Sorry about the fire drill, but something came in overnight. Sit, please."

She thumbed the wall panel, and with a pneumatic sigh, the projection screen rolled down. An overhead view of Pearl Harbor blinked into focus, crisp as a war room feed. Next to it, Castellano had taped three 8x10 satellite photos, each marked with circles and times. She gestured at them with the remote.

"Here, here, and here," she said. "Three different base perimeters, three dates. In each, this figure, she zoomed, is Souza. This isn't open source. This is from a suite of optical satellites that the Navy runs for force protection. They flagged him at Makaha, at Schofield, and at Kaneohe. Each visit is two to five days before a killing."

The first officer, a bull-necked man named Chang, raised a finger. "Was he trespassing, or at the fence line?"

"Close enough to make security nervous," Castellano replied. "In every frame, he's got a camera. Not a phone. A Canon with a telephoto lens, two grand retail." She looked straight at Leilani. "You called it. He was casing the bases before each event."

A ripple of silence. Leilani let her hand rest flat on the table. "If he's still on the island, we need to find him fast."

Castellano keyed up the next slide. A screenshot of an internet forum with the username pohaku42 highlighted. The posting is a 1200-word screed about foreign occupation and the need for ritual cleansing of colonizer sites. Attached, a stock photo of Schofield's main gate.

"Same IP as the one he uses for his university correspondence," said the second officer, a weedy Navy LT whose name Leilani didn't catch. "We flagged this last night. It posted two hours after midnight."

Castellano switched to the next slide. Security-camera footage from the university, time stamped two weeks prior. In the grainy black-and-white, Souza walked with Holt. Both wore casual clothes, but Holt's posture screamed I'm being lectured. Souza's hand chopped the air for emphasis.

"He met with our original suspect more times than he admitted in his interviews," Castellano said. "And according to personnel logs, Souza's badge accessed restricted corridors in the last 24 hours, including the cultural artifact archive. That's a hard pass for any non-staff, and even most faculty members can't get in without a guard."

Leilani registered the pulse in her neck jump. "Has he taken anything?"

"Still working the inventory," said the Navy LT. "But at least two antique clubs and a feathered helmet are unaccounted for."

Isaac slid the folder onto the table, opened to a page of Naalei's handwriting. "We need to add this to the mix. Souza used community contacts for details on the death rites. We believe he manipulated my partner's mother and several of the other elders into giving him specifics about the protocols. She kept detailed notes."

The officers exchanged glances. Castellano paused, then picked up the book and leafed through it. "This matches the ritual elements found at every scene. Down to the cordage, even the pigment."

Leilani let the line hang, then added. "It gets worse.

My mother says he's already reached out to several other cultural practitioners. He's crowd-sourcing authenticity."

Chang grunted, leaning forward. "He's an academic. No way he's the type to get his hands dirty."

"Respectfully, sir," said Leilani. "That's exactly how he avoids detection. He lets others do the physical work, and he scripts the rituals. He's not looking for credit or a legacy."

Castellano slid a printout down the table. "This is the kicker. NCIS intercepted an encrypted message sent from Souza's university account to an address in the Philippines. The text is a string of metaphors, but the subtext is clear. He's recruiting. He's ready for a new cycle."

A cold weight settled in the room. Even the officers seemed to absorb the shift.

Isaac spoke low and even. "He won't do the work himself, but he'll enable the next Holt. He probably already has."

Castellano nodded. "That's why we're here at oh-six-hundred, instead of eating doughnuts upstairs." Her eyes, sharp and deliberate, settled on Leilani. "You were right to push reopening the case. I'm not above saying it. We should have seen this coming."

It felt like a rare and precious thing, that admission, and it changed the temperature in the room.

"What's our play?" asked Chang, all business now.

"We start with Souza's last known associates. Anyone he's called or texted in the last month," said

Castellano. "We'll lock down every base and public event he's mentioned in his postings. He won't be able to walk a block without running into someone in uniform."

Isaac tapped the table. "I'll run the artifacts angle. If he needs more objects, he'll have to hit a collector or a black market contact."

The Navy LT finally spoke. "If he's talking to someone in the Philippines, he might be prepping an escape. You want us to flag the airport?"

"Do it," said Castellano, already moving. "And get facial recognition on every harbor camera for the last 48 hours. If he's headed for a boat, I want to know before he sets foot on the dock."

She turned to Leilani. "Can you have your mother reach out to her network again? If he's sniffing around for details, she'll hear it first."

Leilani nodded, the pieces falling into place.

The two officers left, hurrying out with a sense of purpose. The door swung shut behind them.

For the first time that morning, Castellano exhaled. She ran a hand over her face and looked at Leilani as a partner.

"He's planning something bigger," Castellano said, quiet now. "We can't let him finish."

She didn't add "this time," but the words lingered, anyway.

They cleaned up the evidence boards, stacking files in tidy columns, and Leilani felt like she might be closing in on the spiral instead of circling its edge. Outside, the day had gone from gold to hot white. But the cold in the basement hadn't budged. And across the island, the next move had already begun.

Chapter Forty-Seven

Isaac's cubicle looked like a crash site for a bad paper airplane contest. Printouts spewed from the tiny black-and-white laser printer in wild, half-curled streams. Open laptops fought for real estate with three legal pads, each bristling with colored tabs and the occasional dried-out highlighter. He sat cross-legged on his rolling chair, a cup of vending-machine espresso balanced in one hand, and tapped out numbers on a TI calculator older than most of the interns.

He'd been at it for hours, following the money. The route wound from Pearl's accounting logs to offshore banks, then bounced to obscure antique shops and eBay sellers. A half-dozen wire transfers, all sub-ten-thousand to avoid SAR flags, but the patterns were the same. He always paid in cryptocurrency, always routed through shell corporations that led to a Singapore entity called Kupu Heritage Foundation.

He keyed up the next PDF. It was an invoice for weapons restoration, Kehlani & Sons. Four traditional clubs, three sets of feathered adornments, and a handmade koa-wood dagger. He matched the serial numbers on the invoice to the catalog numbers at the Bishop Museum, where, according to the records, the pieces were on temporary display pending repatriation. That was bullshit. The repatriation had already happened, just not to the museum.

A dull ache formed behind his eyes. He reached for the cold espresso, took a sip, then found Leilani stalking the bullpen, phone to her ear and brows furrowed. He called out low. "Lei, you need to see this."

She clicked off her call and walked into the cubicle. Her hair was back in a no-nonsense bun, and her gaze cut right through the mess. "What have you got?"

He swiveled the laptop, pointing to the screen. "Souza's account is the spine of the entire operation. He buys the weapons, the cordage, even the pigment, and then he distributes them to his people. I found an email to Holt's known burner phone, referencing a necessary gift for the first ceremony."

Leilani bent over the screen, her hands braced on the desk. "This is a koa dagger?"

"Custom. Market value's north of ten grand, and they're only made by three craftsmen." He flicked to a set of eBay receipts. "Souza bought two, delivered to two different PO boxes. Both were forwarded to a third location, a storage locker in Kalihi. I'm betting that's where he staged every kill kit."

She nodded, tight and controlled. "Did you match anything to the last two murders?"

He riffled through the printouts. "Yes. Same seller, same account. For the fifth murder, Souza upgraded. The invoice is for a two-handed war club. It's exactly what forensics found at the last scene."

Leilani straightened. "He was building up. Each kill, more elaborate. He's not just preserving tradition. He's escalating."

"Exactly." Isaac stabbed a finger at the next printout. "And look at this. In the last week, he made a bulk order of ti leaves, salt, and five hundred feet of woven cordage. That's three times what was needed for all prior murders combined."

She looked at him, eyes flat. "He's planning a group event or something for mass effect."

Isaac nodded, the queasy satisfaction of the puzzle coming together. "It fits. Souza's house is cleared out, his office stripped. The university says he's on an unplanned sabbatical, effective yesterday. He's not running. He's deploying."

Leilani focused on the timeline on the wall. "He's got the supplies, the gear and a new set of hands to do the work."

He held her gaze. "You think he'll do it himself this time?"

She considered that. "He's the priest. He needs an offering. He'll pick another proxy."

Isaac pointed at the screen. "We have to find the new proxy."

She let the thought percolate; the silence thick with anticipation and dread.

Isaac leaned back, a smile ghosting the corners of his mouth. "Not bad for a day's work."

Leilani grinned, fierce and fleeting. "We're not finished."

He nodded. "Never said we were."

She scribbled a note on her phone. "Set up an ops meeting. Pull everything we have on anyone in Souza's sphere. Students, former associates, everyone with a grudge against the military. Grab Espinoza; he can help. Coordinate with Castellano's team and cross-reference our list with theirs. Let's see if anyone pops to the top."

Isaac looked around at the tangle of printouts, the mosaic of clues, and the stack of half-drunk coffees. For a moment, he let himself enjoy the pride. He caught her watching him, and the look they shared said it all. It was a race now.

He started a new folder, labeled it "Escalation," and began the countdown.

Outside the window, the sun blazed, and the city shimmered. But in the conference room at HPD, the hunt had entered its next phase, and the island's oldest war had found a new battlefield.

Chapter Forty-Eight

The Halawa interview room felt colder than the rest of the prison. A metal table sat bolted to the tile, with two chairs for the interviewers and one for the prisoner, which sat an inch lower, just enough to establish hierarchy. The lights glared with the violence of a place that didn't care if you blinked or not.

Holt sat in his orange jumpsuit, hands cuffed and chained to the table leg, but he looked more like an athlete at rest than a convict awaiting transfer. His posture ramrod-straight, eyes steady and his hair trimmed close enough to reveal the scars on his scalp. In the brightness, the dark circles under his eyes stood out like a fighter's mask.

Leilani and Castellano entered together, Castellano dropping a manila envelope with a thud before she'd even pulled out her chair. Leilani took the seat across from Holt, her hands clasped and silent, refusing the legal pad this time.

Castellano got straight to it. "We know you didn't act alone. We know you had help before, and you're covering for him now. Why?"

Holt's gaze flickered. The left corner of his mouth quirked up, but he didn't speak.

Leilani fanned out the photos from the envelope. Souza at the protest, Souza in a meeting with Holt, Souza's email headers, and even the weapon invoices. She let the images speak for themselves. She tapped the one where Souza's hand sat on Holt's shoulder.

"We know he taught you," she said. "We know he supplied the weapons. And we know he's setting up someone else for what comes next."

Holt's eyes dropped to the photos. He studied each for a long moment. "You think you're the first to catch him in a lie?"

Castellano slammed her palm against the table. The cuffs rattled. "Stop talking in riddles. People are going to die if you don't help us stop him."

He grinned at her like a predator eyeing its next meal. He turned to Leilani. "She doesn't get it," he said. "She thinks it's about weapons, or bodies. But Souza, he's more patient than either of you. He's not after a headline."

Leilani said nothing; instead she watched the way his pupils narrowed as she pushed the last photo closer.

"You were his trial run," she said. "Now he's looking for a true believer to finish the ritual."

Holt's fingers curled against the table. "I was never supposed to finish," he said. "That wasn't the point."

Castellano bit back a curse. "So what is? What does Souza want?"

"He wants the old world back," Holt said, his voice eerily calm. "He wants it to mean something again. The murders were a message, but the message needed to be answered. That's why I did what I did."

Leilani leaned so that their shadows merged on the table. "He's recruited a new acolyte. If you know who it is, you need to tell us."

He closed his eyes, lips pressed together. When he opened them, the blue was gone, replaced by something almost black. "The next one's not like me. He's younger and angrier. He'll do whatever Souza asks, because he thinks he's the only one who's ever understood him."

A chill crept up Leilani's neck. "Who is he?"

"Look at Souza's student lists," Holt said slowly. "Start with anyone who failed out, anyone who got disciplined for violence. He likes his warriors unbalanced."

Castellano made a note, then stared Holt down. "You're still an accessory. If people die, it's on you."

He didn't flinch. "I've already paid."

The silence settled, heavy as a grave.

Finally, Leilani stood and gathered the photos. She paused, her hand on the door.

"Why did you let yourself get caught?" she asked, not looking back.

Holt smiled, teeth too white for prison. "Because you have to draw the line somewhere. He told me to go out on my shield, but I'm not a fool. If you catch him, burn every piece of him to ashes. If you don't, the next cycle of killings is on your head."

Outside, in the hall, Castellano walked ahead, not speaking until they reached the checkpoint.

"We don't have enough for a warrant," she said. "But if Holt's right, Souza will make his next move soon."

Leilani nodded. She played back Holt's words. "He wants the old world back. The murders were a message, but the message needed to be answered." She thought of the bulk orders, the student files, and the growing instability on Oahu.

Souza hadn't just used Holt as a pawn; he'd set the entire law enforcement apparatus on fire, kept them circling the wrong enemy, while his actual operation gathered in the dark. As they reached the sally port, Leilani exhaled, slow and controlled.

Castellano caught her gaze. "What are you thinking?"

"That the last murder is only the beginning," Leilani said. "He wants to make a point. And we're the intended audience."

Castellano nodded. "We stop him before the curtain call."

They moved fast, each in their lane. The air outside the prison shimmered with heat and the promise of violence. Leilani thought she knew exactly what she was up against. Holt had been a weapon. Souza was the war. And the clock was running out.

Chapter Forty-Nine

Chief Mori's office looked nothing like the precinct war rooms or the tactical conference spaces in the federal building. Her space was all sharp edges and smooth surfaces, broken only by the old-school map of Oahu that spanned the back wall, each district outlined by hand in red. In front of the map, a sideboard with neat stacks of case folders, each tabbed and color-coded. The only sign of disorder: the three dry-erase boards set at an angle, each one crowded with names, dates and a lattice of colored lines converging on the same half-dozen place names.

Mori sat behind a Koa wood desk, her fingers steepled beneath her chin. She watched Leilani, Isaac and Castellano file in, then gestured to the three visitor chairs set directly across from her.

"Let's get to it," she said.

Castellano opened, her voice stripped of the usual sarcasm. "We have confirmation that Professor Tao Souza is the intellectual author of the base murders, and likely the orchestrator of an imminent attack or escalation. The evidence is clear: financials, artifact sourcing, encrypted communication, and repeated presence at key locations just prior to each incident."

Mori's eyes flicked from Castellano to Leilani. "You agree?"

"Yes, Chief," said Leilani. "Holt was the weapon. Souza's the strategist. We think he's identified a new proxy. All signs point to an imminent escalation."

Mori picked up a yellow legal pad and scribbled a date. "Targets?"

Isaac stepped in. "He's mapped all his prior activity to symbolic locations, heiaus, ancient battlegrounds, and now, likely the Aliamanu Crater. There's been a surge in purchases of ceremonial materials. We think it'll be an open-air ritual, not a hidden kill."

Mori circled a spot on the map and nodded. "So, did we have the wrong man in lockup all this time?"

Leilani's jaw clenched. "Not wrong. Incomplete. Holt killed five, but Souza enabled it. Holt confessed, but everything he did was scripted by someone else."

Castellano added, "Military intelligence now rates Souza as a Tier 2 insider threat. His writings advocate for a cleansing of military presence, and he's got a documented history of access to both secure and public areas."

A pause, long enough to make Isaac shift in his seat.

Mori glared at the map, eyes narrowed, then leaned back. "And what's your proposed solution?"

Leilani laid out the plan. "We deploy simultaneous coverage on the top three locations. We bring in the university's security, the shore patrol and every HPD officer within call range. No uniforms: we go low-visibility, low-profile. We flag every registered weapon purchase within Souza's known circle. And we monitor communications on the hour."

Mori digested this, then nodded. "Do it."

She picked up her phone and speed-dialed the duty officer. "Kainoa. Activate a code red for the city and the shoreline. All traffic out of the city gets checked, all ports, all airstrips. Send the order to every unit commander. And tell legal to have the warrants on my desk by six."

She disconnected the call, then addressed Leilani directly. "He's coming for you next."

It wasn't a question.

Leilani felt a chill but didn't blink. "He wants a public ending. My gut says it will happen at the history presentations at Kai's school."

Mori's face softened, just a crack. "Stay close to your family. Don't let Kai or your mother out of your sight."

Leilani nodded, feeling the gravity of the moment.

Mori folded her hands, the gesture absolute. "If you need anything, I'll burn down half the city to get it for you. Understood?"

"Understood, Chief."

The meeting ended. Outside, the sky had turned a steely blue, as a storm rolled in from the west. In the elevator, Castellano let out a breath she'd held since the meeting started.

"She's scared for you," Castellano said, her voice almost gentle.

"She's scared for everyone," Leilani replied.

They rode in silence, each ticking off their next moves.

By the time the doors opened, the precinct was

already buzzing, phones and radios chirping at maximum tempo. The red marks on the map were real now, no longer just theories. Every available officer was on alert, and the city had gone from routine to a locked-down crucible in a single briefing.

But in Leilani's head, the war wasn't over. Not until she'd caught Souza or stopped whatever new cycle he'd set in motion. She thought of her mother and Kai, both unaware, both waiting at home, both bright spots in the coming darkness. She needed to stop this before it started. No more ghosts. No more spirals. This time, the story would end on her terms.

Chapter Fifty

The kitchen was a bubble of light while everything else was blue shadow and the distant susurrus of trade winds battering the louvers. Leilani sat at the island, her laptop open, and her phone buzzing with a relentless stream of group texts, alerts from the chief, status checks from Isaac, and last-minute updates from the teams staking out Souza's suspected haunts. But tonight, for the next thirty minutes, the war would have to wait. Her son sat cross-legged on a stool, bent over a poster board and a shoebox full of printed images, a strip of double-sided tape stuck to his forehead like a tribal mark.

She glanced at the mockup. The title in block letters (Ancient Hawaiian Warriors), a line of petroglyph cutouts, and a series of weapons and heiau images glued in neat progression. He had even drawn a cartoon version of a feathered helmet, bright orange and red, captioned "Ali'i Power!" in a bubble.

"Nice touch," she said, pointing to the cartoon. "That's very mana."

Kai beamed. "Grandma said the ali'i never went anywhere without their helmet. Even for breakfast."

He snorted, then peeled another photo, this one of a carved spear, and stuck it down, tongue between his teeth. "Do you think my teacher will like it?"

"She'll love it," Leilani said, trying to keep her own voice from shaking. She'd lived through riots, death threats, and more than one shootout, but the idea of someone taking this moment from her made her want to burn the world to ash.

She set her phone on silent, swept the worst of the tension off her face, and helped Kai punch out the title letters for his display. When he lost interest, he pulled a sheet from his folder and handed it over.

"My report," he said, proud. "You said to check the spelling."

She scanned it. The first paragraph was a cut-and-paste from Wikipedia, but the rest was pure Kai.

When the first warriors came to Hawaii, they learned to fight the land and the sea. The chiefs protected the people by being brave and strong. But sometimes they had to do scary things so the spirits would not get mad. My grandma taught me about this because her job is to remember old stuff.

She smiled, just a little.

Kai grabbed a marker, scribbled out a line, then said, "Mom?"

"Yeah?"

"Professor Souza helped me a lot with my research. He gave me books and said you would be proud."

She remembered Mori's warning. "He's coming for you next", and felt the cold, electric certainty of the net closing.

"Did you see him anywhere else?" she asked, as evenly as she could.

Kai shrugged. "At the grocery store. He saw Grandma there last week. And he walked past my soccer practice, but that's because the university is across the field." He looked at her, puzzled. "Why?"

She forced a smile. "Making sure I thank him in person. Did he ever give you anything besides books?"

"A shell necklace," Kai said. "Said it would bring me luck. See?" He pulled it out from under his shirt. Cowrie shells strung with blue cord. A subtle signature, easy to miss.

She cupped his chin and made him look her in the eye. "Listen, bug. If you ever see anyone who acts weird, you go straight to your teacher, okay? Don't talk to them, don't take anything from them, just get safe. You remember what we practiced?"

He went solemn. "Yes, Mom. Emergency code, find a grown-up, stay put."

She ruffled his hair, tried not to let her hands shake. "That's my warrior."

She set her phone to vibrate, called up the recent calls and found Isaac's number.

He answered on the first ring, voice taut. "Yeah?"

"I still think he's going to target the school's open house tomorrow. He knows I'll be there."

"We can lock it down and fill the school with uniforms," said Isaac. "How do you want to play it?"

"Let's keep it low-key," she said. "Borrow a couple of plainclothes officers from the surveillance unit. He wants a spectacle. I don't think he wants to kill me or my family. He's coming to finish his ritual with an audience."

“We’ll be ready,” Isaac said. “Do not let Kai out of your sight. I’ll get eyes on the campus tonight.”

“Copy that,” she said, already moving to her go-bag in the pantry.

She looked at her son, who was now coloring the border of his poster with glitter markers, oblivious. For a moment, she let herself watch him. The line of his jaw, just like hers, and the fierce set of his mouth when he concentrated. She memorized every bit.

She called Naalei. “Mom, I’m going to send a patrol car to pick you up for the school’s open house. In the meantime, keep your doors locked, and if you see anyone near the house call 911. I’ll drop Kai and his project off at school and then come back for the presentation.”

Her mother didn’t ask questions. “No problem. I love you, Lei.”

“I love you, too,” Leilani said. She hit the red button before her own voice broke.

The night was calm, the kitchen thick with the smell of glue and printer ink, and the steady thrum of an island holding its breath. At midnight, as Kai snored softly in his room, Leilani sat by the door, badge in one hand and the old notebook from Naalei in the other. She flipped to the page with the circled word, the last, most important lesson:

Kūpaʻa: Stand firm. Even when you standalone.

She would. In the morning, she would go to war. Not with clubs or knives, but with the truth, and the hope that her boy would live to write his own story.

The old world could try to reclaim itself. But this time, it would have to get through her first.

Chapter Fifty-One

The HPD task force conference room looked nothing like it had twenty-four hours ago. Every spare inch of whiteboard bristled with satellite photos, evacuation flowcharts, and hand-drawn maps of Kai's elementary school, side entrances, fire lanes, field layouts, all cross-referenced with faculty rosters and even the schedule for the school's cafeteria deliveries. The air hummed with the aroma of burned coffee and dry-erase marker, and the lingering static charge of a department on Code Red.

Leilani paced the far wall, her fingertips tracing the edges of the printed school floor plans, the other hand clenched around a half-crushed water bottle. Every few seconds, she glanced at the cluster at the table, where Castellano, Isaac and a uniformed patrol supervisor argued in clipped, professional bursts. The last time she'd seen this much focus, it had been in the immediate aftermath of a line-of-duty shooting. Now the threat came not from a shooter, but from the oldest, strangest part of her own history.

Castellano held court at the head of the table, her eyes bloodshot but her voice hard. She used a black Sharpie to sketch triangles on the map, each one a plainclothes officer, every approach road bracketed by unmarked vehicles, and every entry watched by a tight circle of undercover officers disguised as volunteer dads, teachers, even a janitor with an actual mop and keys. She didn't so much speak as dictate.

"No one moves in or out without passing two

checkpoints," Castellano said. "Every adult in the building gets facial recognition at the door, and we cycle through the visitor list every ten minutes. The minute Souza is visible, he gets flagged, and we green light the intercept."

Isaac sipped from his thermos, his tie already loosened, tapping notes into a tablet. "We're running comms on three nets, one for interior, one for perimeter, and one off-books encrypted. My guys have the entire surveillance system mirrored on the fusion center servers." He flicked to a digital copy of the same floor plan, this one peppered with icons and color-coded overlays. "If he tries to jam or cut the feeds, we'll know before he does."

Leilani said nothing but took in every detail. She stood close enough to see the glisten of caffeine sweat on Castellano's brow, the jitter in Isaac's leg, and the silent, measured breaths of the patrol supervisor as she reviewed the assignments. The plan, on paper, left little to chance. But in her gut, Leilani could already feel where the holes would open, what the textbook never captured, and what the textbooks would never admit about people like Souza.

Her own prep went far beyond the maps. A printed sheet with Souza's most recent driver's license photo lay on the table, weighed down by a paper cup. She picked it up, studied the details: the nose wider than memory suggested, the faint scar near the right eye, and the way his hair seemed to thin from year to year. She forced herself to remember the little things: his habit of keeping his hands steepled, his tendency to walk with one shoulder hunched a fraction higher than the other. Even with all the digital muscle in the world, it would come down to someone seeing him with their own eyes.

Castellano paused in her briefing, catching Leilani's stare. "You got input?" she said, not hostile, but not friendly either.

Leilani answered without hesitation. "He'll use the event itself as cover. Too many parents, too many moving bodies. He'll walk in with the crowd and rely on no one looking for him in plain sight. I don't care how many off-duty officers you pack into the gym, he'll outsmart anyone who expects a Hollywood bad guy in a mask."

The patrol supervisor added, "He'll have a backup plan. Even if we spot him, he won't panic. He'll let us move in, then use the distraction to slip away."

"Or to get to the real target," Isaac added. He looked at Leilani, eyebrow raised. "You think it's about you or about Kai?"

Leilani noticed the question tighten her spine. "He's obsessed with the narrative, the ritual. If he's here to make a statement, he wants me to watch it happen. It's about what comes after, whether we fall apart or stand up."

Castellano snapped the marker in half and tossed the dead side in the bin. "We put you front and center. You attend as a parent, play it normal, but we put a two-person detail within ten feet. No comms earpiece, and nothing visible."

Leilani's voice remained even. "And what about my

mother? She'll be there as well. She's as stubborn as," she caught herself, shrugged, "as the rest of us."

"She's not trained," Castellano said flatly.

"She's not going to take no for an answer," Leilani replied.

The door swung open, and for a moment everyone in the room braced, expecting either the chief or, worse, a last-minute press liaison. Instead, it was Naalei. She wore a dark blue muʻumuʻu and her gray hair pinned back, but the set of her jaw could have cracked granite. She held no bags, no phone, only the steely self-assurance of a kumu hula walking into a room of unfriendly judges.

She didn't wait for introductions. "I'll be there," she announced to the room. "He'll recognize me, and I'll recognize him. If he's disguised or if he tries to act as someone else, I'll see through it. I taught him most of what he knows."

Castellano rose a fraction from her seat, her body language a challenge. "We already have cultural experts in the crowd. Police volunteers, university staff—"

Naalei cut her off. "And Souza has spent the last decade teaching his followers how to fake ancient traditions for a crowd. He'll mimic what he's seen, but he'll leave a signature in the way he ties his sash or the way he kneels. He can't help it."

Silence, heavy as concrete.

Isaac broke it. "She's got a point. It makes sense to make the statement to the person who knows the code."

Leilani stepped forward, placing herself between her mother and the hard stare of Castellano. "She'll be safe with me. If Souza wants a cultural audience, we make it clear that's all he gets."

Castellano shifted, weighing the risk. "If either of you gets hurt, it's my badge and yours."

"I won't let that happen," Leilani said.

Naalei's gaze softened, and she let a hand brush her daughter's arm. "We do this together."

The supervisor scribbled something on her pad, then spoke up. "We can place her in the audience, three rows back, flanked by our undercover units. She observes, nothing more. If she sees him first, she texts or signals the detail and falls back."

Castellano exhaled. "Fine. But if it turns, you both clear the scene. Immediately."

Naalei's smile came from somewhere much older than the room, or the case, or even the island. "That's the plan."

They ran through the logistics twice more, Castellano running the scenarios, Isaac cross-checking for gaps. The teams would rotate in waves, no group on for more than ninety minutes. The interior corridors would be watched by two rotating details, with spotters planted at the gym, the outdoor lunch area, and every choke point between the parking lot and the classroom. Kai's class will present at 10:10 AM, just after the school's ceremonial hula and the principal's address. There would be no intercom announcement; the whole thing would unfold in real time, the oldest trap in the book.

In the hour before the operation, Leilani caught her mother by the coffee station, filling two paper cups with weak, over-stewed brew. Neither spoke, but stood side-by-side, watching the tactical ballet unfold beyond the glass partition.

Naalei handed her a cup. "He'll try to talk, first. He always did. You let him. He wants to be heard before he ends it."

Leilani sipped and allowed herself to want something more than justice. "What if he says the right thing? What if I want to believe him?"

Her mother's voice gentled, "You already know the truth. Your job isn't to believe or not believe, but to listen and decide what needs to be done."

They lingered in the silence until the first team mustered at the door, tactical vests hidden beneath windbreakers, weapons stowed out of sight.

Back in the conference room, Isaac waited with a packet of earpieces, all individually sealed. He handed one to Leilani. "Wear it," he said. "For me."

She pressed it into her palm and nodded. "Only because I like your voice better than the rest."

He managed a tired grin. He turned to Castellano. "You're sure about the cross-check on the volunteer IDs?"

Castellano barely glanced up from her phone. "Triple-checked. Any more secure and we'd have to lock down the PTA, too."

They walked together to the elevator, silence stretching like taffy, the sense of finality settling over them. This was the last prep, the last chance to say what had been left unsaid.

At the threshold, Castellano turned to Leilani. "Don't improvise. If you see him, you step back and let the team take it."

"I'll try," Leilani said.

Castellano smiled, the first real one all week. "You won't. But I had to say it."

They exited into the lot. The city glittered in the pre-dawn, all the rain washed away by trade winds, the sky that bone-clear blue that only happened in the hour before sunup.

Leilani stood with her mother, the two of them ringed by the sound of the engines, the urgent footfalls of a department readying for siege. Above them, the stars were already fading, and the old ghosts of the island retreated before the coming light.

She took Naalei's hand, squeezed it. "We're ready," she said.

Her mother smiled. "We'll see."

The car doors opened, and the women got in, the glass swallowing them whole. Tomorrow, everything will be different. But today, at least, the Kealoha family went to battle together.

Chapter Fifty-Two

Leilani drove the battered Explorer east, headlights off, letting the waxing dawn set the world into existence one shade at a time. The city had not yet woken; no traffic on the Pali, no runners in neon bibs, just the wind in the ironwoods and the ocean's hush, a half-mile off. In the passenger seat, Naalei rode with her hands in her lap, her gaze fixed on the oncoming blue of morning, not even pretending to check her phone.

The heiau they aimed for didn't appear on most tourist maps. It crouched low on a bluff above the water, a horseshoe of moss-stained basalt blocks ringed by plumeria gone wild and the spindly, almost comical grass of the island's old goat trails. They parked at the maintenance pullout and walked the last hundred yards, the sky overhead already milked with the first streaks of orange and pink.

No one else was there, not even the usual clutch of early-bird meditators, who sometimes gathered at the perimeter to hum or snap selfies. The silence belonged only to the birds, the clatter of the sea wind, and the measured footfalls of the Kealoha women.

At the boundary of the stone, Naalei stopped. She opened her small shoulder bag and took out a tied cloth bundle. Ti leaves folded and bound, a packet of sea salt, two glossy kukui nuts, and a stub of 'awa root, pale and almost toothlike. She lined them up on the flattest stone and pressed her thumb to the center of each item, a gesture half-invocation, half-inspection.

For the first time, Leilani noticed her mother's hands trembled as she worked.

"You cold?" she said, as lightly as she could.

Naalei shook her head, but didn't look up. "My mother used to say the ancestors hated the taste of morning. Too clean. Too honest."

Leilani watched the methodical arrangement of the leaves and salt. "You never told me she did this."

Naalei almost smiled. "She never told me either. She just showed up every morning and expected me to remember." She paused, searching her daughter's face. "That's why I asked you to come."

They worked together. Leilani found a flat spot on the stone and took the items as they came, salt, then kukui, then the root. Each time she took one, Naalei's hand brushed hers, the tremor bolder than before. Still, the old woman's eyes stayed sharp.

"Sit," she said. Leilani did, folding her knees under her and letting the chill of the rock seep through her jeans.

The ritual was not for tourists. It belonged to mornings like this, when the world was still soft around the edges and the only company was the expectation that something, someone, might be listening. Naalei untied the bundle and scattered the salt in a thin, deliberate arc before them. She pressed the kukui nuts together and rolled them between her palms, muttering a short chant so low it seemed to come from the stone itself. The ʻawa root she placed at the apex of the arc, then spat in her palm, wiped it clean, and set the leaves upright like a small, defiant flag.

Leilani waited, holding her breath. In the growing light, her mother's profile looked both ancient and newly fragile. The woman who'd survived the birth of a child alone, three hurricanes, and a decade of city council budget cuts now struggled to keep her fingers steady. But her voice, when it rose for the chant, cut through the salt air like a bell. It carried none of the museum-pronunciation stiffness of the mainland experts or the over-practiced showmanship of the hula festival. It was the unembellished language of someone asking for protection, not a favor.

Naalei finished the chant, then scooped up a palmful of dew from the ti leaves and pressed it to her daughter's forehead. "Kūpa'a," she said, the word echoing in the shell of Leilani's ear. "Stand firm. Even if you standalone."

A small silence, then Naalei sat next to her, not touching, just shoulder to shoulder. The horizon blazed up with the first spike of the yellow sun.

Leilani's eyes bore into the stone, the arc of salt, the little tableau of tradition held together by nothing but faith and muscle memory. "He's going to use the ritual, Mom. The old one. Only he's changed it. He's made it into something that kills."

"He doesn't know what he's doing," said Naalei, soft but certain.

"He knows enough. He's twisted everything you taught."

Naalei's jaw flexed. "That's how it works.

Knowledge and pain, mixed without wisdom, become weapons."

They watched the sea in silence. A single shearwater looped overhead, the same bird that haunted the bluff every morning, sharp-beaked and hungry. Leilani let the wind numb her, let the salt air do its work.

She said, "You told me the old rituals weren't about hurting people."

"They weren't." Naalei considered the words. "They were about keeping the story whole. If you fought, it was to protect. If you buried the dead, you did it to guide them to peace. Even the darkest ceremonies had a reason: to stop the curse, not to make it grow."

"Souza doesn't believe that. He thinks the island needs to be cleansed. That's his word."

Naalei nodded. "He's not the first."

"Why him?" asked Leilani. "Why now?"

Her mother wrapped the ti leaves into a tight bundle, then bound them with a twist of her own gray hair, pulled straight from the bun. "When you have the gift of the ancient ways, it's a kind of hunger. You think if you use it loud enough, you'll fill the hole inside you. Some people use it to heal. Some can only break what they touch."

She tucked the bundle into Leilani's jacket, right over her heart. "Don't let him trick you into thinking you're the same."

Leilani let her head fall forward, eyes squeezed

shut. “What if he’s right? What if I’m just trying to control the story instead of fix it?”

Naalei reached over, set her palm on her daughter’s chest, gentle but absolute. “You listen to the ancestors, but you choose for yourself. If you ever forget the difference, you’ll turn into him.”

The sun now cleared the ocean’s rim, burning away the morning blue. With it came the first sounds of traffic, a distant engine rev, the lost call of a radio somewhere in town. They sat a few minutes longer. When the salt ring had scattered and the last of the dew had dried from Leilani’s skin, they stood together and gathered the ritual refuse.

Naalei lingered near the stones, one hand trailing over the moss as if to say a private goodbye. She fell in step with her daughter, lighter now, or at least, steadier. In the Explorer, with the heater blasting out the damp, Leilani started the ignition. She didn’t look at her mother, but she didn’t need to. The weight in her chest had changed, subtle but real. Not lighter, exactly, but settled. Understood. They drove back in silence, the city waking up around them, and the world now flooded with color and noise. At the stoplight near Kai’s school, Naalei finally spoke.

“If you have to choose between catching him and saving your boy, you know what you have to do.”

Leilani gripped the wheel and nodded once. “I do.”

They pulled up to the curb, the first of the school’s families already crowding the sidewalk, poster boards and potluck casseroles in hand. The air was thick with expectation, nerves and the perfume of every flowered lei within a five-mile radius.

"Ready?" said Naalei.

"No," said Leilani, but she smiled. "Let's do it anyway."

They left the car, shouldered their bags, and walked into the bright, dangerous morning, ready to stand together for whatever came next.

Chapter Fifty-Three

Isaac hunched over his laptop, the glow from the monitor painting his face ghost-white in the dim HPD conference room. Coffee rings bloomed on every flat surface, and the floor shimmered with a confetti of PowerBar wrappers, sticky notes, and half-shredded printouts. The bullpen behind him pulsed with low voices, the nervous tempo of a department living on pure caffeine and last warnings.

Castellano stalked the length of the room, her arms folded, and her blazer half-on and half-off as if she'd been interrupted in mid-molt. She kept checking her phone, thumbing the screen for updates, then glancing at the door like she expected a SWAT team to burst through at any moment.

"How much longer?" she barked. Her voice was as flat as a tire.

Isaac didn't even look up. "It's not a password. It's a logic gate, custom-coded. Whoever built this, they really didn't want anyone snooping." His fingers blurred across the keys. "But it's all brute force in the end."

Castellano grunted. "I've got base security combing every port, every private airstrip. Still no sign. I don't like working blind."

He sniffed, then turned the laptop to face her. "Give me a word Souza would use for a folder with his most precious ideas."

She scowled and thought for a beat. "Kupuna, or

Kuleana. I saw that on half his published manifestos."

Isaac typed in the permutations. The last one worked.

A file tree exploded across the screen. Nested inside the dense forest of PDFs and lesson plans lay a single folder, marked by a blue spiral icon. He double-clicked. Pages of handwritten text loaded, each scanned with the discipline of an archivist and dated as recently as last night.

He leaned in, reading. Castellano hovered over his shoulder. She started reading aloud.

"The islands must be purified in the ancient way. Every sacrifice removes the stain of occupation. The final offering will awaken all Hawaii to the truth. They will see, at last, that our strength is not in the sword, but in the memory of who we once were."

She paged down, eyes raking the screen. "He lists the victims," Castellano said, voice growing tight. "Each one isn't random. They're chosen for maximum impact, symbolic to both the military and to Hawaiian sovereignty nuts. He's got names, ranks, even times."

Isaac swore, low and sharp. "It's not just Kai's school. He's planning simultaneous events, or at least, he wants us to think he is. There's a reference here to a final symbolic act that will echo across the Pacific."

Castellano's jaw flexed. "He's not going to kill a single target. He wants a spectacle like a hostage situation or worse."

Isaac scanned ahead, eyes narrowing. "There's more. He calls it the Reckoning of Wākea. Old cosmology. It means a reset, the return to zero." He stopped. "He wants to trigger a chain reaction, not just one killing. Like a martyr, but bigger."

They stared at each other; the implication settled like silt.

Castellano pulled out her phone and dialed with surgical precision. "Get every plainclothes unit to Kai's school and double the detail. Lock down every exit and entrance. Notify the base command and put security details on every flagged target. We have a credible manifesto and an imminent threat. Move."

She tried Leilani's number. It rang four times and went to voicemail. She tried again. Still nothing.

"He's already there," Isaac said. "Or he's waiting for her to show up."

Castellano jammed her files into a bag. "We need to move."

They sprinted through the bullpen, weaving past a uniformed officer shouting into a radio and a detective who looked like he'd been sleeping on the copy machine. In the elevator, Castellano hit the button three times, as if force could bend physics.

Isaac glanced at her. "Do you ever get the feeling we're the last to the party?"

She huffed. "We're not late until the first shot goes off."

The elevator doors parted, and they bolted, two shadows racing the morning sun. In the parking garage, as they slid into the pool car, Castellano called HQ one more time. "Activate city-wide lockdown protocols.

And send a chopper to circle the school. If you see anything out of place, you go full red."

Isaac watched the city whip past, already plotting the run from the curb to the auditorium. The thought of Leilani and her boy in the crosshairs felt like the bitter edge of déjà vu, a childhood of waiting for the bad news call, the certainty that the world always took the wrong parent.

"We'll get there," Castellano said, as if reading his mind.

He nodded, gripping the wheel, with his eyes locked on the road and on the impossible. And behind them, in the empty precinct, the digital glow of Souza's manifesto burned through the screen, the words a spell waiting to be broken.

Chapter Fifty-Four

The gymnasium at Kahala Elementary School swelled with the noise only a hundred nervous families could make. Paper banners looped the rafters, every color of the rainbow, hand-painted with kids' names and stick-figure soldiers. The folding chairs were set in rigid rows, but every aisle overflowed with parents in Aloha shirts, siblings running loose, and teachers shepherding packs of students like anxious duck mothers.

Leilani paused inside the main entrance and surveyed the crowd. To a civilian, it looked like any end-of-year history fair. But she saw the shapes in the margins, the undercover HPD officer at the sign-in table, a plainclothes marine dad manning the bake sale, the PTA member whose injured knee gave her an excuse to linger in the doorway with a suspicious bulge beneath her sundress. Near the side exit, the janitor with a mop and bucket worked the same five square feet for fifteen minutes, his stance too controlled to fool anyone who'd done time in surveillance. The security net, such as it was, wouldn't stop a suicide bomber or a spree shooter. But it was tight enough to catch a man like Souza. Unless, of course, he decided not to show up at all.

She spotted Kai and Naalei near the stage, her mother fussing over the boy's shirt, combing his hair with her fingers and straightening the shell necklace at his throat. He stood still for it, only rolling his eyes when he thought no one was looking. When he saw

Leilani, he flashed her a thumbs-up, then mimed putting on a samurai helmet with an exaggerated flourish.

She smiled, letting the sight of her son sink in for a second, then slipped through the crowd to her assigned seat. The ti leaf bundle still rested over her heart, tight against the body armor she wore beneath her blouse. She felt ridiculous for it, but then remembered the taste of sea salt and her mother's thumb pressing her forehead at dawn.

Kai's teacher took the mic. "We'll begin with the fourth grade. Thank you for being here, and please silence your phones until the end of the program."

There was a shuffling of bodies, the hush of adults trying to be on their best behavior.

Kai's class lined up along the stage, holding their project boards above their heads. The parade of posters—"King Kamehameha's Conquests," "Hula is Not Just a Dance," "The Day the Ali'i Died"—each one illustrated in marker and crayon. Kai's board was front and center. His title, "Real Warriors," crowned a collage of battle scenes, club-wielding men, and a photo of him and Naalei at Pu'uloa.

He took the mic, voice steady but high-pitched. "In ancient times, warriors protected the people and the land. Sometimes they had to be strong. Sometimes they had to be gentle, like the Ali'i who saved a baby by hiding her in a cave." He paused, looked at the crowd, finding his mother. "We remember the old stories because they tell us how to be brave. My grandma says you have to stand firm even when you're alone. That's called Kūpa‘a. Thank you."

The applause was surprisingly loud; the pride in the room is palpable. Leilani clapped with the rest, even as her eyes tracked the doors and the shifting figures in the wings. She caught Castellano's gaze at the back of the gym. The agent gave the barest nod and touched her earpiece.

The rest of the event unfolded with clockwork precision. There were no unexpected faces, no mysterious gifts delivered, and no bomb threats called into the office. The constant churn of parents trading seats and teachers wrangling their classes.

After the last act, a folk dance performed by half the student body, families flooded the floor. Children dragged their parents to the bake sale or the buffet or to see their poster up close. Leilani made her way through the crowd, heart still thudding, expecting at any second to see Souza's face or sense the sharp tug of adrenaline that signaled an imminent threat.

Instead, she found Kai and Naalei at the juice table, filling paper cups for the other kids.

"You did good, bug," Leilani said, ruffling Kai's hair.

He beamed. "Grandma says I sounded like a real chief."

"Better than a chief," said Naalei. "You told the truth."

Kai handed his mother a cup of juice. "Did you see my board? I put the picture of us in front of the cave."

She glanced at the collage, her heart catching on the

sight of her family in the middle of the carnage of paper warriors. "I saw," she said. "You put us right into the story."

A flicker of movement near the side door made her turn. But it was Castellano, scanning the crowd with the same suspicion Leilani felt. The agent made her way over, her stride relaxed, but her eyes sharp.

"Status?" Castellano murmured.

"Nothing so far," said Leilani. "Maybe he's bailing, waiting for the next act."

"He's not here," Castellano said. "Surveillance says no matches at any entry. But we're keeping everyone in place until the building is empty."

Leilani nodded, the sense of anticlimax mixing with relief and a fresh, sour dread. "What if this is all misdirection?"

"That's why we doubled the detail at the base. Isaac is on-site with three tactical teams. If Souza wants to escalate, he'll do it loud and publicly."

Naalei pulled Leilani aside. "You should check the perimeter yourself. If he means to make a scene, it might not be in here. He might want to catch you off guard."

"Or he wants to catch me alone," Leilani said.

They moved through the gym together, Castellano joining Leilani's flank, her hand never far from her concealed weapon. The three of them checked every side entrance, every fire door, and even the janitor's closet where one of the plainclothes officers was already reporting in.

Outside, the day was bright and almost unbearably hot. The playground teemed with children, now unchained from their parents and teachers. On the far side of the parking lot, Leilani saw a security team positioned in a semicircle, sunglasses up, hands on hips, scanning for trouble. She checked the street, looked for odd cars or lingerers, saw nothing but the steady pulse of Oahu in motion.

Her phone buzzed. Unknown caller. She answered.

"Detective Kealoha."

The line was quiet for a moment, then a familiar voice spoke.

"You don't know me, but you know my work," said Souza.

Leilani's jaw clenched. "You're late. I expected you at the main event."

Souza laughed, low and musical. "Why would I come to a trap? You made it too obvious. But I want you to know the story is already moving. You'll see soon enough."

A click, then dead air.

She relayed the call to Castellano, who cursed. "He's already made his move. We missed it."

The two of them rushed back inside. She found Kai standing on tiptoe by the bake sale, holding a brownie with both hands. She wrapped him in a hug, squeezed tighter than she meant to. "Stay with Grandma. I have to go."

He looked at her with the straightforward worry of

a child who's lived too long in a world of adult emergencies. "Will you be back?"

"Always," she said, the word a promise and a prayer.

She kissed his hair, nodded to Naalei, and took off. Castellano matched her stride.

"Where to?" Leilani asked.

Castellano's phone pinged. She read the text, eyes widening.

"Admiral Okada's house. He lives in the executive housing on the base. His security is breached, and he's not answering."

They ran for the car, heels scraping pavement, and their lungs burning.

The drive took twenty minutes, but the scene was already chaos, sirens, shore patrol cars, and a chopper thudding overhead. In the driveway, two MPs were doubled over, handcuffed together with a strip of blue cloth. The front door stood ajar.

Leilani drew her weapon and led the way in. The foyer was empty, but a wet trail marked the floor, and something like red ochre paint was smeared on the wall in a spiral pattern. They followed it room to room until they reached the study.

Inside, the admiral was gone. The only thing left was a single feathered cape, arranged on the chair like a body. In the middle of the desk, a clay bowl filled with salt and water.

Castellano stared, the color draining from her face.

"He took him right out from under our fucking noses."

"He wanted the attention on the school," said Leilani. "He knew we'd put our resources there. This was always his real stage."

The radio crackled. "We have a visual on the suspect vehicle heading east, a black SUV with several occupants. Matches the description of a vehicle that passed through the gate a half an hour ago."

"Let's go," Leilani said.

They ran for their SUVs, hearts pounding and the story in freefall. As they sped towards the next intersection, sirens grew louder, and Leilani realized she had never truly understood what it meant to be the hunted as well as the hunter.

Behind them, the base faded. Ahead, the road curved and vanished into salt haze. Leilani gunned the accelerator and raced the ancient ghosts to their conclusion.

Chapter Fifty-Five

The command center was a blur of activity. Every console beeped, every monitor streamed conflicting feeds, and the air vibrated with the overlapping noise of radio chatter, clipped status reports, and the constant stomp of boots across linoleum. The map of Oahu spread across the center table, creased and patched with sticky notes, formed the gravitational center of the chaos.

Leilani leaned over it, shoulders squared, a half-drunk Diet Coke sweating beside her elbow. Naalei and Castellano stood on either side, both with the same tight, unblinking gaze. Someone had marked three sites with red Sharpie circles, numbers in the margins. One at Kaniakapupu, buried in the wet green belly of the Koʻolau range, one at the ancient platform on Puʻu o Mahuka, perched over the north shore, and the last, high above Pearl Harbor, at the old execution bluff, a spot the locals avoided after sundown.

Castellano stabbed a finger at the north shore site. "All three have line-of-sight to major military installations. If Souza wants to make a statement, he'll go for maximum visibility."

"He doesn't care about the bases themselves," said Leilani, voice low. "He wants to finish the cycle. The ritual has to mean something, not just send a message."

Naalei shuffled closer, her eyes never leaving the map. She traced the lines of ancient trails leading to each site. "Puʻu o Mahuka belonged to the luakini class," she said. "Dedicated to Kū. Human sacrifice was public there, meant to terrify the next village into submission." She pointed to the Ko'olau site. "Kaniakapupu, only a few bones were ever recovered. Mostly political executions, done in secret, for power, not war."

"And Pearl?" asked Castellano.

Naalei tapped the spot. "It was a warning post. Every time the old chiefs made an example of a traitor, they did it here. No one from the valley could miss it."

Leilani gripped the table. "He's got the Admiral. He's going for spectacle. He'll want the world to see it happen."

From the far end, Isaac leaned over a bank of laptops, phone pinched to his ear, his eyes flicking from feed to feed. He finished his call and closed the gap to the map, setting down a fresh printout. "We got movement at all three. Drone flyover at Pu'u o Mahuka caught a rental van arriving fifteen minutes ago, but nobody's out yet. There's a campus event near Kaniakapupu, and half the neighborhood is parked along the trailhead."

He slapped a photo onto the table, grainy but clear enough. A figure hauling something heavy up the bluff behind Pearl, silhouetted against the city lights. "Our guy," said Isaac.

Castellano barely blinked. "We have assets at each site?"

"Two plainclothes teams at each. SWAT is staged on call, but they're five out unless we want to go loud."

Leilani moved her thumb over the Pearl site,

pressing hard enough to leave a mark. "He'll see the teams coming. If we rush him, he'll kill the Admiral before we're even close."

Naalei's face was set in stone. "If you can get close enough, talk to him. There's a way to interrupt the ritual. He'll have to respond. That's the rule."

Castellano fixed her with a look. "You trust the old rules to hold against someone this far gone?"

Naalei ignored her, speaking only to Leilani. "He's never broken the protocol before. It's the one line he won't cross."

A new feed hit the main monitor: a shaky phone video, uploaded and shared, already circulating on local social media feeds. The thumbnail showed a man, face painted blue and black, hauling a body-sized bundle wrapped in tapa up the bluff. In the background, the city glowed, and military helicopters prowled the air above the base.

"Shit," said Isaac. "He's livestreaming this."

Leilani pulled her badge off and dropped it into her bag. "I go up there alone. With the right protocol, he'll let me get close enough to stall him. You bring the team in on my signal."

Castellano opened her mouth, then stopped. She glanced at Naalei, saw the unblinking certainty, and nodded once. "We do it your way."

Isaac started barking orders to the comms desk, his voice rising over the growing din. "We need a drone in the air, five hundred yards out. Set up a command line, patch the video to the perimeter team. And lock down all roads for half a mile around the bluff. Nothing moves in or out without my go."

As the orders rippled out, Castellano handed Leilani a ballistic vest. "You don't go unarmed."

Leilani shrugged the vest under her jacket and checked the pistol in her holster. She looked at her mother. "If I don't make it—"

Naalei stopped her with a gesture, and closed the space between them. She set her hands on either side of Leilani's face, pulling her in until their foreheads pressed together, breath mingling.

"Kūpaʻa," whispered Naalei. "No matter what happens. You stand until the end."

Leilani closed her eyes. "I'll come back."

Naalei's hands lingered a moment, before slipping away. She said, louder, "The wind is with you, daughter."

Castellano watched the exchange in silence, arms folded, the hard lines of her face softening for a breath.

Isaac handed Leilani the tactical radio and an earbud, set to a private channel. "We're all here," he said. "Give the word."

The room quieted for a moment as the teams moved out, the old patterns of trust and fear settling in. As Leilani and Castellano made for the exit, Castellano paused and pulled Leilani back a step.

"Hey. Whatever happens, you did good. You kept your head."

Leilani half-grinned. "You saying that for the

record?"

Castellano rolled her eyes, then smiled, tight and real. "Don't get dead."

The two slipped out, the weight of the moment only now beginning to settle. Behind them, the command center shifted gears, the focus narrowing, and the voices sharpening into one thin, lethal wire.

Chapter Fifty-Six

The bluff loomed black against the sky as they gunned the Explorer up the last stretch of access road. Each switchback shrank the city behind them and magnified the silence ahead. They parked a quarter mile out, not daring the engine noise any closer.

Castellano checked the chamber on her sidearm, slotted the magazine back in, and glanced at Leilani. "You sure you're good for this?"

"I'm the only one who can get close," Leilani said.

They slid out of the Explorer and softly closed the doors. Castellano scanned the ridgeline, then moved into the trees, every movement silent and deliberate. They hiked the last stretch side by side, the path alternately choking them with brush and opening into fields of broken volcanic rock. The old airfield's fence gleamed in the distance, but the real stage was higher, at the very lip of the bluff.

Dusk arrived slowly, crawling over the ridge in fat streaks of purple and bruised gold. Leilani counted each step on the old access trail, breathing through her mouth to block out the stench of rotting ironwood and wind-stale salt. Behind her, Castellano moved with the mechanical steadiness of someone built for stakeouts and breach entries, weapon cradled in both hands, and every step soundless.

At the last switchback, the path thinned to little more than broken rock and tufts of fern. The city below blinked alive, each sodium streetlamp a flare, the distant ships of Pearl Harbor arranged in sharp, white lines on the black. Leilani crouched, finger pressed to her lips, and pointed up the next rise. "He set torches. No one's here by accident."

Castellano followed the line of her gesture, then swept the area with her weapon. "Movement on the left. Two, three minutes ahead of us."

Leilani studied the undergrowth. "You see the ti leaves?"

Castellano squinted. "Looks like a bundle every ten feet. Some are upright, some are bent into knots."

Leilani crawled forward, heart sprinting. "He's making a passage. Ritual approach. In the old days, the victim had to walk it, but now he's doing it for them. Each knot is a curse or a blessing. Depends on the direction."

They crested the rise. The torches flanked a level platform, just wide enough for two people to stand side by side. In the center, someone had arranged a circle of volcanic rocks, the edges dusted with what looked like bone-white sand.

"Salt," Leilani said. "He's mapped out the cardinal points. There—north, south, east, west. Every old execution, they purified the air with it before they killed."

Castellano's gaze never left the shadows. "What about the bowls?"

Leilani peered into the circle. Each salt mound sat in a cracked stone bowl, ancient but not original to the site. They were battered, stained, one still with a sticker from a tourist shop. "Salt's for cleansing, but also for keeping the old ghosts from interfering. He's broadcasting this for anyone watching. He wants the spirits on his side."

Their radios hissed. Isaac's voice sounded thin but urgent: "Both secondary sites are negative. Puʻu o Mahuka's van was a decoy—two dummy targets and a torch, nothing else. All teams redirected to the bluff."

"Copy," Castellano whispered, hand cupped over the mic. She eyed the ridgeline. "Best sightline is from the old airfield. If he wants us to see it, he'll start as soon as it's full dark."

Leilani scanned the platform, every detail wired into her nerves. She saw it, a mound covered in pale fabric, nearly invisible against the stone. Not a bundle, but a body: the Admiral, upright, bound with what looked like coconut fiber. Someone had pulled his arms tight behind him and lashed his ankles to a post, then draped his uniform shirt back over his shoulders. Over his chest, a thick band of kapa cloth, stenciled in blue. His face was streaked with pigment, eyes open, jaw clenched.

"He's alive," Leilani breathed, crouching lower.

Castellano sized up the platform, measuring distance and wind, every move deliberate. "How long before he notices we're here?"

Leilani pointed to a scuffed trail on the rock, fresh prints from split-toe sandals. "He knows. He's watching."

Castellano caught her eye, the usual sarcasm

replaced with an iron focus. "He's got the high ground, at least one sidearm, and probably a backup blade. We're sitting ducks."

"I'll distract," Leilani said. "You move left, get a better angle. If he tries to cut the Admiral, you take the shot."

Castellano shook her head. "That's not how this ends. He's not a lone psycho. He's a fucking zealot. He'll wait for you, force you to play by the rules."

Leilani gripped the ti leaf tucked into her vest. "Let's make him break them."

A crow cawed above. They moved, Leilani slow and open-handed, Castellano crouched and hidden, stalking the edge. The salt in the air now stung her nose, and with every step, the sense of entering someone else's grave thickened.

At the top, city lights flickered in the valley below, but here the wind carried only the smell of wet grass. The torches set into the stones cast a wavering circle of light. In the center, bound with old-style rope and stripped to the waist, the Admiral kneeled on a woven mat, his eyes open and glazed with fear, but alive.

Leilani called out, voice pitched to carry but not to threaten. "I'm here, Souza. Come out."

Fifty feet back, in the shadows, Souza waited. He wore a skirt of kapa, chest bare, streaked with blue and black, and his arms painted in spirals and bands. In his right hand, the war club, teeth of obsidian lashed to a hardwood haft. In his left hand, a short staff, the end carved into a sharp wedge.

He looked up as Leilani entered the circle. The old protocols thrummed in the air, as if every ancestor in the dirt watched from beneath the grass.

He spoke in Hawaiian first, harsh and guttural, the cadence of someone raised on legend, not language. He switched to English. "Stop. Any closer and the admiral dies."

Leilani kept her hands up. "He's not your enemy, Tao. You don't have to do this."

Souza's laugh cut the air. "He's every reason I have to do this." He drew the club through the air, tracing the boundary of the circle. "One last offering. That's all the world needs to change."

Castellano, pressed behind a rock, whispered into her radio. "He's armed with a flare gun and a club. Ready to breach on your signal."

Leilani halted at the ring of white stones, raised her empty hands, and spoke in a clear voice.

"I come as witness, not as enemy. I seek only truth."

Souza's face flickered in the torchlight, all bone, and fire. "You seek to end this."

"Not if the story's not done," said Leilani.

He regarded her, gesturing with the staff. "Come forward."

Behind her, Castellano melted into the shadows, positioning herself at a flank, hidden but close. Leilani stepped over the stones, heart slamming in her ribs.

Souza pointed to the bound admiral. "Do you know what this man has done?"

“He commands a fleet,” said Leilani.

Souza’s mouth curled. “He desecrated the land. Buried poisons, burned the bones of the dead, and built his empire on graves. The ancient traditions say this crime has but one answer.”

Leilani looked at the Admiral. He met her gaze, his face pale but steady. Sweat slicked his skin, but he didn’t plead.

Souza lifted the club. “You, too, come from traitors. The police were the first to betray our people.”

She flinched, then steadied herself. “We also remembered. We kept the names. And we know the rules. The rule says you don’t kill an innocent for the crimes of a crowd.”

He looked amused. “You think he’s innocent?”

“No,” said Leilani. “But I don’t think you’re the judge, either.”

A shadow flickered on the path behind Souza as Castellano moved closer, her weapon in both hands.

Souza saw it too and laughed, the sound wild in the dark. “You brought a second?”

“I brought a witness,” Leilani said.

The Admiral’s eyes found Leilani. They glistened, fear and shame locked together. “Help,” he mouthed, almost too small to see.

Souza heard it. He pressed the club to the Admiral’s temple. “Don’t,” he said. “You’ll ruin it.”

Leilani stepped forward, her voice steady. “You

already ruined it, Tao. The old rituals, if you cared about them, you'd know they don't need blood now. That's not how we remember."

Souza smiled, a smile that belonged in a painting of hell. "But the world remembers only the bloody things. You, me, this—this is how the island lives again."

She tried again. "You want me instead, right? I'll trade. Let the Admiral go."

Souza barked a short, cruel laugh. "You'd die for a traitor? Why? He wouldn't die for you."

She reached for the script, the language of old rituals. "In the name of Kānāwai, I claim the right of substitution. Take me. Finish the rite. I know the words."

He paused, the club lowering. He wanted it to matter, she realized. He wanted the audience. "Come into the circle," he said.

Leilani moved slowly, never breaking eye contact. Castellano shadowed her on the left, fifty feet and closing.

When Leilani stepped across the salt, she felt her heart hammer against her ribs. Souza stared at her, the blue lines on his face shining in the torchlight.

"Why did you do it?" she whispered.

Souza's expression flickered. "They said we had to remember. I just wanted to give them something worth remembering."

He jerked the club at the Admiral. "You want him to live? Say the words."

Leilani inhaled, reciting the ancient lines Naalei had drilled into her as a child. Each one a petition for mercy, not for death. "Ua ola, ua ola, ua ola no..."

Souza blinked, a hitch in his breath. "That's not the rite."

She moved closer, dropped to her knees in front of the Admiral. "Let him speak. That's all the old stories ever wanted. Not blood—confession."

He kneeled beside the Admiral and raised the club. "Witness the end." He circled them both, monologuing now, part Kahuna, part late-night host to the abyss. "The haole built their world on the bones of ours. All you do is mop up their blood and call it honor. You're no different. You protect the occupiers, and you betray every ancestor every time you pick up that badge."

Leilani met his fury head-on. "I didn't come to be different. I came to be better. That's what the old ways are for, making it better. You want to kill? Go ahead. But you're not the one who gets to write the ending. Let me do it," Leilani said, her voice sharp.

Souza looked up, startled. "You?"

"I'm the descendant of the kahu. I know the protocol. If it has to end, let me do it."

He weighed this; the club wavering.

Behind her, Castellano inched forward, gun now aimed directly at Souza's head.

Souza lowered the club. "Prove you know the words."

Leilani stepped forward, heart stuttering. She spoke

the old invocation, the one Naalei had taught her for funerals. Each line unspooled in the night, her voice carrying farther than she thought possible. Souza's face changed as she spoke; the rage drained, replaced by something like relief.

He handed her the club, the obsidian edge sharp as language.

She kneeled in front of the Admiral and set the club to the ground.

Souza nodded. "Do it."

Leilani looked at the admiral. "I'm sorry," she said, and twisted, smashing the club up and into Souza's jaw, catching him off balance. He stumbled, howling.

Castellano launched from cover, closed the space, and drove her knee into Souza's spine. He collapsed, club clattering to the stones, and she cuffed his hands with a zip tie.

It took ten seconds. The night rang with shouts and the heavy tread of SWAT boots.

The admiral blinked, and sagged against the ropes, his eyes wide. Leilani cut him loose. He stared at her, wordless, nodded once, grateful.

Souza lay on his side, his jaw hanging loose from his face and blood covering the ground. He glared at Leilani. "You broke the cycle," he said, but it came out distorted.

Leilani stood over him and looked him in the eye. "Yeah. But you don't get to finish the story."

Sirens cut through the night as the teams converged.

Leilani stood, wiped her hands on her jeans, and let the chilly wind clear her mind.

At the bluff, she watched the first light of morning pale the city below. For a moment, all was quiet. Naalei's words returned to her, the ritual not for the dead, but for the living.

Kūpaʻa. Stand firm, even if you stand alone. She turned from the edge, ready to write the rest of the story herself.

Castellano stood next to her and took in the blinking lights of the base.

She studied Leilani, her voice barely above a whisper. "You okay?"

Leilani nodded, hands shaking. "He never wanted to kill. He wanted to be remembered."

Castellano watched as two SWAT officers zip-tied Souza's wrists and yanked him to his knees. She turned to face him. "He'll be remembered, all right. Every headline for the next year will see to that."

Leilani helped the Admiral to his feet. He staggered and leaned on her, breathing hard.

The three stood in the circle, battered but alive, the city glimmering below as the last of the sun died on the water.

Souza sobbed, and laughed, face streaked with blood and blue pigment. His lower jaw hanging by a piece of skin. He glared at Leilani, wild-eyed. He tried to speak, but the words never materialized.

They walked the admiral to the edge and watched

the city lights flicker. Above them, the moon sat hard and perfect, a witness to everything.

The Admiral spat blood and grinned. “Nicely done.”

They turned and headed down the path. At the end, Naalei appeared at the trailhead, not out of breath, not afraid, but holding herself the way the elders did when there was nothing more to say.

Her mother pressed their foreheads together. “You did it, Lei.”

“It’s not over,” Leilani said.

Naalei’s hands were gentle and steady. “It never is.”

They turned the admiral over to the waiting paramedics and watched as they loaded him into the ambulance. Souza, with his hanging jaw wrapped in bandages, was loaded into a second ambulance followed by two SWAT officers. The ambulance pulled out, and they waited for the forensic team to arrive. It was going to be another long night.

Above them, the moon followed, pale as bone, a silent reminder that the oldest wars never ended. They only waited, in the stone and the salt, for someone else to carry the memory forward.

Chapter Fifty-Seven

The interview room at Halawa Correctional Complex did not pretend to comfort. The cinderblock walls pressed in from every angle, the flicker of the overhead light buzzing in its own private Morse code. A stainless-steel table separated the two folding chairs, one bolted to the floor, the other free-floating, as if an invitation to escape would ever be extended. The air hung heavy with the scent of disinfectant and the undertones of human waste.

Leilani sat with her back straight, elbows braced on the table, and the ballpoint pen in her right hand. Her notebook lay open, its pages squared to the edge of the metal. Across from her, the man in the jumpsuit looked nothing like the beast the media had made him out to be. Holt, just Holt now, since the news had long ago stripped him of rank and first name, slumped in his seat, wrists cuffed, the pale chain snaking around his waist. His head listed to one side, like the weight of his own thoughts had bent his neck for good.

He fixed his gaze on the shiny tabletop, his eyes never meeting hers. His hands trembled in the space between them, jittering even at rest. Up close, the wounds of their prior confrontation had healed; a splintered scar traced his right eyebrow, and both wrists bore raw, pink chafe marks where earlier restraints had worn through his skin. He looked smaller than she remembered, as if the air itself compressed him every time the door clicked shut.

She clicked her pen, the sound sharper than she'd

meant.

Holt flinched. “Where do you want me to start?”

“Souza,” Leilani said. “Begin at your first contact. Don’t stop unless I say so.”

A muscle twitched in his jaw. “He found me after my first article fifteen. That was when I transferred from the mainland. I’d been in the Navy six months. Got into a bar fight on Kalakaua, took out three Marines. Nobody wanted to be seen with me after that, except for the guys who wanted a show. Then he showed up.”

Leilani didn’t move. She let him spool out the thread.

Holt kept talking. “He was lecturing at the base. Something about cultural resilience under colonial pressure. I sat in the back, in uniform, trying not to look awake. But the way he spoke, he said the ancient ways never left, they merely slept. That the islands needed warriors, not caretakers. It hit me differently.” He drew a slow breath. “I’d never heard anyone talk like that. My dad always told me not to bring up bloodlines, and the Navy said culture was fine, as long as it stayed outside the uniform.”

“So Souza targeted you.” Leilani’s tone never wavered. She wrote as he spoke.

Holt nodded. “He came to the rec room after, found me alone, nursing a Coke. He called me Aliʻi on shore leave. I thought he was bullshitting, but then he recited my great-grandfather’s name, the one from the Queen’s Guard. Nobody outside my family ever knew that." Holt looked up for a second, met her gaze, then dropped it back to the table. "I let him talk. He made me feel like someone worth saving."

"Did he mention violence?" she asked.

"Not at first," Holt said. "He talked about strength. How the world's better if we make ourselves into weapons. It started as history lessons. We'd go hiking, he said the trails were old highways, that every inch of ground was mapped by the battles nobody remembered. Before long it turned to training. He had me come to his house near Waimanalo. In the garage, he had all the old weapons. Clubs, daggers, shark teeth. He made me hold them, said they'd wake up a memory if I let them."

Leilani pressed the tip of her pen into the paper. "He groomed you."

Holt shrugged. "I didn't see it as grooming. I thought it was respect." His voice hollowed. "He'd show me the pattern of the knots. How to tie someone so they couldn't escape, even with a blade. He showed me how to hold the club, said you have to feel the body's weight through your hand, not swing for effect. He taught me how to prepare, but he also taught me how to look at people. To see their soft parts."

He stopped, eyes glazed. "There was a point where I would have done anything he asked. Even before he had ever mentioned a target."

Leilani watched his knuckles, the way they tightened and then opened again. "When did he bring up the first victim?"

Holt grimaced. “He called it just cause. Said the admiral on the base was spitting on the flag of my ancestors. That he ran exercises through sacred sites and destroyed bones, not even caring what was underfoot. He gave me a folder full of satellite images and timelines. Half of it looked like declassified intel. He told me, they won’t listen if you speak; you have to show them something they can’t ignore.”

I said, “you want me to scare him?”

Souza said, “No. I want you to make him disappear, like he made your people disappear.”

Holt’s hands trembled again. “I laughed it off. But he left the club for me. He put it in my bag when I wasn’t looking.”

Leilani flipped the page, never interrupting the rhythm.

“He said it was tradition,” Holt continued. “But when the first guy died, and I saw it on the news, Souza called me within the hour. He said, ‘Now they’ll listen. Now they know we’re not extinct.’ He made it sound like I’d joined something bigger.”

He shuddered as if the memory itself chilled him. “After that, it got easier. The names kept coming. Souza never touched anything. I’d show up at his place, and he’d have the next assignment ready. He’d tell me the old stories, about when they’d tear out a traitor’s tongue, or how they’d strip the flesh so the bones could walk free to the afterlife. Every time I hesitated, he’d say, ‘If you don’t act, you’re letting them erase you.’”

Leilani watched, silent, letting him flounder in his own guilt before tossing the next line.

"What about the cultural elements, the salt, the ti, the burial positions?" she asked.

Holt's lips twisted. "He said the old gods needed witnesses. That if I did it right, it would unlock the island's protection. At first, I copied what he said, but later, he made me watch while he set up an altar in his backyard. He'd walk the perimeter, chant the old phrases, and scatter salt in the corners. I didn't know what any of it meant, not really. But he said it didn't matter. As long as I believed. That was enough to make it real. He gave me the blue pigment for the last one. Said it was what the priests used for purification. The smell stuck to my clothes for days. I can't forget it. Every time I closed my eyes, I could see the spiral he drew for me in the notebook. I still see it now."

Leilani steeled herself. "Souza picked you for a reason. What did he tell you about yourself?"

Holt swallowed, hard enough to make his Adam's apple jump. "He said I was born for reclamation. That my service made me invisible to the outsiders, but my blood made me the perfect messenger. He said I could walk in both worlds, military, and Hawaiian. That nobody else could."

"Do you believe him?" she asked.

Holt's jaw worked. "I want to say no, but at the time I did. I thought if I just followed the script, something good would come out of it. That the killings would be a message, not just murder." He squeezed his hands together, the cuff chain rattling. "I know it sounds stupid, but he made me believe I was fixing something. I didn't even hate the people he pointed at. I just hated the emptiness he left when he wasn't around. I wanted to be what he saw."

He blinked, and the tears made two quick tracks down his face. He tried to wipe them away, but the cuffs scraped his jaw instead.

Leilani kept her voice steady. "How did Souza justify the violence?"

"He called it restoration." Holt's voice went low. "He said America only understands power, never empathy. He said the only way to stop the erasure was to make them fear erasure themselves. He never talked about the law, never said the word murder. Every time, it was the work, the cause or the return. He made me believe there was no other way. That if I stopped, the entire island would rot out from under us."

The muscles in his shoulders shook now, his exhaustion leaking through every pore. "He'd check in after each one. Not even to say good job, but to give me a new lesson. Like he was just marking off chapters in some old textbook."

"And when you got caught?" Leilani asked.

He closed his eyes. "He called me just once. Said the old stories always end in sacrifice. That I had to go out on my shield, or none of it mattered. He told me to confess, but to never give them his name. 'You'll make it to the legends if you keep the truth safe,' he said. 'Otherwise, you'll just die a number.'"

His voice cracked. "I almost did it. I almost held on,

like he told me. But after you visited me, after the last one, I saw what I'd really done. You looked at me as if I were something you'd seen before. And I realized I'd just been the club in someone else's hand."

Holt shuddered, and for a long stretch of time, said nothing. When he finally looked up, his eyes had a glassy, post-storm calm. "I'm not innocent. I know that. But Souza, he's the one who made it all happen. He's the reason the spiral kept turning."

Leilani nodded and wrote it down. She studied the curve of his fingers, the ragged arc of his thumbnail, and the tiny tattoo, half-faded on his wrist.

"If there was anything you could say to Souza right now, what would it be?" she asked.

Holt met her gaze, eyes bright and vacant. "I'd ask him why he picked me. Why he wanted to see me rot, instead of seeing the world change." His mouth bent, almost a smile. "But I know what he'd say. He'd say the only thing that matters is that the story keeps going. That the next one's already in the chamber, and that the first round was just a warning shot."

He coughed, a wet, broken sound. "But that's not what I want. I want it to end."

Leilani finished her notes, shut the pad, and rose. Her knuckles ached from the pressure she'd used to hold the pen. The old ghosts in her chest had gone quiet, replaced by a new, sharper pain. As she gathered her things, she hesitated at the door.

"You did one right thing," she said.

Holt's eyes lit. "Yeah?"

"You told the truth."

He sagged, as if the words themselves added ten pounds to each shoulder. "Do you think it'll help?"

"Not right away." Leilani paused, hand on the handle. "But in the end, stories are all we have."

He nodded, mouth set in a crooked line. "Kūpa'a."

The word hung in the room, silent and stubborn. Leilani let it stand.

She entered the corridor, her hands still trembling, but her resolve sharper than the cold steel behind her. Holt's voice echoed after her, chasing down the ghosts she'd carried in. She let them walk beside her as she crossed the yard, the morning sun low and unrepentant. The cycle might never end. But at least today, the spiral had a name.

Chapter Fifty-Eight

Leilani's desk sat at the center of a paper archipelago of stacked binders, scattershot printouts and loose evidence photos pasted with tabs in her sharp, no-nonsense script. Two empty coffee cups had staged a coup on her coaster, and a third had recently gone cold, left perched beside a dog-eared manila folder. Outside, the city went about its morning, waves of traffic washing up against the cinderblock of the precinct, but inside her office the silence stayed as thick as molasses.

She skimmed the last page of the confession transcript. Holt's words echoed through her mind, still hot and raw, the ink from her own notes not yet dry. She tried to catalogue her feelings about the interview. It mingled with the smaller, sharper sense of loss that came with every case she put to bed. Today's version tasted bitter, like burned rice.

A shadow fell in the doorway. "You busy?"

Castellano stepped inside without waiting for permission. She wore her suit jacket draped over one shoulder, tie askew, and a stack of folders cradled in the crook of her arm. Under that, a bundle wrapped in brown paper.

Leilani set her pen aside. "Didn't figure you for the courtesy knock, Vic."

The agent grunted. "My last act before I'm back to my regular life." Castellano set the folders on the desk, then stood looking at them as if expecting them to sprout teeth. She tapped the top folder. "This is everything NCIS has on Souza. Chain of custody, forensic files, and all the back-channel emails from his groupies."

Leilani nodded. "Thanks." She opened the file and scanned the first few pages. "Did you vet it yourself?"

"Twice," said Castellano. "Had to lean on a couple of old friends in D.C. They found his name on a PACOM incident report from ten years ago, flagged as a potential force multiplier for local unrest." Castellano let the sarcasm hang a moment. "Your guy's been at it a long time."

"Yeah, well, this time he's not going anywhere but Halawa." Leilani closed the folder and slid it to the top of a pile marked TO REVIEW.

She glanced at Castellano, who still hadn't moved. "You bring the whole Smithsonian?"

The agent flushed. "It's a thank you or something." She slid the brown-paper bundle onto the desk, peeling the tape as if it might detonate. She unwrapped it slowly, and Leilani recognized the shape even before the cover came into full view. A hardbound book, old but intact, the title stamped in faded gold. He Moʻolelo o Nā Koa, a rare anthology of warrior chants and genealogies.

Leilani touched the cover, tracing the uneven edge where someone had once glued the library barcode. "This is out of print."

"I know," said Castellano. "I found this in a rare bookstore in Kapahulu. I paid their asking price plus a donation to a cultural society. I want you to look it over, make sure it's the real thing. If it is, I'd like you to have your mom get it to someone who can preserve it and donate it to the Cultural Center. My treat."

Leilani blinked. "Why?"

Castellano hesitated, her arms folded like she wanted to hug herself but wouldn't dare. "This case made me realize I've spent a career pretending all this cultural stuff was just window dressing. Every time you went off protocol, or Naalei did her thing, I rolled my eyes. But you were right. None of this makes sense if you ignore the roots." Her lips twitched. "I figure it's time I started acting like I've learned something."

Leilani opened the book, thumbing the brittle pages. A slip of paper fell out, folded into quarters and held by static. She read the first line. Stand firm, even if you stand alone. It looked like someone's marginalia, but to her, it felt like a message smuggled through the years.

She looked up at Castellano, studying the lines around her mouth, the caution in her stance. "This is legit," she said. "Thank you. I'll have my mom take it to the preservation office. This will be a nice addition to their exhibits."

"Don't thank me yet. I want you to write the foreword for the center. They said they'd pay you, but I told them you'd do it for free."

Leilani gave a short laugh. "Smooth. You always close the case with an extra assignment?"

Castellano shrugged. "Keeps the paperwork going."

They shared a silence, the old animosity replaced with something that felt a little like respect, or at least mutual exhaustion. Leilani put the book aside, careful not to bend the cover. "You got what you need from the case?"

"Yeah," said Castellano. "He's going to jail for life. Souza might get the death penalty, but I doubt it'll matter. He'll run the same con from behind the fence. Guy like that? He never quits. Of course, he'll also spend the rest of his life eating through a straw thanks to you. Couldn't happen to a nicer guy."

A smile. "You should come work for us. You've got a hell of a nose for bullshit. That's a compliment."

Leilani rolled her eyes. "I'll stick to HPD. At least here, the pay is low, but the dress code is forgiving."

Castellano straightened. She seemed about to say something else, then just nodded. "They're having a commendation at the chief's office in twenty. Full dress blues. You better not be late, or she'll have my badge."

"Wouldn't dream of it," Leilani said. She watched as Castellano pulled the jacket on, the shift in posture automatic, every inch the federal agent again. But as she turned to leave, she paused.

"I meant what I said," Castellano said. "Without you and your mother, we'd have missed the spiral."

Leilani tapped the notebook, now closed. "Without you, I'd have missed the part where stories only matter if people believe them."

Castellano's expression flickered, then steadied.

“Goodbye, Detective.”

“See you, Agent.”

The door closed, leaving the office brighter than before.

Leilani exhaled. She set the book on top of her own files, then texted a photo to Naalei. She allowed herself a moment of pride before she got up to face the next round of public-facing bureaucracy.

Sometimes, the job left no time for grace notes. Today, she would take the small victory. As she filed the evidence away, the last page of her old notebook slid open. She wrote in block letters: THE STORY IS NEVER FINISHED. She set the pen down and went to suit up for the next chapter.

The main corridor of HPD HQ vibrated with the energy of bodies crammed into a space two sizes too small for the moment. Desks had been shoved to the walls, chairs stacked and ignored, the usual clatter of phones and radios dulled by the mass of blue- and black-jacketed law enforcement. HPD’s rank and file packed the main drag in an untidy cordon, shoulder to shoulder with the stiffer, more reserved silhouettes of the NCIS team. The only thing the two crowds shared, besides the case, was a history of mutual suspicion.

At the center stood Chief Mori, hands folded at her belt, blazer buttoned so crisp you could set a clock by the lapel. She cut a line of calm through the buzzing huddle, eyes sweeping left and right before she spoke.

“Let’s keep this short,” Mori said, voice ringing off the concrete and into the bones of every officer in the building.

Silence crashed down. Even the city beyond seemed to hush, just for a second.

Mori faced the group, but her attention arrowed straight to Leilani and Castellano, who stood side by side at the front of the crowd. Neither of them had bothered with the at-ease posture, but both kept their arms at their sides and heads high, the only ones in the room not braced for a scolding or a canned morale speech.

"As most of you know, the joint task force closed the Souza case yesterday," said Chief Mori. "The suspect and his accomplices are in custody; the threat to both civilian and military assets has been neutralized, and thanks to the efforts of this department and our federal partners, the damage was contained to a minimum." Mori's gaze ticked to Isaac, whose mouth twitched when she said a minimum, but he kept his poker face in place.

"Detective Kealoha," Mori continued, "displayed exceptional tenacity and, more importantly, cultural awareness, which proved to be the hinge on which this case turned."

A ripple of nods ran through the HPD side. The NCIS crew remained stone-faced, but several looked Leilani's way with something close to respect.

"NCIS Special Agent Castellano," Mori said, her voice shifting subtly. "Brought the resources, the reach and the muscle of the entire Pacific Command to bear. At every step, she coordinated with our local officers, never once losing sight of the jurisdictional line, though I understand there were spirited discussions." She permitted herself a thin smile, which landed like an inside joke on both sides.

A snort escaped Isaac before he caught himself.

"Let's be clear," Mori said, her voice sharpening again. "This case was a mess. The city watched every mistake we made in real time. But it also saw how we worked together. The Navy's reach and the city's roots. Federal and local. Mainland and island." Her jaw set. "I want this to be the rule, not the exception."

She let that hang, then produced two blue folders from the lectern behind her. "Detective Kealoha. Special Agent Castellano." She called them forward, and Leilani noticed that even the older officers, the ones who never clapped for anything, brought their hands together as she crossed the space. Castellano took the folder with a nod so tiny you'd have missed it if you weren't watching for it. Leilani felt Mori's hand on her shoulder, a squeeze that lasted a fraction too long before the Chief let go.

"Starting next quarter," Mori announced, "HPD will coordinate with NCIS and the FBI on a joint training program. Every new class of recruits will get a rotation through local cultural centers, and our federal partners will be required to complete training on native protocol and island history." She looked at Isaac. "You're running point."

Isaac gave a stiff salute. "Yes, Chief."

Mori nodded once more. "Dismissed."

The silence dissolved into a slow-building buzz. On

the NCIS side, Castellano fielded a few quiet claps on the back, her face never changing, but her eyes a shade less steely. On the HPD end, Leilani caught Akira's broad grin and the upward chin-jerk from the oldest detective in the room. She heard her own name pass through the crowd, the sound of it no longer a punchline or a test of who could pronounce it right.

The crowd drifted towards the break room, the old battle lines blurring. Mori melted away as fast as she'd appeared, already on the phone before she cleared the glass doors.

Isaac cornered Leilani. "See what you did? Now I have to hang out with the Feds every month."

She nudged his elbow. "You love it. Maybe they'll teach you how to iron your shirts."

Isaac leaned closer, voice low. "You did good, Lei. This one could've turned ugly."

She shrugged. "Not like I had a choice."

"Still," he said, "next time you go head-to-head with a serial killer, bring backup sooner. I'm running out of ulcers."

She promised nothing.

Across the room, Castellano hovered near the exit. Her folder tucked under one arm, she scanned the room as if already halfway out the door. Leilani caught her eye. Castellano nodded once, but with all the intent of a handshake. She slipped away, the doors swinging shut behind her.

Leilani lingered for a moment, the echoes of the room swirling around her, the tension replaced by a sense of something resolved, or at least, rebalanced. She ran a finger along the embossed seal on the folder, then tucked it under her arm and joined the migration to the break room.

The precinct felt light. Not healed, but not broken either. There would be new cases, new messes, and more than enough ghosts for everyone. But today, at least, the teams stood together. And that counted for something.

Chapter Fifty-Nine

The air inside the Waimānalo Cultural Center pulsed with the mingled scents of plumeria, ti and fresh bread rising in the back kitchen. The long, open-sided hall hummed with more life than usual. Helpers, teens in matching black T-shirts, kupuna in their best Sunday wear, flitted between the folding tables, arms loaded with bundles of greenery and containers of coarse salt. The late-morning sun stretched gold across the floor, carving shadows that danced in time to the rustle of leaves and the sharp, practiced voices directing the final setup.

At the center of it all moved Naalei, her movements more conductor than participant. She wove through the traffic with a steadying word here, a lifted eyebrow there, correcting the angle of a salt bowl, retying a braided lei that drooped, adjusting the symmetry of the altar's offerings until every element fell into place. She never stopped moving, but never rushed. Leilani watched, a blend of pride and disbelief at how her mother could command a battalion of volunteers without raising her voice.

"Set the awa root there," Naalei said, gesturing with two fingers. "And make sure the ends face mauka. Otherwise, the ancestors won't find it." Her hair, now fully silver, shimmered in the light, and her blue dress bore a garland of shell flowers that made her look equal parts bishop and field general.

Leilani joined her at the altar, arms full of ti leaves, the thick stalks cool and waxy in her hands. "You want these stacked or fanned out?"

"Fanned," said Naalei. "But only in threes. Odd numbers hold better."

"Copy that," Leilani said, and got to work. She could feel her mother's presence like a lodestone. They shared a silence, interrupted by the soft clatter of shells as Leilani arranged the leaves just so.

Victims' families arrived first, ushered in by volunteers who spoke in hushes and led them to the padded benches that curved along the far wall. Many walked with a stiffness that Leilani recognized. The stiffness of people forced into the spotlight by tragedy, unable to relax even in a safe space. Some faces she recognized from interviews, others only from the crime scene file. But every one of them scanned the room, looking for a reason to trust the moment.

The doors remained open as the room filled. Uniformed HPD officers lined the perimeter, mingling in subdued clusters, their badges and dark blue contrasting with the riot of color on the tables. Military representatives, mostly junior officers and a few civilians, clustered together near the back, standing out with their posture and their tendency to avoid direct eye contact. A handful of media lingered near the entrance, their cameras turned off by strict order, but their notepads ready.

Leilani played a kind of host, checking in on families, then ducking behind the altar to help her mother. She kept one eye on the crowd, watching for trouble but also for the first appearance of Agent Castellano, whose RSVP had been as reluctant as every word out of her mouth.

She spotted Castellano hovering at the threshold, wearing an outfit so uncharacteristic that it stole Leilani's breath for a second. A modest black dress, a string of pearls, and her hair pulled back in a loose knot. No badge, no weapon in sight. She looked as if she'd stumbled into a wake and seemed unsure whether to step inside.

Leilani intercepted her with a small wave. "Didn't expect you to dress up."

"Didn't want to disrespect the vibe," said Castellano, glancing at the sea of color and floral prints. "Is this okay?"

Leilani smiled. "You're good. Besides, you're the only one here who could pull off a suit of armor and not get side-eye."

Castellano snorted, and looked around, the severity melting. "What do you want me to do?"

"Watch for now," said Leilani. "I'll explain as we go."

They slipped through the crowd and took seats on the bench reserved for law enforcement. The bench bore two signs, HPD, and NCIS, but neither of the agencies' brass had bothered to send their top ranks. Leilani took that as a sign that, for once, nobody wanted to own the limelight.

At the front, the altar took shape. Naalei stood beside it, arms folded, face calm and unreadable as she surveyed the gathering. She nodded at the last-minute adjustments, and when the time seemed right, she picked up a conch shell and raised it to her lips. The sound, deep and old, rolled through the hall, silencing every conversation in its path. People settled, and Naalei addressed the crowd.

"We are gathered here today," she said, her voice carrying with practiced strength. "Not to erase what happened, but to heal what was broken." She swept her gaze over the families, the police, the sailors, and the quietly bristling island of the press. "In the old days, a perversion of the rituals called down sickness on the land. When the story of the people was twisted into violence, it damaged not just the bodies, but the spirit of the entire community."

She let the silence breathe, then continued. "My daughter and many others worked to find the truth, but finding truth does not erase pain. Only together can we put things right."

She beckoned to the rows of salt bowls and ti bundles. "These are offerings, not apologies. We invite the families of those lost, and anyone who seeks to mend what was torn, to take part. This is your right, not your obligation."

A young woman in the front row rose, face tight and blotched from days of crying, and crossed to the altar. She hesitated, but Naalei guided her hands, showing how to scatter a pinch of salt at the base of the bundle. Other families followed. A uniformed Navy Lieutenant waited his turn, then offered a crisp bow, eyes watery but jaw set. Even some of the HPD officers took their time, stepping up with deliberate movements, as if each action filed a rough edge off the memory of the case.

Leilani noticed Castellano watching the ritual, chin lifted and eyes narrowed as she tried to decode the purpose. When it was their turn, Leilani beckoned her forward.

"Here's the trick," she whispered. "You grab a little salt. It doesn't matter from which bowl. You sprinkle it left to right for luck. If you want, you say something to the person you lost."

Castellano pinched some salt, held it for a second. "What if you lost respect for the person you used to be?"

Leilani shrugged. "Works for that, too."

Castellano scattered the salt, and nodded, stepping away without drama.

As the last of the offerings landed, Naalei chanted. Her voice started low before climbing, the cadence uneven to western ears but perfectly measured in its own ancient logic. The words curled around the room, softening the silence until even the smallest children on the floor stopped squirming.

A hush settled, thick and tender. At the end, Naalei joined Leilani at the altar. They finished the rite together, lifting the ti bundle and placing it in a calabash bowl at the center. The symbolism ran clear, even to the uninitiated: what had been scattered, gathered in again. What was sundered, is made whole.

Naalei pressed her palm to her daughter's cheek, a gesture so familiar and so rare that Leilani had to close her eyes to hold it.

After a time, the crowd broke apart, softer and

slower than before. The families talked in clusters, voices hushed, the air less tense. The HPD officers lingered in the corner, sharing a box of malasadas, even passing some to the NCIS crew. The military representatives fell into easy chat with the older community leaders, the differences in rank fading as the walls dissolved.

Castellano stood alone, hands folded. Her posture, always tight, always braced for a fight, now looked at rest. When Leilani joined her, Castellano didn't say anything at first.

"Thank you for letting me come," Castellano said.

"You earned it," Leilani said.

Castellano eyed her, the faintest smile breaking through. "I still don't get half the words. But I get the point. You don't just solve a case and move on. You fix things."

"Sometimes," said Leilani. "Sometimes you just learn how to live with what you can't fix."

Castellano held her gaze unblinkingly. "You think the others will try something like this again?"

Leilani didn't hesitate. "There's always a new spiral. But now people know how to see it coming."

They stood together, watching as Naalei greeted the last of the families, her hands gentle, her words soft enough to stitch closed what remained of the pain.

As the sun angled lower, the room flushed with color, every face framed in gold and green. Leilani glanced at Castellano, and for a heartbeat they shared a silence that felt like trust.

"We did good," Castellano said.

"We did what we had to," Leilani replied.

They left the center together, stepping into the clear, salty air. The old world waited, but for now, the spiral had been unwound. And for once, that was enough.

Chapter Sixty

Naalei's kitchen never went quiet for long. The gentle thump of the poi pounder set the base rhythm, punctuated by the sizzle of onions and garlic in the battered steel pan, and over all of it, the sound of the ocean that drifted through the open lanai doors. Even with the midafternoon sun glazing the louvered windows, the house felt cool, one part cross-breeze, one part the magic of a century-old plantation home, and all shaded by mango and plumeria.

Leilani had never gotten used to cooking with her mother. Alone, she measured and weighed, precise as a crime lab. With Naalei, nothing followed a script. Spices rained from palm to pan in a blur. Fish landed on banana leaves, filleted by touch, not by sight. The only concession to modernity was the battered rice cooker, humming in the corner, a wedding gift that outlasted one husband and three generations of family meals.

"Watch your fingers," said Naalei, elbowing her daughter aside as she slid the sashimi knife through a slab of ahi. "You cut like you're still at work, aggressive, but no finesse."

Leilani grinned, wiped her hands on a dish towel, and scooped diced green onions into the poke bowl. "You say that every time. And every time, nobody loses a finger."

"Yet," Naalei muttered, but the smile on her face took the sting out of it.

From the dining room, Kai's voice piped up. "Mom, where's the good napkins? The ones with turtles on them?"

"Second drawer, right side," Leilani called back.

He rummaged, then appeared in the doorway, a roll of napkins clutched in both hands. "I put the forks the American way. Grandma said it was okay because our guests are haole." He looked at her, wide-eyed. "Do you think they'll care?"

"I think they'll be impressed you remembered," said Leilani. "And they'll teach you a better way."

Kai beamed, the swirl of freckles on his nose nearly disappearing under the force of his smile. He disappeared, trailed by the pop of plastic cups being snapped apart. Leilani stacked the completed platters. Chicken long rice, salt-and-pepper shrimp, and a salad bright with mango and red onion. She caught her mother eyeing the tray.

"Is that enough food?" she asked, only half joking.

Naalei snorted. "For four? You look like you're feeding half the precinct." She started on the haupia squares, slicing them with surgical precision, before arranging them on a koa tray lined with ti leaves.

The doorbell rang.

Kai raced to answer, almost tripping on the mat. "I'll get it!"

Leilani smoothed her shirt and took a slow breath. She heard Kai's rapid-fire intro. "You're Special Agent Castellano, right? My mom says you catch bad guys too!" There was a deeper, unfamiliar laugh.

Castellano's, she realized. She doubted the agent had ever set foot in a Hawaiian living room, let alone at dinner with the Kealohas.

Castellano entered, bracing herself against the expectations of company. Her blazer had been replaced with a pressed oxford and, impossibly, a lei of tiny white orchids. She held a bottle of wine in one hand and a flat, tissue-wrapped package in the other.

"For you," Castellano said to Naalei, her voice two notches softer than work protocol. "It's from a friend's bakery in Kapahulu. I didn't want to show up empty-handed."

Naalei accepted the gift with a nod. "Mahalo. You want some juice or tea?"

"Whatever you're having," said Castellano, eyes darting to the spread on the counter. "It smells amazing in here."

Kai looked at Castellano's lei. "You look like you're going to a graduation, not dinner."

She blinked and grinned, the lines in her face relaxing. "I got nervous. My boss said it's rude to show up without a lei, and the lady at the store put it on me before I could say no."

Naalei turned away quickly, but Leilani caught her fighting down a laugh. Isaac arrived fifteen minutes later, the slouch of his old athletic walk unmistakable. He wore an open-collar shirt and carried a six-pack of local craft beer in one hand and a bag of chips in the other.

"Figured we'd need backup snacks," he said,

dropping both on the kitchen table.

Leilani gave him a quick hug, his stubble grazing her cheek. "If you eat more than Kai tonight, I'll be impressed."

Isaac leaned down to Kai, stage-whispering, "Think your mom will let us have seconds?"

Kai puffed his chest. "If you can beat me to the table. I've been training."

Castellano stood in the living room, looking at the surfing trophies lined up on the fireplace mantle.

"These yours?" Castellano asked, lifting her chin at the display.

Leilani shrugged. "Mom won't let me take them down. Says she needs proof I was ever good at anything."

Naalei clucked her tongue, ladling stew into bowls with military precision. "Don't listen to her. She used to sleep with that one next to her pillow." She pointed with a steamy spoon at the largest, a bronzed surfer perched atop a blue-glass wave, the plaque etched: ISLANDS INVITATIONAL—1st Place Women's Open.

Leilani rolled her eyes, but she couldn't stop the flush in her ears. "That was years ago."

"Impressive," Castellano said, and the word wasn't sarcastic for once. She left her place at the table, drifted over to the hearth, and picked up one of the smaller trophies, a miniature surfboard mounted on a slab of reclaimed koa. "You never mentioned you were a pro."

"I wasn't. Just a lot of weekends and some sponsors who liked local faces." Leilani kept her voice breezy, but she could feel the weight of Castellano's gaze. "My dad surfed. He taught me early. Mom says it's the only way to keep me out of trouble."

Kai, eavesdropping from the couch, piped up. "She's famous. They still have her picture in the surf shop by the mall."

"That's just for a free discount," Leilani called back. "No one cares about old scores."

Castellano turned the trophy in her hand. "I never learned. Didn't know anyone who surfed when I was growing up back east. My stepdad said if the ocean wanted you, she'd take you. He never set foot past the pier."

Leilani snorted. "That's one way to get out of swim class."

Castellano smiled, a small thing, but real. She put the trophy down carefully, then, after a beat, asked, "Would you teach me? Sometime?"

Silence rolled through the room, broken only by the hiss of onions on the stovetop.

"Are you serious?" Leilani said.

Castellano met her gaze. "I am. I figure if I'm going to be around here for a while, I should at least understand the stuff everyone else here grew up on. Might help with my island etiquette."

Naalei laughed, a round, generous sound. "You might be the first haole ever to admit that."

Isaac whistled. "Better pack extra Advil. When Lei taught me, I nearly broke my tailbone."

"I'll wear a helmet," Castellano said, grinning. "But only if you go easy on me."

Leilani sipped her whiskey, measuring Castellano for the punchline that never came. Instead, she pictured the agent out on a longboard, legs straddling foam, every muscle knotted with the effort to balance and not lose control. The thought was better than dessert.

"We'll start easy," Leilani said. "There's a break near Sandy's; it's sheltered from the wind. Perfect spot for beginners, and nobody around to heckle you."

Castellano's smile spread, wider now, as if she'd just won a small bet with herself. "I'm in."

They set the date—tomorrow, late afternoon, right after Kai's soccer practice, with a promise of cold beer to follow.

Dinner migrated onto the back lanai, overlooking a strip of sun-bleached lawn and the infinite blue beyond. The table, covered in a faded pareo, glowed under the battery-powered lanterns strung from the beams above.

They ate in fits and starts. At first, the conversation creaked, job talk, small talk and silence. Castellano nursed her glass of wine, shifting in her seat every time Naalei looked her way.

Leilani finally broke the ice. "Did you ever cook for your family, Vic?"

Castellano looked surprised, then thoughtful. "Not much. My mom worked doubles, and by the time she got home, I'd already made ramen or boxed mac and cheese. Later, I got good at sandwiches."

Naalei gave her a look. "So you're a city girl."

"San Diego, Navy base, FBI dorm. Never anywhere like this," said Castellano.

Isaac cut in, a chunk of shrimp balanced on his fork. "You ever miss it? The city?"

She considered. "No. Honestly, I like the noise here better. It's a different kind, but it feels real."

Kai chimed in. "The ocean's loud, too. If you sleep with the window open, sometimes it's like being underwater all night."

Leilani smiled, then turned to Castellano. "You seem to know your way around the food, though."

Castellano flushed, took another bite of poke. "I, uh, started a cultural awareness course. They gave us homework. I watched three hours of YouTube on Hawaiian cooking and tried to practice at home."

Naalei nodded, lips pursed in mock approval. "Better than most of the officers who show up at our fundraisers. Last time, someone brought a Costco cheese tray and thought it was exotic."

Kai bounced in his seat. "My teacher says when you

eat someone's food, it's like saying you respect their family."

Naalei locked eyes with her grandson. "Your teacher is smart."

A lull stretched. Isaac reached for another beer, then turned to Leilani. "When did you know you wanted to be a cop?"

Leilani peeled a lychee, juice slicking her hands. "My dad. For as long as I could remember, I wanted to be like him. I didn't realize how much of it was people."

Castellano smirked. "That's every job. Even in NCIS, ninety percent people, ten percent paperwork, one percent anything you see on TV."

"What about you?" Leilani asked. "Did you always want to chase criminals?"

Castellano shook her head. "I wanted to teach or be a coach. I couldn't afford college, so I enlisted. Turns out, I enjoy investigating more than classroom discipline."

Kai swallowed his mouthful, then cleared his throat. "I did a project about warriors. Mom helped. We got an award."

Leilani raised her glass. "He wrote about ancient warriors and made a model heiau out of Legos. Then he turned it into a guide for the other kids about how not to mess up someone's culture."

Isaac whooped. "That's my guy."

Castellano leaned forward. "What's your number

one rule, Kai?"

He beamed. "Ask before you touch. Number two, if you don't know how to say it, ask someone to teach you. Number three," he paused, looking at Naalei. "Don't make a joke if it's about someone else's family."

A laugh rippled around the table.

Leilani glanced at Castellano. "You hear that? Could be a good start for next year's training program."

Castellano tipped her glass. "I'll suggest it to the brass."

As the sky faded to dark, dessert appeared. Mango bread and the bakery treat from Castellano, a guava chiffon cake, impossibly pink and light as a cloud. Plates passed from hand to hand, napkins wadded and swapped, and somewhere between seconds and thirds, the last barriers crumbled.

Isaac told a story about his rookie year as an FBI agent, chasing a chicken thief through downtown, losing a shoe in the mud. Castellano countered with the time she tried to go undercover at a surf shop and got sunburned so badly her face peeled in sheets. Even Naalei joined in, sharing a legend about the trickster gods and how they always made a mess before they made anything good.

Leilani caught her mother watching her; the pride soft but unmistakable. For the first time in years, she felt the two halves of her life connect, no tension, no double-checking which part of her belonged in the room. Only the sense that she had built a family capable of holding both the past and the future.

After the last plate had been scraped, Kai dragged Isaac and Castellano outside to see the best star view in Hawaii. Leilani lingered, helping her mother pack leftovers and clear the table.

"You okay, Mom?" she asked.

Naalei smiled, eyes full. "You did good, Lei. Your dad would've liked this. Not the chaos," she nodded towards the sliding glass, where the others hollered at some constellation or another, "but the company."

Leilani set the last bowl in the sink, wiped her hands, and pressed her forehead to her mother's. "Thank you. For everything."

They stood like that, just breathing, until the voices outside called them to join. Leilani stepped onto the lanai. She saw her son, her mother, her partner and her friend, all pointing at the night sky. She let herself feel the comfort, the weight, the relief of finally having somewhere to belong.

The tide, the laughter, the click of empty bottles on the rail, she committed it all to memory, a perfect contradiction. The old world and the new, joined at one small, bright table.

In the dark, Naalei's voice threaded over the group. "This is how you remember. You feed the people, and you let them tell their stories. That's all the old ones ever wanted."

And for once, Leilani didn't have to argue. She simply listened and knew the world would wait for them in the morning, steady as ever. Outside, the air had shifted. The scent of dinner faded under the clean sharpness of night, and the world's edge glimmered with a fuzz of brine and starlight. Leilani slipped off her shoes at the lanai steps and padded down the path to the sand, Isaac close behind.

Chapter Sixty-One

The moon hung so low and so fat above the ocean it looked like it might slide right off the horizon. Its light washed the beach in silver, sharpening the ripples where the tide inched up to erase their prints. She took the lead, letting the sea's hush clear her head.

After a stretch, Isaac broke the silence. "Your mom can throw a party. Never saw Castellano go back for seconds at any function, ever."

Leilani snorted. "She only did because she thought Mom was grading her."

"Was she?" asked Isaac.

"She grades everyone," said Leilani. She let the sand sift through her toes, still warm from the long sun, then said, quieter, "She used to grade me the harshest."

Isaac looked at her, that cop's tilt to his head. "You think she does now?"

Leilani shook her head. "Not anymore. I think she wanted to see if I could make both sides work. Being Hawaiian and being a cop. Used to feel like I had to split myself down the middle just to keep up."

He nodded, and they walked another fifty feet in silence, broken only by the gulls screaming at some far-off bait ball.

Isaac stopped and picked up a chunk of driftwood, spinning it like a baton. "Can I tell you something?"

"Sure."

He drew a deep breath; the words heavier than she'd expected. "When this case started, I kept my distance because I thought I'd screw it up. Personally and professionally, I mean. I wanted to be your partner, but I didn't want to mess up the good part by blurring it with feelings. In my last job, that didn't end well."

Leilani laughed, but the sound caught sideways. "You didn't screw it up. I think if you hadn't kept your boundaries, we'd both be dead by now."

Isaac tossed the stick into the waves and watched it vanish in the whitewater. "Still. Sometimes I wish I'd told you sooner."

She bumped him with her hip. "Sometimes I wish you had, too. But then I'd have to pretend to be nice to you at work, and I enjoy being a pain in your ass."

Isaac grinned. "I noticed."

They kept walking. The houses behind them receded, lights blinking off as the hour grew late. The world felt smaller and more private, each step measured against the others.

Isaac spoke again. "You know, you were right about Souza. I spent weeks looking for a monster and missed the human part. That's your gift, Lei. You see both."

She blushed in the dark. "It's not always a gift. Sometimes it hurts too much."

"That's what makes you the best at this," he said, and he sounded like he meant it.

They reached the spot where the sandbank curved into a hook and the beach narrowed. The waves crashed closer, throwing salty mist in their faces.

Leilani turned, the wind catching her hair, and looked at him. The moon cast his face in sharp planes and soft shadows, equal parts familiar and strange.

"I'm still figuring out who I am when I'm not chasing the job," she admitted. "For so long, I thought I could outwork my doubts. But now, I think the only way through is to accept both sides. The cop and the girl who chanted on her grandma's porch every morning."

Isaac took her hands, cold but steady. "You don't have to pick, you know. You're both already."

She laughed. "What if it's never enough?"

He looked her straight in the eye. "Then we'll fail together. At least you won't be alone."

For a moment, neither said anything. The ocean filled the space. Leilani stared at his hands holding hers. Scarred knuckles, the old burn at the base of his thumb from some distant arrest gone bad. He held on like he meant it.

She stepped into his space, their foreheads almost touching, and let herself think about tomorrow. Not in the abstract, or as a series of problems to solve, but as a string of days with room for more than just survival.

They stood at the tide line, bare feet sinking into cold, wet sand, and letting the moonlight soak their faces. Leilani realized she'd stopped flinching at the future. She liked the feel of his hand in hers. She liked even more that she could take it, or let go, and either way she'd still be whole.

She leaned in and kissed him. The salt on his lips

tasted like memory, and possibility, and a little like freedom.

For now, that was enough. The waves behind them wrote and rewrote their footprints, the night erasing what it didn't need. Ahead, the world stretched out, dark and endless. But they walked into it anyway, together.

Chapter Sixty-Two

The next evening, Leilani arrived early. The chosen cove was so far from the main road that you had to park by a chained-off trailhead, hop a cattle fence, and hike through ankle-high grass prickled with lantana. At the end, the land slouched down to a ribbon of perfect sand, abutted by two rocky outcrops and a sprinkle of wild palms. If there were better breaks for teaching a stubborn mainlander, she didn't know them.

She laid her board and Kai's shorter foamie in the dry sand, then dropped her duffel beside a clump of naupaka. She wore her oldest pair of navy bikini bottoms, the elastic softened by years of salt and sun, and a blue rash guard. She stretched, checked the leash cords, then turned her focus to the sea. The water shimmered, bands of turquoise and glassy blue, the surface scattered with lazy lines of swell. Only knee-high, but gentle enough for anyone with a spine.

She sat cross-legged on her blanket, listening to the pulse of the water and trying not to overthink the next hour. She ran through teaching scripts in her head: the funny metaphors, the safety warnings, the awkward bits about straddling the board. She'd done it a dozen times for the department's summer programs, even once for the Lieutenant Governor, but this was the first lesson that felt like a challenge.

A car crunched over the distant gravel, and a few minutes later Castellano came into view, moving with the wariness of someone sure she was being watched by hidden cameras. She carried a faded REI blanket, a cooler bag in the other hand, and wore an unzipped rash guard over a bikini patterned in bright florals that looked more boutique than department store. For a moment, Leilani couldn't decide whether to laugh or stare.

"Hey," Leilani called, lifting a hand.

Castellano returned the wave, set the blanket down next to Leilani's, and parked the cooler with a soft grunt.

"I brought hydration," she said, pulling two cans of Longboard Lager from a bed of melting ice packs.

"Nice," Leilani said. "That's actually rule number one: You can't surf without a beer first."

Castellano arched an eyebrow. "Isn't that against the law?"

"Only if you drink before ten a.m.," Leilani said. "This is what we call harm reduction."

They popped the tops and clinked; the sound drowned out by the nearest wave. Castellano took a sip, then surveyed the boards.

"I expected you to bring one of those big ones. This looks like a toy."

Leilani nodded at the shorter board. "That's Kai's. You get it until you're ready to upgrade. You'll want the extra stability." She eyed Castellano, whose arms and shoulders, though lean, were defined with the muscle of someone who'd never skipped a morning run. "I give you, what, fifteen minutes before you demand something faster?"

Castellano laughed, surprisingly unguarded. "I'll just try not to eat sand for the first hour."

"Deal." Leilani finished her beer and let the silence stretch, the two of them watching the sets roll in, gentle and perfect.

"So, what's the first lesson?" Castellano asked.

"Come here," Leilani said, patting the sand. "Start by lying down on the board, chest at the midline."

Castellano complied, placing the foamie down and lying flat, her skin gleaming with a faint dusting of sunscreen and sweat. The bikini cut low, revealing the slope of her lower back, and for a moment, Leilani found it hard to focus on anything but the smoothness of her body against the board.

"Good," Leilani said, keeping it professional. "Now, you're going to paddle using big strokes. Imagine you're reaching for something just out of arm's reach."

Castellano gave three strong pulls. "Like this?"

Leilani corrected her hands, guiding her wrists and elbows into a more efficient scoop. "Yeah, but less splash. You want to conserve energy. Here, watch." She lay down next to her, demonstrating the movement, then propped herself on her elbows, inches away from Castellano's face. The agent's expression was intent, but not uncomfortable.

"Got it," Castellano said, repeating the motion. "Feels weird. Like I'm trying too hard."

"That's normal," Leilani said. "Next part's the pop-up. This is where you'll make or break it."

She stood and offered a hand, pulling Castellano upright. She motioned for her to crouch behind the board, knees bent.

"You want to plant your hands on the rail, then pop up to a low squat in one quick move. Keep your weight centered. Like this." She showed the pop-up, nimble, the movement practiced to muscle memory.

Castellano mirrored the position, then tried to vault herself up. The first attempt went sideways; the board flipping out from under her. She landed in the sand and spat a curse.

"Try again," Leilani said, holding back a grin.

They did it again. And again. With every repetition, Castellano's motion smoothed out, her balance improving, her embarrassment fading. Leilani moved in to adjust her stance, hands on Castellano's hips, realigning her feet.

"You're leading too much with your shoulders. Let your core pull you up."

Castellano nodded, her face inches from Leilani's. "You ever lose anyone in a lesson?"

"Only to sharks," Leilani said. "But today feels pretty safe."

They laughed, the last bit of awkwardness rinsed away by effort and the quickened pace of their breathing.

For the next forty minutes, Leilani coached Castellano through drills: paddling, popping up, and finding the sweet spot on the board. Every time Castellano faltered, she pushed through with grim determination, only allowing herself a self-deprecating laugh when Leilani proved her wrong.

As the sun dipped lower, their bodies warmed, the sheen of sweat and salt glimmering on their skin. The air had that blue-gold cast of a late Hawaiian afternoon, turning everything softer at the edges. From the water, laughter echoed; some kids fishing off the rocks, otherwise no one for a mile.

They sat down on the blanket, breathing hard. Castellano finished her second beer and wiped a line of sweat from her brow.

"How am I doing?" she asked.

Leilani appraised her. "You're a lot better than my average recruit. Plus, you haven't called me a liar or threatened to sue."

"That's only because you haven't thrown me in yet."

Leilani shrugged, and for the first time all day, allowed herself to really look at Castellano: the curve of her shoulders, the firmness of her breasts, the narrow line of her waist, and the way her legs, athletic and shapely, caught the light. Her hair, damp from the humidity, clung to the sides of her neck in dark ropes.

"You want to get wet, or are you scared?" Leilani teased.

"I'm always ready to get wet," Castellano said, and it was less bravado than an admission. "But don't rescue me unless it's an actual emergency."

Leilani grinned and gathered the boards. "Last rule: if you fall, fall flat. Don't dive. The water is shallow here."

Castellano picked up the foamie and followed, hips rolling with every step.

They stood at the water's edge; the Pacific stretched endlessly before them. The breeze smelled of salt and plumeria, and the only sound was the patient hush of the tide.

"Thanks," Castellano said, voice suddenly earnest.

"For what?" Leilani asked, scanning the horizon.

"For not making fun of me. For giving me the real thing. I know I appear a hard-ass, but—" She trailed off.

Leilani let the silence fill in. "No worries. Out here, none of the rest matters."

She shot Castellano a look, saw a flash of the woman beneath the agent, softer, a little more vulnerable.

"All right," Leilani said. "Let's do this."

They waded in, the first rush of water cold at their ankles, then sweet and warm as it covered their legs. Leilani looked back once, saw their footprints side by side on the empty sand, and felt a quick jolt of something like nostalgia for a moment that wasn't even over yet.

She paddled out, with Castellano close behind. The boards bounced over the whitewater, then coasted smoothly as the sea calmed. Out beyond the impact zone, they sat astride their boards, catching their breath.

The light had turned amber; the shore behind them painted in stripes of gold and blue shadow. There, on the open water, the city's troubles seemed half a planet away.

"You ready for your first wave?" Leilani called.

Castellano nodded. "Born ready."

Leilani smiled and turned her board to face the sets, feeling the old thrill, the mix of responsibility and reckless possibility.

A set was building. Leilani caught the first one, turned, and paddled with a few quick, efficient strokes. She caught the wave, stood, and rode it all the way in, her body moving with the familiar rhythm, the board alive beneath her feet. At the shore, she turned and watched as Castellano lined up for the second.

She paddled hard, caught the face, and then, too slow on the pop, crashed sideways in a spectacular wipeout. She surfaced, spluttering, but laughing hard enough to make Leilani smile.

They repeated the process again, with Castellano lasting a few seconds longer each time. Every fall was less dramatic; every pop-up was more controlled. On the fourth attempt, she rode a tiny roller nearly to shore, fists in the air like an Olympic finish.

She turned, grinning, eyes lit with adrenaline and pure pride. "Did you see that?" she called.

Leilani clapped from the water, feeling a surge of genuine pride.

They paddled in, waterlogged and hungry, and sprawled on the towels, watching the last scraps of sunlight disappear behind the mountains. They shared two more beers, the silence easy now, and the sound of their breathing matching the slow roll of the tide.

Leilani watched Castellano, who sat with her knees pulled up, watching the horizon with a strange, thoughtful expression.

"You ever miss the mainland?" Leilani asked softly.

Castellano shook her head. "Not really. Out here, I don't have to pretend. It's like—" She groped for words. "Like maybe I could belong if I worked at it."

Leilani considered that. "You'll belong," she said. "Might take time, but it happens."

Castellano looked at her, then back at the sea. "I want to believe that."

For a moment, they just sat side by side, two silhouettes against the world's edge.

Leilani let the feeling settle in, sharp and warm.

"Next time," she said, "we'll try the north side. If you think you're up for it."

"I'm up for anything," Castellano said. "Especially if you're the one teaching."

Leilani turned, their faces closer than she'd realized, and for a split second, neither of them moved. Something electric hovered, unspoken but there, and Leilani let herself want, just a little.

Then she leaned back, grinning, and offered another toast. "To new beginnings," she said.

Castellano bumped her can and smiled, the smile

that belonged nowhere but here.

The light faded. The world grew soft, the air thick with salt and the hum of all the stories yet to be written. They lingered on the sand, talking and not talking, the city just a memory, the future wide open as the sea.

Chapter Sixty-Three

The sky had gone from blood orange to the bruised purple of early night. The wind kicked up just enough to raise goosebumps on their skin, but the air held on to the day's warmth, heat pooling between body and sand.

Castellano shook the water from her hair, then dropped onto the blanket with a grateful exhale. She reached into the cooler and tossed Leilani another beer.

"Here," she said, voice husky from shouting over the surf. "You've earned it."

Leilani took it, popped the top, and let the foam bleed over her knuckles. She drained half in one go, wiped her mouth with the back of her hand, then leaned back and stretched her calves until they ached.

"Not bad for your first day," Leilani said, and she meant it.

Castellano looked at her, really looked, with the admiration that would've made Leilani squirm in the past. "You're very impressive," Castellano said, the compliment raw and simple, stripped of sarcasm.

Leilani froze, not used to the directness. She waited for the punchline, but none came.

"Thanks," she said, unsure what else to say.

They sat side by side, silent, letting the rush of the waves fill in everything unsaid. The stars pressed through the thinning dusk, scattered and bright as the city lights beginning to flicker in the far-off valley.

Leilani felt her own heart slow, the beer settling her into a pleasant haze. Castellano's thigh pressed warm against hers, an accident at first, but neither moved away.

After a while, Castellano propped herself up on her elbow, looking at Leilani with a searching expression. "Do you ever just... let yourself enjoy this?" she asked, gesturing with her chin at the water, the sky, the stretch of empty sand.

Leilani shrugged, unsure how to answer. "Sometimes. It usually feels like there's always something next."

"Maybe there doesn't have to be," Castellano said, voice lower now. She brushed a wet strand of hair off Leilani's cheek. "Just a thought."

Leilani didn't respond, but she didn't look away either.

For a long minute, they watched the horizon together. The waves broke and receded, every so often a rogue crest sending fine spray into the air, misting their skin with salt. Leilani finished her beer, set it aside, and lay back, arms folded behind her head.

Castellano watched her, then lay back too, close enough that their shoulders touched. The world contracted to the radius of their bodies and the sweep of the ocean in front of them.

Eventually, Castellano turned, propped herself up again, and reached over to rest her hand gently on Leilani's stomach, right above the seam of the rash guard.

"You're really something," she said, then leaned down and pressed her lips to Leilani's.

The kiss started soft, a question more than an answer. Castellano's lips tasted like beer and ocean, a little chapped from the wind, and they lingered against Leilani's until she felt her own mouth soften in reply. Castellano didn't force it, just waited, thumb tracing slow circles through the thin fabric.

After a moment, Castellano kissed her again, this time with more certainty, her hand sliding up the line of the rash guard until it cupped the side of Leilani's ribcage.

Leilani exhaled, her body melting into the sand beneath her. She let the hand stay there, felt the warmth of it spreading in measured, patient increments. She parted her lips, inviting the press of Castellano's tongue, the slow tasting of salt and breath and heat.

The sound of the waves faded. Time unspooled.

Castellano unzipped Leilani's rash guard with steady, deliberate fingers, pulling the slider down an inch at a time until the blue fabric parted, exposing the top of Leilani's breasts and the subtle vee of tanned skin.

Castellano kissed her again, soft and hot. Castellano's hand moved inside the open zipper, sliding over Leilani's breast, her warm palm on bare skin.

Leilani's breath caught. She reached up and grabbed a handful of the blanket, anchoring herself against the rush of sensation as Castellano's thumb circled her nipple, then pinched it, gently at first, then harder when she didn't pull away.

"Are you okay?" Castellano whispered, her voice sandpaper-rough.

"Yeah," Leilani said.

They made out in slow motion, Castellano's hands exploring with the same patience she brought to every interview and search. Leilani allowed herself to go slack, let herself be guided and tasted and claimed, at least for tonight.

Leilani slowly pushed Castellano off and lay back in the sand. This was not how she expected the end of the day to go, and she was a little unsure of what came next.

She reached up and unzipped the rash guard the rest of the way and let the fabric fall to the side, exposing her large, firm breasts. She rolled onto her elbow, smiled at Castellano, and leaned in closer.

Chapter Sixty-Four

Sunrise came soft, almost bashful, the first pink hint of it prying open the sky above Waimānalo like a secret. The beach lay empty except for a strip of footprints leading from Naalei's back gate to the tide line, the edges already blurring as the morning breeze lifted sand across the surface.

Leilani stood at the edge of the world, her toes numb in the wet sand. She'd risen before even the birds, slipping out while the house held its breath in post-party sleep. She wore her surfing wetsuit, zipped to the hips, and a pa'u skirt in faded indigo that fluttered around her knees. Across one shoulder, she'd slung the small handwoven basket she'd finished last night, filled with ti leaves, yellow plumeria, a few coins of mango, and a single shell scavenged from a beach on a day long past. Under her arm, she carried her battered surfboard.

She walked the length of the shore with measured steps, recalling the old chant under her breath. Each word tasted different in the hush of morning, softer, stripped of its performance. This was for her and for the ones who'd walked here before, not for the world or for anyone watching.

A line from her mother echoed in her head. The old ones don't want you perfect. They just want you to show up, whole.

She waded in until the chill stung her shins, then kneeled at the boundary where the ocean met the earth. The basket looked small against the long, flat sprawl of the sea.

She whispered the blessing, old syllables looping into her new story. "He ali'i ka 'āina, he kauwā ke kanaka." The land is chief; man is its servant. A lesson, a warning and a benediction.

She set the basket on the surface and watched it bob, dip, and finally float free, spinning once before the current tugged it towards the reef. The offerings drifted away in silence, no trumpets, no audience, just the faint hiss of foam and the scrabble of pebbles under her knees.

Leilani stood and faced the sun. It burned higher now, gold and greedy, painting her in silhouette against the white-bleached east. She let the skirt fall away, stripped to the wetsuit, and jogged up to where her board waited. The old sticker on the nose, HPD 415, caught the first light.

She pulled her ponytail tight, tucked the shell necklace inside her suit, and carried the board to the break. In the water, her arms remembered every stroke, the old strength returning without protest. She paddled past the shore break, sat up, and drifted.

She floated there, letting the board rock her, the brine and light and memory all mixed. The story inside her got quiet, not gone, but no longer something to fight. She belonged here, neither traitor nor saint, neither cop nor crusader. A woman in the water, waiting for the next set.

She glanced shoreward. Behind her, the house looked small, Naalei's silhouette in the window. Ahead, the world stretched open, full of clean blue and salt. She shut her eyes, breathed deeply, and waited for the perfect wave. When it came, she paddled hard, caught the drop, and rode it all the way in.

The sun kept climbing. The old wounds faded, replaced by something bright, something she'd earned. Tomorrow, the city will call her back. The job, the world, the next spiral. But for now, she let herself float in the gold of the morning, a woman at peace in both her skins. Somewhere beyond the reef, her offering kept moving. So did she.

Acknowledgments

A special thank-you to my daughter Christina J. Morgan, my unofficial collaborator.

Any mistakes the reader may find are solely the responsibility of the author.

Special thanks to my daughter Stephanie Morgan, my beta reader. Stephanie has read every novel in its rough stages and rarely gets to see the completed product. Her insight and critique have been critical to ensuring the stories make sense.

Also, I would like to thank my family for their encouragement. I have been telling them stories since they were little, and I always told them that someone should be writing this stuff down. I decided to write it down myself.

I want to thank my closest friend, Trish Moakler-Herud. She has been encouraging me for years to write my stories down. I hope this will make her proud.

A special thanks to my late wife, Jane. She pushed me for years to become a writer, and my biggest regret is that she didn't live long enough to see it happen. I love her with all my heart and miss her every day. I think she would be pleased.

Finally, thanks to the readers. Without you, none of this would be important.

About the Author

2019 Pacific Book Awards Best Mystery Finalist . . . ***Crime Delayed***

2020 Pacific Book Awards Best Mystery Winner . . . ***Crime Denied***

2020 Chanticleer International Book Awards: 1st Place Blue Ribbon, CLUE Book Awards for Suspense, Thriller Fiction . . . ***Crime Denied***

2021 Chanticleer International Book Awards Finalist, CLUE Book Awards for Suspense, Thriller Fiction . . . ***Crime Conspiracy***

2021 Chanticleer International Book Awards Finalist, Book Series, CLUE Book Awards for Suspense, Thriller Fiction . . . Crime Series, The Buck Taylor Novels

2022 Chanticleer International Book Awards Finalist, CLUE Book Awards for Suspense, Thriller Fiction . . . ***Crime Exploded***

2022 Chanticleer International Book Awards Finalist, CLUE Book Awards for Suspense, Thriller Fiction . . . ***Crime Spree***

2023 Chanticleer International Book Awards Finalist, CLUE Book Awards for Suspense, Thriller Fiction . . . ***Crime Scene***

2023 Chanticleer International Book Awards Series Finalist, Mystery & Mayhem Book Awards . . . *Crime Series*

Chuck Morgan is a Colorado-based crime and thriller author whose work blends procedural authenticity, emotional depth, and high-stakes suspense. A graduate of Seton Hall University and Regis College, he spent thirty-five years as a construction project manager before turning his focus to writing full-time. An avid outdoorsman, Eagle Scout, and licensed private pilot, he draws inspiration from a lifetime of camping, hiking, mountain biking, and fly-fishing across the American West.

Besides his acclaimed crime fiction, Chuck wrote Her Name Was Jane, a deeply personal memoir chronicling his late wife's nine-year battle with breast cancer. He is the father of three, grandfather of four, and dog-dad to a Siberian Husky. He resides in Lone Tree, Colorado.

Chuck is the creator of multiple thriller series, including:

The Buck Taylor Crime Series (Colorado Bureau of Investigation):

Crime Interrupted • Crime Delayed • Crime Unsolved • Crime Exposed • Crime Denied • Crime Conspiracy • Crime Unknown • Crime Exploded • Crime Spree • Crime Family • Crime Scene • Crime Victims • Crime Unraveled • Cold Justice

The Delia Cahill Assassin Series:

The Assassin's Heart • Edge of Betrayal

The Leilani Kealoha Hawaiian Thriller Series”

Murder in Paradise • The Eye of the Navigator • The Last Spiral

The Mike Branik Series:

Preserve, Protect, and Defend

And

Chimera, a standalone psychological thriller

His novels are known for their vivid settings, layered investigations, and interesting characters, earning him a loyal readership across the crime, mystery, and thriller genres.

Other Books in this Series

The Leilani Kealoha series follows an Honolulu detective caught between modern crime and the ancient forces shaping Hawai'i's future—where corruption runs deep, family history cuts sharp, and every case pulls her closer to the secrets her islands refuse to bury. Murder in Paradise, The Eye of the Navigator, and The Last Spiral are a trilogy and should be read in order.

Happy Reading,

Chuck Morgan

"She thought she knew her island—until the murders began."

Murder in Paradise by Chuck Morgan is an exciting and engaging read. It is a thrilling journey filled with death, danger, dark

secrets, and retribution. The story is fast-paced, with action kicking off from the very first page and never letting up. *Reader's Favorites Review.*

"Paradise Has a Price—And Detective Leilani Kealoha Is Paying It."

Chuck Morgan fascinates us with contradictions, as paradise is shrouded with murder and crime becomes a game in this conspiracy thriller, The Eye of the Navigator. Detective Leilani Kealoha treasures her heritage of the Hawaiian Islands, and she strives to keep it safe. *Reader's Favorite Review.*

"When the truth is buried, justice becomes personal."

☆☆☆☆☆ **Chuck Morgan is the author of numerous series, and Leilani Kealoha is one of his toughest female protagonists. She needs to deal with everything that's thrown at her. There's a hand-to-hand combat scene that lasts an entire chapter, which had me gasping and cheering, then gasping again.** ***Reader's Favorite Review***

"It's not about money, Detective. Someone took this because they wanted to erase what it means."

☆☆☆☆☆ **Guardians of the Drums by Chuck Morgan is an outstanding thriller that kept me on the edge of my seat from beginning to end. The story moves at a brisk pace, yet allows readers just enough time to absorb each event before the next twist unfolds. I was completely captivated from the**

first page and found it impossible to put the book down. *Reader's Favorite Review*

www.ingramcontent.com/pod-product-compliance
Lightning Source LLC
LaVergne TN
LVHW041100080826
845145LV00007B/1639

* 9 7 8 1 9 6 8 1 7 9 6 8 7 *